the MIND BOX

MAIN

the

MIND BOX

A.J. DIEHL

Midnight Ink
Woodbury, Minnesota

First Edition
First Printing, 2005

Author photo by Jeff Nicholson
Book design by Donna Burch
Cover design by Kevin R. Brown
Cover computer image © 2005 by PhotoDisc
Cover woman image © 2005 by clipart.com
Editing by Valerie Valentine

Midnight Ink, an imprint of Llewellyn Publications

Library of Congress Cataloging-in-Publication Data
Diehl, A. J., 1958-
    The mind box / A.J. Diehl. —1st ed.
      p. cm.
   ISBN 0-7387-0820-8
    1. Police—California—Los Angeles—Fiction. 2. Motion picture producers and directors—Crimes against—Fiction. 3. Motion pictures—Moral and ethical aspects—Fiction. 4. Murder vctims' families—Fiction. 5. Los Angeles (Calif.)—Fiction. 6. Problem families—Fiction. 7. Policewomen—Fiction. I. Title.

PS3604.I344M56 2005
813'.6—dc22

200543755

Midnight Ink
Llewellyn Publications
2143 Wooddale Drive, Dept. 0-7387-0820-8
Woodbury, MN 55164-0383, U.S.A.
www.midnightinkbooks.com

Printed in the United States of America

To George and Stephanie Diehl;
For unforgettable memories, for lives courageous and profound.

... his brain momentarily seemed to catch fire, and in an extraordinary rush, all his vital forces were at their highest tension. The sense of life, the consciousness of self, were multiplied almost ten times at these moments which lasted no longer than a flash of lightning.

—Fyodor Dostoyevsky, *The Idiot*

PROLOGUE

Thursday, June 23

ON HIS COMPUTER SCREEN, the email's images opened: a white gift box with a blue ribbon that untied itself and fell to a virtual floor. As if removed by invisible hands, the top of the box lifted. From inside came pictures so vivid, so alive, they shamed his Oscar-winning films. The young woman. Drops of red appeared, smearing her with their implication. The heart beating like something out of Poe's worst nightmare. He had to admit, it was the most terrifying gift a person could receive— one's worst memories. Untraceable; he'd checked twice. His estate manager hovered, watching. Was he in with them or not?

Feeling exposed, Eddie Ealing reached for his Scotch, then remembered he'd stopped drinking a decade ago. First his mind grayed, like cooling ash, until the replaying images stoked and fired him, enraged him. He'd been accused of propagating violence, but his exploits paled against the horrors conjured by the perfectly honorable monsters he knew. What they'd done. What they would do, if allowed.

At last, Eddie's plan was in place. The deadline—July 4. They could terrorize, manipulate, and threaten him, but they wouldn't win with him alive, and they couldn't kill him. Not now. The one redemptive deal in his life would be this—stopping them. He expected the next waves of dark haze icing his brain, but not the tears that dropped to his cheeks as he tried to quell the violent shaking in his gut. The damn memories filled him again.

ONE

Tuesday, July 5

THE CALL INTERRUPTED AN epic beach morning.

Lane Daily had just settled into her sand chair, the aches of last night's chase melting from her legs in the strong Hermosa Beach sun. She'd finished her first glass of fumé blanc, had just started a new book, and had just forgotten she was an LAPD homicide detective. She answered her cell phone with more of a sigh than a word.

"They're saying it's the strangest murder ever seen in LA." It was her partner, J. D. Nestor.

"Real funny. First day off—"

"—in three weeks," he finished. "I'm not messing with you. More media here than God, and they're calling it the chart-topper."

"Worse than Tate/La Bianca?"

"More personal. All the sick stuff directed at one guy." Nestor paused. "Eddie Ealing."

The wine soured in her stomach. "*The* Eddie Ealing? Where? How?"

3

"His place. Off Mulholland. Haven't seen the how; I'm on my way now. The lieutenant's been trying to reach you. Hear it's colorful." Nestor gave her the address and said he'd see her there.

As she gathered her beach gear, the wind nipped at Daily's chestnut hair and relief coursed through her. Even now, she couldn't entirely relax near the ocean, no matter how she tried. Too much to remember. *Systematic desensitization*, her best friend called it: settling near your fears until they don't conjure up the demons anymore. But Daily's demons weren't in the sea, they were in her head.

It was early, but already the smells of a grill tickled her nose. At the yellow beach house, the cute guy manning the barbecue waved at her and smiled. He ate burgers for breakfast. She certainly couldn't criticize, given her dry white nourishment this morning—the first sip of relaxation she'd allowed herself in twenty days. She tried to remember his name. Tad? Todd?

"Leaving already, Lane?" He knew hers. "The day's young and long . . ."

———————

Mulholland was jammed with news cameras, vans, reporters. In sight was the canyon road that separated the Hollywood Division of the LAPD from the turf of the LA County Sheriff. If Ealing had been murdered a block west, she'd still be on the beach. The lieutenant had reached Daily right after Nestor. Even though the call was out of rotation for her team, he wanted her there. Like Nestor, he'd been unwilling to discuss any details until they were at the scene.

Daily navigated her unmarked car through the media glut and the sun bounced a glare off the rearview. She adjusted the mirror; the reflection of three nonstop weeks stared back at her. Her olive skin looked unusually pale. Red irritation nagged her brown eyes for sleep. Feeling much older than thirty-three, she stretched tired shoulders and wiped the sweat beading her brow. This July was already the hottest in decades, worse than the spikes a couple months back, and the crime rate had hiked in harmony.

The Crown Victoria's churning air conditioner was worthless. She made a mental note to have the Freon checked and rolled down the window. Her unruly mane danced in the arroyo gusts. She reached in her bag for a hair clip, the biggest one she could find, yet it couldn't contain the chaos of her hair. The unsure, loose waves came from her Italian mother, the dense curls beneath from her half-Bahamian, half-British father. The whole mess framed her dad's willful cheeks and nose, her mom's ample lips. Lane Daily was the "other" box on every form and application. Small wonder her hair didn't know if it was coming or going. Her skin prickled and the mirror showed her neck and chest flushing. It wasn't the heat; it happened when she was stuck, as if her blood was trying to jump out of its skin. She needed to move.

She opened the car's glove compartment. Provisions. The notion of real food evaporated when Daily rode a case. In its place came one of two cravings—salt or chocolate. She tore a cellophane cashew packet open with her teeth, downed the warm nuts, then finished off two more packs and stuffed the empty bags under the seat. If Nestor laid eyes on the stuff, she'd get another lecture. Ever since she'd shot the perp that was about to unload a nine into her partner, Nestor felt it was his duty to save Daily from her junk food diet, her ex-husband, and her life. She loved Nestor like a brother, but he could be a pill.

An officer spotted Daily's car and yelled at the plug of vehicles to let her pass. She edged the Crown Victoria past Kelly Spreck, the blonde from Channel Six News pitching fast and hard to her camera. Daily listened.

"High-powered and hot-tempered entertainment executive Eddie Ealing has been killed in exactly the fashion he lived: loudly, violently, and as the center of attention," Spreck reported. "A hundred people attended the Fourth of July party thrown by Ealing last night here at his estate. While no cameras were allowed inside, News Six caught the mogul smiling as he returned home in his car yesterday. But this morning, Ealing was found dead in what's certainly the strangest murder the Southland has seen in years."

Kelly cut it there, barked at her cameraman to follow her past the gate. Daily watched as two patrol officers stopped her.

"Just doing my job," the reporter protested.

Daily rolled by in her car. "Outside, Kelly."

"Daily—nice shirt. It'll play great on camera. Tell me—"

"Not now."

"Hey, I've been good to you. Help me out."

"I am. You leave a trace inside this line, you get to be a suspect."

"Is it true? About his tongue?"

"I just got here, Kel."

The reporter leaned in. "You'll talk to me first? Tell me the truth?"

"Someone always talks. The truth is another matter." Daily passed the last news van and gunned the gas.

She drove up a road that meandered past mature pines and oaks. Three acres, easy. Looked like horse country, not a couple miles from the Sunset Strip. The ME's van and several patrol cars were parked in the curved driveway of an estate five times as big as the Hollywood Police Station. Pitched roofs, gables, two enormous chimneys. Shingles coddled the place in a rich coat of cedar. Edging red brick, the mansion's wood gleamed in the July sun. She parked and badged the two uniformed officers stationed at the home's entrance. After signing her name to the crime scene log, she entered a porte-cochère. Arches hovered over a succession of iron lanterns. To her right was a garden filled with rosemary and lavender. A fountain in the corner. To her left, multipaned windows framed the opulence inside. Daily entered a pristine foyer filled with three more officers talking in somber tones. Their radios were louder than their words, but she caught a few.

Heinous.

Bizarre.

Psychopath.

Daily's eyes took in spaces filled with antiques. A long public room was graced by a Steinway baby grand at one end, a mahogany dining table and tapestry chairs at the other. Crystal vases coddled blooms of blue irises set off by branches of red hypericum berries. Punctuating the walls were irregularly sized windows, leather bench seats beneath two of them. Party invitations and small American flags were strewn on a secretary desk in the corner. Even the messy spots in the mansion looked arranged. At homicides in the bowels of Hollywood, Daily usually stood out as well-dressed, fastidious, confident. But here, in the world of Mulholland, every imperfection of her knock-off suit screamed mediocrity. She shook off her nerves and asked to see the scene. Senior officer Carl Hastings led her toward open doors that spilled them onto a marble deck above a pool squared in emerald grass. The lawn was Disneyland green, perfect. She'd read about genetically programmed grass seed in the *Times*. Eddie Ealing could afford it.

"Hell of a party," Hastings said. "Hear the tab was quarter of a mil."

"For how many people?"

"Hundred and change."

"That's one expensive plate. More than my wedding, anyway."

"Even more than my divorce," Hastings grumbled. "They had theme buffets, according to one of the TV vultures at the gate last night. Departing guests were talking Caribbean, Indonesian, Brazilian, Indian, you name it. A caviar bar with five kinds of fish eggs and fifty kinds of vodka. Wine tasting, Cuban cigars."

"No sparklers?"

"Just the stars themselves. Both Toms, Julia, Brad and the little lady, plus a bunch of others. The news guy said Ealing was his usual self. Nothing out of the ordinary."

"Nothing in Ealing's life was ordinary."

"Nothing different, then."

"The reporter have tape?"

Hastings shook his head. "Nope. And no cameras allowed inside."

Past a rising berm and ash trees on the other side of the pool, panels of glass steepled skyward. A chapel? She couldn't envision a tyrant like Eddie Ealing believing in higher powers of any sort but these days who knew? The man had won Oscars *and* a Grammy and winners always thanked God, implying the losers were unrepentant pagans. Daily figured the Big Guy had more important things on his mind than the statuette for best special effects. Then again, maybe the privileged prayed to a different god.

Officer Hastings motioned toward the steepled glass. "The vic's in there. Conservatory. That's what the estate manager calls it, anyway. Helmut Ulgrod. He's the one who called."

Conservatory. Place for growing plants.

Daily entered what was more of a luxurious pool house than a greenhouse, though tropicals and palms lined the walls. In the middle of the space, an azure pool snaked from one corner to the other. Rock steps at one end draped waterfalls into a spa that steamed in the shafts of morning light. Golden sandstone encircled the main pool, while flagstone walkways led to a black marble wet bar. White phalaenopsis orchids pouted in successive urns.

J. D. Nestor stared at a chaise longue and rubbed his forty-four-year-old chin with a consternation Daily rarely saw. Nestor was six-foot-two, with the build of a tight end gone long on calories. He shook his head at the chair.

Her gut clenched. The smell of pool chemicals engulfed her. Daily typically saw death in its usual milieu—murder was mostly impulsive, dirty, or sloppy. But here death lay decadent, lounging in a magnificent summerhouse. Eddie Ealing's body had been split open. Fat spilled from either side of the wound that ran from his breastbone down his abdomen. There was a noticeable lack of blood. The large man's nostrils were filled with something dark. A small brown trail had oozed from one nostril and withered dry on his cheek. His thick ash hair stuck to his head as if it had been wet and then air-dried without benefit of a towel. His eyes were open but instead of pupils, the raw backs of his eyeballs glared back at Daily. From the victim's open mouth spilled a yellow mass. She looked down at the abdominal cut. The skin on one side of his belly crumpled in. The fat in his mouth was his own.

Nestor stared at the wound bisecting Ealing. "Stomach, intestines, and liver are intact. I think."

"The knife?"

"If it's here, we haven't found it."

"Prints?"

"More than words can say. Some of the guests found Eddie's pool house to their liking."

"Stuffing his mouth." Daily's pulse rushed. "Packing his nose. Eyes turned inward. That's three of the five senses. Was there a recording playing when he was found?"

Nestor nodded. "Phone conversations. Eddie Ealing himself, tearing new assholes across America."

"That covers sound. What was he touching?"

Nestor handed Daily four pages, a guest list for the party. "That's a copy. Slam's got the original over there. It was rolled and stuck in Ealing's right hand."

"*Sense of Life.*" Daily pointed to a framed film poster near the bar. "Six years ago. It's not exactly how the victim in the movie died. But it's mighty close."

Nestor snorted. "Wouldn't know. I don't pay to see that kind of crap."

"Several million people did. And the book was a bestseller before Ealing made it into a movie."

"Double the pleasure. You sure it was Ealing's movie?"

"Absolutely. Won for best actor and best adapted screenplay."

Nestor studied the other movie one-sheets: *Mercy Seasons. Lifeline. Break the Chain. The Currency of Souls. Sense of Life.*

"He was one of the producers on *Sense of Life*," Daily said. "He took the lion's share of the credit at the awards. The whole premise was the ultimate death for a narcissist. The perfect comeuppance. Every one of the victim's five senses was filled with himself as he died."

"How in God's name is that entertainment?"

"I'd rather people work out their dark sides at the multiplex than this."

Nestor's eyes challenged her, but she wasn't about to engage in one of his what's-wrong-with-the-country debates. Daily scanned the names on the guest list, noticed the tally on the last page. Fifty-seven. Some with one guest, some with more than one. On the other side of the body, Daily saw coroner's investigator Slancio "Slam" Damas, one of the senior CIs, the word CORONER boxed in yellow letters on the heart of the dark windbreaker. Today he also wore a nose/mouth mask as he made notes on a clipboard—his field report. The CI had first pass at the victim, and it was critical that no one else work the body until he gave the go-ahead in order to prevent defense attorneys from crying foul on tainted evidence. Two men from Scientific Investigation Division, the LAPD's own crime lab, talked with the police photographer. Daily saw open tackle boxes, which meant Slam had already cleared SID to work the outer perimeter. They were farther along than she realized. Traffic on the freeways had been hell—hungover holiday drivers had slammed four jams in the city's arteries. Cars had run into dogs scared loose after a night of fireworks; the fifth of July was first in dog deaths. Even detours had been a mess, and a drive that should have taken forty-five minutes had taken ninety.

Daily rolled on a latex glove. Flashes fired as the police photographer started on a fresh angle. Careful to stay behind the working area of the CI and the photographer, she circled Ealing's body.

Nestor trailed her. "Ealing's live-in estate manager, a guy named Helmy, found him just before ten. Said the boss liked to crash out here after a swim to relax. Mess by the door is this morning's breakfast. Helmy dropped the tray when he walked in and saw this carnival. Called us, then passed out upstairs according to Helmy's wife, Berta, who's also housekeeper. Helmy went bonkers when he came to. She gave him a chill pill, Xanax. Slam pulled the guest list out of the vic's hands. Berta gave us a copy from inside. The lists match. There were several copies around the house for Ealing's reference during the party, including one in here."

Daily looked at Ealing's gaping wound. "Sure his fat is the only thing cut out?"

"Only your medical examiner knows for sure."

The photographer bumped Daily. Blasts of light strobed. She moved out of his way and again caught the sharp odor that sent her reeling.

"The pool man go heavy on chemicals?"

"It's not the pool, it's *the body*," Nestor said. "Washed in stuff we found in the maintenance cabinet. Muriatic acid. Mostly evaporated with the sun, but Slam's being careful. Recommends we do the same within three feet of the vic." Nestor shot his chin at a small bag of the masks.

"I don't remember chemicals in the movie." Daily slipped on a mask and stooped to study the sandstone. Close to the body, even with the mask on, her nostrils burned. Enough to clear five pools by the smell of it. Here, drops on the floor from Ealing's abdomen were clear, tinged with brown. Muriatic acid and oxidized blood. A rivulet had coursed toward a drain.

Nestor said, "Not only do we have acid all over our vic, we got a friggin' Hansel and Gretel trail of powdered chemicals leading out the back door of this place."

"You're telling me we have no tracks?"

"We have a trail of powdered chlorine. Perp gets a gold star."

"Tire treads out back?"

"Hundreds. This edge of the property butts up to where valet parked all the cars last night."

Hundreds. Daily soaked in the scene and let her thoughts swim.

A story made real. Aspects mimicked.

"What about his tongue? In the movie, the victim's tongue was cut out and put—"

Nestor turned to the CI. "You got a mobile tongue anywhere, Slam?"

"Negative."

Daily had seen unbridled rage and she'd seen the meticulous planning of sociopaths. This felt like neither—or both.

Some aspects missed or left out. Contradictions.

SID criminalist Roger Kerns was scanning the floor for trace evidence: hair, blood, fibers. Kerns was a film buff.

"How many people wanted the guy dead?" Daily asked him. "In the film?"

Kerns blinked at her with eyes that were processing facts in some other universe. "Five. Five senses, five suspects."

"*Sense of Life* had five. *Murder on the Orient Express* had twelve. We get fifty-seven plus. What about the chemicals, the acid? Am I forgetting? Or was that not in the movie?"

Kerns' nose was back in the tiles. "Not in the movie."

Daily and Nestor watched Slam cock his head under Ealing's chaise as he scanned for more damage on the body. He caught their stares.

"The chief's moving things around to get ready for this puppy," Slam said. "Lots of problems with it. Estimated time of death between two and four AM, factoring in the vented abdomen. Right hand shows some abrasions."

"Right-handed or left-handed cut?"

"You tell me where the killer was standing, Nestor, I'll be a fountain of answers."

"Evidence of sexual assault?" Daily asked.

"Not that I can see externally, but you know how that goes. One molar is broken. Contusion here consistent with a blow to the cheek that could have split the tooth. We'll run swabs when we get him downtown, but he's been sloshed pretty good with the muriatic and water."

"Any of the perp's blood?"

"That isn't oxidized to hell from the acid? No's your short answer. I'd say you're going to need something other than blood. Your man Kerns has worked miracles before. Call one in."

Kerns grunted at the floor.

"Hairs?" Daily asked Kerns.

"Can't even find one consistent with the vic so far. Floor's so clean, I think it was vacuumed. Not with the Oreck in the maintenance closet over there, something else."

The scene around Ealing meticulous. Blood and evidence washed in acid.

Obsessive. Careful.

Slam gently tweezed the swell of fatty tissue from Ealing's mouth.

"Posterior head wound on the left side," he said. "Looks like he was banged against the side of this iron lounge chair. This all may be clean now, but it was ugly at some point."

Butchered like in his own movie.

Certain things matching. Certain things missing.

Contradictions.

At the back of the conservatory Daily eyed the trail of damp white powder that led out the rear door. It would be near impossible to scoop or vacuum it without compromising evidence.

"Where's the estate manager now?"

"Upstairs in the house with Burns and Pierce," Nestor said. "Guy's pretty wrecked; they'll radio as soon as he's coherent." He studied Daily's copper suit. It was her last clean outfit, but the linen had creased after sitting in the discount store bag for days. Nestor cocked his head. "Donna Karan?"

"Not at forty-nine dollars, it isn't. But thanks for trying."

He leaned in, caught her breath. "Visit the vineyard already?"

Daily reached for her Altoids. "I'm allowed a drink on my first day off after three weeks on those ecstasy scumbags."

"I was there, too. The difference is, I sleep at night."

Daily didn't answer. His stare was protective and annoying.

Nestor shrugged. "Okay by me if RHD takes this mess—"

"Don't start," Daily cut him off. He knew just how to press her buttons. Robbery-Homicide, the LAPD's elite detective team based out of headquarters, would love to step in on this one. But as much as she felt out of her depths, Daily wanted to prove she could handle it, for a lot of reasons. "Tell me the rest."

Nestor read from his notepad—other details of Eddie Ealing's party that echoed what she'd heard on Mulholland from the Channel Six reporter. Kelly Spreck always seemed to scoop everyone else in town, from the network affiliates to news radio. Daily wondered who the reporter's source was, wondered if she had more than one.

"Was the recording of his voice cued to anything in particular?"

"Nope. Recordable CD. Set on continuous replay." Moving to the audio rack behind the bar, Nestor flicked a switch. Eddie Ealing's booming voice filled the room.

"What are you—a moron?"

"No . . ." A male voice.

"This was a good use of my money?"

"Probably not."

"So I'm the moron then?"

Daily walked to the player, hit STOP. Remembered something she'd read about Ealing. "In a *Times* interview, Eddie once said his job description was 'navigating the stupidity of others.' He called it 'shorting excellence.'"

"That's too cynical," Nestor chuffed. "Even for me."

Daily appraised the amenities in the conservatory. "A very rich cynic." She made a note to identify other voices from the disc, then looked at the whole scene. "The theatrics don't match the rest, Nestor. Half of this mess is staged for the drama, to match his movie, the other half screams impulse killing. The acid, the powder on the floor. Stuff found here on the premises."

"The whole thing looks like a problem," he said. "I'm serious about RHD, Daily. You look like shit. Even the nice duds don't hide the fact that you're running on fumes."

"Gee, thanks."

He leaned in close to her and looked down. "And you got two different socks on. Chili peppers on black and flying basketballs on brown."

Flustered, Daily lifted her pant legs. "They're flying oranges."

Nestor smirked. "This just keeps getting better."

"My head's in the game, not my accessories."

"Whatever you say. Tellin' you, Robbery-Homicide's going to want this puppy. Lots of media. Lots of heat."

She felt the morning's hollowness ebb; in its place came adrenaline. "RHD's not the only crew that can deal with heat," she said. "And they've got their hands full."

Most of the Robbery-Homicide team was currently embroiled in a volatile double homicide. A local rap star and a visiting baseball pro had exchanged gunfire outside a concert. Black against white; both died. Thirty witnesses, no consistency. Truth shifting like the San Andreas. The baseball player's family claimed the LAPD had been bribed by the rap star's record company. The rap star's relatives said the white athlete was the member of a right-wing militia that had sympathizers inside the LA force. Ever since the Rampart scandal, the police had to respond to all claims with a landslide of facts to the contrary, in addition to clearing cases. Guilty until proven impotent.

"I'll be done with my first pass in a couple minutes," Slam said as he pulled at Ealing's eyelids with tweezers. "Then he's yours for close-ups."

Daily's eyes watered as Slam poked. She worried that RHD would, in fact, try and take over this case. As the female homicide detective with the LAPD's best clearance rate, Daily was a rumored candidate for the select squad, but in truth she wanted to stay in the Hollywood Division. Less bureaucracy, less hazing.

Less pressure?

She quashed that notion; she could take it. But fitting in with the bulls at headquarters would require full-time political maneuvers, or she'd be pegged the "administrative one." She'd had drinks with a female RHD detective who drew a pie chart on a cocktail napkin: less than ten percent of her time was spent investigating. Daily didn't want the promotion, even the raise, if it meant becoming a glorified paperpusher and poster child for diversification. At the Hollywood station no one cared about Daily's plumbing, her skin color or her politics, just her skills. And the people who lived in her division—the struggling creatives, the crew people, the Latino families, the Russian immigrants, the retirees who spoke of the old studio system and the golden age of Hollywood, even the *cognoscenti* cresting Mulholland—most of them just wanted a safe place to live.

But Eddie frigging Ealing. Sweet Jesus. This was no ordinary murder; this was top block news, front page. The loo had called her and Nestor to the scene and it wasn't even their rotation; something was definitely up. She told herself she could handle it as well as RHD, maybe better without the downtown bullshit. But the media . . . if she got it and failed, well, she'd swan dive on the national news.

Slam was done with Ealing's body. Kerns and his SID crew still canvassed the edges of the room. Daily walked toward the victim and made her first contact. The corpse was stiffening; rigor would peak between six to twelve hours after death. The long incision in his middle wasn't jagged; it was a confident cut, free of hesitation marks. She checked Ealing's eyelids for petechiae, the telltale pinpoints of blood that could accompany heart attacks, aneurysms, or strangulation. A mere eleven pounds of compression on the carotid arteries wiped a victim unconscious in ten to fifteen seconds.

"None in the eyes," Slam narrated as her fingers searched. "But I'm guessing those are livor petechiae on his back, not contusions. Lowest point on him, the way he's lying with that leg rest on the chair angled up. ME will be able to tell you for sure."

"The eyes and the fat were cut out post mortem?"

"Affirmative. The gut cut isn't what killed him."

"And the tongue isn't taken," Daily said. "Ealing's greatest weapon, arguably. If someone wanted to mimic the murder in *Sense of Life*, why *wouldn't* they cut it out? Lack of time? Fragmented thinking? Interruption? Or is it some other kind of message?"

Ealing's hands were already bagged to preserve any scrapings underneath the nails. The coroner's team would clip each one, keep them in clearly marked manila envelopes, and study them one by one.

She stared at Ealing's inverted eyes. What had they last seen? One blow had broken a tooth, another slammed the back of his skull. During the examination of a body it was critical that Daily see everything in sharp detail, without emotion. But after that, she put the logic away. Impressions took over as she tuned into the entire scene. Like a Rauschenberg collage, the disparate pieces could make sense only when you stepped back and experienced them whole.

Some aspects obsessive. Careful. Others screaming impulse. Mess.
Butchered like his own movie. Theatrical.
Certain things matching. Certain things missing. Contradictions.
Fifty-seven names . . . more than one killer? One killer with two minds?

Her skin felt hot, but her bones chilled. Dizziness swayed her, the same lightheadedness she felt near the ocean. Daily thought she smelled warm salt air, stale and fetid. She asked if the pool was fresh or saltwater; Nestor said fresh. Her imagination, then, or something else—the spin of the chemicals. She could stomach the foulest of crime scene odors, but here, the muriatic acid was mixing with her fatigue and the trails of wine in her system to create some sort of toxic cocktail.

"You okay?" Nestor asked as Daily gripped the chaise's frame.

"Yeah. Just trying to piece it together. If someone wanted him dead, there's easier ways. Shoot him, drug him, stab him."

"Hell, he was swimming before. Perp could have just held his head under, drowned him."

Daily's ribs tightened. She couldn't catch her breath. *The rumble of waves. Hands. Choking.* Damn the ocean this morning, damn desensitization. This was a pool house. She wasn't afraid of pools at all, she loved their containment, their clarity. Nothing hidden. She told herself to focus. The blood pulsing in her head was so loud she almost didn't hear Nestor.

"You all right, Daily?"

She found her breath. "Just thinking."

Nestor didn't look convinced. "This screams a lot more than murder."

Daily nodded. The mess shrieked at something inside her, something familiar. She willed it away. She was just tired. Amid the conflicts there was clarity, if she could just get her head above it.

She found her voice, steadied it. "He was killed right here in his own haven, butchered like the victim in one of his own movies. And that's the clearest message of all."

TWO

THE TALL, IMPOSING FIGURE of Lieutenant Theo Powell strode into Eddie Ealing's first-floor library. The room was two stories tall, with first-edition books and collectors' videos filling four walls. Nestor often joked that Lt. Powell was like basketball coach Phil Jackson in Samuel L. Jackson's body. He exuded a Zen-like calm that belied the storm inside. Powell nodded at Daily and Nestor without a word, then handed Daily the search warrant—not required to check the home or business of a clear homicide victim, but preferred in a case where the victim was as well-known, and as vilified, as Eddie Ealing.

As he donned a latex glove, Powell perused a set of shelves filled with awards, photos, and souvenirs. The detectives knew enough to let the loo initiate conversation. He stared at a pair of Elton John's glasses, then a pair of Shaquille O'Neal's tennis shoes. Photos of Ealing with Elton and Shaq hung above the items. Powell walked to the television sitting in the open armoire, turned it on.

Reporter Kelly Spreck's head filled the screen. *"News Six has tape of the victim's father, Dr. Reece Ealing, last weekend, as he joined senate*

frontrunner Paul Tidell in Los Angeles to speak at the summit meeting
of the National Organization for Better Literature and Entertainment—
NOBLE, as they're more commonly known."

On the taped broadcast of his speech, conservative lion Dr. Reece Ealing comported himself as if he was still twenty-five and head of the pride, even though he was pushing seventy. His signature white hair didn't reflect light, it seemed to emanate it. With his patrician countenance and paternal smile, he could be St. Peter's stand-in at the pearly gates, Daily thought, just lose the Brooks Brothers for a robe. In a deep and commanding voice, Doc spoke of the psychological merit of the "right" kind of entertainment, of the moral corruption all too prevalent in books, music, and movies being fed to young minds today. No mention of the right parenting, Daily noticed.

Nestor mumbled to Daily. "The guy who wrote the book is Eddie Ealing's dad?"

"*Safe Minds, Sound Lives.*"

"I read it. Mother of God, Eddie wasn't exactly a chip off the old block, was he?"

Lt. Powell interrupted them. "Daily—you won a NOBLE award last year?"

"Yes, sir. Youth Mentors program."

Powell's gaze fixed on Nestor. "You still have one cheek on my shit list." He looked back at Daily. "Burns and Pierce are yours for the duration."

"It's ours, not RHD?"

Powell confirmed it. "It's ours. It's yours. You're lead, Daily. All of this is based on RHD's current preoccupation with the arena shooting and some other trade-offs I had to make. One of them is Pierce. She's won three NOBLE commendations."

Daily and Nestor exchanged a rocky glance. Their excitement dimmed at the mention of the insufferable junior detective.

"There a problem?" asked the lieutenant.

"No problem with me or Nestor, sir. But Pierce—"

"What about her?"

"You think she's up to this? She's only been on homicide—"

"You do the Hollywood dance, Daily. Pierce is good with blue bloods. Doc Ealing knows someone she knows from Yale, et cetera, et cetera." Lt. Powell sighed. "Seemed important to the old man that he speak with someone who's *simpatico*, as he put it."

"Doc Ealing has spoken to Pierce?"

"The mayor first. Then Pierce."

"How does this follow protocol?" Daily's voice revealed her irritation.

"It doesn't. It's going to be different on a whole lot of levels and I don't have a choice in the matter. *Simpatico?* The chief and I expect your full cooperation as a team. I'll give you all the additional manpower you need. Make it work." The lieutenant stared hard at Daily.

"What'd I do now?"

"No maverick stuff this time. I let you have your head when it's just us girls, but there's lots of folks watching. Important folks. Political critical."

Daily bit her lip. "Loo, aside from Doc Ealing, we're going to be talking to more than fifty people from *Eddie's* world—they clam up if you come at them too hard. Pierce makes Rush Limbaugh look easygoing." Daily found the smirk tugging at Lt. Powell's mouth disconcerting, but she continued. "Nestor, Burns, and I . . . we've learned how to talk to these folks. Play the nuances. Pierce gets all dogmatic and righteous. She comes off like some hard-ass militant and that's going to shut every door and mouth in the entertainment communi—"

Taryn Pierce's nasal, hyperefficient voice shot from behind Daily.

"Last person to see the vic alive was Helmy Ulgrod, Ealing's personal assistant. Found Ealing sleeping after his swim. Covered up to the chest with a blanket on the chair. Didn't disturb him. Says Ealing often slept out there in the summer, didn't like to be wakened when he nodded off. Helmy found the vic, 10:10 AM, made the call."

Daily reddened. Lt. Powell smiled and said, "Come in and continue, Pierce."

Pierce acted like she hadn't overheard Daily's comments. "The housekeeper, Helmy's wife Berta, wouldn't stop talking. I didn't want her to pollute the guy's recollections, so when Helmy came to I took him aside and got his statement. Had a panic attack talking about Eddie, went to the bathroom and swallowed too many Xanax. He's upstairs now, knocked out again. I took the wife's statement in the meantime."

The loo didn't mention Pierce's dance around the chain of command, didn't give Daily a chance to ask. Instead he said, "Keep me posted. *Team.* Got to go feed some worms to the birds." He tipped his head at the news coverage on TV and left.

Daily and Taryn Pierce assessed one another, as they had so many times at the station. In contrast to Daily's lanky frame, dark eyes, and careful manner, Pierce was a sparkplug of blonde impulse. Everything about her was quick, furtive, and snappy, from her blunt haircut to her scrubbed face and machine-gun patter. Daily had given Pierce a lot of thought when the younger detective arrived in March. She tried to serve as the kind of mentor she'd wished she'd had when she first got bumped up to homicide, a tough gig made tougher on women, but Pierce rejected Daily's attempts at bonding. Daily didn't know if it was because Pierce was Ivy League educated, an elitist, or both, but after a series of rebuffs, Daily let it slide.

Nestor held up one of the guest lists to break the tension. "Fifty-seven live ones. Opportunity abounds. Not to mention guests of the guests."

Daily said, "They weren't necessarily guaranteed an invite themselves, or admittance, so let's focus on the invited guests and the help first."

"We have the knife?" Pierce asked her.

"Not yet. Looks like it's single-edged. No ricasso marks on the vic. Clean, sure cut, but it's not what killed him. Slam's guess is blunt force trauma to the head."

"Before or after—the rest?"

"Before."

"Got as many motives as we got people," Nestor grumbled.

"Top ten," Daily said. "Love, sex, fear, rage, possession, revenge, blackmail, madness, secrets."

"That's nine," said Pierce.

"And money," Daily finished. "Who gets Ealing's?"

"His attorney's on vacation," Detective Clem Burns said as he entered the library.

The small, saturnine man was close to retirement. Daily and Nestor, who pegged people to their animal analogs to pass time on stakeouts, had dubbed him "The Crab." Tough shell, soft inside, snatched his facts and his perps when people least expected it, from an angle. Nothing got to Burns, not even his partner, Pierce.

Burns said, "A partner at the firm says Ealing's lawyer is the only one who knows where his last will is. But he's not out of town, he's just off. We can find him at the Equestrian Center later today, if we have to."

"We have to," Daily said. "How about relatives?"

"Ealing's wife is an ex. Not in the vicinity last night or any time in the last three years."

Pierce added, "Sister Aubrey lives in New York. Mother's deceased. Brother Peter was here at the party last night along with Doc Ealing, surprisingly. I spoke with him. They heard from the news first."

Hell of a way to find out, thought Daily. "Pierce, check into the exact aspects of the movie Ealing produced—"

"*Sense of Life*. The director has a production deal with Crescent—Ealing's company—as I'm sure you know, considering your extensive contacts in Hollywood." Pierce shot a look at Daily, then recapped the details of the death in the film and the parallels to the homicide. With distaste, she recited what was in the movie victim's nostrils.

"That's just dirt in our vic's nose." Daily was interested in the differences. Every single one.

"Potting soil from one of the planters," Nestor added. "Kerns said some trailed."

"The fat matches. So does the replay of the victim's voice. The guy in *Sense of Life* is left holding five business cards—"

"Cards from his Rolodex," Pierce corrected. "All of the five people hated him, wanted him dead. The director says that part was Eddie's idea."

"It was Agatha Christie's."

"Shakespeare," Burns mumbled.

"You want conspiracy, you want Romans." Pierce went for the last word, as usual. "*Let us bathe our hands in Caesar's blood.*"

Nestor rolled his eyes and Daily knew what they were both thinking: *Why the hell did this college-degree-freak showoff ever want to be a cop?*

Through the window, Daily could see the coroner's van backing up to the conservatory. The narrow stone walkway was lined by a phalanx of white camellias in tall pots so the vehicle had to park twenty feet away from the pool house door. Daily heard the churn of sliced air—a news copter she couldn't see from inside the house. She wished the coroner's attendants would hurry and put Ealing's body bag in the van before the sky cam could shoot the whole damned thing in living color.

Pierce pointed at one wall in the library, filled floor to ceiling with tomes. "See this? I ran a rough count earlier. The guy has more than five hundred murder mysteries, thrillers, true-crime books. Obsessed with death."

"His company produced thrillers," Nestor said.

Daily went to the wall, thumbed the titles:

Serial Killers in North America.

The Rutledge Guide to Mass Murderers.

The Root of Rage.

Daily knew the rhetoric all too well. "Psychologists say it comes from childhood trauma—people with an inordinate interest in this stuff."

"They say that about cops," Nestor said.

Pierce added, "They say that about killers."

Through the windows, Daily watched as the coroner's men carried the bagged victim to the open doors of the van.

"Movies," Nestor scoffed, "give people sick ideas. You know how many creeps cite flicks and music as influences? Richard Ramirez, Manson, the Columbine kids."

Pierce said, "He's right. Sociopaths are—"

"Ticking time bombs." Daily watched the coroner's crew on the berm. "If it isn't Nine Inch Nails, it's that girl that said 'No,' or a book, or a lousy meal that sets them off. The Taliban allowed no music, no movies and still found plenty of 'reasons' to kill. You really want to censor Dickens and Surf Burgers?"

"A bad burger doesn't glamorize murder, for God's sake." Nestor wiped his face.

"God wasn't at this party," Daily said.

Outside, Slam placed the remnants of Eddie Ealing in a small ice cooler, the same kind most people took to the beach. Above the pool house, the Channel Six News copter dropped in for a shot. An orb was attached to the chopper, a color video camera with a precision broadcast gimbal designed for long-range surveillance or live news shots. A close-up of their crime scene.

"You want to clean something up, Nestor? Go sanitize that." Daily shot her chin at the TV.

On the live broadcast, Kelly Spreck's voice distorted with excitement. *"Our Sky Cam has these exclusive shots of the scene and we must warn you—some of the images are graphic and disturbing, so if you have children . . . "*

Tiny images of Daily and Nestor stood next to the sunlit sprawl of Eddie Ealing split open on his chaise. Tape from twenty minutes ago, she guessed. Better-funded media outlets now had equipment that could shoot video, read lips and record voices up to a quarter-mile away.

"They shot through the damn skylight," Nestor said, disgusted. "Yesterday, it was night vision when we were nailing those other perps. Damn defense technologies on a media budget. Unlimited access. Friggin' first amendment gone malignant." Nestor exhaled. "Unreal."

Pierce agreed. "Out of control."

Nestor went on, "No rules for anyone, but I'm hogtied six ways from Sunday just trying to keep this place safe for people who want to turn it into hell's rodeo."

Daily had enough. "Pierce—you and Burns head back to the station, make copies of the guest list. Powell's giving extra manpower. Use it. Start calling names from the top. I want to know who was in the pool house, when, why, how, and what Ealing's mood was last night, minute by minute. Get me copies of the records Eddie worked on, and all his films on tape. The ones in which he had a major role or credit."

"Popcorn and bonbons too?" Pierce muttered.

Daily ignored her and addressed Nestor. "Let's go see if Helmut Ulgrod's coherent yet."

"I already took his statement," Pierce said. "And the wife's. You weren't here."

Daily felt her jaw clench. "Appreciate it, Pierce, but I want to talk to him myself."

The junior detective blinked back disdain. "Of course you do."

In the second-floor quarters of the northwest wing of Eddie Ealing's estate, Helmut Ulgrod lay groaning on a settee. His wife Berta consoled him in a language that sounded like German. Everything about Helmy Ulgrod was narrow and thin except for his round head. His russet hair was uncombed and wet from sweat. Red patches mottled his cheeks and high forehead. At the sound of their arrival, Helmy rubbed his face, opened groggy eyes, and tried to focus. Long, pale fingers crawled toward his heart. Daily pulled up a chair. She placed Pierce's notes on her lap for comparison.

"Mr. Ulgrod? I'm Detective Daily. This is Detective Nestor. We're in charge of Eddie's case. Anything you can tell us that might help?"

Helmy's expression froze, then crumpled. His answer was a moan.

"Did anyone threaten Eddie recently?"

An interminable pause. "Every day." His words were a whisper.

"Do you know who killed him?"

Helmy turned toward his wife's shoulder, shaking his head, no. More red grazed his neck.

"The guests from the party—did Eddie argue with any of them?"

"Some." His accent was noticeable now. "Not yesterday only. Eddie like to rub people's faces in things." *Tings.*

"Did he rub your face in things?" Nestor asked.

Helmy began to hyperventilate—tight, quick breaths.

The wife glowered at the detectives. Her accent was thicker than her husband's. "The other police ask us already. Helmy has bad heart—he need rest now."

Daily chose her words carefully. "I'm the lead investigator, and I may need to ask some questions several times, in different ways. It helps witnesses think of new details, and right now, we need every single one." Daily touched Helmy's shaking hand; it was cold. "Is there anything else you can recall?"

Berta said, "We say everything—to other one. Look how upset he is—you want he should have heart attack? He should die too?"

"Of course not, Mrs. Ulgrod. But your husband is the one who discovered—the situation. His recollections are the most important."

"Later. All this will put him in hospital again."

"I appreciate Mr. Ulgrod's condition and we'll do everything we can to make sure his health isn't jeopardized. But I'm sure you don't want to give the killer any advantage. After forty-eight hours, our chances of catching the murderer nosedive. That's just the way the statistics play out in homicides. The ones we don't catch can kill again."

Berta Ulgrod sniffed and sat back.

Memories rifled Helmut Ulgrod's rheumy eyes. "God," he gasped. "It's all my fault."

Daily and Nestor stiffened.

Shock blared on Berta Ulgrod's face. She draped her arm over her husband's shoulder, cooed to him like a child. "You're upset, Helmut. Don't talk nonsense—"

"It's not nonsense, Mama!" Helmy's voice broke. "Is God's truth—"

"Helmut, don't get—"

"Enough!" Helmut Ulgrod's tone was sharp.

Berta's lips made small smacking noises. Her expression tap-danced to some debate in her head. Daily waited for what seemed like an interminable length of time, letting silence do its work.

"Mike send gift to Eddie," Helmy said finally. "I call no one. I should have call the police."

Daily struggled to keep her expression calm. "Mike?"

"It was a woman's heart. Mike's Gifts send him a woman's heart."

THREE

It was going to be one hell of a news day. Dr. Paulette Sohl strode through the newsroom at Channel Ten, her ponytail glazed to the sweat on her back. A damn scorcher outside. Her ample hips knocked a stack of mail off the desk she shared with one of the late side writers. Books with cover photos of skinny women laughed at her. Her deskmate was working on *The Five Best Diets of the Year*. Paulette had tried them all and failed.

The assistant news director, Davis Jacoby, approached with a predatory look: tight jaw, dark hair falling loose in his eyes, serious grinding of white teeth that was supposed to pass for a management smile. Breaking news, new psycho, new story. She looked down until his fingertips tapped their arrival on Paulette's desktop.

"The next cut-in, Paulette. I need one minute at eleven-thirty-seven. Just your educated guess."

Everyone wanted the instant answers from her, the station's freelance shrink. Cartoon Lucy five-cent analysis. She was about to tell Davis she expected more of an educated man, but instant news meant ratings and Davis' gig. Thankful she was only a consultant, she said, "I'm here to tape the workplace sex thing for early. That's all."

"One minute. Just your overall impression of the killer—"

"I don't do knee-jerk diagnosis." Paulette bent to pick up the letters and postcards she had knocked to the floor:

Dr. Paulette Sohl ℅ News 10.

Doc Soul ℅ Top News 10.

TV Shrink, News Ten.

Screw You, Dr. Jew.

Marry Me Paulette ℅ News 10.

Hey Shrink Rap: What Do You Know About Me?

Thanks Dr. Sohl. Gardena Family Mental Health Center.

They were out there, each one of them, watching the Channel Ten News. Most of them had a hard enough time dealing with reality, and already Davis wanted to provide a phantom killer. Ludicrous, these endless, incendiary postulations. It could have been a lover, a business partner, an extremist, a hundred people with a thousand reasons. Don't bite Davis' head off, she told herself. Ratings proved people watched the guess-perts no matter how uninformed they were. Sadly, there seemed to be no saturation point; enough people kept tuning in to make it a market—a hot one. After forty-three years of life and more than a dozen in psychology, Paulette realized human behavior could still baffle her. She gave herself a paper cut as she stacked the postcards into two piles: respond or don't respond. Paulette stood and looked at Davis. "When there's more information—"

"It'll be old news. C'mon. You used to be all over this forensic stuff."

"Past tense. No one knows enough about this story yet. You want an accurate psychological profile or a bad one?"

"This is breaking now. People want your opinion. *Now*."

"You need my opinion—now—because there are only bits and pieces of something that sounds pretty ghastly and has all kinds of ramifications for the media and Hollywood, and you want me to fill in the blanks, and I won't do that, Davis. I won't make up shit."

"Calm down. Who asked you to make up shit?"

"How can I possibly make any intelligent statements that relate to the profile of this killer now?"

"Gozman's doing it over at Six. Says the killer's a young male, eighteen to twenty-four, with neo-Nazi leanings who may have tried to break into the movies and been rejected."

Paulette willed her anger back. "Gozman's a loon who should have his license burned."

"Tell me how you really feel."

"This is how I really feel: this piece of news scares the hell out of me. Not because it's gruesome, not because it's a copycat killing of a movie plot, not even because the victim is someone as invincible as Eddie Ealing. It scares me because it might *not* be a psycho thing."

The assistant news director paled. "What do you mean?"

"Psychos are easy. It's how we explain away the dark, rogue pieces of society we don't like very much. '*Oh, he's psycho.*' We just put it in a box and lock it up. Well, this might not be that. A lot of people have had enough of the endless chaos and violence around them and they want it stopped in the media, stopped in their movies and music, stopped on the news, and stopped in their world. Period." Her pulse revved. It wasn't like her to feel so agitated.

"You think someone in their *right* mind did that?" he asked.

"I'm not sure. But I'll tell you this—if it's *not* a psycho, you have much bigger problems than your next news break."

FOUR

"EDDIE TOLD ME SAY nothing about the heart," Helmy Ulgrod told Daily and Nestor. "It look ripped out, not even cut. Awful. Bloody. He was—so upset."

"Did you also see the delivery from Mike's Gifts, Mrs. Ulgrod?"

Berta said she hadn't. Daily stood and paced the room. Taryn Pierce had interviewed the Ulgrods separately. Why hadn't she discovered this critical piece of information? Had Helmy withheld it out of fear? Or was Pierce holding back? Daily asked Berta to leave the room so they could discuss the heart alone with Helmy, but she refused.

"I know how much he can take, you don't," Berta protested. "I stay or I call his doctor. He will make you leave Helmy alone."

Daily suppressed her irritation. She couldn't risk precious time, and right now the man clearly wanted to purge his memory. "Mr. Ulgrod, are you positive it was a human heart? Sometimes people use organs as scare tactics or pranks. Animal hearts. Someone sent Marcia Clark a sheep's heart when she was working the O. J. trial."

Helmy thought about it. "Berta and I, we cook. We butcher our own meat where we come from, in Alsace. It could have been animal heart, could have been human. Of course—I see few human hearts in my life. I check Mr. Ealing's incoming email, and—you can imagine—I hardly knew how to give him this message."

Daily stopped pacing. "This *gift* was an email?"

Helmy nodded. "It was, how you say—virtual. You click message and picture of gift box appear, like little movie. It open by itself and there is the heart. Bloody. Horrible."

"A cartoon? Animation?"

"Real looking. Real heart, believe me. Make me sick."

"Eddie received other mean-spirited messages in the past?"

"Yes. Before 9/11 attacks we receive bad packages, bad mail sometime. I return unexpected things now, unopened. This just email . . . but worse for him." He stifled a moan.

"Why show it to Eddie then? Why not delete it?"

Helmy's shoulder curled. "You have to know Eddie. He want to see things like that. Everything. Always. Want to know who is trying—how you say—'wind him up.' In '99, Eddie get bomb threat, next year voodoo doll with pins in—you know—bad places. Sometime disgusting things in bags, dead flower. Sick things. Now just bad email."

Nestor asked, "What makes you think this one had anything to do with his murder?"

"It was only one that ever upset him."

Interesting, Daily thought. Or an interesting lie. "And the sender was named 'Mike'?"

"Blue card that open in email say 'Mike's Gifts.' No way to find who sent. I try."

"Did any of the previous deliveries or email messages ever come from Mike's?"

"No."

"Is Mike's Gifts a shop? A website?"

"I call several shops in U.S. with this name; none send email gift like this."

Like they'd admit it if they did. The LAPD techs would find out soon enough. "You said it was a woman's heart. How would you know?"

"Photo next to heart—young woman, dark hair, dark eyes. Eddie recognize her. I do not. It make Eddie more upset than heart. Blood on her photo, too. Whole thing—whole message—like something awful happen to her—like this is *her* heart."

Lord, Daily thought, how could Pierce miss this? "Did you or Eddie print the email, the images?"

"I did not. He look at message, replay it several time, close library door. Next time I use computer, message is gone. He never mention again."

"As upset as Eddie was, you didn't ask him more about it? Look for printouts? You didn't call in a computer specialist to track the sender, or call the ISP?"

Berta said, "We work for Mr. Ealing and those decision he make! Is not Helmy's fault he is dead!"

"I didn't say it was, ma'am." Daily turned back to Helmy. "When did it come?"

The strange-looking man thought about it. "June twenty-third. We have dinner party for Eddie's music guys, some others. Message come middle of day. After flowers. Before air shipment with caviar. I go to service entrance, sign for things—help come in and out on party days."

Daily took the names of the florist and the caterer; they'd interview the people working at that time and see if anyone slipped into the library to mess with the PC. "Do you think Eddie might have made a printout and hid it somewhere?"

Helmy shook no and shrugged.

"Show me where he kept his private items."

———————

Helmy hesitated in Eddie's library and looked at his wife. She was clearly steamed at him for telling the police about the virtual delivery from Mike's Gifts. Daily wondered if it was protective instinct or something more. Helmy directed Daily to Ealing's antique mahogany desk. He weaved and his wife grabbed his arm, then helped him sit down.

"This is where Eddie like to think," he said. "He spend most work time here."

The library Eddie's brain haven, the pool house his escape, Daily thought. Nestor's mind was in sync with hers—he radioed out to the SID crew in the conservatory, told them to look for a computer printout of a dark-haired young woman, a heart, or both. Nestor asked the voice on the other end of the walkie-talkie to hang on. "How big is the image?" Nestor asked Helmy.

"It fill screen on computer, when gift box open."

"No, the part with the girl."

"Ah—like for wallet. Smaller."

"Color?"

"Color."

"Professional or family photo?"

Helmy considered. "Like you get at shopping center. Curtain behind."

Nestor paraphrased the description into his radio while Daily started on a desk drawer. Helmy Ulgrod might be pushing focus in one direction to serve his own agenda. The wife grew more peeved by the minute. Daily's gloved hand found a stack of statements from attorneys, banks in New York, Los Angeles, Switzerland. The balance at Ealing's Beverly Hills branch alone was more than Daily made in five years. On a piece of paper were the name and phone of a national TV newsmagazine host.

"Cray Wrightman? Of *TimeLine?*"

Helmy squinted. "Eddie try get him to come to party. He did not."

Daily saw notes scribbled by the dates: *5-23 Not in, msg. 5-24 Not in, msg. 5-28 Asst PMS, hung up. Send wine...*

"He made all these calls to Wrightman himself?"

"Yes. They knew each other long time ago."

"He call all his guests personally?"

"No. This was first time we invite Cray Wrightman. Long as I know."

Daily filed the message. "You said Eddie recognized the woman in the photo?"

"Yes. When he look at her, there was lot of pain in his face."

"First you called her a woman, now a girl. Which was she?"

"Her face look young. Nineteen, twenty, maybe. But her eyes— they knew lot. Like woman who live through things." *Tings* again.

"She was never here? Eddie never said her name?"

"No."

"Tell me again what happened last night, chronologically."

Berta snorted. "We told other one. That little *Zündkerze.*"

Daily prodded Helmy to repeat his story to see if anything changed.

He said, "Party is over. Catering clean up and loaded. Tents, rentals, also done. I go to check in conservatory; he like to swim lap before bed. It relax him. Inside he is sleeping on chaise so I cover him with blanket. He hate to be waken. So hard for him to fall asleep in first place."

Verbatim what Taryn Pierce had reported. Truth or a script? Daily said, "There was no sign of anything unusual?"

"No, he look like he always does when he sleep. Head to side, mouth open." Helmy held his breath. "There was one thing."

"Yes?"

"I find glass on pool bar and bottle of Glenlivet. Eddie not drink in long time. Recovery alcoholic. Now, he addict for sports drinks."

Nestor said, "You kept booze in the house when Eddie was an alcoholic?"

"He entertain often. We serve guests what they want. Eddie good about not drinking. Never in all time we work for him. Nine years."

"Ten," Berta corrected Helmy.

"What time did you find him sleeping in the pool house?" Daily asked him.

"One-fifteen, one-thirty."

"Could someone else have left the scotch out?"

"No, there was cleanup after party, but before he swim. Nothing left out."

"It didn't alarm you that Eddie had taken a drink of hard liquor?"

Helmy and Berta shared a look. Helmy said, "In our work, we see lot and make no comment. Is not our place."

At first skim, Daily found nothing remarkable in Eddie's desk drawers. Moving to the chair next to Helmy, she scanned his fingers for cuts or abrasions. One scrape on the top knuckle of his right index finger. Daily flipped through her notepad.

"Was Eddie's hair wet when you saw him sleeping on the chaise?"

"Wet? No. I don't think so."

Daily nodded at the abrasion. "How'd you scrape your hand like that?"

Berta stood. "You accuse Helmut, we get lawyer—"

"Mama, please. Sit." Berta sat down. He explained, "One of bartender for party lose knife in disposal. I had to go in and get. His name is Mario. You check, he tell you."

As Berta glared, Daily looked back over her notes. "The blanket that covered Eddie last night wasn't covering him when you walked in this morning."

Helmy quivered. "No."

"The recording of Eddie's voice was playing in the pool house."

"Yes."

Her pen tapped triplets on the small pad. "We think Eddie was killed between two and four AM, Mr. Ulgrod. Did you hear anything during that time?"

"I tell other one—something woke me, two-thirty, I think. I look out, think I hear something by conservatory. Main light turn off, but pool bar lamp on inside."

"You didn't feel compelled to go down and see what was happening?"

Indignance flared across Helmy's face. "Lot of thing maybe odd to you are not odd to us. Eddie often make call in early hour to London, Paris. Eddie do business international. We make many call around globe."

The royal "we" suddenly. Guilt over not checking as thoroughly as he should have or more that *we* weren't telling?

"We also have intercom. I buzz conservatory, ask Eddie, 'Everything all right?' He say he is fine." Helmy sighed. "Kind of fine that mean, 'Leave me alone.' Most important skill for us—when to help, when to leave alone. Require timing and experience."

"Separate pro from amateur," Berta gave the last word its French pronunciation.

Daily didn't point out that their special sense of timing had failed last night. "I'm sorry, I'm confused. At one-thirty, after the party, you *intuitively* knew that you should enter the pool house to check on Eddie Ealing because he had 'nodded off' after his swim? Yet at two-thirty, you somehow chose to use the intercom instead and *not* enter the pool house?"

Annoyed, Helmy exhaled. "I *use* intercom. I always check intercom before bother Eddie. Is when he *not* answer I go down and follow up, cover him with blanket. I go in first time because no answer. He is sleeping in conservatory. Second time I buzz him, at two-thirty, he say he is fine. 'Leave me *alone*' fine."

"Gonna need a damn decoder for this," Nestor groused.

Daily tried to read Helmy Ulgrod's sincerity, yet she knew from hours of behavioral sciences training, there was no foolproof visual indication if someone was lying. This homicide screamed *staging*, but Helmy seemed scared shitless, center stage without a clue. Again, Daily felt the tug: something personal, the reverberating strains of manipulation. Then again, with her history, she was prone to feeling tugs that weren't even there. *The facts. Stick to clarity.*

"The same phone lines are in the house and the conservatory?" she asked Helmy.

"Yes."

"Did you hear the call come in?"

"Which call?"

"You said Eddie was on a call—when you looked out."

"I say I hear noise, then see light on in conservatory."

"You assumed he was talking on the phone."

Helmy reddened. "Yes."

"But you never heard a call come in."

"No."

"Then either Eddie made an outgoing call, he was calling from a cell phone—

"—Eddie's cell was here, inside—"

"—he was talking to someone who was there, or he was talking to himself. The last option is that you simply heard the recording of Ealing. The one the killer left playing."

Helmy groaned.

Daily let it settle, then asked, "The virtual card and box from Mike's Gifts—anything distinctive?"

"Image of white box, card with name: 'Mike's Gifts.' Dark blue ink."

Daily looked at the strange constellation of notes staring back at her from her pad. Helmy was either terrified or a terrific actor. Impatient, she let frustration spill into her voice as she asked if any other strange gifts had arrived the same day. None had.

"You didn't mention the Mike's Gifts delivery to anyone else? Friends? Family?"

"No. Is just us two here. We hire help for parties, gardening, pool, but even when no entertaining, we have no time for friends. Family we have is back in Europe. We work six-day week, long hour, one day off when we have own errand to do, pay bill, send money and things home. Don't know what we do now. Have to find other position."

Berta's eyes had grown wet. She swallowed hard and studied her husband with a look that softened her face.

"How about Eddie's family?" Daily asked. "Are they close?"

Helmy thought a moment. "No. Mother pass. Sister, Aubrey, live in New York. Brother Peter is brainy guy, scientist. Doc and Peter, both here last night. They don't fit good with Eddie's guests. Doc like to argue with Eddie regarding Hollywood. But last night they stay off to self, with others from institute."

"What institute?"

"Temperel. Party was fundraiser for Temperel Foundation. Brain study. Eddie's mother has the Alzheimer before she die. Institute is in her honor. Peter is director. All Ealings on board."

"Was Eddie at odds with any of them?"

"Usual family things. Eddie always say his father tyrant. Doc say Eddie play his own game. Brother Peter never involved . . . he always, ah . . . *Anspruch genommen* . . . off his own planet . . . super IQ.

"Eddie have any recent business conflicts or problems?"

"Nothing new," Berta said. "Plenty of people argue with Eddie, but is his business. You expect some bad things. But not like that." She cocked her head toward the window facing the pool house.

Daily said, "What about jealousy? Revenge? Love?"

"No love," said Helmy. "Eddie had lot of girlfriends. He see them two, three time, then on to next. None serious. All girls stop in May."

"What happened in May?"

Berta shrugged. "No more centerfold or supergirls."

"Super*models*," Helmy corrected her.

Perplexed, Nestor studied the photos of Ealing on the wall. "Lots of brunette-browns, but I don't see any Cindy Crawfords or Catherine Zeta-Joneses here. In fact, these women look more like—"

"Got it." Daily wrote: *EE women—Bimbos? Pros $$? Brunettes/ Browns* . . . "Who was Eddie's date for the party last night?"

"No date," Helmy answered.

"Did he keep a safe here in the house?"

Helmy said he did, but he didn't use it. Ealing kept his currency and paper at the bank or with his business manager. The only items of real value at the house were those Ealing wanted displayed: memorabilia lining the walls and shelves—Shaq's shoes, celebrity pictures, platinum albums, awards, remarkable souvenirs.

"What are you doing?" Helmy barked as Nestor peered into one enormous tennis shoe. "Put it back!"

"You'd be surprised where people put things." Nestor's forearm lost itself in the size-22 sneaker, came out empty-handed. Next, he removed a framed photo and began undoing the back mat with his pocket knife.

"Careful—you will damage everything!" Helmy behaved as if Eddie Ealing might still chastise him. The detectives took apart the layers inside every frame searching for hidden material. No luck. Daily set the last frame back on the wall. She picked up Ealing's statuette for Best Producer on *Sense of Life*. The little gold man was heavier than he looked. She scanned the base for anything underneath then set it back in its place. An old 8mm camera stood next to it. She picked it up. PAILLARD-BOLEX read the metal strip under the lens.

"Eddie shot first home movie with that as boy in New York," Helmy explained. "He say camera show him better storyteller than director. No good eye for technical, just—how Eddie call it . . . 'Vision inside and passion to will things into being.'"

She studied Helmy. "Sounds like you admired him, Mr. Ulgrod. Unlike some other people."

"He was not—a bad man—I think maybe . . . tough with scars."

Will things into being. Vision inside. Daily pulled at the silver ring on the side of the camera, twisted it.

"Please—is delicate—" Helmy pleaded.

The camera popped open in Daily's hand. Inside, where a roll of 8mm film would have spooled, were two small, square photos tucked in place. Daily pulled out the first and turned it into the sunlight.

Helmy looked at it. "Eddie's mother. Monique. She die when just forty."

Daily reached in the camera for the second image. A color printout on computer paper. The mysterious dark beauty, a half-smile parting her lips, was as captivating as Helmy had described, but for the faded smear of crimson across her face.

FIVE

PAULETTE'S CELL PHONE CHIRPED as she left the TV station.

"I take today, no contest," Lane Daily's voice pronounced.

Paulette was the detective's former therapist, current landlord, and local television personality. The two women kept a running tally of who handled more insanity in a given day. Usually it was a release-valve, a way to step back and decompress after hours of immersion in minds gone off the deep end. Today it was just the sad truth.

"Think we can keep this one church and state, my friend?" Paulette meant it. The Ealing murder was going to be one big riptide, tangling police and media.

"You switching from psychology to investigative reporting?"

"No, Lane."

"Still just the News Ten guest shrink, job doctor, sexpert, and marriage guru?"

"Your *ex*-marriage guru. And *occasional* commentator for news insight."

"Then I'm not worried. Unless Ten made you a full-time staff offer today, covering the crime beat."

"They couldn't afford me, Detective Daily. And if the station doesn't start appreciating my freelance work more, I'll go back to magazine articles. Same work, less pancake."

Lane laughed, but Paulette heard the tension in her voice. Privately, Paulette was dying to ask her about the Ealing homicide, but she knew Lane preferred to mete out bits of case information on her own. If pushed, she'd shut down.

Paulette first met Helena Saggeza Daily four years ago, when the detective needed counseling to weather a divorce from her LAPD spouse but stay sane on the job. After she was done with therapy and splitting, Lane moved into one of the loft units by Paulette's Hermosa Beach condo—close to her budget and far from her ex. Paulette and her husband owned Lane's fourplex; Paulette managed it while Gerry, a road manager for rock bands, traveled about eight months of each year. Lane got a good deal; both women gained a friend.

Lane exhaled and finally asked Paulette what she'd heard about Ealing at the TV station.

Paulette relayed the rumors—the inverted eyes, the fat, the chemical-washed body. "Davis in the newsroom wants me to give viewers my 'first take' on the mind that did it. I told him no. He's pressing for something by tonight; I said tomorrow at the earliest, if at all. That's not fishing, by the way. I'll do my own research. I refuse to just slap together some half-baked profile to make the slot, like that media hog, Gozman."

"Understood." Lane paused. "Paulette, there's information out there that shouldn't be. Who knows the most in your newsroom?"

"Honestly? No one. Davis was getting everything he had from Kelly Spreck's pieces on Six . . . *Six*, of all places, not one of the big stations. That's what riled him. Our reporters are just recycling. Was it really like *Sense of Life?*"

"Close enough."

Paulette tried to clear the strain from her throat and couldn't. "The day is definitely yours, then. Maybe the year. I just have my Tuesday narci at two, then a new foot fetish."

"You know what they say about foot fetishes."

"They're the sick puppies. This one's been stalking Julia Roberts. He's convinced she needs her instep licked."

Usually Paulette could crack Lane's seriousness, distract her from the grim realities of her job, and in the process feel better herself. Today she just felt wired; everything played like gallows humor. She told Lane not to go too deep trying to figure everything out—Lane could go dangerously deep.

"Look who's talking."

"Speaking as an expert, as a matter of fact. Got to let it go at the end of the day."

"It's not the end yet," Lane said.

"That's your other problem, you never stop. You're not going to want to cook when you get home tonight. I'm making mahi-mahi in chipotle sauce, I'll leave some on your stove."

"Thanks." She hesitated. "Paulette—if you're still up—"

The tone in Lane's voice was disturbing. Paulette's friend had handled an uncertain childhood, a rollercoaster with the ex, and murder for a living. Through it all, Lane had learned to stay cool, to take charge, to make things right. But in all the time she'd known her, Paulette had never heard Lane sound as apprehensive as she did now.

"I'll be there."

SIX

THE SHRINK WAS GOING to be a problem, Tee thought as he put his headphones on the car seat next to him and braked two cars behind Daily's Crown Victoria. Sinfully easy to capture calls if you had the right system, he thought, just stay one step ahead of the latest technology. He'd have to listen in on their get-together tonight, but he was ready; he had the best equipment. *Anticipate.* If there was anything he'd learned after all the combat, the losses, it was to anticipate. He hadn't known Daily was tight with a psych, however. One who worked at a *TV* station, of all the luck. He would need to keep her away from Daily and off track. Whatever it took. Once a soldier, always a soldier.

President Truman's 1946 brainchild of putting ex-war equipment and soldiers to use was a worthy one. Now, generations later, Tee wondered what Truman would say about the notion, its evolution spawning surprising new strategies in undeclared wars of will and conscience, fighting erosion of a country and values that used to stand for something.

Gotta do what you gotta do, Tee.

Maybe. Maybe not.

Things getting a little out of hand, Tee? Can you handle it when you're in charge? When there's no military contract, no directive, no DynCorp operation, just you?"

"I can if it's for a good reason, Harry." Talking out loud to presidents helped Tee clarify matters.

What reason is that, Tee?

As he pondered his answer, he saw Daily pull into the Hollywood police station and park. Walking through the lot, she wiped her brow and stopped to fuss with some clip that wouldn't hold her mass of dark, willful hair. Watching, Tee felt the stirrings, then quelled them as he did all emotions. Everything about Lane Daily was willful, and that thrilled Tee even more than her coltish good looks.

"It's the right thing," Tee answered Harry Truman. "Someone has to stand up and do the right thing."

SEVEN

THE CARVED WOOD SIGN over Lt. Powell's desk said: *Hollywood Homicide. Our Day Begins When Yours Ends.* Daily sat across from the loo, her cup of Kona on his desk. Nestor straddled a backwards chair. Clem Burns parked himself in the corner, while Taryn Pierce paced.

The lieutenant scratched his head. "He's sure it was a real heart?"

Daily nodded. "Could have been an animal heart. Or a donor organ."

"What's a stolen heart?" Burns grumbled. "Grand theft?"

"But what made this Helmy fellow think this heart was *that woman's*? That's a big leap," the loo asked.

"Eddie Ealing's reaction." Daily pulled out an evidence bag. "This photo was in the message along with the heart from Mike's Gifts. Looks like Eddie cut the picture out and trashed the rest. The Ulgrods don't know the woman, but Helmy was sure Eddie did. We pressed him pretty hard on it."

Pierce tapped her fingernails on the back of Daily's chair. "Easier to press him when he's not floored on Xanax."

Daily shook off the barb; Pierce was just pissed because she had missed critical evidence and now it was hanging there in front of the lieutenant. *Magna cum screw up, Pierce.*

"Kerns called from the lab," Burns continued. "He's got at least one unidentified dark hair from the back door of the place—"

"The pool house," Nestor clarified. "Maybe it belongs to the woman in the picture. Maybe it's a hair from the woman's lover. Some guy stews when his woman hooks up with Eddie, the guy kills Eddie in a rage."

Daily said, "Maybe *Eddie* kills the woman in the photo. The lover, husband, brother, father retaliates by killing Eddie."

Without reacting to either idea, Burns studied his toothpick. "Kerns wants to show Quixote the hair when he gets back from court. See what the trace-to-case-king thinks."

Quixote was a celebrated hair and fiber expert at the LAPD's Scientific Investigation Division—he collected hairs of note from around the globe, from feral pigs on Kauai to dogs in TV commercials.

Daily moved to the sound recordings. "I sent the CD-R to Barber for voice analysis. Whoever killed Ealing knew he recorded people. CDs of his conversations were underneath the music discs, in a drawer you wouldn't just stumble into."

"That narrows it down to someone who observed Ealing recording or playing back conversations, or was told about it," said Nestor.

"Like Helmy Ulgrod?"

"If he left to go back out to the pool house between two and four, we'd either see him on one of the main house cameras or we'd see resets on the system, to open a door."

The lieutenant's knees cracked as he stood. "Search the databases and use every aspect of this to make a list of possible perps and keywords: *mimics, movies, media* . . . in case our killer's expressed his feelings before. Add aliases and work histories. Who worked security at this party?"

"ProStance," said Daily. "I already spoke with the owner. He'll have his supervisors call Burns with their reports. Owner had his best people on the event, none of them saw anything suspicious. Piece of cake compared to concerts at the Palladium."

"Speaks even more to an insider. What's the track on Mike's Gifts?"

"Four of the party guests I've interviewed have mentioned it," Pierce said. "It's an underground service that delivers gifts to jerks that need humbling."

"They deliver murder?"

"Anyone that sends images of a heart in a box should be put away. It's sick."

Drama, Daily thought. A heart in a box. A certain photo. Mike's Gifts. Something that could terrify a bear like Eddie Ealing. It wasn't about the heart, or the delivery, it was the *meaning*. The dreadful context was known only to sender and recipient, and Daily would need to get inside their heads to understand. Subtext. Implications. Swells of something she couldn't see on the surface of the case. Daily said she would run Mike's Gifts through a host of web and database searches.

"I've already found five results online," Pierce said. "A store in Omaha, a webpage for some kid's birthday party, and three sites on the Mike's Gifts that we want."

"A guy who does this has websites?"

Pierce shrugged. "Not him. They're fan sites."

Nestor chortled. "He has fans?"

"Just people talking about the gifts. Big underground hit apparently—and most of the postings seem recent. It's not just an LA thing. Plenty of activity back east and elsewhere. From the comments on the sites, it looks like everyone loves Mike's Gifts as long as they're not the recipient."

Pierce led the others to the computer on her desk, one of several homicide desks grouped together in a corner of the station. She clicked on a couple keys, brought up *www.themindbox.com.*

"This fan site, The Mind Box, is the most complete. Here's Mike's first gift. 1989. Mike ran an ad in the paper telling people to bring all their dead Christmas trees to 414 Yula Place for recycling." Pierce waited for recognition on the address, then grew impatient. "Joe Freed's house."

"President of IMT," Daily acknowledged. "Famous for that memo that got printed everywhere, 'Christmas is no day at the beach.' Made all his employees work the holidays. *People* or *Us* or someone called him 'The New Scrooge.'"

Pierce enlarged a photo on the webpage: dead Christmas trees piled six feet high. "Thirty-five hundred evergreens on his lawn."

"Whoopee. So Mike dumped on a putz. Big deal." Nestor rubbed the aggressive stubble on his chin.

Pierce clicked to a different page. "Here it says Mike is responsible for hiring that Nicole Brown Simpson lookalike that played the golf courses behind O. J. for a month." She went to another site. "This one says Mike arranged for all the hotel televisions on one of John Rocker's road trips to play *The Twilight Zone* movie episode with Vic Morrow. That's the segment where he's the racist and suddenly things are switched around—"

"We know it." Powell waved her along.

"There's page after page, plenty of people we know and hate— from Linda Tripp and the Menendez brothers to Pinochet and Imelda Marcos—plus others I hadn't heard of, but they all sound like—"

"Dickheads," Nestor said.

Pierce blinked. "I was going to say people with low morals and no character. Over a hundred gifts. Mike might be someone with a vendetta, a psychological bent against immorality. A heightened sense of injustice."

53

"Mike could be more than one person," said Nestor. "Who runs the site?"

"Computer geek. Clean as can be, just a freak for odd trivia like this."

Daily said, "Conjecture later. Right now, copy the team on the list of Mike's Gifts and the photo of our mystery woman. There's still thirty-five more guests to interview."

"And ninety new cold calls," Pierce added. "The power of the media."

"Ninety-two," Nestor corrected. "Not counting Captain Kirk, the Human Radio and four calls from supposed psychics."

"We interview everyone in the family?" Lt. Powell asked.

Pierce said, "I spoke with the sister, Aubrey. Lives in New York City. Only talked to Eddie on holidays. Mother's deceased, Alzheimer's. Brother Peter lives out here. Montecito. He was at Eddie's party last night, along with Doc Ealing, who's bicoastal."

"Doc's next," Daily added. "He's waiting for us now in Calabasas. We'll go see Peter after that. He works near Santa Barbara, at the Temperel Institute. They study memory."

"Refresh mine," Lt. Powell said. "Eddie have a beef with any of them?"

"All the Ealings are on the board at Temperel, but so are several others. The event last night was a fundraiser for Temperel. There were some family differences, but the housekeepers said none of it was new."

"Any business deals heat up or fall apart this week?"

Nestor said, "I'm heading over to the Equestrian Center to see Ealing's attorney. He's taking the week off, but he's around. No one else at the firm knows where the latest will is; Ealing changed it a few times, according to the lawyer's girl."

"Assistant," Daily corrected. "The Ulgrods said it was business as usual on other fronts. They had no idea what happened at Eddie's office because he was never there anymore. He spent most days in his library, other days working from bed. Helmy helped with faxes, letters. Eddie did most of his business by phone. No one needed to help this guy talk."

The lieutenant was paged; he picked up the phone. His brows rose then furrowed. "Send them back." He looked up at the four detectives. "Doc Ealing didn't feel like waiting in Calabasas."

The thick white hair on Doc Ealing's head caught Daily's eye immediately. The neat coif seen on the man's book jackets and TV talk shows was mussed. Two patrol officers recognized the man and offered their condolences. Trailing Doc, a dark-haired man asked the officers a question. Doc approached with a purposeful stride, the dark-haired man walking evenly behind him.

He said too loudly, "I'm Dr. Reece Ealing, Edward's father."

Every muscle on Doc's tall, sinewy frame seemed taut, Daily noticed. The lieutenant indicated that Daily was the lead detective and Doc shook her hand with a strength that belied his age. His eyes blazed, their edges red and angry.

The younger man was forty-something and confident. "I'm John Safford. Deputy Director of NOBLE. The National Organization for Better Literature and Entertainment. We've given the LAPD—"

"Dozens of commendations since your inception," Lt. Powell finished.

"Exactly. Your chief assures us we'll have the department's full attention."

Daily pondered the "we" part.

"Of course," said Lt. Powell "We'd like to ask—"

"This sociopath needs to be apprehended before he does any more damage," Safford interrupted.

Daily said, "We'd like to ask Dr. Ealing some questions, Mr. Safford. My people were on their way to see you, but since you're here—"

"Yes. We're here. Since you people seem to be moving so slow."

Daily ignored Safford and turned to Doc. "You were at Eddie's party last night?"

"Yes."

"You too, Mr. Safford?"

"Yes."

"You serve as Dr. Ealing's attorney?"

"Well—no."

"Then we'd like to talk to you separately—"

"Not necessary," Lt. Powell cut her off.

Daily searched the lieutenant's face. A silent order. Later, she told herself. She addressed Doc Ealing and Safford. "What time did each of you leave?"

"We came and left together," Safford answered while stealing a long look at Taryn Pierce. "We arrived as dinner was served in the garden, around seven. We left right after the virtual fireworks. That was around eleven. Eleven-fifteen, maybe."

"Virtual fireworks?" Pierce asked.

"Holographic and computer-generated images. Created by some special effects expert from one of Eddie's films."

Doc's eyes seemed to focus on images in his head. "They started out tiny—small explosions over a small model of an American town by the creek. All the guests remarked that they felt huge watching the miniatures—like giants. The images grew until they surrounded us in the dark garden. Very strange effect that had—made us feel as if we were floating in the sky for a few minutes, along with the fireworks."

"You saw Eddie during the virtual fireworks?"

"Couldn't miss him. He was bragging about the technology the whole time."

"And afterward?"

"We—I—"

Safford cut in. "There were a lot of people crowding around Eddie after that. We tried to catch his attention before we left but couldn't."

"That was the last time you saw him, then?"

"Yes." Doc's single word weighed heavily.

"And you didn't speak to him by phone after that?"

"No." Safford again.

"What exactly do you do as Deputy Director of NOBLE, Mr. Safford?"

"I serve as an extension of Doc, in whatever capacity he needs me, from spokesperson to attaché. It's my job to put Doc's long-term strategies into real time, Detective, from NOBLE's internal and external channels down to the tactical executions."

Business babble as what—overcompensation? Defensiveness? Daily wondered how much John Safford annoyed Eddie Ealing. Taryn Pierce looked impressed by the man's rhetoric, and Daily had no doubt the junior detective would have smiled—maybe even beamed—at Safford if the occasion for their meeting had been anything other than a homicide.

"Who drove to the party?" Daily continued.

"I did," Safford said.

"You picked up Doc and drove him home?"

Safford's chest filled. "We live next door to one another. Practical, since we work on NOBLE around the clock more days than not."

Taryn nodded as if Safford had landed on the moon.

"Did Eddie seem agitated about anything this week?" Daily said. "Upset?"

Doc dropped into a chair. "Edward always had issues with someone. Trauma and drama. The newswoman who coined that phrase years ago first used it in a feature on my son. That says it all, I'm afraid."

"Trauma and drama?"

"Edward didn't feel alive unless he was fighting with somebody over something—anything. Ever since he was a kid. Like those stunt men, those thrill seekers that always have to push the envelope. Eddie pushed people to see how much farther he could get with them. That made a lot of folks angry."

"Mad enough to kill him?"

A weary sigh. "My son used to brag about his death threats as if they were some measure of his impact. As if the violence and noise he called entertainment weren't enough. Good God, his own idea ended up killing him! The murder in that movie fermented in the mind of some psychopath out there—until it came back to take his life." Doc's shoulders rode a long breath. "I want you to find who did this. I'll arrange any additional resources you need—"

Pierce fawned, "We'll leave no stone unturned, sir."

Nestor looked away and Daily pressed her temples. Pierce was going to drive them each crazy.

Doc shook his head. "I only wish we'd been there to rescue Eddie from—"

"His life?" Daily said.

Doc Ealing blinked as if he hadn't heard right. Even Daily wasn't sure why she'd blurted it out.

Safford glowered. "There may have been philosophical differences between us, but we never told Eddie how to live."

More us. We.

Daily searched Safford for signs of grief. He appeared to be irritated rather than upset, but Daily knew that happened with control freaks. People who talked about strategies and tactics. Murder messed with their buttons. It served up mortality.

"I have to assume Eddie was something of a sore topic for you both," Daily said. "After all, NOBLE stands for the National Organization for Better Literature and Entertainment. And, as you just pointed out, Eddie's work in the film and music industries was—controversial."

Doc narrowed his eyes but didn't reply.

"We commended you last year," John Safford edged the words at Daily.

"I'm most grateful. Even so, there are questions we have to ask. Most murders are committed by someone who knows the victim. And Doc's name was one of the—"

"Fifty-seven stuffed in his hand?" Safford caught Daily's surprise. "It's all over the news already. The names were the VIP list. Yes, Doc was invited. Yes, I joined him. You can't possibly insinuate that just because Eddie invited his father that—"

"It does seem odd, doesn't it? Inviting you both to a party with guests who create so much that NOBLE finds objectionable?"

The lieutenant blinked Daily a look that said *careful.*

Safford's jaw adjusted then set. "The party was a fundraiser. For the Temperel Foundation."

"The trust started in my wife's name. Edward's mother," Doc said softly. "The foundation allots money to people who can't afford care for Alzheimer's, Parkinson's."

"We had our differences, but we were grown men," Safford continued. "When it was appropriate to put things aside for a good cause, we were adults about it."

"Are you related to Eddie Ealing?" Daily asked.

"No. I'm speaking for Doc, of course."

"Of course." Daily looked at Doc. "Who gets Eddie's money?"

"No one in the family needs money," Safford sniped. "Your energies would best be spent finding the killer, Detective. We can help each other."

Her irritation burned. Tired of tap dancing, Daily needed straight answers. Facts. "Fine. Get me a list of all relatives and business associates you're aware of. Include names, numbers, and any motives. Like it or not, that includes insurance, wills, assets—"

"This was done by a sociopath." Doc's voice was hoarse.

"Even sociopaths have reasons, Dr. Ealing. And relatives."

Doc stood and glared. For a split second, Daily thought he might slap her. She watched as pain broke over his stone confidence.

"I'd like to know where we stand on a viable suspect," he said.

"And this Mike person," Safford added.

Daily reeled. "Who told you about Mike?"

"Helmy Ulgrod," Doc said. "When I called to get an update an hour ago."

Her heart pounded. "As soon as we have something salient—"

"For God's sake, woman, this is his *son!*" Safford's voice rose. "We're hearing more on TV and radio than we are from—"

Doc's scowl cooled Safford.

"This is going well." Pierce said just loud enough for Daily.

Lt. Powell smoothed the air with his hands. "Dr. Ealing, I don't like the media coverage any more than you do. It compromises our investigation in ways I can't even begin to list. Nonetheless, we have progress. We've eliminated fifteen people altogether and we're interviewing the others. Mike's Gifts is one of the latest developments."

Daily reached for the picture found at Eddie's. "Do either of you know this woman?"

Safford studied it, shook his head.

Doc wiped his face. "Familiar, but I can't place her. One of Eddie's girls?"

Safford mumbled that no one could keep up with Eddie's women.

"That blood?" Doc pointed to the red smears.

"It's a computer image, so there's no way to tell."

No reaction Daily could read.

"I'm going to want to bury my son with the rest of our family," Doc said. "I need to make arrangements and the coroner's office keeps giving me the runaround. Won't even give me a release date."

The lieutenant measured his words. "There's a significant amount of . . . autopsy information present in this case. I'm sure you want them to be thorough."

"We also want updates." Safford eyed Daily. "Perhaps your lead detective could be more responsive to our messages. We've left several."

"We simply want this animal apprehended," Doc added. "NOBLE has tremendous resources. My contacts at various agencies have already pledged their assistance."

A flicker crossed the lieutenant's face. "I appreciate your intent, sir, but bringing in others can hinder my people more than it can help."

"I don't see how more manpower can hurt—"

"Daily has one of the top clearance rates in the city. Nestor has worked on my toughest cases, knows how to take the heat. So does Burns. Both are ex-Marines with over twenty years on the squad. Pierce has the commendations of your former academic associates. And I've got the rest of my best committed solely to this matter on every front. The quickest way to find your son's killer is to let them work without a lot of other agencies interfering."

"Now I'm meddling?"

"That's not what I said."

Lt. Powell and Doc Ealing gauged one another.

After a long moment, Doc said, "I have little tolerance for criminals, lieutenant."

Powell didn't blink. "Around here, we don't have any."

———

After Doc Ealing and Safford left, Daily followed Lt. Powell down the hall toward the restroom. He stopped at the men's door. "I am potty-trained, Daily."

"I don't understand."

"It means I can use the facilities—"

"You let Pierce slide on the Ulgrods. You didn't want Doc Ealing and Safford interviewed separately. I don't get it."

"I didn't let Pierce *slide* on the Ulgrods. You took forever and a day to get to Ealing's—"

"Traffic was hell."

"—Pierce called your cell and your pager, couldn't get you. She cleared the first Ulgrod interviews with me. As for Doc Ealing, the chief and the mayor both want him treated with kid gloves. If we don't, Doc *will* call in favors and you won't be running anything but circles. The man's a huge supporter of law enforcement and right now the crowd's a little thin on the LAPD's end of the bleachers."

Daily released a long breath. "Right."

"Safford's an agitator, but that's in his job description. And he's right. We're behind the clock with this many suspects. Split up the crew."

Daily kept her frustration corked. The sense of purpose that had come with this case was fast being replaced by trepidation and rancor.

"Political critical, Daily. Keep that in mind."

She suppressed the retort on her tongue, smiled, and hated herself for it. "Yes, sir. It's burned on my brain."

EIGHT

LT. POWELL WANTED THE crew split, so Nestor went to interview the ex-wife, Eddie's attorney, and eleven of the party guests. Clem Burns and Taryn Pierce divided their share of the guest list, and Daily made the trek north to the Temperel Institute. Traffic picked up in Ventura, and so did the wind—it nearly sent Daily into another lane when she'd passed through the city that rode the sheath in the coast range and spilled against the sea. The town had originally been named Buena Ventura—good wind. An understatement.

Nestor called on the cell. "I spoke with the company that handles security for Doc Ealing's place in Calabasas," he told Daily. "Allegiant Line Security. One of their patrol units saw Doc's Jag return before midnight. Security cam shows Doc, Safford, and Peter Ealing get out of the Jag and walk into the residence, just like they said. You're going to ask me if it's the same company Eddie used and the answer is no. Allegiant Line tries for family deals, discounts on packages, but Eddie declined and used his own private contractor."

"Does Peter Ealing use them?"

"Allegiant Line doesn't 'do' Montecito. Peter's complex has its own security. Anyway, Allegiant's ops manager will send us the camera tapes plus their patrol reports. There's a unit that circuits Mulholland every hour. Saw nothing suspicious on first pass. We'll keep them digging."

Daily thanked Nestor for the update. He admonished her to get some carrot juice at his favorite organic store in Santa Barbara, said it would fight her free radicals. She knew a serious drink was the only thing that would put her radicals to rest tonight.

On news radio, the murder hogged the airwaves. Daily flipped through three stations, and stopped when she heard one announcer talk about a virtual gift delivery to Eddie Ealing that showed a real heart. They even referred to "The Mind Box" website.

Daily cursed; this would fuel everyone from legit journalists to the tabloids, zealots, and wackos. On *Talk Six*, sister station to Channel Six TV, the host was a hack of righteous indignation whom Daily loathed. She couldn't believe the cretin got paid, let alone to speak on morality. When Daily had been a patrol officer, the man had been arrested for soliciting transvestites on La Brea. He slid out of charges with a high-priced defense attorney and some community service. Now he was on the airwaves calling Daily's new homicide *The Case with No Conscience* . . . and *Hollywood Hellion Pays His Tab*. Daily switched to KNX and KFWB to see what they had. One of LA's more solid reporters spoke.

"Our station put in calls to numerous media figureheads that have worked with Eddie Ealing over the years," he said. "Their offices sent condolences, but no one would speak with us on the record, Frank."

"Didn't most of these people have rough dealings with Ealing?"

"Par for the course, these days. Cost of doing business. Not just in media and entertainment, of course. With Wall Street, conglomeration, and brutal bottom lines, sociopathic behavior can be an asset, not a psychological malady."

"What did they say about the Mike's Gifts development? This Mind Box?"

Daily's knuckles tightened around the wheel.

"Even less than they would about Ealing, Frank. There's rumors that MIKE is an acronym, that it stands for a coalition of some kind. In any case, my sources tell me that power brokers are already toning down their acts, behaving like model citizens. Some assistants I know forwarded emails, one from the office of a major player in New York. He's already apologized to everyone on his staff for 'accidentally' throwing paperweights and telephones when he's stressed."

"This guy's employed?"

"He's a heavyweight. I have dozens of emails. Some include mention of other rumored gifts, like the Grant Totter incident. The TelePrompTer."

Daily remembered that. The blush-nosed morning anchor, Totter, reciting his own slanted rhetoric on TV. *The mutant scum of Los Angeles.* Totter was oblivious as his eyes bounced. *This cesspool of alien DNA from crackhead daddies and unwed mothers.* He smeared five-and-a-half minorities before they cut to commercial.

"That got him fired," the radio commentary continued.

"Lawsuit and countersuit, actually. Totter didn't want to admit the words were the same ones he spouted off the air; the station was embarrassed that someone had pranked the Prompter. We'll never know what really happened. Six hired Totter for *The Hard Truth* after that."

The newsmen talked of executives across the entertainment industry stepping up their security, from people who worked on *Hannibal* to *American Psycho*.

"There's been copycat murders before," Frank said. "The *Scream* thing."

"But this time someone killed the creator in the same way as their work."

"So the fear of another Mike's Gifts murder is putting people on the straight and narrow, eh? Who said negative motivation doesn't work?"

———————

North of Santa Barbara, Daily caught the sign announcing Goleta's population of sixty-six thousand. Goleta had launched an aggressive campaign to attract clean industry when the area's aerospace contracts dwindled. They'd been more than successful, and Temperel was now one of its many research and development jewels. She passed the signs for the University of California at Santa Barbara and the small airport, then saw her exit. Eucalyptus trees lined the roads, then came groves of avocados and lemons. On her left, industrial complexes appeared—buildings of cold glass and concrete. Several companies hid back from the road, barricaded by hedges or walls.

Temperel's rolling lawn and wide, slate compound were hard to miss. The grass was greener than Eddie Ealing's—surreal in the stark July sun. The simple but elegant Temperel logo was carved into a title stone near the driveway. Daily parked and noticed neat landscaping that coddled a postmodern glass and steel entranceway. Inside the lobby, sign posts displayed a brief schedule: *Orientation 2:00–3:30 PM Open House 3:30–6:00 PM*. Daily told a pleasant security guard she needed to see Dr. Peter Ealing. He said she would need to meet with Dr. Rena Ross first.

"Actually, I don't. I'm here on an official investigation." Daily flashed her badge.

"No disrespect meant, Detective. Dr. Ross is the only one who knows where Dr. Peter Ealing is right now, and she's in the middle of orientation. You can talk to her when she's done."

The guard directed her to the auditorium at the end of a hall decorated with photos, bios of the scientists and board members. Doc Ealing and Eddie's images stared at her. A host of other faces surrounded them. The largest photo belonged to "Peter Ealing, PhD, Executive Director." Wire-rimmed glasses framed intelligent but tentative eyes. Aquiline bone structure that couldn't be more different from Eddie's thick features. The image of a keen-eyed brunette hung next to Peter's: "Rena Ross, MD, PhD." An amplified voice echoed through doors that opened for a man exiting in a lab coat.

As Daily entered the auditorium, darkness overwhelmed her and she stopped to let her eyes adjust. On a huge screen above the stage, giant neurons glowed red. Ganglia ignited, impulses exploded across synapses. Faces in the auditorium were illuminated by the incandescence of the images. Now that she could see better, Daily made her way down the aisle. Her footsteps clacked between a microphone's peals of feedback.

Behind a podium, Dr. Rena Ross adjusted her lavaliere mic. She looked forty going on Vogue, hipper than her photo. Dark wiry waves of hair, cut blunt just below the ears. A thin but arched nose. High forehead over remarkably clear, piercing eyes—green or blue. Displaying expressive hands and a measured comportment, Dr. Ross walked in front of the enormous screen and continued addressing the audience.

"You're each here today because you've been carefully screened for certain characteristics that make you ideal subjects in our newest phase of memory studies. Many of you have led particularly challenging lives due to circumstances beyond your control; others have always felt a little bit different, a little bit 'outside.' I assure you that no matter what has happened to you before, you're special to us here at Temperel."

Dr. Ross smiled at the audience; her warmth almost maternal. A quiver tugged her lips. She looked up at the screen's giant neurons, alive with computer-generated color.

"You are all damaged. Damaged in terms of your genetics, environment, experiences, chemicals, illness, toxins or—in some cases—pain.

Whatever the reason, you are aberrant from the norm. But here this difference can be a good thing, indeed, something quite special. You're starting at Temperel today precisely because those factors have created, in your brains, an amazing and groundbreaking opportunity. While I don't usually like words like 'normal' or 'average,' I'll use them here in the context of comparison to illustrate why your minds are especially remarkable. The images you've been watching above me are what we would consider 'normal' synapses processing information, emotions, and reactions at an 'average' rate."

A new image flashed on the screen. These synapses erupted with brighter light and a furious energy that exploded across the nerve endings like fireworks gone awry.

"By contrast, these are synapses like *yours*, processing the same experience."

Dr. Ross stared at the captivated faces; Daily could now see hundreds of them.

"Our screenings have selected you because your brains run on 'high.' You record data more readily. You actually *feel* more than the average person—higher, lower, deeper, harder. At times, you may have thought that it's a blessing, making you more creative or sensitive, more aware. It's also likely you've cursed the same qualities—as you experienced levels of depression, grief, or pain unknown to others."

Daily sensed agreement in the audience; several heads nodded.

"Here are scans of two brains which measure metabolic activity and cerebral blood flow. In the past, you may have had people tell you that things were all in your head. Little did they know how right they were."

Shards of laughter.

"This brain, on the left, is an average brain. But here, inside the brain to the right, the circuits run hotter, metabolically speaking. You can see the increased areas of what we've colloquially dubbed 'heat' here, especially in regions of the brain that play a part in retrieving memory."

Daily grew anxious. Ridiculous, she thought, but slices of these minds made her more uneasy than an autopsy. Two different minds above with millions of choices ahead of them. The giant images seemed beyond comprehension. How the hell did a normal person control all that going on inside her head? Let alone a person who was damaged?

Dr. Ross smiled again. "The good news is that because you're different—regardless of what you've endured in the past—you're now going to be involved in the most profound brain research of all time."

When the orientation ended, Daily waited for the crowd to thin around Dr. Ross, then trailed her down the hall. She'd culled some key facts about the scientist from the bio under her photo: Princeton undergrad, Harvard Medical School, a PhD from the University of Cologne studying some brain protein that Daily couldn't pronounce. An enzyme that she and Peter Ealing had identified bore their names. The doctor belonged to Mensa and an exalted scientific community that called her studies of the human brain and memory "remarkable."

Daily caught up with her. "Dr. Ross? I'm Detective Lane Daily, LAPD. Impressive facility you have here."

Dr. Ross acknowledged Daily but kept walking. Up close, her eyes were light blue grazed with gray. "We're proud of our work. You're here about Eddie Ealing, of course." Dozens of people milled past them and many surrounded Eddie's photo down the hall. "Let's step in here for some privacy."

She motioned Daily toward a door that led to a maze of offices. Hers was spacious and tasteful. Biedermeier furniture. A large Ansel Adams print over calla lilies in a Waterford vase. Dr. Ross offered a beverage from a small refrigerator. When Daily declined, the doctor poured a grapefruit juice for herself. She sat in the chair next to Daily's, both saffron-colored rhomboids with cushions a mile deep. Daily preferred to ask the smart ones open-ended questions. Plenty of latitude. It forced them to make telling choices. She asked Dr. Ross what she knew about Eddie and the party.

"I was with Peter and Doc last night. Not really our sort of thing, but it was for the foundation's in-need recipients, after all." As Dr. Ross recounted the night's events, she emphasized her proximity to Doc and Peter frequently. Too frequently.

"Where is Peter?"

"Out."

"Out where?"

"The end of State Beach, where it's quiet. Peter's incredibly sensitive anyway, and Eddie's death just devastated him." She sighed. "Orientation days are hard for him under normal circumstances, all the noise and racket of the tours. But he'll be back. This is where he lives, practically."

"Did you drive to LA together?"

"No, I went with Gil Amanpour, one of the board members. Philanthropist. Peter drove down earlier in the day to see Doc in Calabasas. We met at Eddie's party around seven, kept to our own group at dinner. Even though the celebrities were there for the Foundation, most of us don't feel comfortable mingling in Eddie's world. All the brainpower in the world and we have no idea what to say to a movie star." Dr. Ross tossed Daily a smirk and got nothing back. "Eddie was good with the people who could make that sort of thing successful. He rallied the right ones together. Bullied the ones he couldn't rally."

"Bullied?"

"That way they do down there." She made it sound like Dante's Inferno.

"He forced people to donate?"

"He persuaded people to direct their donations our way. Instead of other ways."

Daily studied Dr. Ross's even gaze and waited.

"I'm not explaining it well, am I? Eddie threw his weight around to get what he wanted. I'm the wrong person to ask about the boundaries because I don't understand their rules in the first place." Dr. Ross took a deep breath. "You want to know if what I saw could be of any help. Eddie was his usual self. Alternately gregarious, irascible. Always volatile."

"What kind of things set him off last night?"

"God knows. Some waiter getting a singer the wrong drink. A tray of seared Japanese snapper not being rare enough in the middle. There was something theatrical about it, I suppose, but so much with Eddie *was*. He seemed to be enjoying himself later. He was quite taken with his virtual fireworks demonstration."

"What time did you and Mr. Amanpour leave?"

"Right after the fireworks. Eleven or so."

"Did you see Doc or Peter as you were leaving?"

"We waited together while the valets brought our cars."

"Whose car came first?"

"Doc's Jaguar. John Safford was driving him, as usual. Peter left with them."

Daily asked the doctor if she had heard of "Mike's Gifts."

"The news mentioned it. They said Eddie had received a vicious gift two weeks ago, via email. A human heart in a box that opened up on the screen."

Everybody knew everything. As infuriating as it was, Daily had no time to track leaks right now. She didn't say anything, but found it interesting that Ross called it human. "Any idea who might have sent it?"

"I wouldn't *want* to know anyone who would do such a thing."

"Had you heard of 'Mike's Gifts' prior to the news?"

"Never."

"Did you see or overhear anything at the party that would indicate someone else was particularly upset with Eddie?"

"You mean did I eavesdrop on others' conversations? Hard not to at a function like that. So many of those people talk as if they're performing." Dr. Ross caught herself, sipped some juice. "Did I overhear anyone who was mad with Eddie? Not mad, per se."

"What then?"

"The usual. They fawned over him when he was in their circle. As soon as he left, they would rip him to shreds. Lovely town, Los Angeles."

She asked if Dr. Ross knew the names of the badmouthing guests; she didn't. Daily asked if it was just typical dish.

"More than dish, more than *Schadenfreude*. Sounded like they had business issues. Something about Eddie and another man competing to buy their radio stations."

Daily circled that note. "Anyone else?"

"A brunette. She was there with that actor from the asteroid movie, the one where they need to go into space to seed it with explosives. Not a sound plot from a scientific standpoint, mind you. In any case, this woman didn't have too many nice things to say about Eddie. She'd had one too many martinis, and it was hard not to catch her rants. Said Eddie had the class of a sloth and the breath of a swine and—other things."

"What other things?"

"I really don't—"

"It's important that we get everything."

Dr. Ross exhaled. "The sexual stamina of a hummingbird."

Daily wrote it down verbatim. "Did she speak to Eddie during the party?"

"Just spilled on him." Dr. Ross read Daily's confusion. "A plate of food from the Indian buffet."

"Did you ever see the movie Eddie produced, *Sense of Life?*"

"No. The world has enough violence; I don't need to see films with more of it."

"It got decent reviews, won big awards."

"Politics at play. I don't pretend to understand the maneuvers of the media or people like Eddie who buy their control of information."

Buy. Control. Information. The doctor's impressions of Eddie's world were hardly unbiased; if this condescension got to Daily in one interview, it must have driven Eddie nuts. "You understand the maneuvers of science?" Daily asked.

A strange look crossed Dr. Ross's face. "Yes, I do."

"Did you have any issues with Eddie Ealing, Dr. Ross?"

The scientist studied Daily a long time. "That suit you're wearing— it's not a Karan, is it?" Dr. Ross spoke as if she could see straight through Daily to the knock-off label in her jacket.

Daily smoothed the wrinkles in her pants. "I asked if you had any issues with Eddie Ealing."

"He could be a bit of a beast in the board meetings. He thought we were patronizing him because he wasn't a scientist."

"Are the other board members scientists?"

"Not necessarily. Gil Amanpour was the head of a publishing firm before he retired to philanthropy. We also have a well-known painter whose father succumbed to Parkinson's."

"So it's fair to say they wouldn't understand some of the scientific jargon either?"

"I suppose, although they're very bright. They grasp concepts quickly. Eddie grew frustrated easily. If he didn't get something the first time, he grew impatient."

"Abusive?"

"Not abusive, exactly. Not with Doc present."

"And when Doc wasn't present?"

"I can't think of a time that Eddie was at a board meeting when Doc wasn't. Doc shows up like clockwork, no matter what time of year."

"What does time of year have to do with it?"

"Doc spends summers here in California. Fall and spring at his place in New York. Winters he bounces between the Caribbean and New York. Christmas in the city, New Year's in St. Bart's, that sort of thing. The board meetings occur about once a month. More often, lately, with the venture capital decisions pending."

"Doc said no one's in need of money."

"It's about whose money you're aligned with. In the last year, we've been approached by venture capitalists and even some of our competitors—larger companies—about alliances."

"Was there any friction over these alliances? Between Eddie and the board?"

Dr. Ross ran a French-manicured nail along her lower lip. "Every single one of us just wants what's best for the company, for Temperel. The work we do here is going to make quite a difference. It's only natural that we've had our disagreements about whose money we accept and on what terms. Any alliance means new people, new input. They all have different goals. Debating the best match has been taxing."

"Did Eddie have a different point of view from everyone else?"

Dr. Ross iced. "He felt strongly that we should form an alliance with one of our competitors. Florian or Stulles. They're both well-known, large companies. He said it would increase market share and eliminate duplication of efforts."

"What's the downside?"

"Significant loss of control."

"Was Eddie the only one who wanted an alliance?"

"No. The board remains fractured. But most of us lean toward maintaining stewardship of our own future even if it means more risk financially."

"What about Peter and Doc?"

"Doc is emphatic that we don't give up control. He wants Temperel to get full credit for our work. Peter—Peter just wants to be a scientist."

"He must care one way or the other."

Dr. Ross grew peevish with Daily. "You have to *understand*. Peter's mind—his IQ is off the charts. He doesn't process information the way the rest of us do. But bottom line I don't think Peter would like any arrangement that would dictate or corral his process. Even if it's a better business decision."

"Were Eddie and his family close?"

A hard sigh. "The Ealings are old money. They were in New York before God docked. Peter said Doc tried not speaking to Eddie for a couple of years. It didn't work. For better or worse, the family sticks it out, thank heavens, for this place."

Daily asked who would inherit Eddie's money, and Dr. Ross said she had no idea, in a tone that insinuated it was rude to ask. The scientist's condescension escalated on the topics of Temperel and money, Daily noticed. She was either fiercely protective of the institute, hiding something, or both. Daily handed Dr. Ross the copy of the picture found in Eddie Ealing's old camera. The original was now at the police lab.

"We found this at Eddie's house. From the email. Do you know this woman?"

Dr. Ross's face blanched. "My God. These streaks—blood?"

"Do you know her?"

"This is Alma. One of the girls from our evening cleanup crew. I haven't seen her in some time. *Eddie* had this?"

"It was in the message from Mike's Gifts. When the virtual gift opened, the heart was one image, this was the other."

Dr. Ross dropped the photo on her desk. "I'm sorry. It's such a cruel message."

"There's no evidence yet that the heart was hers or that it was even human."

"I didn't think twice about Alma being gone until now. Our maintenance people come and go. They find other jobs, move on. Some of them have families in Mexico or abroad who need them to come home."

Something in the doctor's tone made Daily bristle. "Who set Alma's schedule?"

"We contract out for maintenance. Cyrus Services. Several of the research and biotech companies use them. They run the background checks, screen people for health and suitability. Run payroll."

"So you have no paycheck stubs, no address."

The doctor's head shook as she stared at the sun-streaked sky outside. "One check to the contractor every month. We do issue pass cards, though." She went to her computer. "Here she is. Morada is the last name. Alma Morada. She last swiped her maintenance pass card here on May twenty-second. We had a board meeting that day, she swiped out late. Conference room cleanup."

"You knew Alma's first name before you looked her up."

"I often work late. She was part of the evening crew."

"How many maintenance people are on that shift?"

"Five to ten, depending on the workload, I guess."

"And they change often."

"Not infrequently. I don't remember all their names."

"Yet you remembered Alma. What was it about her?"

Dr. Ross let a sad laugh escape. "She sang. Like an angel."

NINE

DR. ROSS LED DAILY down a long hallway. "Alma worked in and around the same labs as the senior subjects. Most of them do lab work when they're not in a study phase themselves. Extra money."

A woman approached, handing a data log to the doctor who scanned it.

"No shipments from here to Eddie's home on June twenty-third, or the days on either side," Dr. Ross told Daily after she dismissed the assistant. "These records show packages by department, name, destination, number. No shipment could have left here untracked. We're quite vigilant about that."

The scientist seemed short of breath since she'd seen Alma's photo. Distracted too. It was as if some other dialogue was going on in her head, one Daily couldn't hear. Daily asked more about Temperel.

"As baby boomers age, we're going to have one hell of a mass memory lapse," Dr. Ross explained. "Other problems as well. The drug companies are putting up billions for compounds to fight brain disease—Parkinson's, Alzheimer's. The strides we've been making the last few years with NTs—neurotransmitters—and memory, it's all quite amazing. Even to someone like me."

"I've heard there's a vaccine for Alzheimer's?"

"Several prototypes. We're involved in one. Same basic principle as all vaccines: weakened or defused elements that cause the disease can elicit an immunity to it later."

"You don't sound sold on the idea."

"The drug companies want the compounds cleared for market so everyone moves at fever pitch to get them to the millions who need them. But anything that has an effect on the brain, its chemicals, its processes—there's just no way to tell what some of the long-term repercussions might be. I believe in thorough testing. Otherwise what seems like a godsend can turn out to be hell."

Edgy on that last sentence, Daily noticed. "Speaking from experience?"

Dr. Ross' eyes flared. "My scientific record is impeccable."

Daily was going to investigate her relationships, family, money. She'd met business and creative virtuosos who were complete failures in other parts of their lives, the expansive mind of a genius leaving no room for common sense. Daily moved to neutral ground. "Wouldn't most people with Alzheimer's be willing to risk the trade-offs? I'd rather live five good years *with* my mind than twenty without it."

"You concur with our TR-4 Alzheimer's trial patients—our test program for clinically terminal patients who have tried everything else. We've made some strides. But in all cases, they've been told they have no more than a few months to live. And they've willingly signed away all risk to have a few more 'clear' months. The program works for them. But what are the effects of the drugs on those who live longer? I'm just not that big on human guinea pigs."

They turned and Daily heard the sounds of squealing from behind two swinging lab doors. "As opposed to real guinea pigs?"

"I'm not fond of hurting any creature if I can help it. But given the choices? Yes, it's better to discover such ramifications on rabbits or rats."

"You and Peter are considered the leading experts in the study of memory—"

"Uncorrupted memory *recall*," she corrected. "The term memory means a lot of different things to different people—emotional memories, false or repressed memories, dreams. I've devoted my life to understanding how the brain records things that actually happened. That's where my passion lies. Making sure the memories are *genuine*." Dr. Ross paused to let the implications sink in. "The police applications of our research will be staggering, Detective. You know, even better than me, that eyewitness testimony is the least dependable evidence you can take to a case. But if science bears me out we'll be able to provide neutral, accurate witnesses in a courtroom. We'll enable people to recount *exactly* what they saw—without any emotional shadings."

The impact hit Daily full force as she remembered the failings of warped memories: a rapist released because the victim picked the wrong guy out of a lineup. A gangbanger set free because a witness could only see red in the mind's eye of her husband's brutal stabbing, yet the perp was a Crip who would never wear Blood colors. Lovers who tried to kill each other over conflicting perceptions and often succeeded.

Daily realized she'd stopped breathing. Her ribs were tight and the top of her chest had flushed red. Dr. Ross asked if she was all right, and she said yes, it was just disturbing to remember how many criminals got off because there wasn't irrefutable proof of their acts. She didn't add that proof of uncorrupted memories in her own past would have changed her entire life.

"Memories are tied to emotions, aren't they?" Daily asked.

"Not necessarily. Recall is a fairly involved process: some calibration of a subject's impressions against hard data, some sequencing of brain chemicals, some behavioral conditioning. Now we capture computer models of the process. But eventually we're going to retrieve raw brain records—memories—without distortion. Pure truth."

"A truth the courts may not accept for years."

Dr. Ross shrugged. "Would it stop you from wanting to know it?"

Daily thought of what it could mean to cops on the street. To juries and judges. To victims too traumatized to see anything clearly the rest of their lives. To children whose stories weren't believed. Then cold logic slammed in and sobered her.

Dr. Ross read her mind. "This isn't sci-fi stuff. This is the data actually *recorded* on our sensory systems as original input. A couple of private investigation firms have tried our witness recall techniques with some success. You should let us see what we can do on this case. I know we'd all like answers."

Now the scientist was offering the institute's help, but it sounded more like a directive than a suggestion. The maternal manner Dr. Ross evinced in the auditorium had steeled into protectiveness. Daily would stay with the "enlighten me" tack.

A whooping monkey rattled a cage as Dr. Ross led Daily into ANIMAL LAB A. Inside, two men and one woman wore casual clothes under open white lab coats. The sandy-haired man juggled oranges in front of a chimp. Giggling, a group of four orientation students watched as the monkey mimicked the man's hand motions.

"Don't tease him, Burg," said Dr. Ross. She herded the new arrivals outside and toward another lab. Then she turned and addressed the three wearing lab coats. "Everyone, this is Detective Daily of the LAPD. She has some questions."

Dr. Ross nodded at sandy-hair. Surf-washed, tan. Thirty-something. About six feet. His blue eyes smiled even as his strong jaw and full mouth remained set. She said, "This is Steven Woydyno, but everyone calls him Burg."

"He's from Pittsburgh," the other man added as explanation. Looking a bit older than Burg, this one had a Brillo of ebony hair shaved close at the sides, tall on top. Cinnamon skin. Six-two. Wide shoulders, athlete's build. Strong, wide features, impulsive brown eyes and a mouth in motion—chewing itself with nervous energy. He hand-passed a piece of fruit, shot it into the cage. The chimp made a hoop with its arms, clapped after the fruit sailed through. The monkey held up three fingers.

"Our hoop star here is Jerome Martin; everyone calls him Wood," said Dr. Ross.

Burg was straight-faced. "He's from Hollywood."

"And hiding in the corner, as usual, is our dear little bookworm Karen."

Turning away from her microscope Karen removed her glasses. Dark blonde, she was a short but large-boned woman with a small way about her, as if cowed into reducing her own presence.

"I'm not little and I'm not hiding. I'm working," Karen said.

Wood moved one step too close to Daily. "Up from El-Lay, Detective?"

"On the Eddie Ealing case. Tell me, the young woman who helped clean up at night, Alma Morada, did she ever mention knowing Eddie?"

A pained look crossed Karen's face. "Alma's gone."

"We think she may have known Ealing."

"Alma played some singing gigs in LA." Wood dropped the sass. "I don't know where, or for who."

"Whom," Karen corrected. "I never heard Alma say she knew the guy, but then, Alma was way private."

"Any of you talk to her before she—left? Did she say she was leaving town?"

They shook their heads no.

"Any of you in LA last night?"

Karen said, "I went to a party in Isla Vista."

"Played some one-on-one," said Wood. "Then the movies with Burg."

"Got your stubs?"

Without hesitation Burg pulled a ticket from his jeans. The Arlington Theater on State Street. Daily noted some scrapes on both men's arms. Scabs on Wood's palms.

"Where'd you get the skids, guys?"

"City college," said Wood. "We use the asphalt court when the gym's taken."

"Must play hard. Where were you later—between one and three AM?"

Burg thought. "Watched *Butch Cassidy and the Sundance Kid* on AMC." With his grin, Daily thought he didn't look unlike a young Robert Redford himself.

Wood made loud snoring noises.

"I was asleep too." Karen shrugged. "One beer and I'm out."

"Anyone with you? To verify?"

In turn each of them said no. The doctor hovered, her gaze intense. Daily needed to get her out of the room. "Dr. Ross, could you get me data logs of their times in and out for the last week . . . now?"

"Sure." Dr. Ross sounded anything but sure as she left them.

The three techs loosened up noticeably with Dr. Ross gone.

"You guys arrive at Temperel around the same time?" Daily asked them.

Burg said, "I was first, then Karen, then Wood."

"Do a lot of people from LA sign up for the clinical trials here?"

Wood shrugged. "For the artistically inclined, it beats slinging burgers or selling CDs. And we're just ninety minutes away if we want to jump back into the cauldron."

"When did Alma begin working here?"

"About the same time I came," Wood said. "Just under a year ago."

"You all work late a lot?"

They shrugged. "Here and there," Wood said.

"Alma work late, too?"

More nods.

"You talk to Alma while she was cleaning?"

"Some," Karen said.

"You ever see Eddie Ealing around?"

"Board-meeting days," Wood sniped.

"Eddie and Alma talk to one another? Ever see them pass in the hall, acknowledge each other?"

Three heads shook no.

"You never asked Alma where she was from? How she came to work here? If she had family, a kid?" Their blank stares puzzled Daily. "You guys study memory, right? If Alma, a maid, knew Eddie Ealing, a multimillionaire and one of Temperel's board members, wouldn't she mention it? And wouldn't you remember it?"

Their glances read *who's going to explain it to her?*

"The work we do here is pretty intense," Burg said. "Especially when we're in the test phases. After-hours, you just want to kick it."

Daily was getting no traction; she wasn't buying it. "You never *once* talked about Alma's life with her?"

"Hey, you have any idea what it's like?" Wood snapped. "In recall, I get to railroad back down the track of a father who wanted to kill *me* because my mother screwed around. Him taking me to the cops and having me arrested for twenty-nine kinds of shit he fabricated. Then I get to soak in the stench of the wacks next to me in juvie all over again. So, no—I don't want to *share* afterwards, *De-tec-tive.*" Wood was breathing hard. "When I'm off, I'd rather pound through some one-on-one, then knock back some eighty-proof memory-loss."

Karen exhaled. "It's not all like that. Some of us are just born a little more aware," Karen told Daily. "We didn't get *damaged* or any of that other nonsense."

"Bag the act, princess," Wood groused.

Daily studied Karen—not part of Wood and Burg's fraternity.

"Relax, you two, she has to ask." Burg turned to Daily. His eyes were calm, his voice even. "We hardly ever talk about ourselves. It screws up the studies if we talk about the same things we process."

"But Alma Morada never participated in any studies. She just cleaned up."

Wood chuffed. "Far as we know."

"Honestly, no one with the maintenance crew talks much," said Burg. "They do their thing quietly; we're usually finishing tests, putting things away for the day."

"She hummed," Karen said quietly. "And sometimes she sang. In Spanish."

Daily strolled past the shelves of bottles, studied the labels:

8-OH-DPAT

S-76 SCOPOLAMINE

MP-98 MPTP

Q-65 QUELDEN

TR-4 TEMPEREL TRIAL #4

TR-3 TEMPEREL TRIAL #3

"Process . . . " Daily echoed Burg's term. "Using new drugs?"

Dr. Ross caught the question as she returned with the new data logs. "Certain compounds help maintain a subject's awareness—clarity of experience while disengaging the emotional reactions that can warp accurate recall."

Daily pointed at one of the tinctures. "Wasn't this used on POWs?"

"That's only used on animals here. Any drugs administered in the clinical trials are extremely safe, they've been tested and fully sanctioned by the FDA. They're quite mild; they simply reduce anxiety, tension, mood swings during the recall studies."

"Stepford lives," Karen mumbled.

Dr. Ross shook her head. "The subjects in our tests already see, taste, hear, and smell at more heightened levels than the average person; that's why they're part of the trials. Some 'sensitives' record input more acutely, and that can cause reactions that affect the integrity of the memory recall. Some of these drugs keep them balanced—"

"In line," Karen interrupted.

Dr. Ross raised her voice, "—and remove the accompanying fragility found in highly-attenuated individuals who would otherwise find their memories and sensations unbearable."

"You make them sound like machines," Daily said. "Human cameras."

"You want to know what Dr. Ross isn't telling," carped Wood. "Join the club."

Dr. Ross's look silenced him. "I'm not hiding anything," she said to Daily. "As with any endeavor, scientific or technological, that aspires to break conventional boundaries, we take a lot of heat from those who don't fully understand what we're doing." The doctor walked to a counter and showed Daily colored graphs. "Look at these matches from the latest trials—our work will show that when the brain maps original data, it's nothing but the truth. It can't be anything else. It's our emotional tags to it, our other *experiences*—our playback filters—that change the way the information is processed and recalled."

"There's a margin of error?"

"There won't be."

"There's a margin of error now."

Dr. Ross' face darkened. "You came here asking for my help."

"So I did." Daily turned back to the three techs, asked them if they'd ever heard of Mike's Gifts.

Karen frowned. "What's that?"

"An underground service that apparently sends gifts to people to mess with their minds. Eddie Ealing's 'gift' was a virtual one. An email with images of a real heart and Alma's photograph."

Karen paled. "Alma's heart?"

"I'm guessing it was an animal heart."

Burg wiped his face. "Who would do that?"

"Someone who hated Eddie Ealing a great deal, I imagine."

Wood leaned into a counter. "The news says everyone hated him."

"Not everyone." The voice was weak but certain.

Dr. Peter Ealing, his eyes bloodshot and pained, his ash hair tossed by the winds, stood in the doorway. In contrast to Eddie Ealing's large and corpulent frame, Peter was thin, almost wiry, thick ash hair the only attribute he shared with his dead brother. Peter inhabited the sinewy frame of someone who ran a lot. She imagined his aquiline features were handsome under normal circumstances, but now every part of him was drawn, except for his eyes, which were ripe with grief. He lifted his wire-framed glasses, pressed his lids with splayed fingers.

Karen offered him a weak smile of condolence. Burg and Wood returned to their lab tasks without a word.

Dr. Ross said, "Peter, this is Detective Daily. She's in charge of Eddie's investigation."

He extended a tired hand. "I'm sorry I wasn't here when you arrived. I needed to . . . " He didn't finish. One of the monkeys in the cage pealed at Peter and his expression warmed. He approached the animal, touched its outstretched fingers.

Dr. Ross touched Peter's arm. "Let's go back to your office." She motioned for Daily to follow her. Peter stayed at the cage. The monkey climbed up the bars to study Peter's eyes. It touched its own eyes and reached out for his. He stroked the animal's hand, then tucked it back inside the cage with care.

"Little Beatrice," Peter said softly. "It's not a good day, indeed."

TEN

THE ASSISTANT NEWS DIRECTOR called Paulette at home to say that the guest list from Eddie's party was now posted on the Internet. For the sixth time he asked her to profile Ealing's killer on the air.

"Maybe tomorrow," Paulette told him for the sixth time.

"There's other people I can use, you know. People who would give their right arm to be talking about this on TV."

"And they'll spill bad guesses to a few million people, Davis. You want that on your head?"

He groaned, then said, "You promise me tomorrow?"

"I promise I'll do the research. Whether I'll talk about what I find, I can't say."

The list was right where Paulette had expected to find it, on the most popular gossip websites, but she didn't expect to see Jordan Krasinski's name on it. Paulette had counseled Jordan, a cameraman, through years of nerve-frying investigative documentaries. She'd helped him move into *writing* pieces instead of living them. During the time she'd been his therapist, she'd often wondered how a guy that good-looking could have worked in Hollywood that long and not been dragged in front of a camera.

Paulette found Jordan's new place in Manhattan Beach in fifteen minutes. He'd sent her a dozen invitations to his new three-level oceanfront including two housewarmings, one celebration for a well-known Polish director, and several fêtes heralding features in solid magazines. She pulled her Karmann Ghia behind his Land Rover; she'd only be a few minutes. Paulette expected he'd be tearing apart a new camera or a new story, his hair back in a messy ponytail.

Jordan was in front of his house looking anything but messy. His hair was cut above the collar, his skin was burnished. Twelve people sipped white wine in the front yard, a square of Mexican tile and California garden that faced the Pacific Ocean. The sun dripped orange above a smear of clouds on the horizon. Double-edged Los Angeles air—it dusted your lungs but painted spectacular sunsets.

Jordan spotted her. "Be still my heart. Am I delusional or has Dr. Sohl finally found time in her busy schedule for me?"

Paulette entered the waist-high teak gate. "Nice," she said, meaning more than the woodwork. "Saw your piece in *Vanity Fair*, Jordan. Congratulations, writer."

He announced to his guests, "This is Paulette, everyone. You've seen her on News Ten. My new life's all her fault and she's come to take her ten percent, I'm sure."

Laughter. Someone cracked that she should ask for a third. Paulette denied any responsibility for Jordan's talent, said she just helped him recognize it.

Jordan's smile played as he came closer. "Still married, soul doctor?"

"Last time I checked." She caught herself fiddling with her ring and stopped.

"Where's the mystery husband no one's ever met?"

"He's a road manager. He's road managing."

"And now that I'm no longer patienting, you still won't let me make you some of my *bigos* and homemade bread, eh?" Jordan's playing to an audience, Paulette thought. Surely there was a woman at the party who wouldn't like it and he knew it. There she was: short dark hair, clear eyes, lips pruned in anger. Jordan may have found his career calling via therapy, but he still had a long way to go on the relationship front. Jordan, like many patients, had quit at the brink of his toughest discoveries.

Paulette asked to speak to him alone. He led her inside and upstairs to an office facing the ocean. He closed the door and motioned for her to sit.

"Eddie Ealing," she said.

He sighed. "It's fucking unbelievable. I was there—at the party last night."

"I know. Your name's on the guest list, which is now on the worldwide web."

He looked shocked. "The cops didn't mention that. Eddie a patient of yours?"

"No," Paulette said. "Channel Ten's asked me to do an educated profile of his killer. I'm educating before I comment. How'd you know him?"

"Shot that exposé, the surgeon without the license. Crescent Media, Eddie's company, produced it. You and I talked mostly about the director, Über Prick."

"Right. Why were you at Eddie's party, if you'd quit?"

He grew stiff. "I don't want my name used in this."

Paulette gave Jordan her word, then waited to see how much trust she'd earned.

"Eddie pushed for me to land a peach assignment with CTC News. This was network, not local. Writing *and* producing, no shooting. Without his clout, that would have taken me years. Piece was on teens and guns. School shootings. Why they do it."

"I saw it. Powerful."

"Thanks. But I didn't just get the 'opportunity;' he got CTC to pay me full pop *squared*."

Paulette surveyed Jordan's furnishings. "Clearly. And in return?"

"Eddie wanted me to write and produce a piece on this disease. A project he'd had on the back burner. Said he was going to deliver it to one of the major network news magazines. Exclusive. He wanted to talk about that more than anything. After what he'd just done for me, I couldn't say no. I have no idea why he was so obsessed with it. But now he's—" Jordan shrugged. "Shit, Paulette, it's all pretty weird."

"What was the disease?"

"*Kuru.*"

"Kuru." A distant bell in Paulette's head.

"Laughing death," Jordan explained. "Kuru. Dementia. Found in New Guinea, in headhunters who eat the brains of others."

ELEVEN

Eddie's ex-wife, Donia Ealing, greeted J. D. Nestor in the library of her Bel Air estate, a sunny room with good light and art that could shame a small museum. Donia could have been thirty-five or fifty, it was hard to tell. Tall and trim. Arctic-ice eyes brushed by brown bangs that fell into a shoulder-length blunt cut. A slate sweater topped alert nipples that caught Nestor off guard. He dropped his glance to her silk pants, recited his reason for calling, then reddened when he realized he was talking to her crotch. She led Nestor to a sunroom where they sat on a sofa the color of Nestor's father's beloved homegrown eggplants. The old family garden—that was a safe place for his mind to go. Eggplants, not nipples. He tried to relax, turned to his notes.

Donia had worked as a New York-based fashion model until she'd met Eddie and married him in 1979. They'd filed for divorce two weeks after her fortieth birthday, she told Nestor. Since then, she'd invested her energy and money as a patron of the arts.

She didn't seem upset or surprised that Eddie was dead. Not happy, either. Blank, thought Nestor. A drape over a blank easel. Probably what happened to a woman in Eddie's world, only room for one ego, one consuming identity. Nestor wondered what she identified with now. If the answer was as vacant as her glazed expression, she was as good as dead, too.

"I don't have anything to hide," she said. "My lawyer said he was going to come by and join us. I had to let him know you'd called, of course."

"Of course." Nestor watched Donia work a series of practiced expressions through the silence. Performing for her own security cameras or maybe just habit. He found it loopy. The maid led a pale man into the sunroom. Expensive suit. Satchel. Attorney. The guy took Donia aside, asked her a few questions. He whispered something and finally allowed them to proceed. Nestor asked how Donia had originally met Eddie. Her answers matched the information possessed by the LAPD, with added emphasis on her modeling career.

"Don't get me wrong," Donia added. "Eddie was already making his mark. With his sense of timing, he always seemed to have a feel for the next trend. But his money-management skills were abominable. I'm the one that showed him how to invest, how to maximize income and diversify. If we hadn't stashed some away, he would have burned through his cash in no time. Amazing, given the family he came from. You think he'd have prudence in his genes."

"Did you socialize with the family?"

Oddly, Donia guffawed. "Not as much as I would have liked. God knows it wasn't for my lack of trying. But Eddie was the renegade in a family of bluebloods, intellectuals, doctors. I'd grown up an orphan, shuttled between foster homes for years. I said to him a thousand times that a family with differences is better than no family at all. He'd say, 'That's what you think.' He'd just spout off nonsense, change the subject. Say things like, 'Their kind of love leaves you damaged.'"

The attorney whispered to Donia.

She nodded and said, "On Harold's advice, I'd like to answer the rest of that question after the will is read. You understand. Eddie may have had his differences with the Ealing family, but I always found them *charming*." Her sudden smile was out of place, a magazine cover from twenty years ago.

Nestor asked who would have wanted Eddie dead.

"Eddie had a horde of enemies, but that's such a nebulous term in business today. Anyone who's had any modicum of success has enemies, that's the game. Nice guys can't even make the race."

"You're saying it was inflated? Eddie's reputation as—"

"A major *asshole*?" Donia's face didn't flinch. "Look, the same accusations have been leveled against all his contemporaries. Books have been written about these men. They don't follow the rules, they're obsessed and crazy, but they produce results, don't they? Whatever anyone's said, no one ever doubted that Eddie Ealing made things happen. Seismic things."

"Why'd you get divorced?"

The magazine cover faded. "Our issues weren't business. We were good there."

Nestor sat forward. "Where weren't you so good?"

Donia traded looks with the lawyer. "My approaching forty seemed to be a bigger hurdle for Eddie than for me."

"Other women?"

Donia laughed without mirth. "Other everything."

"Let's wait on that, too," the attorney said.

Nestor was about to remind the prick this was a homicide, then remembered Daily had told the lieutenant how well they handled *these people*. He eased back, tossed out a couple of gimmes before asking if Donia had an alibi for the hours in question.

The attorney snapped, "You can't possibly insinuate that she had anything to do with that mutilation."

Nestor said he had to ask since most homicides involved someone close to the victim.

"I was in bed asleep," Donia said. "If I so much as stir, my Irish Setter barks for an hour. You can check with the maid and the cook. They're live-ins. They'll both tell you it was a quiet night." Her tone grew hard. "Let's cut to it, Detective. If I'd wanted to kill my ex-husband, I'd have done it when we were married. When I still felt something for him."

Her attorney leaned over, but this time she waved him off.

"But if I wanted Eddie to *continue* to pay for all the wrongs against me during the course of our marriage?" Her eyes landed on a Picasso, then a Jasper Johns. "Well, I'd want Eddie very much *alive.*"

―――――――――

Each gleaming horse that cantered past the rail at the Equestrian Center cost more than the new Ford Explorer in Nestor's garage, he was sure of that. That one over there, with the long black tail and the coat like a spit shine might even be worth more than the first house he'd bought in Upland in the seventies, when he still had a wife and dreams of greatness.

The smell of horses and hay took Jesus Dimitri Nestor back to Bonsall, to the ranch where his Greek father cleaned stables and his Mexican mother worked in the kitchen, serving up chili verde in sauce made from her own tomatillos. At the Western riding camp, young Jesus Dimitri helped with the horses, showing the rich, gumby-backed greenhorns from Orange County and San Diego how to take charge of a quarter horse, how to nudge it to another gait with the quiver of one's thighs, how to pace a *gymkhana* to win. When he was fourteen, his senses shifted into overdrive along with his body, and he suddenly wanted to be called J. D. instead of Jesus Dimitri. It was way too heavy being called Jesus and, well, Dimitri was so *disco*. He certainly wasn't going to be Jessie or Dim, so he became—against his mother's protestations and his father's two-year scowl—simply "J. D." The new J. D. would have endured any amount of parental wrath in exchange for the long looks from sweet-smelling girls like Marian McDonnell and her friend Lindsey, their long, blonde hair gleaming like Palomino tails, their breasts sprouting. Their easy giggles smelled of peppermint. Just after the Fourth of July that year; he remembered it too well. Twilight.

J. D.! J. D.! They called . . . come into the barn, J. D!

He walked into games he didn't understand. At first he played along, waiting for the joke. Later, somewhere in the haystack, with his sweat-soaked shirt off and his pants down he heard the laughter of a dozen girls and realized *he* was the joke. He was not one of these bright, shining people. He was different. He was an outsider. He was ashamed and he didn't know why. To this day, Nestor hated the smell of peppermint.

Now, he scanned the riders at the Equestrian Center. Plenty of females with their high boots and stiff posture who looked like they belonged in the English countryside. The only man who looked to be blonde and thirty-five was walking this way with reins and a mahogany bay in his wake.

"Adam Vanderberg? J. D. Nestor. LAPD. You told me to meet you here."

Vanderberg's face registered apprehension before discomfort. Nestor turned to walk with him. He worked the guy gently, acknowledged his reputation as an attorney, warmed him up. Then Nestor asked why he was out riding, given his client's murder.

The lawyer's jaw shifted. "First of all, I didn't hear about Eddie's death until I was here this morning. Second, it's my first week off in years and this training is costing me a small fortune. I pay either way.

Finally, there's not much real work I can do until all the brouhaha dies down. I'm certainly *not* going into the office this week."

"Makes perfect sense then, doesn't it?"

Vanderberg eyed Nestor to see if he was being a smart-ass. Nestor smiled. Big.

The attorney ignored it. "From Eddie's party, we drove to the bar at The Standard around twelve. My wife's an art dealer. A client was spending the evening with us and my wife wanted to discuss the final price on a Pollock in a different setting. Things went well; we left there around one-thirty. We dropped the client at home in Beverly Hills and made it to the gates of Bell Canyon, where we live, around two-twenty. There's twenty-four-hour security in The Bell Estates guard house, you can check with them." Vanderberg's tone rose as he checked to see who was in earshot. "You know, Detective, if I had something to do with Eddie's death, I certainly wouldn't have stuffed my *name* in his hand. Besides, there were far more than fifty-seven people that wanted Eddie Ealing dead."

Nestor was silent. The guy bristled in his skin, breathed too fast.

"Don't go rifling through my private life; I had nothing to do with it."

Nestor waited for the backstory he knew was there.

After several false starts, the guy unloaded. "You hear this from me, it's solid, all right? You don't need to go double or triple checking it. I can't have trouble. *I won't.*"

Nestor told him to calm down. That's all he needed now: a lawyer having a damn stroke.

"Things went swimmingly with Eddie the first few years he was my client. We got on well; I didn't understand all the stink about him being so difficult. We invested together. We went on a business trip to raise money from Pacific Rim rich boys who wanted a stake in Hollywood, especially with content going digital. In Thailand—"

Vanderberg stopped as two women passed and said hello. American women talking like they were British. Nestor wondered if that was something they picked up at prep school, Britglish.

"In Thailand—" Nestor repeated.

Vanderberg reddened. "God, the gall—"

Nestor lost his patience, said he'd heard it all before, cut to it.

"Eddie had me videotaped *flagrante delicto* with—" He stopped.

A hooker, a cucumber, an orgy of pygmies, a blowup doll . . . same old shit.

"Look, I'm not gay or anything, but in Bangkok, the young boys do this incredible thing with—eels and marbles—"

Nestor's mouth twitched as he fought to keep a straight face.

"Eddie threatened to leak the photos to my wife and the press if I didn't sell him my shares in two of our joint companies. If the projects had gone south, he'd have used the same photos to get me to buy his shares, inflated. How do you think Eddie became so powerful? Thank-you cards and candy?"

"You stayed his attorney. You went to his party last night."

"Keep your friends close—"

"Your enemies closer."

"A lot of people despised Eddie, but he always had his hands in the next big thing. Usually first. The rest of us just circled around for the spoils and he knew it."

"You ever hear of Mike's Gifts?"

Vanderberg eyed Nestor's worn belt. "A private rumor inside high-placed—"

"Not anymore. There are websites. Fans. People talking about him."

"*Really* . . ." His eyes met Nestor's. "Can't imagine Mike would like that at all."

"You know him?"

This time Vanderberg's glare was pure insolence. "No one *knows* Mike. Mike's isn't a storefront, or a shop you can look up in the Yellow Pages. The phone number's a secret, the password's hard to get. But no one delivers revenge quite like Mike."

The wind kicked up dust from the perimeter of the ring; Nestor shielded his eyes as he told Vanderberg he'd need to see Eddie's last will as soon as possible.

"I can recite the damn thing from memory. As of his death, Eddie had about seventeen million in net personal assets. Some of his holdings will be sold or absorbed to pay off outstanding debt, but that seventeen is free and clear."

Nestor chortled. "So his ex-wife's contention that he was bad with money wasn't exactly accurate."

The attorney hesitated. "The Eddie Ealing I knew was always exceptionally good with his money. I can't speak to her issues."

"Hidden assets, in other words."

Vanderberg didn't bite. "Eddie changed his will all the time, but the last alteration was in late May. The pertinent change notation is the 'Temperel Business Combination Amendment.' That revision says that Temperel would receive all of Eddie's money and shares only if Temperel was sold or added to a business combination in which another company was the majority, managing partner."

"Nothing to the family members directly?"

"Not a cent."

Weird, Nestor thought. Rewarding Temperel only if they *gave up* control. "And before the May change?"

"The money went primarily to Temperel."

"Let me get this straight—in May, Eddie changes it so that Temperel will get his money for research only if and when they are sold or managed by *another* company."

"Correct."

"And what if they aren't?"

"Then all his money goes to the Florian Corporation thirty days later."

"What's Florian?"

"Research institute up by Stanford. Menlo Park. Brain studies."

"Like Temperel."

"Bigger," said Vanderberg. "They've tried to acquire Temperel several times."

Nestor's mind raced. Why the hell would Ealing want a competitor to have control of Temperel? The final word in a power struggle? The last *screw-you*? Or something bigger? The slippery feeling in Nestor's gut said he'd just lost more ground than he'd gained.

"The Ealings know this?"

"Absolutely. Eddie insisted that his father, brother, and sister be copied."

That killed motive for anyone in the family wanting Eddie dead. At least until one of them could change his mind.

Nestor wiped his eyes against a new blast of wind. "Does your firm represent the Florian Corporation?"

The attorney cooled. "We run conflict-of-interest checks before we take clients on and we advise them of those situations."

"You haven't answered my question."

"We've done some work for Florian in the past. They also employ a number of other firms for various projects. Not uncommon these days."

"What kind of work did *your* firm do for Florian?"

"I'm not at liberty to say."

"This is a homicide."

"Do what you have to do. My time is up. You know where to reach me if there's anything more on the business front."

From anxious sexual skin diver to arrogant wall of the law in the span of ten minutes, Nestor thought.

Vanderberg took his horse by the reins and walked away.

TWELVE

PETER EALING SAT ACROSS from Daily in his office. She waited while he sipped steaming tea. Odd for July, but then he'd been walking near the ocean and had little fat on his bones. Heat singed his lips and he winced. A pang of empathy shot through Daily. Past the crow's-feet and the few filaments of silver in his cropped hair, Peter seemed more like the quiet, shy kid at the back of class than the director of a ground-breaking scientific institute. He took off his glasses, rubbed his eyes again. His gaze was gentle, almost timid, his voice a soft contrast to the rants of his brother on the CD-R found in the pool house.

"The news says it may be a serial killer," he said.

"There's no evidence of that."

Peter didn't seem to know how to respond. From above came bang-ing sounds and a hum. He looked up. "My apologies. You'd think with fifteen million spent on this place. . . . They're running a program on the large screen in the conference room upstairs. Part of orientation."

She couldn't tell if he was embarrassed or agitated. "The party at Eddie's last night was for Temperel, I understand."

"For the Foundation. An important distinction. Temperel is a corporation, a business." He pronounced *business* in three syllables.

Daily thought he'd elaborate. He didn't. Lost in thoughts no tea leaves could read.

"The Foundation isn't a business?"

Peter blinked back to the moment. "The Foundation is a charitable organization, a trust started by my mother before she died, to help less fortunate people who are afflicted by Alzheimer's and other conditions that involve memory. The Foundation receives some donations from Temperel proper, of course, but a large part of its money is from my mother's charitable trust—money she raised during her years in New York—plus new donations and fundraising. The Foundation has had a static income over the years, but the need for our science, our answers, increases exponentially as people age. We need to do what it takes. Events like last night."

"Meaning you wouldn't normally go to a party at Eddie's house?"

"That's not what I meant."

"What time did you last see Eddie?"

He swallowed. "Around eleven PM, the fireworks. After that, Dad wanted to get back to his place. He was exhausted. John Safford drove us back to Calabasas. My car was there." The answer matched the others.

"You came back up to Santa Barbara last night?"

"No. Early in the morning, around 7:30 AM. Alone. Before the news—"

Daily asked for his home address. When she looked up his eyes had welled with moisture.

"I'm sorry," he said, ashamed as he dabbed back emotion. He cleared his throat.

She asked, "You've seen Eddie's film, *Sense of Life*?"

"No. Newspapers told me more than I wanted to know when it came out."

"You didn't approve."

"Well, my God," he whispered. "Look where it got him."

"You have any idea who might be behind it?"

Peter seemed to be struggling to get a full breath. "Eddie never let go of anything. He held grudges and exacted revenge. There were always people who were angry at him. I can't begin to speculate which one of them would do . . ." He couldn't finish the sentence. When asked about the past, Peter explained that they were close as kids, but when Eddie hit middle school, he became what teachers called a problem child. From there, Eddie seemed set on avoiding the Ealing family path.

"What path is that?" Daily asked.

"Work hard, study hard, carry the knowledge and good works along. I imagine that sounds idealistic, but it's an edict that's served the Ealing family for generations."

"Eddie didn't want to work hard?"

"He worked like a maniac, he just seemed hell-bent on the dark side. Presented with a new idea, Eddie would find the fallacy in it. Faced with a choice, he selected 'the lesser of two evils.' Given a gift, Eddie wondered what the giver's agenda was."

"You're familiar with the delivery—"

"Heard about it driving back here from the beach, yes. It's abominable, even in his milieu."

Daily asked if Peter had heard of Mike's Gifts, he said only from the news. Daily pulled the photo of Alma Morada from her bag. She watched Peter study it. Puzzlement morphed to recognition.

"She worked at the café here."

"No, maintenance, the late shift. That picture was in the email message with the photo of the heart sent to Eddie. Did you ever see them together?"

"I can't recall when I last saw her. Not recently. You think Eddie's death had something to do with this woman?" As if Eddie would actually interact with *the help*.

"We're not sure. When's your next board meeting?"

"Tomorrow." Sarcasm soured him. "Never mind how this affects our family. This tragedy is what our bankers and a couple of our board members call a 'PR nightmare.' They insist we formulate a plan to deal with the media." His mouth rode the last word hard, as if it was something foul.

"To be honest, I'm a little surprised that Eddie had any interest in serving on the board of Temperel, given everything else. It seems odd."

"It was my mother's wish and mandate that we all serve on the board. Eddie respected her wish, so did Dad, Aubrey, and I. Perfect evidence of how people can come together for a good cause. We're on the brink of helping millions of people. But the wrong kind of press can devastate it. Everything we've worked for until now."

"Dr. Ross seems to think you've got a lock on some profound developments."

He chewed on his lower lip. "There's no such thing as a *lock* in science anymore."

Outside Peter's office, Dr. Ross handed Daily two files. "These are the cleaning route schedules on Alma's shifts. When you're done, I'll need the files back."

"And I'll need copies."

Daily turned to see John Safford of NOBLE standing in the doorway.

"They told me I'd find you up here." Safford seemed delighted to catch Daily off guard. Daily and Safford held each other's stares as Dr.

105

Ross left and a copy machine churned out of sight. Dr. Ross returned, handed one file to Daily, one to Safford.

"Doc Ealing requested the same information," she answered Daily's puzzlement. "Let me know if I can be of further assistance, Detective." Dr. Ross didn't address Safford as she showed Daily to the lobby. "I meant what I said earlier. Goodbye."

Daily found Safford was trailing her in the parking lot.

"What did Dr. Ross mean by that—'what she said earlier'?" he called out.

Daily kept walking, didn't respond.

Safford was now at her heels. "Did you see the scrapes on those two? Wood and Burke?"

"Burg," Daily said. "As in Pittsburgh."

"You establish their whereabouts?"

How the hell did Safford know she'd spoken to them?

"I've left a dozen messages for you," he went on. "We're not receiving the updates we expect. We're getting all our information from television. Do you realize how insulting that is? What kind of investigation are you running here? Maybe I should be working with Detective Pierce—"

Daily spun and faced him. "I realize you work for a national icon and you think we're barely capable of earning our Girl Scout merit badges, so don't take this the wrong way, but this is not *your* investigation to direct. We'll update Doc when we have salient information. In the meantime, I don't report to you, I don't owe *you* any explanations about how we find our suspects and I *hate* being shadowed and micromanaged." Her head was going to explode.

Safford laughed. "Glad we cleared that up."

"If and when I choose to divulge information about this homicide, it will be on my terms. Are we clear?"

"Very." Patronizing. Safford blocked her from the Crown Vic's door. She tried to elbow him aside but he wouldn't move. He said, "Eddie was his *son*."

"And from what I've gathered so far, a disgrace to the Ealing legacy." She could have sworn he almost said *we* again and caught himself.

"Doc deserves to know what happened to his son."

THIRTEEN

TEE CLOSED HIS EYES, put his mind and memory into flight again. The only way to deal with the rage was to remember the point. Remember one of the OV-10 Broncos, over the jungle in Bermuda shorts and a Hawaiian shirt. More than one jungle. More than one mission. Couldn't dress like a Parrothead on the current job, but it was a small price to pay to get where you had to go.

You always were a solo player, eh?

Harry always got right to the heart of it, but that's why he'd been a great President.

Tee said, "I get so tired of hearing people say they want to make things better without any follow-through. Follow-through is everything."

Hard to find follow-through these days. Rare quality.

"You said it, Harry."

You ever not follow through, Tee?

Hard to stomach that one. "You know the answer to that, Harry."

Think you might be overcompensating?

Christ. Tee's heart ricocheted in five directions. It was all there again—suddenly—the odors and sounds of the shitty hospital where his Jay lay hemorrhaging from the shot. A younger Tee never even saw him get hit.

"We weren't supposed to talk about the mission, Harry. We never used our real names. We weren't supposed to be there. We didn't exist on anyone's radar." Tee thought of all the unofficial wars. Unaccounted-for collateral damage. As bad as the scumbags were, no civilized culture wanted to admit that it underwrote the only kind of tactics that ever really made a difference with guerillas or terrorists. They were animals. Back then, the newspaper stories they caught every few weeks were relentless:

"Critics in Washington question whether private contractors slip through the net of Congressional restrictions on aid to foreign countries in the areas of antiterrorist and antinarcotic efforts, and if some of those private contractors may be linked to human rights abuses."

God, almighty—human rights abuses? These were creatures they were fighting with. They didn't know human. Didn't deserve to be in the same hemisphere as a human.

Ironically, it was one of the more beautiful days in that last God-forsaken piece of rainforest when Jay and Tee had walked back to their camp. They needed to tend to Jay's ankle, swelling from a nasty sprain and gash at the river.

They smelled it before they saw it. The fire pit's hot embers smoked with a stench. Burnt meat. Charred well past cooked. Then they heard the weeping of the village women. As they approached, the wailing pierced Tee's soul. They saw the rifle barrels jammed against the napes of the kneeling females. The scumbags were forcing the women, their hands roped behind their backs, to eat off the stones of the pit. When they dropped the food in the dirt, the creeps laughed at them, made them eat it anyway. Jay said he couldn't figure the meat, there'd been none in camp that morning. They were lucky to get rice from the poor villagers helping them. Fruits or a fish were cause for celebration. If the guerillas killed a pig, they certainly wouldn't share it with the villagers. Tee could translate what the scumbags were saying now. Pieces of it, anyway.

"Eat the meat, you stupid bitch. Eat until you vomit your traitor blood."

What were they making them eat? Burnt animal excrement? Tee had heard of that, but had never witnessed it. Certainly helping the American mercenaries was a heinous infraction in the warped minds of these psycho-creeps, but the people in this sad camp had no politics, they were just trying to survive, to make it through the madness.

One of the scumbags slapped the woman closest to him. "Whore traitor! Using your mouth to betray us to the Americans. Use your mouth now, whore!" She refused to eat any more, and the creep slammed the butt of his rifle into her head, sending her reeling into the hot spit and the charred meat. The cries of hell burned from her lungs.

"Use your mouth now. Eat!"

Dazed and weary, the woman craned her neck and swallowed a mouthful of meat from the spit. She weaved on all fours, then choked on her own retches and passed out.

No one moved to help her.

Jay fell against Tee, suddenly weak from the realization. "The men . . . there's no men . . . they're all missing," Jay whispered. "They're making them eat their men—"

"My God—" Tee's cry was too loud.

Like a pack the guerillas turned. One man aimed his rifle at Jay.

Jay yelled, "Cover me—" He ran as well as he could on his gimp leg.

Tee stood frozen, his hands paralyzed on his gun. They're making them eat their men. Tee's entire body clenched; he reeled at the horror of it. Jay called to him and he felt himself stumbling toward his friend's voice. Tears burned Tee's eyes as branches and vines whipped his face. Petrified as never before, he couldn't shoot, only run. He found Jay, tried to support him. Shouting, then more gunfire behind them. They slid their bodies into a mudpit until the guerillas passed. Tee pressed on Jay's wound with leaves, but the bleeding wouldn't stop. By the time Tee got Jay to the medics, the memory, like a bad tape, replayed time and again. Tee's soul had frozen in time. Fear had filled him with disbelief, impotence.

... the men ...

Tee had failed, he had locked up, for identifying with the poor women. Emotion. Fucking emotion. That night, as he prayed for Jay to make it, as he prayed to every god in heaven and some in other places, Tee vowed, if they got home, to start over again. Vowed that emotion would never again get in the way of doing the right thing.

FOURTEEN

"I ALWAYS SAID I could have killed him, but God, not like that," the woman who'd worked Eddie's party told J. D. Nestor. *Gawd.* Something of New England played with her vowels. She poured peanuts into a bag, took a customer's money, and pulled her faded baseball cap tight. Nestor noted the emblem: Red Sox. She'd said she'd be off work at Farmer's Market fifteen minutes ago, but her boss had sensed her hurry and made her clean the iced tea dispenser twice. Nestor knocked out two unproductive phone interviews then bought an organic pear the size of Rhode Island and wolfed it down while he waited. Hanna Morgenstern removed her apron and motioned Nestor to a table far from the crowd. She handed him a bag of complimentary nuts in honey-roasted coating that repulsed him. He'd save them for Daily.

"I'm confused," Nestor said to Hanna. "You worked Eddie's party as a caterer, but on the phone you said you used to date Eddie."

Hanna's smile was sad. "I cater now. And work here. Eddie snagged me a part in one of his first pictures about ten years ago. We were an item then. Had big plans for me, provided I was willing to make some 'changes.'" She lifted her cap, pulled dark hair away from her scalp. A wig. Her fingers grazed scars as thick as tripe. Nestor's stomach lurched at the ropes of angry skin that slashed from her temple into her jagged hairline.

"Did Eddie do that—?"

"Nah, E. E. just told me which doc to use—supposed plastic surgeon to the stars—but the guy had a problem. Man was a walking pharmacy the morning he did me. Pictures of me ended up on The Discovery Channel: *Bodies Gone Wrong*. The doc shimmied out of it, lumped me into some percentage of people that scar weird, as if it was *my* fault. Said a notice 'to that effect' was in the paperwork I'd signed, if I'd paid *attention*. Also my fault, you know what I'm sayin'?"

Nestor tried not to look as disturbed as he felt. "You felt okay employed at Eddie's parties? Considering?"

"Hey, I need the work. Not Eddie's fault the doc screwed up. Besides, E. E. attracted people who matter." She read Nestor's vexation. "I'd became a different kind of 'attraction.' There's parts in town for . . . unusual-looking people. If you're in the loop."

Nestor's bile mixed with disgust—that a scumbag doctor could deliver such wreckage and have the stones to blame it on her. That Eddie Ealing brokered her freakishness into a commodity. That Hanna Morgenstern accepted her fate so readily.

"I did other favors for him," she continued. "Six months ago, Eddie asked me to interrupt him halfway through a meeting with a guy selling some radio stations. They were fixing on a price, Eddie wanted me to throw him off. I brought in their sandwiches and made sure my wig 'accidentally' fell off. I played it up, bumped right into the dude when I went to pick up my hair. I told him disfigurement was no big deal, grabbed his hand to touch the scars and all. I'm a damn good actress. The guy got so freaked he said yes to Eddie's price just to get the meeting over."

Nestor asked for the name of the seller.

Hanna could only offer a general description: conservative suit, corpulent body, balding pate. "You don't resent being used like that?" he asked.

"Hey, the use paid real well. And Eddie always made sure I got to work at his parties if I wanted to. I finished last night's gig about midnight, then wound down at The Firefly Bar with an old friend of mine. As in, older than Hollywood wants to hire. He took me home, tucked me into bed. That's been my story for a while, you know. Just getting through each day's enough. I certainly don't have the energy to participate in some plot to have Eddie killed."

"Ever hear of Mike's Gifts?"

"Sure, 'cause of the circles I moved in when I looked good. Tried to hire Mike to get back at the doc when I was fired up, in my anger stage. Never heard back."

Nestor wanted to pay a personal visit to the physician responsible for wrecking this woman and pound a few slices into his face just to see how *his* scars would heal. He asked if Hanna had a phone number for Mike.

"Anyone trying to hire Mike has to go through this maze of directions," she explained. "They change every day. Every hour, sometimes. I was told to mail my request to a PO box in Jersey. If Mike wanted the job, I'd hear back. Never did. Some say Mike quit. Others say he's dead. Some say Mike doesn't exist."

Nestor asked her to try and find the PO box address. She promised to check, although she said it wouldn't matter by now. Mike moved fast and often. He asked if Hanna had worked Eddie's party on June twenty-third; she nodded.

"You remember seeing anyone go into the library besides Eddie or the Ulgrods?"

Hanna frowned. "No, but there was a lot goin' on. Caviar shipment. Flowers. Stargazers and irises. FedEx showed up with all these Dean and DeLuca blinis." Off Nestor's expression she said, "They're these little round pancake things, all the same size, for the caviar. I'd use Bisquick with some buckwheat thrown in, myself. Sorry I can't remember more."

"You're doing pretty good." Nestor waited while she squeezed her memory, came up dry.

"Can't think of anything else."

"Memories have a funny way of coming back when you least expect them to." He showed her the picture found inside Ealing's camera. "Ever see this woman with Eddie?"

Hanna's eyes flickered. "Can't say I have. But that's a woman Eddie would have to know. That was Eddie's big line—when he saw an attractive woman he wanted to meet, he'd saunter over and say something like, 'I just couldn't help myself, even though I'm here tonight with—insert the bimbo—Tori, Lori, Heather, Feather, Skippy, Muffy—I just *have* to know you.'" She chortled. "It worked really well, so he kept using it. I watched them come and go, all the women he *had* to know."

Must have been hard, Nestor thought, yet Hanna kept watching. "You ever hear of Mike sending anyone body parts, organs? Or photos of organs?"

"God, no. The thing about Mike's—all these years—the gifts are always something of the asshole's own making, you know? That's what's so righteous about it. It's not revenge. It's not horror. It's a *mirror*. Mike just sends the jerks their own history."

Nestor looked down at his hand. He'd nearly decimated the bag of candy-coated nuts without realizing it. He stood, thanked Hanna Morgenstern for her time. As he looked at this once-whole woman, every paternal instinct in him surged; he wanted to right the wrongs, avenge

115

her, protect her and tell her to get out of this warped reality and go live with real people again. He tried to keep pity out of his voice as he fumbled through his gratitude a second time.

"Hope you find who did it," Hanna said. "Creepy to think that the person who did that to Eddie is out there now."

Nestor nodded. If most civilians only knew what was *out there now.* As the feeling overwhelmed him again, the feeling that he'd never move as fast as the animals trailing the human wreckage in the City of Angels and the rest of the world, he reminded himself that he could only solve one problem at a time. He ambled toward the parking lot, his stomach in knots.

FIFTEEN

As she watched John Safford's blue Suburban leave the Temperel parking lot, Daily used the privacy of her Crown Vic to call the station. Lt. Powell said Nestor was still out, while Burns and Pierce were eliminating more leads than they were finding. Daily said she was sure that Dr. Ross and one or two of the senior lab techs knew more than they were telling. She finished by telling the loo she finally had a name to match the blood-streaked photograph—Alma Morada. Clearly relieved that Daily had given him that morsel of progress, Powell said he'd put the crew at the station on every possible database. Daily would call Alma's last known place of employment herself—Cyrus Services.

Daily dialed the maintenance contractor's headquarters in Camarillo and was transferred to Lyle Pearson, the "group manager" in charge of Temperel's outsourced employees. In guarded tones he asked for verification that she was really LAPD. Daily told him to call the Hollywood station, gave him that number, then her cell. He called back in three minutes.

"Okay, Detective. You wanna know about Morada . . ." Daily heard him tapping computer keys. "No show. Twenty-two of May she worked. Twenty-three of May, she didn't. Got a paycheck that ain't been picked up. Disappearing acts usually take their winnings before they go AWOL."

Daily asked for Alma's basic data, Pearson rattled off what he had, most of it useless. "Emergency contact? Relatives, next of kin? Husband?"

"Zip, nada, zilch."

The guy was a zero on concern so she tried the legal angle. "You let her paperwork go through without it?"

The guy snorted. Pearson said she wasn't an illegal "as far as he knew," said they did everything at Cyrus by the book. He was in charge of meeting his company's goals and projections, not getting personal with the thousands of employees they hired and placed in a year. "This girl didn't want no one notified if she got in trouble? Not my business. You got issues with that, you can speak to the boss."

Pass-the-buck Pearson; she'd interviewed a million of them. This one left her colder than most. She asked for the boss's name and wrote it down.

"You find this Alma Morada, tell her I got her money." Pearson's tone said he wanted to give her a lot more than her paycheck.

Daily ended the call and shook off her distaste. With Safford gone, she wanted to do one thing before leaving Temperel. She walked back inside the main building, told the security guard she'd left something behind. Near LAB A she caught the tech named Karen in the corridor.

"Just who I was looking for. Where's the ladies' room around here?"

"It's down this hall, then two lefts here—" She led Daily.

"Karen . . . you know more about Alma and Eddie than you want to say in front of others."

"What makes you say that?" Karen's face blossomed with red patches.

"A highly tuned instrument called a bullshit detector. Useful in my line of work."

Karen bit back the words until Daily stopped walking and took her arm.

Karen exhaled hard. "Okay, okay. I overheard Eddie Ealing talking to Doc one night, after a meeting. They didn't know I was outside the conference room. Eddie was angry, said something about suicide."

"*Suicide?* Are you sure?"

"Yeah. He said it loud. He was really mad."

"What makes you sure they were talking about Alma?"

"I'm not." Karen's chapped lips quivered. "But whomever they were talking about—well, Eddie said she'd never be singing again."

After calling the Santa Barbara Police Department and the County Sheriff about Alma Morada, Daily churned over what Karen had told her. If Eddie Ealing brought harm to Alma, his death could simply be revenge disguised. But the Mike's Gifts delivery—why? What was the connection? Once she got on the freeway Daily called Nestor's cell, got voicemail. She tried the station. Clem Burns said Nestor was still out.

"He told me to give you a message," Burns said. "The will. Money wasn't left to the Ealings. Left to that place you're leaving, but only if they're managed by someone else. If they're not, his dough goes to a place called Florian—"

"A competitor." Thank God she'd learned to interpret Burns.

"Roger."

Daily tried to field the thoughts hurtling at her. Eddie Ealing wanted Temperel to have different management? Or he wanted his money to go to the institute's competition if current management stayed? Was Eddie working his own deal with Florian? Burns said Nestor was following up on that angle.

"Burns—the photo—the girl's name is Alma Morada."

"The loo told us. Nothing on the search yet."

"We're going to need to start the box. The grid."

Burns' breathing was even but noisy. Forty years of smokes. "You want it laid out on the blackboard or the wipe thing?"

"The wipe board, the big one. The Santa Barbara Sheriff's office has no matches. I'm heading over to SBPD now, they have a couple missing persons matching Alma's description. In the meantime, call the transit authority up here, find out what buses run past Temperel's address between six and midnight. Call me back, give me a route number, a driver. Anyone who might have seen her ride." She read Burns the address for Temperel and added, "By the way, SBPD says the home address Alma listed doesn't exist."

"No green card," Burns said.

Daily didn't need to tell him to check with INS or the hospitals in the area, he was on it. Burns hung up without saying goodbye. The Crab wasn't big on formalities. As Daily neared downtown Santa Barbara and police headquarters, her cell rang. Dr. Ross, sounding like she'd had too much coffee.

"Detective, I wanted to ask if you'd consider not stirring anything up with local law enforcement over the Alma Morada matter. This is a small, intimate area. Everyone knows everything around here. Many of our donors, our investors, they're pillars of the community. I don't— we're already in something of a delicate media situation as it is."

"Working with local departments is routine—"

"Look, I'm asking you—" Dr. Ross eased off her irritation. "Just don't make any insinuations that could be misinterpreted about Temperel, that's all. The people on Cyrus maintenance crews—they're fine, but they have a high rate of turnover. We don't police them for it, and we don't make any leaps in judgments about it under normal circumstances."

Not an hour ago, this woman wanted to do anything to help. Now she was asking Daily to back off. Was someone there with her?

"Leaps aren't much good to me, doctor. Just facts."

"Well good," she replied, her voice all false cheer. "We're clear then."

Daily scored an empty parking space across from Santa Barbara Police headquarters. Entering the warm building, she heard Lieutenant Tim Litton's voice before she had a chance to ask for him.

"Lane! I know, I know . . . you're going to tell me that I look like you *wish* you felt." Litton's hale smile mirrored the one on the poster behind him. Four of Santa Barbara's finest on the beach with a group of teens and a triathlon trophy.

"And you'll say I should stop laying around and work a little," Daily replied.

They would have hugged but for the desk sergeant. Litton led Daily back to a conference room piled with printouts and four dead computers, their cords and wires a tangle. While he explained the fraud case he was working, Daily studied him. His sun-weaved hair was cropped—shorter now. Same good face, a couple more smile lines. He surfed, long board—a soul rider. He had that soul at twenty-three, when he and Daily had shared a case a decade ago. Now he looked even more comfortable in his skin. Their camaraderie was born when they were rookies—the only two thrown in with older egos elbowing for turf on a multiple-homicide case across jurisdictions. Back then, they were too nervous, too driven, and too far away to explore their mutual attraction. Now, she was just driven; he was just far away.

Litton laughed at the computer mess. "When will criminals get it through their heads that delete doesn't really mean delete?"

"Same time they get it through their heads that illegal really means illegal."

"Can't say I'm sorry to see you, Daily, but why all the intrigue on the phone? You have all this free time down in hell to come up and work missing Ps here?"

"Eddie Ealing."

"That's yours? I figured RHD—"

"They're a little preoccupied right now."

"Right. Rap and Jock. You're going Robbery-Homicide soon anyway, right?"

"Who told you that?"

"I got my sources. What does Ealing have to do with Alma Morada?"

"Temperel. The research place in Goleta. Eddie Ealing was on the board of directors there. Doc Ealing—yes, *the* Doc Ealing, the guy who wrote the book on morals and values and all that—is Eddie Ealing's father. Doc and Eddie's sister and brother are on the board as well. Eddie's party last night was a fundraiser for their foundation, the charity arm of Temperel."

"And Alma's someone's illegitimate daughter? Illicit lover? Bookie?"

"Alma Morada was a maintenance technician at Temperel."

"Is that the new politically correct term for cleaning woman?"

"She's missed work for five weeks. Eddie Ealing had her picture." Daily told Litton she'd already checked with the S.O. and come up empty.

"We had no paperwork on anyone named Alma Morada. Period. End of story. But these are the missing Ps that match the physical description you gave me on the phone." He pointed to a couple piles of folders, each stack two-feet high.

Daily looked at her watch. "Okay, let's get to it. Here's the photo."

Litton soaked in the image without emotion and set the picture down on the table. He gave Daily half the folders. They stood next to each other, opening files, comparing young, brown-haired, brown-eyed women between the ages of sixteen and thirty.

"This one looks like you when I met you. 'Course you weren't this wild." Litton passed her the file.

Cedella Rayborne. 28. Daily's olive skin, mixed heritage, the angles, the full hair. *Born: Jamaica. In U.S. on student visa. Hotel management. Missing since last December. Parents in Kingston say daughter never came home for Christmas.* There were two photos of Rayborne, both sent by her parents. One, a student ID from a vocational school in Kingston. The other taken at a party. Buddy Holly glasses perched on the woman's head, holding wild hair back. Rayborne's eyes not so innocent. She knew more at twenty-eight than Daily hoped to know when she died. It was there, the whole sorry story, in that one shot. *Last known place of employment: Minton Hotel. Maid.* Cedella Rayborne didn't get that look in her eyes from studying hotel management.

A dense pain pulled at Daily; she thought of the haunted eyes that tortured *her* so many times. Eyes that could burn with beauty, then ice over with madness. She remembered dead eyes, staring up at her from the sea. *Put it aside, Daily.* She placed her feelings in check as she opened, compared, and closed each file. Each one of these girls was missing. More than half of them would never be found. They were somewhere else now—runaways, petty criminals on the run, hookers, drug addicts, scam artists just getting by. A third were running from themselves, their families, pasts that only looked good in the rear-view. One or two might learn too much too fast and score big with it, maybe take on guys like Eddie Ealing in high-priced bedrooms. The rest would be found dead or they wouldn't be found at all.

Litton made good time with his stack. Standing close, Daily could smell his cologne. Clean. Brisk. Her head was light and Litton's scent was intoxicating as he leaned in front of her. She tried to remember how long it had been since she'd last made love to someone.

"Seven months," he said out loud.

Daily dropped two folders to the floor. "What?"

"This last one. She looks a lot like your woman, but she's been missing seven months. You said Alma Morada's only been gone for five or six weeks, right?"

Daily blushed and hoped he didn't notice. "Right."

Litton showed her the photograph.

"No, Alma's lips are different."

"Good eye. Well, that's my half. No match." He slapped the last folder shut.

She finished her stack. Nothing. "Where do people dump bodies up here?"

"You mean from all those homicides we have every day? This is civilization, Daily. We don't have a lot of killing, pillaging, and maiming. People actually live here. It's nice. They have days off and they have husbands and holidays and kids and—"

"Get some new material, Tim. Now if someone was going to dump a theoretical body in a theoretical place in this *paradise*, where would that theoretical place be?"

"No need to get edgy, woman. If I was a perp, I'd dump my victim in Devil's Canyon, the ocean, or somewhere along the beach. Rocky, preferably.

"Temperel. I know it's sheriff turf, but you ever hear of trouble around there?"

"Something stirs but I'm not nailing it. Let me ask Kieve."

Litton left Daily alone in the conference room. She felt rattled. He was rested, sated, relaxed. She was tired, hungry and, of all things, horny.

She took the deep breaths recommended by Paulette and composed herself.

"Temperel had a couple guys making GHB," Litton said as he returned. Gamma-hydroxy-butyrate was similar to date-rape drugs that could be put undetected in drinks; it rendered people helpless or comatose. Mixed with alcohol, it often killed. "Kieve says the arrests happened a few months back; school was in session. The perps were two trial subjects at the institute. They sold their stuff around schools up here, at local parties."

"No one on the Temperel staff linked to it?"

"Nope. In fact, Temperel wanted the GHB boys given maximum penalties. Didn't want its reputation tarnished and all that. Here's the names of the perps."

Drugs. Made sense. A research lab. Young people who liked the new-tech highs. Signing up as subjects.

"This bust make noise in the local media?"

Litton thought about it. "Can't remember."

"Let me know if anything comes back to you."

He gave her a slow smile. "Ah, the things that I wish *would* come back."

"Tim, I want to stay low profile on this. Can you check in with the perps serving time for the GHB? See what they have to say about it now?"

"And I'm going to be asking . . . why?"

"Say you have a suspicion there's some new guys at Temperel doing it now."

"Not SBPD business. County."

"These jokers don't know that."

"Their attorneys will."

"Tie it into 'new GHB sales in your jurisdiction,' then. Ask them if anyone there might be imitating their old system, making the drug there now. Ask how they were busted and see if they think anyone at Temperel snitched on them. And see what they have to say about these people, if anything." Daily handed Litton Temperel letterhead that listed the board members. She added the names of the lab workers she'd interviewed.

Litton put the sheet in his pocket. "I'm going to call in this favor."

"I know you will."

Back in the car, Daily called the coroner's office and asked them to add GHB to the tox screen. Temperel. Labs. Drugs. The correlation should have hit her head-on, and she missed it. Too wiped out. Then the notion tremored through her, the one she hated the most. *You miss things.* Someday they might find out. Everyone—the department, the city, her friends and family, the whole damned world—would discover that for all her organization and drive and merits, she could, she *would*, miss things.

A crucial link in a case.

Her husband Rob. His passive-aggressiveness; the affair she refused to see.

Betrayals by people she trusted the most in her life.

Excuses for the dangers alive in her own flesh and blood.

Things you don't want to see. Things you can't see. If they found out she could short-circuit like that, miss reality head-on, she'd be through—discovered, naked, humiliated. Taryn Pierce would use Daily's screw-ups as jet fuel. Dread washed over her. The biggest case of her career and she could blow it because of her damn mind blindness.

Dr. Ross had talked about drugs that could take away—what had she called it? *The accompanying fragility found in highly attenuated individuals who would otherwise find their memories and sensations unbearable.* Daily's memories didn't help. Neither did her emotions. She was one of them indeed: damaged. Outside, a great faker. Inside, defective. The car seemed void of oxygen. She smelled stale salt air, yet the windows were up. She rolled hers down and the breeze that hit her was fresh and moist, not stale at all.

Clem Burns called, told her where to find the bus depot that handled Goleta and Temperel. When she got there, Daily left a copy of Alma's photograph with the shift manager. She asked him to make sure all the bus drivers took a look at the picture. The matter breezed past him as he hit golf balls toward the open mouth of a plastic alligator. He hit one in, and the alligator's toy mouth closed with a mechanical roar.

SIXTEEN

"YOU'VE GOT SOMETHING," DAVIS said to Paulette when he called to badger her again. She could hear the sound of the newsroom behind him. Voices, radios, multiple televisions. Paulette had made a promise to her former patient, Jordan Krasinski, and she intended to keep it. Davis wanted his murder profile; she replied that she was still "researching possibilities."

"For crying out loud, Paulette, with your clientele you had to know someone on that guest list, or someone who knew Eddie Ealing, at least. Spreck and Channel Six are scooping the whole damn DMA, no—the whole damn world—on this story, and I'm sick of it."

"Take some Dramamine."

"That your stab at therapy? Tell me what you know."

Her pulse quickened. "I'm not one of your investigative reporters. You have several. Have them call the LAPD and ask about Eddie Ealing's recent projects."

"For God's sake, just *tell* me. Is this a money thing?"

"No, Davis. It's an ethics thing. I don't talk about confidential patient matters."

His voice was drenched in sarcasm. "Please. Like you never sit around with other doctors or friends and dish on the kooks."

"I prefer to call them reality-challenged and any discussions we may have are always nameless, faceless, and in the most general terms."

He coughed *bullshit* on the other end of the line.

"I'm hanging up now."

"Paulette—wait. I'm sorry."

Tension constricted her breaths. Most of the time she liked Davis; he was usually balanced and fair in the newsroom. But for some reason, this story had him as worked up as a blue-balled teenager. It had Lane coiled too; this murder was jarring some tough psyches.

Davis broke into her thoughts. "Deep Throat."

"I don't watch porn, Davis."

"Watergate. *That* Deep Throat. It was no *accident* that Bernstein and Woodward were the ones who got the information."

"And this has what to do with Eddie Ealing?"

"It's no accident that Kelly Spreck and Six are getting this information. No accident. That's all I'm saying."

Paulette sank into her couch, looked out her deck window, to the sun licking the horizon. "You're saying there's a leak in the LAPD? And it's only to Kelly Spreck?"

"She seems to be riding shotgun on every new turn and we're still in the pit."

"Stop with the sports metaphors."

"That was a racing metaphor."

"I don't buy the leak idea."

"I'm not selling it, Paulette, I'm telling you the facts. Turn on Six and watch. The stuff Spreck knows? It's no accident. No accident at all."

SEVENTEEN

Again, Tee read Daily's old journal entry. It explained so much:

She burned me tonight. We played with fireworks on the driveway. The Gorvicks came over for 4th and Daddy made big burgers. Everything was OK. Then she got that look like . . . when it starts to scare me. She watched all the cones shoot off and stuff but she looked like this zombee. She had this sparkler. She came really close to my arm and I said don't because it was still HOT even after it was done. It GLOWED.

She stuck it in my leg and it burned me. My leg went HISSSSS. At first it didn't hurt. Then it HURT REALLY BAD and I was crying and my skin was peeling hot and I wanted it to stop HURTING. Everyone said it was an accident. She didn't say sorry. She just looked at me funny. Now I can't sleep it burns so bad. Everyone said it was an accident.

EIGHTEEN

BACK ON THE FREEWAY, Daily scanned the radio. Four of five news/ talk stations were now talking about Ealing's death. Mike's Gifts. The Mind Box website with rumors of Mike's history. A wave of paranoia was going to kill more projects than the last few strikes. On one station a well-known slasher-pic director told the host he was thinking about a change, maybe something animated, upbeat. Down the dial, a convicted felon and platinum rapper announced he was going to record a Christmas album with the proceeds going to victims of domestic abuse. This reactivity was insane, and Daily wanted clarity.

Unleashed by stress, the two primal cravings hit her. Chocolate and salt. She rifled the glove compartment and found a half-eaten Slim Jim.

Nestor called from Eddie Ealing's estate. She was relieved to hear his voice. She heard her own replies, cool with a little twist of their banter, just so he'd know she was fine. On her game. She wondered if he could tell she wasn't. They discussed Eddie's will. How family members *wouldn't* want him dead, given its directives. She asked him to repeat his encounter with attorney Vanderberg firsthand. Nestor finished by telling her that the guy wouldn't offer any more information on Florian and he didn't seem the least bit worried about the police pursuing it. "Someone's got his back, and they're bigger than we are."

"Why would Eddie give his money to Temperel's main competitor? There's a million other places he could have willed the money," she said. "Eddie's giving the money to Florian after thirty days, with the specific instructions that *they* be in control of Temperel. That's a clear message."

He said coroner Zaginsky had mentioned Florian before; they did post-stress work with intelligence folks. "The ones who came back from the Middle East missing a few pieces of themselves."

"Literally?"

"Figuratively. Guys who went deep undercover and got a little too lost."

"You know this how?"

"One of my Marine buddies," he said. "When they got him out, he knew who *he* was. But he didn't know who *I* was. Or his wife. Or his kids."

"But that kind of thing has happened in World War II, Korea, Vietnam—"

"This is different. Not posttraumatic stress disorder, where they're all shaky and jumpy at the site or sound of certain stressors. My friend came back happy as a clam. Just has no memory of ever *knowing* us. I'd say we should talk to him now, but he disappeared a couple of years ago. Don't know if he's dead or alive."

Daily asked Nestor to conference Zaginsky into their call. The coroner was working late, as usual, and Daily asked him about the Florian connection.

"Florian's heavy duty," Zaginsky said. "Some say the alphabet agencies have used their scientists on amnesia cases, other sensitive memory problems. Of course those are just rumors. On the record, they don't talk about anything."

"Is Florian government-funded?" Daily asked.

"I'm just a lowly county coroner. Talking on a lowly county phone line."

"Right. Thanks, Zag."

After Zag dropped off the call, Daily said to Nestor, "Why would Eddie want to spite Temperel? That place was founded on the very condition that killed his mother, the only person he admired, according to Helmy." They agreed to put Pierce on Florian, give her a chance to mix it up with some fellow know-it-alls. Then Daily gave Nestor the update on Alma Morada, the link to Temperel, the lack of an address or any trace of the woman since May twenty-second.

"What the hell was Eddie Ealing doing with a maid?" Nestor asked.

"A very beautiful maid."

"Even so—" Nestor paused. "Guys like Ealing. They worry about what kind of car they drive, who they're seen with. No matter how hot she was, it wasn't like he couldn't have his pick of a thousand wannabes. I just don't see Ealing sitting around smoking a Montecristo with the guys, yapping about the new *maid* he just did. No upside."

"Even assholes fall in love."

Nestor's doubt grumbled. "Can't buy me love on this one. Not yet."

"Fine. Blackmail. Alma found out Eddie was planning to sabotage a Temperel deal unless he got his way."

"The kid's that smart, she wouldn't be working *basura* detail. The guys here at Eddie's house got nothing productive from the pool house drain or pipes. The skylight wasn't opened in months. There's a computer program for the temperature control—it tracks a record of air conditioning, heat, skylight, vent activity. Ealing's security system is separate. No meaningful pictures from any of the surveillance cameras. The techs are going to enhance some that look like rectangles of nothing right now. Night shots. Nothing from the computer trace on email. These guys have thrown about two hundred acronyms at me and I haven't got the faintest idea what they're talking about."

"Ask them to explain it."

"Didn't understand their *explanation* of what I didn't understand." Nestor lowered his voice. "Sometimes I get the feeling they aren't sure themselves, they're just throwing around a bunch of terms to make us *think* they know. You ever notice how much these wireheads argue? If it's such an exact science, how much can there be to debate?"

"They expect to know something solid by the briefing tomorrow?"

Daily heard Nestor repeat the question to one of the IT men. Then, a long reply. Nestor chortled. "He said maybe, maybe not."

"Let me talk to him." Daily asked the tech to repeat his answer. Then she asked for him to put Nestor back on the phone.

Nestor said, "Well?"

"He said maybe, maybe not."

Nestor laughed. "I may not speak the language, but evasion I understand. You translate what he's saying at the briefing tomorrow. There's a hand-held vacuum missing from a closet at the estate. And rubber gloves, according to Helmy. They lived in the cupboard where the pool supplies were stashed. We're checking dumpsters in a five-mile radius, farther on the main drags. Already did the trash in the adjacent homes, nothing."

"Quixote going to have a line on that dark hair by tomorrow?"

"Yes."

"Yes is good. Yes is definitive. We can work with yes."

Daily signed off Nestor's call and braked the car at the plug of traffic near the 101-405 interchange. She turned to her favorite rock station, turned it up. U2. *One.* Intense and beautiful, but it made her think of her ex, Rob. She changed the station. Garbage. *I Think I'm Paranoid.* Real funny.

Daily wondered if she had met Mike today at Temperel. Wondered if the message to Ealing was sent by Mike or an impostor. The real Mike had been smart enough to avoid getting caught in over a decade. Someone with an inside track to information and secrets about people. Someone with a strong opinion about things—from Christmas to O. J. to media executives to John Rocker. All of it tinged with an undercurrent. A message. Not foreign or extremist. Pierce had mentioned "gifts" on both coasts, so Mike wasn't obsessed with Los Angeles. No one interviewed had heard of Mike's Gifts killing anyone, but all seemed to agree that this murder was the ultimate comeuppance for a narcissist like Eddie Ealing. Maybe Mike was escalating—growing more angry as time went on. Had Ealing uncovered Mike's identity?

More than one killer? One killer with two minds?

Red brake lights signaled more slow traffic ahead. She felt boxed in on all fronts. Frozen with frustration she cursed the freeway. The surface of her skin prickled hot even as she felt a chill hit her spine—the strangest sensation—hot on the outside, cold within. Again, Daily thought she smelled something stale. She sniffed the air-conditioner vents, the doors, even her clothes. The scent was gone. She closed her eyes.

Boxed in her car.

Boxed in this case.

Boxed in by her own fears and limitations.

Her anger just made her feel more incompetent; she realized there was nothing to do now but wait.

NINETEEN

PAULETTE SOHL STOOD IN Daily's kitchen manning the stove as Daily entered her modest loft in Hermosa Beach, thirty miles away from the Hollywood station but a world away from the insanity. After Daily's divorce, after therapy, they'd exchanged keys and confidences. Daily had stopped to pick up ice-cold Coronas, since Paulette cooked everything on the hot side. Broad cheekbones and a strong nose hinted at Paulette's Eastern European ancestry. Her wide hips and softening jawline were comfortable in mid-forties skin. Paulette looked every part the content, nurturing mother, but for one holdover from her earlier years: the sea-bleached blonde hair that roped down her back in a loose braid, out of the way of the steam rising from the sauté pans.

"What are you doing with more Coronas?" Paulette asked. "There's a six-pack in your grocery delivery. Came right before you did."

Daily stared at the bags of the local market and berated herself for not remembering she'd placed the order in anticipation of her days off. Paulette told her to cut herself some slack, no one else would.

Paulette was the big sister Daily wished she'd had. Paulette genuinely admired her police work, said it took incredible strength of character. Daily respected Paulette's endless patience and insight. They shared everything but the few things Daily could barely think about herself. Things so long gone they didn't matter anyway.

They both liked classic films on video, spicy food, the Discovery Channel, dogs, and the same bands. They both hated crowded social scenes, game shows, wedding and baby showers and fishing because of the worm part. Like Daily, Paulette was a first-generation American. They were the children of dreams, sisters in their differences from others. As the children of immigrants, both expected far too much from themselves. Paulette's father had been a major in the Polish underground. Her mother was half-Jewish, half-Catholic, wholly intellectual. Both parents were studying in Warsaw when the Nazis bombed in '39. They'd fought as long as they could, then escaped to America, arriving in New York with seven dollars and their memories. Paulette never forgot how different her future could have been had they not made that trip.

She was glad they made it, too, thought Daily as she unpacked the bags, the tension of the day bowing her shoulders.

Paulette examined the groceries with mock seriousness. "Insightful diagnostic criteria." She held up the bag of SOS pads. "Overconscientious, scrupulous." Paulette tapped on an egg carton. "Reluctant to confide in others." Oreos. "Persistent consumption of nonnutritive substances." A jar of pickles. "Recurrent and distressing thoughts of a past event."

Daily shrugged. Paulette grabbed the six-pack of Coronas.

"These longnecks, my dear, are phallic symbols, which, I'll remind you, you've been in short supply of since you stopped seeing that cute boy, Tony."

"He's a man, not a boy."

"Sweetie, they're all boys."

"He was sharing his longneck with other women. And I'm sorry to shatter your analysis, but the sink is dirty, I crave pickles and Oreos, and the eggs are easy to cook."

"Denial won't get you anywhere, Detective."

Daily forced a weak laugh then shot up the stairs of the loft to change into something loose and lazy. The bed and main bath were on the top level; an open railing overlooked the narrow living room. The spare condo was perfect for a single woman and Daily loved it, especially the tiny window at the top of the loft, right above the bed. At night she could stare at the stars, even the moon when it decided to sail that way.

She pulled off her copper jacket. Constantly ribbed for dressing up—more by the women than the men—Daily found clothes her one indulgent distraction. Through the years, she'd found just the right fabrics, cuts, and colors she could wear on the job. She'd stopped wearing light colors after her first decomposition case. She pulled off the two mismatched socks she'd put on this morning in her rush. Chili peppers and oranges with wings, indeed. If clothes were her serious indulgence, socks were her whimsy. She had alligators in go-carts, hounds with sunglasses, dancing martini glasses and Elvis juggling coconuts in her drawers and on her feet.

In her cotton bra and panties, Daily gave herself a quick appraisal in the mirror. She certainly wasn't the business executive her family had expected. Her deep-set eyes had soaked up too much hard reality, her skin was unusually pallid, absent the deep caramel tones that could rival her dad's. Her legs and arms were more sinewy than svelte. What the hell, she worked out to stay in shape, not to win contests. Daily threw on a sweatshirt and some shorts, gathered and clipped her hair on top of her head.

The smell of the chipotle sauce hit her as she came downstairs. She took her plate of fish from Paulette and they ate in comfortable silence in the loft's living room. Daily drowned the burn with a long slug of beer.

"I'm on fire, but it's heavenly heat."

"It's good for you," Paulette said. "Insomnia again, eh?"

"That obvious?"

"Those dark circles could be the 'before' picture."

"Ouch. Today was supposed to be the first of three days off. Then this. No way I can stay out of it."

"It screams Robbery-Homicide. Why aren't they handling it downtown?"

"They're neck deep in the arena shooting. And this is the biggest case that's ever hit my—"

"You want the glory, pay the price."

"This has nothing to do with glory." Daily wrestled with discretion, than tossed it. She needed Paulette on this. She retrieved the picture of Alma Morada. "Check this out."

Paulette studied the image, then looked to the shelves, to the photo of Daily at eighteen, her arm slung around a doe-eyed girl. "Haunting. Fragile eyes. Like your friend from high school. The one who killed herself—Mira?"

"Tira." Daily hadn't made the association. "I guess their eyes are similar. This girl's beautiful, but her expression . . . it's like she wants someone to *hear* her, but no one listens. Or maybe I'm just tired, seeing things that aren't there."

Paulette made a strange face, didn't push it. "What does this picture have to do with Eddie Ealing?"

"The woman's name is Alma Morada. Her photo was in the email sent to Eddie from Mike's Gifts."

"No one mentioned this in the newsroom—the girl's picture."

"The heart in the digi-file from Mike's was probably an animal heart, not human. It's more about the message. Someone messing with Ealing's secrets. His memories."

"What are you thinking?" Paulette asked her.

"Why?"

"You've got red on your face and neck. Flushed."

Daily trusted so many secrets to Paulette. Rob, love, anger, parents. Still, she wondered if any human could ever be trusted completely.

"The chipotle," she fibbed. "Anyway, the Ealings are all on the board at Temperel. Research place that studies Alzheimer's, Parkinson's. Alma Morada was a maid there. Contract maintenance. Boss doesn't know where she's gone and I don't think they check green cards as hard as they say they do. Turnover's high. It could be nothing, no link to Eddie's murder. But I pressed one of the women I met in a lab. She said she heard Eddie ranting after a board meeting. Something about suicide and not singing anymore. The maid sang really well, apparently. That's how people knew her."

Color drained from Paulette. "She reminds you of someone you lost."

If Paulette only knew. "Like I said, she doesn't remind me that much of Tira."

"You letting this get personal, Helena?"

Daily didn't answer.

"Be careful, my dear. Take emotion along and she'll distract you."

Paulette was right. Daily finished eating in silence and they watched some of the news. She noticed Paulette's rising agitation at the reports on Eddie Ealing. Daily was usually the one fidgeting. "Personal for you, too?"

Paulette stilled restless hands. "This is personal for everyone. Serial killers and psychopaths—they're horrific, but we watch them

140

from a distance. They're the aberrations. I don't think this is a psychopath at all. And the ramifications of *that*—"

"We'll track him down." Daily hoped she sounded more sure than she felt.

"You should see some of the letters I get at the station—articulate, well-researched arguments about everything from the news to music to movies. There's a lot of regular folks who've had enough. The swell gets big enough, one or two of them may take matters into their own hands."

Daily stood. "I brought home a bag filled with CDs and films Eddie Ealing produced. The titles and topics aren't pretty, but if regular folks don't like it, they should stop buying those CDs and stop going to those movies."

"Preaching to the choir, but think about it. What a way to make a point. If people with strong feelings hit dead ends on the censorship front, they might try other avenues, especially if they have money and power—"

"Doc Ealing was in Calabasas when it happened. And Eddie's death actually complicates things for the family, according to the will. Eddie's money only goes to Temperel if they agree to merge with another company and let them take over management. If not, all his money goes to a competitor, a research firm called Florian. Know them?"

"Heard of them, sure. Bay Area. Guy I knew from the master's program at Berkeley went to work there after he got sick of teaching and therapy."

"Why'd he become a psychologist?"

"He liked mysteries, not people. He's an ace on aberrant behavior."

"He likes you?"

"He dislikes me less than the rest of humanity."

Daily asked Paulette to see if he knew anything about Florian trying to acquire or partner with Temperel.

"Sure. But if they already know about Eddie's bequest, they're going to be tightlipped enough to protect it."

"If they already know, then Florian had a lot to gain from Eddie Ealing being dead. Although, there's also a lot of other people who are thrilled that Eddie's dead and—"

"And?"

"Don't give me that look. You know something—"

Paulette chastised herself. "No names."

"Fine."

"Davis called from the station, told me that Eddie's guest list was posted on the Internet. I saw the name of a former patient on it. I spoke with him today, after your people did, and I asked him why he attended. He's making a name for himself with some projects but he's not A-list yet, by any stretch." Paulette was trying to be informative yet vague for the client's benefit. "He said Eddie helped grease his recent career shift. He worked on some of Eddie's previous projects in another capacity. My guy says Eddie couldn't stop talking about a new investigative project. *Kuru.* Said he was obsessed with it."

"What's *kuru?*"

"Brain disease. You lose your mind, get hysterical, depressed, weak, go mad. Originally found in the natives of New Guinea. Transmitted during cannibalism. The eating of human brains, to be specific."

Daily stiffened. "Good God."

"You went to a research institute. If they study what you say they do, I guarantee they have brains, brain sections, brain slides."

The image of the Temperel labs replayed in Daily's mind. First drugs, now diseases she hadn't thought of correlating. *You miss things.*

"Correct on all counts," she said too quickly. "But Eddie was on the board of the institute. Maybe he just took some images he saw, a piece of information he heard and translated it into something he thought would make a good media hook. A story."

"Maybe. But Jor—my patient—implied that Eddie was messianic about this new thing. The story 'had to be told.' My guy was less enthusiastic. After investigating it, he told Eddie that the disease had been virtually eradicated, it wasn't topical anymore. He suggested they work on something more mainstream, more uplifting. But Eddie told him all that matters is 'what you leave behind.'"

"Cryptic." Daily leaned into her hands. She was too tired to think and too wired to sleep. Definitely too tired to pretend she had the answers.

Paulette seemed to read her thoughts. "You want Pavlov tonight? Help you run into some sleep?"

"If Pavlov doesn't mind workout clothes that smell three weeks sweet."

———————

Daily took the leash from Paulette. Attached was one big, brown dog. Part German shepherd, part golden lab, part God-knows-what, Pavlov licked Daily's knees in anticipation. Paulette offered to do the dishes before she went back to her own condo, so Daily took Pavlov down the stairs and out the front of her fourplex.

"Have a good run and sweet dreams, Detective," Paulette chimed from the doorway. The light behind her cast past braid-loosed hairs. "Be good to my man tonight."

Daily broke into her jog and Pavlov joined, familiar with the drill. At the beach, she let him off the leash. She often ran at night, and Hermosa was safer than most Southern California beaches. Pavlov's size was also intimidating and his rapscallion countenance threw folks off guard. Paulette had originally rescued the mutt from a client who'd dressed the dog—along with his dates—in dresses and hats for the amateur photo pages of magazines like *Crosstown Traffic*. Paulette stopped seeing the client and adopted the dog; Pavlov quit wearing feather boas.

Daily jogged to the hard sand at the water's edge. At night, the ocean didn't spook her; it was much worse during the day. Running next to the dark water, she could practice her *systematic desensitization*. Work on the sounds of the waves one at a time. Think good thoughts with each break.

Pavlov helped too: he ran ahead, splashed into the waves, nipped at nothing in particular, then herded each retreat of the sea. As she ran, Daily thought about the case. Eddie Ealing had been despised by hundreds of people, for years. So why kill him now? What was the catalyst? A pang shot through her. She wished she could talk with her ex about it. Then she remembered the rest and changed her mind.

They had both worked for the LAPD. Rob was a good listener—then. She tried to remember when he closed up. Couple years after she'd passed Detective I, which had happened as a fluke. She'd been assigned to the Hollywood station when they were thin on manpower, thick on unsolved cases. Her drive and tenacity served a fresh tonic to jaded detectives. Homicide had been so impressed with Daily's work, the detectives encouraged her to give the exam a shot. Even Rob supported the test, which she'd passed readily; he just didn't want her working homicide for good. But with too many murders that involved sexual or domestic abuse, female detectives weren't an asset, they were a necessity. Female victims felt more comfortable relating to other women. A woman listened differently, heard certain nuances.

Meanwhile, Rob, a sergeant in the West-LA division, rode a career track as flat as the Mojave. He didn't complain, just disappeared, in more ways than one. He grew less aggressive at work and more contentious with her. When Daily passed Detective II, their celebration dinner turned into an insult-laden debacle. Rob, six years her senior, felt compelled to tell her she was simply a poster child for a police department under serious gender and ethnic heat.

Friends on the force finally told her that Rob was making his own heat with a female patrol officer in his division. Rob said he could "really talk to her," and made lots of noise around the station about how bad his marriage was. That did it. Monogamy was her big one. She loved him even as she'd filed for divorce, afraid she would never find another man who could hold her the way he did, touch her, move her. She'd lost twenty pounds that winter. Too sick to eat. Too proud to take him back.

Daily touched the pylon at the pier, her marker, and turned. Pavlov barreled past her then stopped. She approached and he dashed off again, enjoying the game. She jogged in place; the dog cocked his head. Pavlov tore into the waves and rushed her. His wet body knocked against her legs. Her laughter provoked more barking.

"*Sshh!* The normal people are sleeping."

Now, two and a half years later, the ache over Rob wasn't constant anymore. So she didn't have him around to discuss cases. What she needed from a man right now was something else entirely. Daily cleared her mind of the case, sex, everything. She ran ten more circuits. Drained, she stripped to her maillot and hit the pull-up bars near the pier. The dog sat motionless as her arms worked. Daily found Pavlov's ardent watch alternately humorous and reassuring. *Twenty-five. Twenty-six. Ignore the pain. Put it away. Thirty-five. Burning pain. Ignore . . . the . . . pain . . .* Fifty pull-ups done and her nerves were numb. Daily shook out her arms as she walked to the end of the pier. Pavlov cantered before her and met her under a sputtering light. The salt air filled her nostrils. Real salt air, not the warm, stale stench that had hit her earlier in the day. Pavlov panted; he was tuckered out, too. He dropped to his haunches and watched her as she climbed atop a pylon bearing a red warning sign.

No Diving.

Daily straightened, assumed the posture. A gust nudged her but she held steady, waited for it to subside. *Think of the sea as pleasant.* Her skin puckered with goosebumps. There. The dark ocean lapped at the pier's struts below. *The sound of the ocean is soothing. Good thoughts. Only good thoughts.* The dog sat vigilant; two old fishermen ignored her. She extended her arms, took a long breath, felt the rush. She could do it this time. Her arms swung back, her knees bent to spring and—

The face. The eyes staring up at her again.

Open.

Dead.

Daily's legs crumpled and she fell off the pylon, back onto the pier and Pavlov's cold, wet coat. She bit into her lip, but no tears would come.

TWENTY

DAILY LED THE DOG from the pier to the beach, toward her shoes and his leash. The ocean sounded terrifying to her now, each wave break a taunt. *You can't do it. You can't forget.* Systematic desensitization wasn't cutting it. She needed to wipe her brain clean.

Pavlov growled at a man standing still on the incline of sand above them. Daily said hello. The man didn't answer. Pavlov bared his teeth but the man seemed oblivious. His eyes were fixed on Daily. He wore a *Los Angeles Herald Examiner* windbreaker. The paper had been out of business for decades. His chinos were worn at the knees, frayed at the ankles. On his feet were sneakers, a couple sizes too big. His hands were behind his back. Daily stood in place, her muscles pushing and pulling at her. The man opened his mouth. No teeth. He hesitated, then hissed at her over the rumble of the sea. He turned and proceeded to pull his contraband, a dead octopus on a two-by-four, toward the water. In the shallows, his hands became tangled in the tentacles. He spoke to the lifeless creature, then cursed when he couldn't rid himself of it. Dead, it still wouldn't let go. She led Pavlov back toward the apartment building.

You can't do it. You can't forget. Daily willed her demons to stop. Pleaded with them. They'd been around for years, but *now*, of all times, they demanded center stage. As she opened her front door, the dog bolted past her and headed for the loft upstairs. In her apartment, the light on her answering machine glowed. The beep seemed unusually loud.

"Lane, it's Rob. Saw you got the Ealing case." Long pause with static. On his cell. His voice was hesitant. "Been thinking about you all day; hope you're doing all right." Longer pause. "Miss you, Helena."

Even divorced, they thought of each other at the same time. She could run into oblivion, she could push into deep workout pain, but she couldn't escape her memories. Long ago, the dead eyes in the sea, staring up at her as she stood on the pier. In high school, her best friend's suicide. Now Rob, thoughts of his arms around her, his lips making her feel warm and safe and whole. *Damn him for calling.*

Upstairs she showered and scrubbed with the loofah so hard that she scraped her skin raw in places. She brushed her teeth twice, then slid into bed. Her demons invaded her dreams when no one knew she was grappling with them. The frequency and duration were always up to them. But since this morning, at the scene of Eddie Ealing's murder, they'd been with her all day, accelerating, for what reason she didn't know. Some fuel of theatrics versus facts, lies versus truth, perception versus reality. She was sweating and she'd just showered. She lay still, waiting for the nightmares to begin. But instead, as she drifted into half-consciousness, only Alma's delicate ghost danced in the footlights of Daily's brain, telling her something she couldn't hear.

Daily sat up in bed, jarred awake. She was certain she'd heard someone in the living room below. She listened. Nothing. Pavlov stirred, licked his chops, dropped his head across her feet and let out an inconvenienced groan. She reached for the clock. 1:40 AM. Now she remembered—dinner, dog, run, shower. She'd been dreaming of Alma Morada, a woman she didn't even know. She prayed for sleep to wash back over her, but she couldn't close her eyes. Hypervigilance, Paulette had called it. Even in her nightmares, eyes watched her. She was staring off a phantom, afraid to lose control. People knew about her insomnia, but Daily had not disclosed the real source of her fitfulness to anyone, not even Paulette. If she knew what happened, even so long ago, Paulette would never again see Daily as someone with strength of character. Instead she'd see weakness, revulsion, madness, death.

Daily turned on a lamp. Light made her feel better, as did the dog. Pavlov rolled on his back, all four paws in the air. If she was up, he'd just as soon have his belly scratched. Pavlov waited, prone, then twisted to his feet when Daily didn't respond. He negotiated the bed covers until he was in her face; his warm dog breath and big tongue assailed her.

"You're a fine houseguest. Come on."

Daily would leave between six and seven for the autopsy. Faced with four more hours of insomnia, she decided to work, so she started a pot of Kona and went to the living room where she unpacked the bag of Ealing's videos and CDs on the floor: a semicircle of stories and songs—links to the victim's mind, his engine. She turned on her laptop. When she went back into the kitchen, Pavlov had his nose in the trash and his muzzle was covered in Paulette's chipotle sauce. The dog erupted in furious sneezes. Daily dabbed his nose and mouth with a wet towel, let him sneeze a few more times.

"That's what you get for slumming."

She went to the fridge and took out some turkey slices. Pavlov's wheezing stopped as he gobbled them. She poured herself a steaming cup of adrenaline and downed half quickly, then went to her laptop and sat on the floor. She opened a custom spreadsheet template she'd designed to plot out complicated cases, or those with too much information. Daily had first seen the "Box of Lies" used by the Trial Support Department down at the DA's office. The charts and graphs of contradictions were a celebrated success for the prosecution in a tough case. Daily had morphed her own spreadsheet from this concept, which homicide had since dubbed the "Box of Truth." While the legal eagles downtown found it helpful to illustrate what *didn't* synchronize in a case, Daily wanted to see what *did*. In every lie, even the lies of killers, there was some truth. Mining that truth was the key to motive. She entered her raw data. Saved the computer file once, then saved a copy so she could play with the possibilities free of anyone else's input. Taryn Pierce, for example. Daily's stomach grumbled at the thought of the junior detective, her crisp hair, her papercut tongue. Shifting back into motive mode, Daily directed her thoughts to the people who had the most at stake in Eddie's death. They also had some of the best alibis.

Doc hated what his son represented, but he would lose control of Temperel with Eddie dead. Safford, the moralist capo, a sycophant who seemed like he would jump off a cliff at Doc's command, wouldn't stand to gain if Doc didn't. Dr. Rena Ross had painted Eddie as the luau pig from hell, but she didn't want to share control of Temperel with a partner company any more than Doc did.

Peter Ealing didn't seem to have much affection for his brother; more than anything, his tears had seemed born of confusion. Even so, he wouldn't want another company meddling in his work, telling him what to do.

Someone from Florian? A buyout or stake in Temperel worth murder? Sure, people had been killed for far less, but who had access to

Eddie and the pool house after the party who hadn't been seen on the security cameras? Daily entered the guest list from the party into the spreadsheet so she could sort it myriad ways. Mapped alliances? Commonalities? Staring at the screen, she saw only boxes with names.

An old gift jar of candy-covered chocolates she'd never opened sat on the bookshelf next to her. She removed two-year-old shrink wrap blaring *HAVE A GREAT BIRTHDAY!* She opened the jar and nibbled on one. Stale. She poured a pile of the candies on the floor, correlating the colors to people on the party list. They all knew Eddie Ealing. Eddie Ealing knew them. One big pile of colors. They were at a fundraiser for Temperel. *No, the Temperel Foundation.*

Look at the guests.

Tom and Brad and Julia. Hollywood. Yellow candies. Three of them.

The owner of a newspaper group. Media. One red candy.

The senator from California. Politician. Green candy. The senator from New York. Politician. Green candy.

Dr. Rena Ross and Peter Ealing. Science. Blue candy. *Whose idea was it to make blue candy? Probably a scientist.*

David and Jeffrey and Steven. Hollywood. Three more yellows.

A man wiring the world with cable and now satellites. Media. Red candy.

A congressman from Santa Monica, another from the Valley. Two more greens.

By the time Daily had sorted the guest list this way, there were four piles that stood out in almost equal proportion:

Hollywood Names

Media Moguls

Politicians

Scientists/Science Underwriters

The four groups had some things in common. Power. Ego. Edge. Competition. And something more basic, Daily realized. They thrived on information. Legal or illegal, each of the four groups had to have the latest facts to get ahead, to stay ahead.

Daily bit down on a particularly stale politician. Information was key. Mike's Gifts had information on people. Mike used it to wreak psychological revenge, a mental checkmate that all these power mongers couldn't contest, no matter what their assets or connections. Truth was the truth, even if it was dirty and ugly. Was Temperel sourcing the information? Compiling it? Was Eddie in on it?

The missing woman, Alma, had worked at Temperel. There was no candy for Alma. Alma didn't fit into any of the four groups. Then again, she wasn't at Eddie's party—as far as Daily knew. The link between Eddie and Alma was still a mystery. Sex? Love? Nestor was right—it didn't seem likely, given Eddie's options. Then again, Alma sang. *Like an angel.* Ever the opportunist, Eddie might have heard the songbird and the sound of cash registers. She was pretty and she was Latin—a hot commodity in pop music. Past Pygmalions had certainly brought new icons to life under stranger circumstances. Whatever the link between Alma and Eddie, her photo had caused the jaded magnate to shed tears in front of Helmy Ulgrod.

Eddie's murder was a contradiction from start to finish. If they found GHB in Ealing's blood, he either ingested it on his own or he was dosed. Those who took GHB by choice were usually young and buzzed on immortality, too caught up in a scene to find out they were downing lye and floor stripper. Eddie moved in elite circles and he'd been through twelve-step programs. If he was troubled enough to fall off the wagon, he would do it in high style. He would snort Peruvian. He would down glasses of pricey single-malt Scotch, not drain cleaner out of a sports bottle.

Blunt force as the cause of death—typically an impulse killing. But what followed seemed staged, planned, as if someone had been contemplating a noisy revenge with decibels of rage. Chemical associations roamed through Daily's mind. Muriatic acid. For cleaning pools and tiles. GHB—made from solvent and lye. *Cleaning. Maid. Alma.*

What if Alma Morada had stumbled upon something while she was cleaning that implicated Eddie Ealing? What if she threatened him? What was her motive? It all screamed crosscurrents, multiple agendas.

She ran through dozens of Internet searches of Doc Ealing online, found quotes from his bestseller, *Safe Minds, Sound Lives.* Doc's mantra was, "Live forward." He derided those who wallowed in their pasts or blamed others for their hardships. Daily clicked on a video clip that featured a recent speech:

The only way to be productive is to wipe the slate clean each day and ask, "What can I do now, to better the world I live in, for the future?" We all know how to solve our problems—at this very moment. But we don't act. Instead, we prefer to loll on the comfy couch of introspection, the dense pillows of analysis, weeping about how much we've been wronged, then replaying it endless times to equally lazy friends and relatives or nodding heads who call themselves "doctors," who in fact make more money listening to us regurgitate the past.

Daily wondered how Paulette would feel about his denigration of her trade. Doc derided shrinks, yet he held a PhD in psychology himself. Hatred for his peers? Self-loathing? She found Doc's passage on the *"corruption of tomorrow's minds thanks to the entertainment industry."* No references to his own son, just a bashing of Eddie's trade:

A person can't avoid it today, even if they try. If the rappers don't tell you how to kill someone, the movies do. The news shows it to you with slaughterhouse detachment. Scenes and descriptions that were once considered too horrific to even discuss are now measured in terms of competition—which movie this summer had the most 'outrageous' gore, which

lyrics about killing cops 'just speak the truth of the streets.' And accom-
panying all of it, the raging soundtrack of two-bit criminals and four-
letter words justifying this wildfire hatred in the name of the past.

Doc had her there. More than ever, cops were targets. Protect and serve and wear a bull's-eye on your back. No wonder so many of the guys on the force, like Nestor, found that Doc's book resonated with them. It was better than replaying the mental slide shows of open case files that would stalk some haunted cops to the grave, if they didn't eat their gun first. Daily wondered if she would become one of them, wondered if Dr. Ross had the answer in her labs. Something that could wipe out the nightmares, let you keep only your sweet dreams.

Daily hit the print command for the excerpts from Doc's book. The churning of her printer aroused Pavlov. He surveyed the mess of paperwork between them, chuffed.

Something clashed in Daily's mind. Doc was on the board of Temperel—a research institute whose prime goal was to restore *memory*. But Doc's personal philosophy? Don't live in the past. A conflict? Maybe not. Doc and Temperel wanted people with Alzheimer's to be able to re-member their names, or where they lived. The faces of their children and grandchildren. Different kinds of memories. Doc was against emo-tional memories, the kind that squeezed hormones of anger and sorrow into minds.

She rearranged Eddie's videos and CDs chronologically. From various websites and databases online, she made lists of his storylines, themes, stars, crews, engineers, editors, locations, anything that could play into his murder. No commonalities she could see; Eddie churned through many people who worked on only one project. She pondered the names of the films, the groups, the titles of the albums that had snared Ealing's time: *Mercy Seasons, The Vertical Sins (Film Rights to Novel Purchased), Mimic's Poison (Film Rights to Novel Purchased),*

Lifeline, The Currency of Souls, Break the Chain, Sense of Life, Last Sister's Limit.

Music from artists like Jones Pandora, a pithy-prose rock group, Short Strike, a rapper from Philly, Safe Minds, an angry metal band whose members looked anything but safe. Their name—a jab at Doc's book title. Daily checked the date of the band's first record. Well after Doc's book. If Eddie had suggested the name to the group, it was a real finger to Daddy Ealing. Among all the CDs and movies, there was no link Daily could see. She had video of each film except for the two optioned movies which hadn't been finished, so she searched the Internet to see if either one had moved into development or production. Nothing. Just one announcement by Eddie in the *Hollywood Reporter* that he had purchased the rights to both novels, written by the same author, one Linus Janss. Big picture of Eddie's ash mane, his imperious jowls. Daily went to a book website and ran a search. Both titles were out of print, one written in 1949, the other in 1962. No details on the author. Daily filled out online forms that would allow booksellers across the web to help her find what she was looking for, then sent both forms into cyberspace. Back to the films that had been produced. The ones the public had seen, the killer included. All did well at the box office. The main characters: *A suspended student. An unemployed loner. A struggling musician. An NSA agent with a troubled conscience. A tender kid in a tough ghetto. A deaf but brilliant teenage girl.* Daily slid one of the tapes into her VCR, scanned through the key plot points, fast-forwarding through the action episodes. She scanned another, more quickly this time. Ealing had a penchant for underdogs, outsiders. It was the recurring theme in each of his six completed films.

She pulled the liner notes from the CDs of the music stars Ealing had handpicked for his label. More outsiders, all with lyrics about suffering, hypocrisy, and betrayal. Lean on fluff. Dense on standing up for one's self, no matter what the price. Daily questioned how much was authentic, how much was Eddie's marketing spin. Either way, his recipe for sound and vision had reached millions. Each of his works had everything to do with righting past wrongs, settling scores, overcoming fears. Never forgetting. Another point on which Eddie and Doc squarely disagreed. Doc Ealing told people to move on, *forget.* Eddie Ealing sold songs and stories about *remembering.*

Then there was this bizarre kuru thing. Paulette's unnamed patient said Eddie was pushing for a documentary. Daily ran a search on the strange disease and read the descriptions: *Fore Highlanders of Papua, New Guinea . . . strange, fatal disease . . . dementia . . . laughing death . . . spongiform encephalopathies . . . proteinaceous infectious particles . . . always fatal . . . irritable . . . traced to food and bone meal from infected animals . . . growth hormone from human pituitary glands before recombinant growth hormone became available . . . kuru shown to be transmissible by injecting extracts of diseased brains into the brains of healthy animals . . . unprecedented class of infectious agents, composed only of a modified mammalian protein . . .*

It gave Daily the creeps, but the brain reference did take her back to Temperel. She scoured the Internet for anything on Rena Ross. Linear life, carefully stepped successes. Nothing that didn't match the LAPD's notes. She did the same with Peter Ealing. In all the media, Dr. Ross did the talking for their team. She spoke of Peter's work from his student days at UC San Diego to the present in glowing, almost fawning, terms. In person, she had mothered Peter and coddled him. In the press, she was both his advocate and ardent disciple. His choices seemed to be hers. Temperel was their common dream, restoring memory their ultimate goal. Inside Temperel's walls were the memories of thousands. What if someone's secrets had been captured as a by-product? The power Mike's Gifts held over titans of money and influence was based on the fear evoked. If Mike's Gifts was part of Temperel, it would explain how Mike had the information. Dr. Rena Ross as Mike. Peter Ealing as Mike. Doc Ealing as Mike. Safford as Mike. The Florian Corporation as Mike.

But why send the virtual gift with the heart and Alma's photo to Eddie? To scare him? To threaten him? To force him to change his will? Daily scanned Taryn's list of web addresses for the Mike's Gifts sites, tried to imagine new links . . . to Temperel . . . to Alma . . . to Eddie Ealing. Tried to filter out all the waste and noise in the case. Tried to feel the distillation of it. The essence of it.

She looked at the list of "gifts" again, and the dates. The change in tone—that's what bothered her. The first gifts were vengeful, but also bitingly entertaining. The Christmas trees for the industry scrooge. The TelePrompTer with the changed copy. Then, suddenly, the gifts took on an edge they didn't have before. A champion of human rights who quietly invested in sweatshop clothing factories in Malaysia found his canceled checks to those factories copied and used as party-favor wrappings on the dais at a charity ball. Inside were pairs of designer panties, made at the sweatshops, which were sold stateside for a markup of four thousand percent. At his company Christmas party, the head of a prominent fertility institute and an advisor to the FDA opened a box of caviar on ice, along with a vial of human eggs he'd been reselling to an affluent black market. A Supreme Court justice received pair after pair of designer high heels. The photo of size thirteen lemon mules peeking out from his honor's robe on the eve of a landmark women's rights decision sent *The Hard Truth's* ratings soaring.

Mike had turned up the heat seven years ago. Why? She checked to see what happened to the more recent recipients. Many of them avoided incarceration, but their reputations were ruined. Some part of Daily admired Mike for his balls. He gave these jerks their comeuppance, the silent stones that balanced the scales. As Pierce had done earlier, Daily entered the word "murder" into a search engine. Then she typed "Mike" and "Gifts," adding plus signs in between for a Boolean search. No results showing Mike's tied to homicide. Taryn said most of the gift postings had only made it to the Internet in the last few days. It was as if Mike's Gifts didn't want the information out there until now that Eddie Ealing was dead. With less than an hour to go before she had to leave for the autopsy, Daily was getting sleepy. Perfect. Her mind and body working against each other. She shut her eyes.

The whirring of her hard drive opened them. Her hands were on her coffee mug, not her computer. Her email sounded a new message. She clicked it open. No sender. No title. A file in the email opened on its own, and an image of a light-blue notecard appeared. The notecard spun and settled center screen. Daily recognized the type font— often used for invitations:

MIKE'S GIFTS

She watched in awe as the notecard opened itself. Inside it said:

. . . DOESN'T DO DEATH.

TWENTY-ONE

THE IMAGE CHANGED BEFORE her eyes. Each word became a vague shape, then the note faded. An entirely blank screen stared back at her. She flipped through her notebook on computer crime. There it was. In a seminar, techs had told the detectives about email programmed to last only as long as the sender wanted. *Mike's Gifts doesn't do death.* Now the message was gone and only the cursor blinked on the screen. She clicked **REPLY**. The address showed nothing, but she was going to give it a shot anyway. She typed:

```
Then Mike has nothing to worry about.
```

She hit the send button. Minutes later, a signal. The message came back "undeliverable" with a string indicating an error. Couldn't fix the error if she couldn't see the guy's address in the first place. She printed the notice so she could show the department techs. Pulling the page out of the printer, she saw only the email header and her name. The rest of the page was blank. She looked at the screen. The error message was gone. In its place was a blank email form. A new message arrived. This time it was plain text:

WITH MIKE, NOTHING IS QUITE WHAT IT SEEMS.

Again, the letters morphed and dissipated as she read them. Daily's fingers flew:

```
The Book of Counted Sorrows? or . . . ?
```

Daily was primed this time, ready to print out the undeliverable notice the moment it came. Instead, her cursor moved on the screen without her touching it. It minimized her mail program, opened the computer's notepad function and typed:

WELL, WELL, WELL. WHO WANTS TO BE A MILLIONAIRE? A LITERATE DETECTIVE.

Daily had to keep the mystery messenger engaged. Relax. Think. Tease.

```
We're not all bumbling boobs.
```

She removed her hands from the keyboard. A new line seemed to type itself:

NOT TOUCHING THAT ONE. POLITICALLY INCORRECT.

A wise-ass. She went to hit the print command but a new sentence appeared:

DON'T EVEN THINK ABOUT PRINTING THIS.

Daily retracted her hands. It was as if he could see her, but that was impossible. Her curtains were closed. Her balcony and front doors were bolted and locked. Daily dialed the LAPD's computer tech line. Voice mail. She left her message, speaking softly because of the odd sensation that she could be heard. When she finished, all type on the screen was gone. Her laptop now displayed the last Internet page she'd been reading, before the first email had arrived. She waited, but no new messages came.

"How do I know Mike's Gifts doesn't do death?" Daily spoke to the empty living room. "Damn mind games. Prove it." She slammed her file folders shut, gathered up Eddie Ealing's CDs and videos, put them in bags to take to the briefing that would follow the autopsy. Just as she was about to turn off the laptop, an email arrived:

MIKE'S GIFTS ARE WHAT YOU LEAVE BEHIND.

TWENTY-TWO

Wednesday, July 6

BY SIX-FIFTEEN, DAILY HAD left messages for two computer techs downtown and Nestor. She showered and dressed quickly. A salt craving hit her; she ate three dill pickles standing at the open fridge. She found her key to Paulette's place, roused Pavlov from his dog dreams and walked him to her friend's condo. Paulette was gone.

Nestor reached Daily as her Crown Vic barreled up 190th, toward the 405. He was calling from the Hollywood station with Anjar Mahbubnagar, the police department's lead IT man, conferenced in. Daily told them about emails from Mike. Anjar asked if Daily had a small hole with an "eye" in the back of her laptop. She said she wasn't sure, and told him the model, said she was bringing it in.

"That model is wireless-enabled. It can interface within certain radii," said Anjar. "He hacked into your system, but he did it via a remote."

"But I specifically avoid using wireless for the Internet. For security."

Anjar recited three sentences of jargon as if she had a clue.

Daily stopped him. "Clarity."

"Your computer is wireless-equipped to interact with many *other* similarly-equipped devices, though you may not use it that way yet. Power switches, alarms, even your microwave."

"My laptop makes popcorn?"

"It can send signals to a wireless-enabled microwave to start a predetermined cooking program if you like."

Nestor sang, "It's a Great Big Beautiful Tomorrow . . ." Then he said, "The *old* Disneyland, Daily. Before your time."

She told Nestor she'd pick him up in thirty, told Anjar she'd discuss the rest later, when he could draw her one of his famous diagrams, show her the how.

But who was Mike?

Mike's Gifts doesn't do death. What if there were two Mikes? One a copycat? It would explain the contradictions, but she sure didn't need two of these jerks.

Daily focused her thoughts on Temperel, an institute that studied memory. *Memory recall*, Dr. Ross had corrected her. A lingering disconnect from last night bothered her. Something unfinished. Alma Morada's memory was nowhere to be found, Eddie Ealing's was history. What Daily wouldn't give to see the memories each of them had possessed.

———

When Eddie Ealing's body was received Tuesday, the coroner's staff had photographed it, washed it, and photographed it again. X-rays were completed after that, and the ME had started on the autopsy this morning—the fast track, if ever there was one. As Daily had once explained to the producer of a TV series, in California no one attends an autopsy without the consent of the coroner; technically the police don't have to be invited. The ME calls as a professional courtesy, and ninety-five percent of homicide detectives adjust their schedules to attend. The timing was not in the hands of the police—with over two thousand murders a year in Los Angeles, and two-hundred seventy-eight bodies in the crypt in a day, you went with the flow at the Mission Street facility.

Nestor climbed into Daily's car as it eased to a stop in front of their station.

"Six people have mentioned another Mike's Gift," he told her. "Said to expect one tonight. Big shindig for some broadcasting muckity-mucks. Loo wants us there." Nestor sipped from a steaming paper cup; a dangling tag read DigestiMint Tea.

Daily said, "If it's Mike—whoever that is—putting the rumor out, then we've got ourselves a high-altitude, no-fear psycho shit. And if it's not Mike—then somebody's fucking with Mike and us at the same time."

"*Geez*, Daily, having a foul-mouthed-truck-driver kind of morning?"

"No sleep. What do these six people have in common, other than this rumor?"

"Pierce is running cross-refs, said she'll have them by the briefing." Nestor opened her glove compartment, inventoried the detritus of snacks that spilled out. "For crying out loud, Daily. You're a damn goat." Nestor's glare poured into a smile as he reached behind her seat. "And I thought I'd been making progress with you." He rattled the plastic-wrapped eight-pack of kiddie-sized cereals. "What is this?"

"Traveling breakfast options."

"Intestinal pond scum."

"I like it."

"Junkies like heroin." He opened the top of the Korn Krispies and poured some of her coffee inside.

"What are you doing?"

"Going to show you what you digest."

"I don't want to see it, I want to eat it. You're going to pay for that, Nestor."

"You're going to thank me for it. We'll just let this settle awhile, kind of like it does in your system, for eighteen to twenty-four hours. Then we'll have a look. Guarantee you'll never eat this crap again."

"Do I tell you how to—"

"I want my partner running on all pistons. You got my back."

"What did you have for breakfast?"

"Half a papaya. Organic, with a squeeze of organic lime. One slice of low fat, high-fiber whole grain toast, all-fruit spread, no added sugar. Two ounces of hickory-smoked tofu and this exquisite cup of chamomile tea with ginger."

Daily shook her head. "Put your mess in a container for eighteen hours. It won't fare any better."

"That's where you're wrong. I dare you to compare messes."

Daily sped toward the freeway. "I'm full up on those right now, thanks."

————————

Daily watched as the medical examiner, Jerzy Zaginsky, stared into Eddie Ealing's open mouth with a light, then pulled back, a confused look in his Plexiglas-shielded eyes. His ruddy cheeks were a contrast to his surgical scrubs and the sterile environs. Daily offered thanks that the coroner's office had put Ealing on a rush and the ME cracked that it had nothing to do with her, no offense. The higher-ups on every front were starting to direct traffic on this one, hedging bets against the hindsight analysis of politicians, business interests, and media pundits.

Zaginsky was Daily's favorite ME. He'd come from West Orange, New Jersey to work at the LA County Coroner's Office in August of 1969 to help pay for his schooling as a premed student at USC. Four days after he'd arrived, the Manson family had raided Bel Air to butcher Sharon Tate and four others. The day after that, Leno and Rosemary La Bianca met similar mayhem at the hands of Manson's clan. For Zag, a student initially fascinated with the pathology of disease, it was a sobering and baffling immersion in the pathology of the human mind. His future as a coroner was sealed in a new need to understand, to dissect criminal behavior and its claimants.

"For all this drama, Slam was right," Zaginsky told the detectives. "What killed Eddie Ealing was plain old blunt force trauma to the head. Right parietal lobe. Here."

He pointed to a spot at the top and rear of his own head for reference, since Ealing's skull cap had been removed with a Stryker saw and the brain was no longer in its cranium. "Fix the time of death between one and two AM. Subdural hematoma. We'll get to that in a minute. Victim's fat was excised here, right of the navel. The cut was neat."

"Real neat," said Nestor.

"As in *experienced*. Deliberate. No hilt marks, like you see in stab wounds. Postmortem wound is consistent with a single-edged weapon, V-shaped margin. The point of entry is confident. But here, when the blade passed the last rib, we have an abrasion from the guard that has rust particles embedded in it. This was not a new knife." The coroner peered into Eddie's open abdomen and Daily noticed the whiteness of the chemical burn, like a dusting of confectioneras' sugar on either edge of the slice.

Zag said, "Everything's in place but the chunk of fat. As Slam mentioned, the perp irrigated the abdominal cavity with the muriatic acid. Literally washed him out. I know the whole Western Hemisphere's worked up over the *Sense of Life* angle, but you ever know of the Black Dahlia? 1947? Cut in half, no blood. Tortured, murdered. The killer scrubbed her body and washed her hair."

Daily turned to Nestor. "1947. Can't blame that on Metallica or Stephen King."

Nestor sneered.

Zag said, "The muriatic dousing was post mortem. But it looks like there were two different rinses with it. Bit of time apart. Maybe a half hour, hour."

Daily's head whipped up. "How can you tell?"

Zag fixed his gaze on a hand in a steel receptacle. Zag took the hand and tucked it under his arm. "This other donor wanted to give science a hand, now he is."

Daily laughed gamely. Nestor whispered, "You think *my* jokes suck?"

"I heard that," Zag said. "Daily plays me like the fickle, stringed instrument that I am, and I let her, Nestor. Your partner is a nuanced, complex piece of music. You, on the other hand, are everything I don't like about country music. Predictable, one-dimensional, and always pining about lost love, trucks, or horses." He scanned one cabinet, then another. "Muriatic, muriatic . . . here we go. Muriatic is 31.45 percent hydrochloric acid." Zag took the hand and moved it to a plastic, rectangular tray. He opened the bottle of acid, poured a small amount on the skin of the hand. Vapors rose as the acid hissed into the flesh. Trails of the liquid dripped down the sides.

"Have to remember this trick for Halloween," Nestor mumbled.

"Don't even joke. It's used around pools, but muriatic is nothing to toy with."

As the detectives watched, the thin, outer layer of flesh on the donor hand looked as if it was being peeled back by spidered trails of heat. The other areas remained intact. The contrasts gave the hand a strange, shadowed effect, like two shades of skin coloring.

"Does it keep burning through the layers like that?" Daily asked.

"It seeps in, oxidizes any blood it touches, which is the darkening you see occurring beneath the skin." Zag picked up the tray, motioned for them to join him back at Ealing's body and set the hand on the steel table next to the victim's head. He fingered the victim's temples. "See these shadows or faint stripes in the skin here, on either side of his head? These are the first set of trails from the acid. Like the ones on Mr. Hand. If you were to let that sit, and come back later, and use more acid elsewhere on Eddie's skin, such as here, around his nose and the mouth, you'd see this distinction between the two sets of trails."

"The abdominal acid was only poured once?" Daily asked.

"Looks that way, yes. It also looks like Ealing was rinsed with water after that."

"Why?"

"He was laying over flagstone, right? Muriatic is used to etch concrete, in addition to descaling pool tile. Your perp drips a little on Eddie's head to cover up his tracks on the eyes, it's conceivable he could have done it without gagging. Towel to his face, whatever. But once he started pouring the stuff in the belly, some of it hit the flagstone. And that creates all kinds of new fun."

"Chemically-treated flagstone. For pools."

"Nestor, there's hope for you yet. When it spilled from Ealing's abdominal wound to the ground, the muriatic made some interesting vapors. At that point, your killer had to get out or rinse out."

"He rinsed," Daily realized.

"He rinsed. But it also gave us a fix on each *distinct* acid usage. One was farther along."

Daily asked, "Did Ealing swallow any of the acid while he was alive?"

"No evidence consistent with that."

"Acid screw up all the blood evidence?"

"Enough left in the victim's veins to do what we need to do on him. But have we found anything viable that isn't Ealing's blood? No."

Zag indicated Ealing's nostrils. "It was potting soil. Indicia of plant food."

"The orchids," Daily thought out loud. "Or the plants walling the conservatory."

"Dirt was put up his nose after the douse with the muriatic."

"Same knife used on the eyes?"

"Correct."

"After the first acid wash or before?"

"Found acid in the orbits, your perp wanted to get at more than the rectus muscles and the optic nerve. The acid only traveled as far back into Ealing's head as it did *because* of the damage, the loss of integrity in the orbits."

"Integrity," Nestor chortled.

"No sexual assault, one molar broken," Zag continued. "Contusion on the cheek consistent with it. Ealing bit his tongue, but there's no attempt at excision. Blood's still in the lab, we'll have tox back for you later today or tomorrow. Based on sections of the liver not affected by the acid, I'd say Ealing was a real bon vivant. Weighed in at twenty-five hundred grams. Fatty."

"Used to be an alcoholic. Stopped drinking a few years ago," Daily explained.

"Few years too late. I got your message on adding GHB to the tox screen, got it on a rush. Why GHB?"

"Santa Barbara PD busted two guys who worked at Temperel. Ealing was on the board there. I'm not sure if there's a link between the perps and Ealing, but we won't have a chance to second-guess."

"We may not get a first guess. Half-life on GHB is short. It's also endogenous, so perhaps it's worth more to you than the DA right now." Zaginsky veered toward a steel container. "Now for the grand finale. Movies, muriatic acid, copycats, serial killers, GHB, none of it explains *this*. Look at Ealing's brain."

Daily and Nestor stared at the washed gray mass of a billion nerve cells. Nestor fixed on the dark, deadly hemorrhage. "Nasty knock."

"No, no, no. Look at this *atrophy*. Generalized cerebral atrophy is nonspecific with age, but he was only fifty. This could be *eighty*. There's specific and disproportionate atrophy of the medial temporal lobes." Zag turned it. " And see the hippocampus, here?"

Daily and Nestor traded a glance.

Zag sighed impatiently. "Was Eddie Ealing suffering from dementia?"

"A lot of people would say he was out of his mind," Nestor quipped.

"Clinically speaking. Was he suffering from a loss of any previously-acquired mental abilities? Was he forgetful, disorganized, depressed, volatile? Was he having trouble talking, walking, sleeping?"

"He was always volatile. Had more insomnia recently, according to his housekeepers," Daily said. "That's why he was swimming in the pool house."

Zag set the brain down. "Could be from several different conditions, this shrinkage. Celaya in Neuropath is going to scope everything."

Paulette's words raced through Daily's mind. *Kuru.* Ealing's obsession with the strange brain disorder found in cannibals half a world away. First, Daily wanted Zag's unbiased take. "Was Eddie's brain condition reversible? Curable?"

"We don't know what the condition *is* yet, and I don't want to speculate."

"We have to speculate, Zag. Too many suspects, too little time. And if Eddie Ealing was dying—however slowly—if someone knew it, that may make the difference between putting them in the box or not."

"The stand? Or your infamous Box of Truth?"

"Both. Either."

Zag wiped his forehead with the top of his arm. "Based on a very loose guess—and I mean a *wide* swing here—your man had early-onset Alzheimer's."

Daily's skin prickled. "His mother died of Alzheimer's."

"Could be something else. Whatever it is, it's atypical for his age."

Unprecedented class of infectious agents, composed only of a modified mammalian protein . . .

"Kuru," Daily said.

"What?" Zag and Nestor asked in unison.

"Kuru. Could it be Kuru?"

"*Kuru?*" Zaginsky reeled. "Was Ealing dining with New Guinea cannibals forty years ago? Kuru is history. Why the hell would you ask?"

"Ealing was working up a documentary on the disease. For TV. He was obsessed with it, apparently."

Zag worked his neck. "Thin line between obsession and dementia. Some people who are starting to lose their faculties have inappropriate outbursts, fixations. They grow paranoid: everyone is a bogey man, everything is a plot, a sinister disaster. Kuru. Might make for a creepy piece on TV, but—that's it."

"How long on the sections?" Nestor asked.

"Seven to ten days and don't you two give me those looks. We're moving as fast as we can, even with orders from bigger fish than you. You want to have the budget conversation again?"

Nestor walked back to Ealing's body. "Abrasions?"

"Antemortem, perimortem, *and* postmortem." Zag went to Ealing's side. "This one, on his right hand, for instance, occurred prior to death; coagulation in the grooves indicates the heart was still pumping. This one here, right ankle, weak blood pressure, close to time of death. Some abrasions related to the cuts around the abdomen and the eyes, no blood pressure."

Daily studied the yellow, translucent marks next to the cuts. "Scrapes on a dead man. Our killer mimics every aspect of the film but the tongue. Adds the acid. Why?"

"You're asking a man of science?"

"Maybe the perp just ran out of time. Got interrupted." Nestor said, shaking his head. "Whole lot of questions and suspects going on."

"Some of them hated Eddie Ealing for twenty years," Daily said. "Why was he murdered now?" She thought of the tinctures she'd seen at Temperel in the lab. She looked at her own notepad, Dr. Ross's words. *Any drugs we administer in the clinical trials are extremely safe . . . that's only used on animals here, never humans . . .* "Any injection marks?" she asked the ME.

"Not one."

"It doesn't sync," said Daily. "Certain aspects tie into Eddie's film. Some don't. Can you give me a best-guess chronology?"

Zaginsky's fingertips rattled triplets on the steel table. The ME played drums to jazz records in his spare hours, and Daily wondered what song was coursing through his mind now, helping the beats of a dying man fall into time. The ME's eyes stared at Ealing, but fixed somewhere else. "He's alive. There's a struggle, but it's not protracted. His right hand is abraded as he fights. His head is slammed against the iron bar of the chaise. As he's losing consciousness, his ankle grates against the chair frame, his leg and the rest of him goes limp." Zag paused. "His eyes are cut out. Muriatic acid wash number one. Eyes are inverted and put back in. I found remnants of the lacrimal in his nose and his mouth, which means the eyes and acid wash number one occurred *before* the dirt or the fat. The soil was packed up his nostrils, the fat was excised and placed inside his mouth. Those two are interchangeable on your timeline. Then, another wash with muriatic, more thorough. Inside the gut, inside the sliced stomach, so on. Last but not least, the guest list placed in his hand, since it was relatively dry."

Daily paced down the length of the steel table holding the body. "It's overkill."

"The whys are all yours, Detectives." Zag turned his back on them. The drumbeats of his fingers quickened, signaling his impatience with maybes. "We'll try and finish the tox screen by tomorrow or the day after." Zag walked to the other side of the body. "As a footnote, Ealing had plastic surgery, here and here—jowls and forehead. Can't hide the march of time from me. And he was going near deaf in the left."

The ME dropped a tiny hearing aid in a small steel container with a clank.

"Called his ENT at Cedars, saved you the trouble." Zaginsky flicked Ealing's ear. "Rock and roll just kills 'em."

Nestor grinned at Daily. "What'd I tell you?"

TWENTY-THREE

FIVE, FOUR, THREE, TWO, and . . . cue:

"I'm Chip Vance . . ."

"And I'm Sherry Fox . . ."

"And this is Morning News Ten. It's 8:42, and it looks like it's going to be another scorcher, Sherry."

Paulette Sohl sat at the third seat behind the news desk, off-camera for the moment, wondering how she'd let herself get talked into going on the air when she wasn't ready. Davis had used everything in his quiver, but what finally convinced Paulette was the part about his family and the kids—four markets in five years. The assistant news director couldn't afford to lose this gig. Now she cursed herself. She didn't have complete information, she wasn't prepared, and she'd worried herself through the night after seeing Lane so high-strung. Lane had tried to cover it up, but Paulette sensed something more than the case was knotting every part of her friend.

Camera on Chip. "In a News Ten special report later this hour, we'll show you why law enforcement is especially troubled by the latest crime wave among teens. But first, an update on the murder that has everyone from LA to Washington on edge: the bizarre killing of media mogul Eddie Ealing. Here with News Ten's exclusive insights into the mind of Ealing's killer is our team psychologist, Dr. Paulette Sohl."

Camera close on Paulette, who nodded. They cut to a three-shot—Sherry, Paulette, and Chip at the desk.

Chip addressed her first. "It's no secret that Eddie Ealing had his share of enemies. But what motivated his killer to stage this heinous scene, mimicking one of the very films Ealing himself produced?"

Paulette took a hard breath. "It's risky to try and project what's going on in the mind of someone you've never evaluated in person, Chip."

In the control booth, Davis Jacoby squirmed.

"I can say with certainty that it wasn't just about killing Eddie Ealing. There were simpler, cleaner ways to accomplish that—if it was the killer's only motive. Clearly, it wasn't. The perpetrator was leaving a message."

Paulette's stomach tightened. It just didn't feel like a psycho thing. She worried that the message might be the work of some homegrown alliance, a network of people fed up with Hollywood, but she'd be damned if she was going to broadcast that to several million televisions just yet.

Sherry said, "A lot of people think that this may be the first retaliation of many—for excessive violence in the media."

So much for not fanning the flames. "Consider other controversial issues," Paulette said. "There's strong opinions on both sides of the abortion debate, but the number of people who actually burn down abortion clinics or *kill* abortion doctors is minimal. Most people know that killing doesn't stop killing. And violence won't stop violence, even though a lot of people are upset about the level of it in the media and entertainment these days. If that turns out to be the motive for this killer, then he's an extremist. Someone with different boundaries from the rest of us." Paulette kept referring to a singular killer on purpose. And she wasn't going to say *no* boundaries. Not yet.

Chip sat forward. "Word here in Hollywood is that many upcoming films with violent themes and stories may be in limbo. If they're tabled, the killer may have made his point. Violence *has* stopped violence."

"We don't know the killer, so we don't yet have a firm read on *his* point. Maybe it was personal, just for Eddie Ealing. Maybe it's a bigger message. Trends in art and media are as cyclical as people. So what's scrapped today, no matter how onerous, will be another year's rage. No pun intended."

Sherry chortled. "Earlier, you said it's difficult to analyze someone you've never met in person. But you're a well-respected psychologist who has a number of clients—uh, patients—in entertainment and media. Many of them attended Ealing's party. So it's possible you *have* met someone behind Ealing's murder." Sherry didn't make it to the nation's number two market by lobbing softballs.

Paulette had to respond. "Anything's possible, but we should focus on the facts. Speculation will only cloud the issues and the investigation. That will help the killer's cause, not law enforcement's."

Chip clasped his hands. "The virtual 'delivery' from Mike's Gifts seems to indicate a taunting, even cerebral killer."

"But are the gift and his death connected beyond a doubt? No—"

"Now you sound like Johnnie Cochran."

"Eddie Ealing received lots of threats through the years. But this one grabs the limelight because of its proximity to his death. What if it had *nothing* to do with his killing?"

As the camera held Paulette in a tight shot, Davis approached Chip off-camera and handed him a piece of paper. Chip let Paulette's comments hang while the camera went tight on him. "This breaking news just in—there's been an electronic delivery to the management of this station." Chip paused. "I'm not at liberty to discuss the contents yet, but the sender was Mike's Gifts."

TWENTY-FOUR

TEE TURNED OFF THE TV and sat back, satisfied that the latest delivery to Channel Ten would set the necessary diversion in motion. That shrink Sohl wanted to peel away the mysteries, let her see if she liked what she'd find.

The feelings of accomplishment were fleeting, however. Hypervigilance, a head doctor had called it, typical after deep trauma—feelings of being watched, of lurking danger. Nothing made it go away, not therapy (what a crock), not medication, not all that biofeedback bullshit or behavior modification. No, the only thing that would fix the pain in this world, the damage, was erasing the past and its memories.

Our experiences may be unpleasant, but they teach us things, Tee.

"Then I've learned far too much, Harry. More than any human should have to."

Yes, oblivion would be sweet relief. But before then, Tee still had things to do. Because she wasn't cooperating as anticipated, because she didn't get the bigger picture, there was now a very special gift to deliver to Detective Lane Daily.

TWENTY-FIVE

THE BRIEFING ROOM AT the Hollywood station had filled to capacity. Daily watched a monitor with Taryn Pierce, Clem Burns, J. D. Nestor, Lt. Powell, and two of the computer techs from downtown. A host of officers and detectives stood behind them. On the screen, a videotape showed the back of Eddie Ealing's estate. The conservatory's steepled roof was a fuzzy triangle past gray knolls of grass. The date/time stamp read:

7/5   2:27 AM

Nestor pointed at a figure on the tape. "Here's Helmy Ulgrod heading back from the pool house—eleven minutes after we saw him go out there. He says he checked on Eddie, found him sleeping, covered him with a blanket. Ulgrod looks like the picture of bored servitude here, not like someone who's just gutted Ealing and dressed him like Grandma's turkey."

Pierce's pen beat double time on her desk. "He'd have to be the fastest killer in history to have done all that in eleven minutes, not one speck of mess."

Heads bobbed in agreement. The camera showed a quiet summer night.

"That's it for this view," said Anjar Mahbubnagar. Born in India, he'd attended Stanford before joining the LAPD in civilian duty. He had dark hair and onyx eyes that dissected whatever was before him. His teeth were perfect.

"ME estimates Ealing's head injury occurred up to an hour before the rest." Daily said. "Between one and two."

"The person we're looking for didn't enter the front of the pool house," Anjar explained. "The rear grounds camera—"

"Irised down and went to black," said the second tech. He extended his hand to Daily. "I'm Dave. Dave Bobb. I know it sounds like some Southern thing, but it's just my name. Two Bs, like Bibb lettuce. Bobb." He inserted a different video, used the remote to fastforward. "This is what the rear camera recorded from one-fifty-seven on. Black."

Daily said, "I thought date/time stamps couldn't be altered on these new things."

"Date and time are intact. The *iris* of the camera closed, so no images were coming in. There was a hiccup in the code—not visible with the naked eye on replay. Since most of that camera's point of view is dark at night, unless there's activity, you wouldn't notice anything. The feeds were linked to Eddie's computer screens in the house, anyway."

"The perp could've entered the back of the pool house unseen," Daily said.

"Exactly," said Dave. "He got into Ealing's network—his private one. The parameters were changed—something intercepted his system—the software protocol—"

"Clarity, please," Daily said for the second time today.

Dave Bobb searched for the words. "Something wireless *mimicked* the signals of Eddie's system and 'rode' it. His system followed that signal instead of its own brain."

Lt. Powell spoke. "I thought Ealing's system was state-of-the-art."

"It's also wireless," Anjar said. "People like Ealing have to have the latest thing and that's it. But they're not the most secure, in spite of the advanced technology, even encryption. Eddie's master control could do just about anything he wanted it to. Lights, audio/video, doors. It could signal his car to start and warm up. It was *his* system. But I think he cared more about the bells and whistles than the basics."

Daily nodded. "So if someone got inside Eddie's system's brain— carte blanche—how would they do it?"

"There would have to be a second brain somewhere, but these days, it could be as small as this." Anjar waved his tiny cell. "The audio recordings of Ealing's calls were probably played to drown things out during the murder. Haven't found anything of consequence on them so far. Eddie was a real prick, though."

Taryn Pierce mimicked Anjar's pronunciation. *Preek.* Daily glared.

Dave added, "Eddie's private software and system were installed by a company called 'Archipelago Technology.' Tracks to a shell corporation in the Gambier Islands, South Pacific. Our friends in Virginia are working up an ownership history."

"What came up on our check of Florian Corporation?" Daily asked Pierce.

"I'll get to it, don't worry."

"I'll worry about it—did you do it or not?"

Pierce tossed a look at Lieutenant Powell.

"Don't concern yourself with Florian, folks," Powell said a bit sheepishly. "Bureau's on top of Florian and everything there checks out clean. No need to bring it up or mention it to any of Eddie Ealing's Fourth of July guests, or at tonight's Loquitur Man of the Year function."

What the hell? Daily wondered if Powell had lost his mind or if an alien had simply taken over his body. Nestor was right. Someone bigger than the LAPD had Florian's back and now the lieutenant's balls. They were being dicked around, detoured on purpose. She wondered if Powell was in on it, or just being duped along with them. She couldn't tell; her instincts felt fuzzy, off.

You miss things. She willed the thought back.

Dave Bobb said, "At the party tonight, if someone comes within two miles with the kind of equipment that did this, we'll be prepared to intercept." He walked to a wipe-erase board in the room with programming code scrawled across it. "Here's the command trail that overrode the data stream on a dedicated frequency—"

"Excuse me," Daily interrupted and stood up. "Techs, surveillance—stay here with Dave and Anjar for this. Mere mortals, let's continue in the other room."

Lt. Powell addressed the nontech group. "We've had reports there may be another Mike's Gift 'delivery' at tonight's event. You'll be canvassing for perpetrators based on the best profiling information we have. Those of you assigned to the undercover detail will need to dress accordingly. See me if you don't have anything passable for the soirée, and if you don't know what soirée means, you don't have the right accoutrements."

"Who's the supposed recipient of the next gift?" a young officer asked. Powell said they weren't sure. Pierce added that she had cross-referenced those guests attending tonight's party with Eddie's on July Fourth. There was a list in every person's packet.

It was time for Daily to go over the coroner's protocol. She approached the front of the room and outlined the findings on the knife. One was missing from the maintenance cabinet in the conservatory,

SID had noted, plus Zag said the blade was held facing *out*, a technique used to dress a deer or cut meat. She assigned checks of meat packers, taxidermists, even labs and vets.

"The cut-out heart." Clem Burns said what was on everyone's mind.

Officer O'Rourke piped in, "Seems like an organized crime message. Ealing owned companies with content; the Russians and Chinese are working the digital piracy pipeline like crazy."

Nestor shook his head. "OC says those groups wouldn't have been so noisy about offing Ealing. Last thing those guys want. Publicity."

"The Berman hit was more their style," Lt. Powell added. "Quick and direct."

Daily paused as she thought about Mike contacting her online last night. The loo, Nestor, and the techs knew, but she wouldn't discuss it openly until she could find out if there was a media leak on the inside. She gave the floor to Pierce for the update from a well-known Quantico profiler.

"Okay," Pierce said loudly. "FBI shows several similars, no exacts. To date, none of *those* perps have ever attacked someone like Ealing, who was less commonly known to the public at large. None of them have ever used the victim's own work to stage a crime. Our perp has serious issues with morality and hedonism. One match could be Redgwick Tristone, released from Raiford after serving seven for murder two. Used a knife to kill a music video director who was having an affair with his wife—a 'model,' and I use the term loosely—in a fit of rage. In lock-up, Tristone compulsively washed his cell walls and his body from 'the filth of the endless brown sounds.' Another contestant is Darlyn Sutton, a female working in tandem with a partner, Horton Vargin. She had Horton kill her husband, her boss, then some guy who laughed at her at a package store. He does it because he needs direction, says our expert. A lot of men do." Pierce directed the last part at Burns who didn't blink. "But the FBI's first choice is Bingus Korr."

"The radical?" Nestor said.

"One and the same. Although Korr's crew hasn't used this particular MO before, the feds found a list of 'Human Scum' in the car of one of Korr's followers and Ealing's name was on the Top Ten . . . 'for his body of work' was the direct quote. Other people Korr's crew cited are Marilyn Manson, Larry Flynt, Dennis Rodman, that cosmetics heir who was a date rapist, Wes Craven, Lil' Kim and the guy who built Angel Stadium." Pierce noticed the looks in the room. "Korr says the Big A scoreboard is actually a monument to the devil's phallus." Pierce stumbled on the last word and Daily had to suppress a grin. Reddening, Pierce said the FBI had notified all the people on Korr's list so they could take precautions.

Daily expected Powell to say he'd follow up with the FBI, but instead he changed the subject. "What's the latest on Eddie's message?"

"Dead ends all around," Daily told the room. "No record with the Internet service provider and trails that lead nowhere inside Eddie's PC. Anjar said we're dealing with a serious pro. Someone who knows how to *alter* their footprints, not just cover them."

"What if the message didn't come via the Internet?"

"I asked Anjar that. He said there's a hack that invades your email, then mimics it, adding new messages from another source, like a disc. The problem is, we have no disc."

Nestor said, "There were deliveries for the June twenty-third dinner. Flowers, caviar, blinis—little buckwheat pancakes you put the caviar on. No one seen in Eddie's library, though. If there was a disc, there isn't now. Helmy's the only person who actually saw Eddie's virtual gift: the box that opened with the card, the heart, the photo."

The lieutenant grumbled. "Stay on it. What else do we have?"

Clem Burns' lungs rattled as he walked to the front of the room. He hadn't said much in the briefing. All eyes were wide as he tossed a folded, light blue card on the table in front of them. It read:

MIKE'S GIFTS

TWENTY-SIX

DAILY WAS FLOORED. "WHERE'D you *get* this?"

Burns reached in his pocket, pulled out two more cards just like it, tossed them down. He found four more in his trousers, another straggler in his wallet. Eight cards in total. Identical. He contemplated his mutilated toothpick. "Stationery catalogs." He cleared his throat, walked back to his desk and sat down.

It hit Daily. "Samples. From those big binders at office supply stores."

"Roger." Burns peeled cellophane from a new toothpick, started digging.

Daily thought about the simplicity of it. And if she knew Burns, he was already past that curve. "You know exactly where cards are missing, and if any stock was taken from the catalog company's main office."

Burns nodded. "But we got a souvenir problem now." He chipped at something in his gums. "Catalog company says people have started taking 'em like crazy from all the hype. As souvenirs."

Daily caught Pierce glowering at Burns. He must not have told his partner; but Burns didn't seem to care, he stared at the wipe-erase board where his even lettering filled the grid. Burns said the gift card leads were compromised, thanks to the news coverage and public reaction. With innocent people taking them on the wake of the publicity, finding the ones that may have actually been removed by a perp would be weeks of work. The loo assigned two people to follow up on Burns' findings.

Moving on, Nestor recapped Eddie's will, said it removed motive for some of the typical suspects. Then Daily recapped the alignment of the four types of guests that had attended Eddie's party, leaving out her insomniac process with stale candy.

"They all thrive on information." She walked to the wipe-erase board, with a larger sketch of her proven matrix for complicated input. She hoped the chaos in her head would make more sense once it could be dissected and organized for the group. "The names in the first column have been eliminated from direct physical suspicion. Under all names, motives as to why they might have benefited from someone *else* killing Ealing. Xs cross a number of them out, indicating these folks stood to lose more than they gained from Ealing's death. Eddie's ex-wife, Donia Ealing, falls in this section, as do the people who worked at Crescent Entertainment, Eddie's primary company. Third column contains names of those: 'FAMILIAR WITH RECORDED DISC.' Whoever killed Ealing, whoever went through the trouble to mimic *Sense of Life,* had to know that he recorded conversations. That he had at least one of those recordable CDs in the pool house."

"Could have brought it with them," Nestor postulated.

"Say they did. The perp still *knew* Eddie recorded people. Next column over—Helmy Ulgrod. Facts stated by Eddie Ealing's primary housekeeper, or his wife Berta, that have since been verified. The last guest left just after midnight. Cleanup was finished by one twenty in the morning. The last party worker to leave the estate was the catering manager who drove off the grounds at one forty. At that time, Helmy Ulgrod says Ealing was swimming." Daily grabbed a marker. "Anjar and Dave Bobb say the security camera in back irised down to black at one fifty-seven. That means our perp is in the vicinity, 'riding the signal' of the wireless system, whatever. He enters soon thereafter. He either bashes Eddie's head against the iron chair in spite of Eddie's size and strength, or Eddie was drugged ahead of time and wasn't able to respond."

Pierce's head shot up. "Who said anything about drugs?"

Daily explained the GHB bust at Temperel, the two ousted subjects. "Stay with me on the timeline for now," she said. "Helmy Ulgrod *only* went out to check on Eddie because there was *no* answer on the intercom. Had Eddie responded, Helmy would have stayed upstairs. He assumed the lack of response from Eddie meant the usual."

"Eddie had crashed," Nestor said.

"Right. And, when Helmy comes down to the conservatory he sees Eddie laying on the chaise, a blanket over him—he's seeing exactly what he anticipated he would. But Eddie *wasn't* asleep."

"He was already dead." Lt. Powell's eyes peered over steepled fingers.

"Precisely. But not cut up or maimed, not yet. That fits the coroner's timeline including the delay between death and the post-mortem wounds."

"You're saying the killer was *in* the pool house when Helmy Ulgrod—"

"Inside or he heard Helmy coming and stepped out back. Waited until Helmy was gone. The camera wasn't an issue anymore."

Taryn Pierce flicked her pen: *peck, peck, peck.* "If this perp knew Ealing so well, wouldn't he know that Helmy checked on Eddie if he didn't respond?"

"Say the perp did know. He couldn't predict what time Helmy might use the intercom to check in. If I'm the perp and the disc is part of my plan, I might use it to mimic Eddie's voice when Helmy does call down. Helmy said he didn't check when Eddie did answer; he went down if he *didn't*."

"So Helmy buzzed down before the perp got the disc cued?"

"That's what I'm thinking. Worried that Helmy's on his way, the perp makes it look like Ealing's asleep, covers him with the blanket. He hides. Helmy comes in, does the check, leaves. Now our perp's got time to stage the rest of the scene the way he wants. At some point in the night, about an hour later, Helmy wakes up. Thinks he hears Eddie on the phone down in the pool house. He looks out his window, sees the light on the bar turned on, and *hears Eddie's voice.*"

"The disc." Lt. Powell rubbed his chin.

"Right. But this time, the perp's ready. He uses one of the Eddie soundbytes on the intercom and gets Helmy to buzz off. That's why Helmy thought Ealing was still alive at three thirty, when he'd already been dead for some time."

Pierce gnawed on a nail. "I'm still not clear on the drug connection."

Nestor scanned his notes. "Helmy put six new bottles of blue PowerAde in the conservatory refrigerator at the end of the night for Eddie. Yesterday morning, five of them were found—warm—in one of the cupboards. One was missing."

"Five of the six were put in the cupboard," Daily added. "That means someone wanted Eddie to drink the cold one, the only one left."

"What if Ealing didn't drink any of them, what if some guest did?" Pierce said.

"Helmy confirmed one empty bottle of blue PowerAde and a glass of scotch were sitting on the counter when he went down to check on Eddie at two sixteen," Nestor said. "Helmy threw the PowerAde bottle in the trash. It wasn't there the next morning."

The room came alive with theories. Helmy was lying. Helmy was part of an alliance. Helmy knew the killer and was afraid for his own life.

Daily tapped on the wipe board to quiet everyone. "No matter what, Helmy's our atomic clock—his actions track to several verifiable time stamps." She moved on to Alma Morada, asked if Burns had found any people with that name.

"Ninety-four-year-old woman out of Zihuatanejo, Mexico," he said. "Never left a four-block area in her life, except once, to go to the hospital."

"Okay. Our twenty-something Alma Morada doesn't exist on standard radar, so keep showing the photo. We're running background checks on everyone at the research institute who had any contact with her. Some of them had heard of Mike's Gifts. Then again, everyone has by now." Daily moved to the next column. "The mysterious Mike. What do we know about this guy, except that he's been in a lot of stationery stores?"

Nestor said, "Maybe Mike is Dr. Ross. Lots of her subjects are creative types who've worked down here—what better way to get inside information? She'd have access to all kinds of dirt on moguls, celebrities, media execs, whatever."

Daily reminded them that Dr. Ross didn't want to lose Temperel. "Eddie's death put his will into effect. She was better off with him alive."

Lt. Powell said, "Maybe Eddie Ealing was Mike."

Daily had wondered the same thing. "But then why send yourself the delivery with Alma's photo and the heart? Helmy said Eddie was surprised and shocked by it."

"Maybe someone was on to him. The gift let Eddie know."

"It still doesn't explain the Alma connection." Daily stared at the Box of Truth on the wipe board. "Maybe Mike's Gifts had nothing to do with Eddie."

Silence. Then one nervous cough. The room looked at Daily as if she'd lost her mind.

"Okay, then. We need to find out what the killer did with his clothes. No one in the adjacent homes saw anything?"

Half a dozen heads shook no. Slow, like they were watching a tennis match.

"Latest on the Ealing family?" Daily asked Pierce.

"You know everything I know."

"Share your tree of knowledge with the rest of the room."

Pierce blinked. "Two servants at Doc's place and his security company confirm that Doc, Safford, and Peter Ealing returned to Calabasas before midnight. Doc went to bed. Safford had brandy in the library and read. Peter lives alone in Montecito, but his next-door neighbor confirms that she heard him pull into his garage at one forty AM. The roll-up door is noisy; it woke her up."

"How about Eddie's sister?" Nestor asked Pierce.

"Aubrey Ealing's been in New York for a couple of months straight. Missed the last few Temperel board meetings because of fibromyalgia."

"What's fibromyalgia?"

"You hurt all over for no apparent reason."

Lt. Powell snorted. "So that's what I've got."

"Aubrey's arriving in Santa Barbara for the emergency board meeting at Temperel this afternoon." Pierce spoke of the Ealings as if they were above reproach.

"Is Doc Ealing a medical doctor?" Daily asked Pierce.

"No, but he was integral to developmental studies at Wisconsin and UCSD. Served as an advisor to Rockefeller in Washington. He's also published a number of influential articles and of course, the book, *Safe Minds, Sound Lives.*" Pierce answered the unspoken question. "Eddie was the black sheep, but Aubrey said Doc never stopped believing that someday he'd reform his son. Save him."

An uneasy silence filled the room. As the police knew all too well, some souls didn't want to be saved.

Daily said, "Pierce, double- and triple-check the movements of Doc, Safford, and Peter from the party through Tuesday noon."

"Tuesday *noon*?"

"Phone calls, car mileage, all of it. If there's even one thing that doesn't jibe—"

"Jive."

"No, actually, it's jibe in this context. Look it up. If there's even one thing that doesn't jibe in their stories—"

"Why are we focusing so much on Doc?" Pierce crossed her arms.

"Eddie was a big problem for NOBLE."

"It's the antithesis of everything he stands for. NOBLE is the National Organization for Better Literature and Entertainment. He's trying to *improve* the world, not sink to Eddie's level. Having his son murdered isn't in his makeup."

"You have personal insights on Doc Ealing you want to share with us, Pierce?"

Pierce blanched. "I'm just saying that there are loose ends in town, and now more at Temperel. Doc, Safford, and Peter, in my book, are non-issues."

"They are absolutely *still* issues."

"But Tuesday noon—that doesn't make any sense—"

"You have your assignment."

If Pierce wanted to push now, she'd be risking insubordination in front of the whole room and the lieutenant. Daily waited. Pierce's color returned. A phone call cracked the tension. The lieutenant answered, listened, grunted, then turned to Daily.

"That was Quixote. He's got an ID on that single dark hair found in the pool house. Monkey. Rhesus monkey. The kind used in animal testing. In labs."

TWENTY-SEVEN

"Nestor and I are heading up to Temperel in a few minutes," Daily told Lt. Powell when they were alone.

"No, *you* are. Solo. I don't want the people at Temperel to shut down with Nestor around. He can intimidate people. Downplay the monkey hair. DA just called, told me it's thin legally, could have traveled down on Ealing himself, long before July. So you're tying up a loose end. Special Flights is taking someone up to Fresno, they'll drop you at SB, bring you back on return. Now, talk to me. Just you and me—and your gut."

Daily exhaled. "There are too many contradictions. I don't know."

"I can't work with 'I don't know.' Chief wants us to start disseminating *proactive* statements. Right now, we're playing catch-up with the news. Think this Mike is at Temperel?"

"I sure hope so."

Anxiety pulled at Lt. Powell's usually serene features. "Hope is for the people of the cloth, Daily. Bring me facts."

At her desk, Daily stuffed Alma Morada's Temperel file in her bag with a stack of AutoTrack reports on the VIPs from Eddie's party. *Real* birth dates, not the ones used in magazines. Lots of DBAs, AKAs and addresses that Daily could sell for a fortune if she didn't have a conscience.

Taryn Pierce finished a phone call, looked up at Daily. "You actually told John Safford you didn't owe him any explanations?"

Nestor caught Pierce's tone and his eyes begged Daily not to say what they were both thinking.

"That's out of context." Daily spoke as calmly as she could. "He was in my face, and he knew it. People like Safford can derail an investigation."

"This man's the Deputy Director of NOBLE, Doc's right hand man and you said you *didn't owe him any explanations?*"

Daily stood. "He was behaving like a major jerk. He shouldn't shadow my moves, and technically, *he's* not entitled to any information. Doc's entitled to some, but at our discretion. Don't forget one of the basic tenets of homicide here."

"The will itself clears Doc of motive," Pierce griped. "And Doc's not *any* relative. He advised Nixon on youth and violence. He was the head of a university known for—"

"You're real impressed by titles and power, aren't you, Pierce?"

"I'm impressed by accomplishments like Doc's, sure. He's a good man. He does good things." Pierce snorted. "I can't believe you don't see the bigger picture here. You lecture me on how I talk to people, you tell me not to push too hard on these fragile Hollywood egos, yet you're alienating people who—"

"Could further my career? I'm not in this for the props, and I certainly hope you aren't either. Distractions like that can take your head out of the case."

"You were adversarial—"

"You would know." Daily cursed herself for tangling. "Let's just do our jobs."

"Insinuating I'm not doing mine."

"You're not objective on Doc."

"Then why didn't you just say so in the briefing?"

"There's no point in being confrontational in front of everyone. We're a team."

"Then why did you single me out? Ride me?"

"I'm not riding anybody. I'm leading the investigation."

"No, you made it seem like I'm not covering my bases. Like I'm missing something. That's worse than just being straight, and I don't think the focus of the—"

Daily's cheeks grew hot. "You want straight? Think you can *deal* with straight?"

"All I ever ask for."

"Fine. Here's straight: I'm not interested in what you think the focus should be. And I haven't come close to riding you. If you want to know what that feels like, let me know. Because I want everyone on this case following through with the assignments I deliver. Not second-guessing them. How's your focus now?"

"Crystal clear." Pierce's jaw set. "I just think you could be handling things better."

Daily smiled in spite of the burn filling her cheeks. "Thanks for the feedback." As Pierce strode away, Daily turned to her partner. "God, Burns. Doesn't she *ever* get to you?"

Burns leaned back and considered the holes in the ceiling. "My partner's job is to make sure my fly is up and I'm facing the right direction. The rest I don't worry about."

Nestor came around to Daily's desk and sat on top of it. His mussed hair framed a face that was less sure than it used to be. Nearly getting killed would do that to you.

He said, "You were pretty picky on Pierce, D."

"This much information, we better all be picky, don't you think?"

"We're all tired; we're all pulling heinous shifts. When nerves are frayed—"

"They miss things. Things that are screaming right at them."

Nestor crossed his arms. "Something screaming at you?"

Daily started five retorts and finished none. She loved Nestor, yet she was about to unload on him, too.

He sensed it, changed the subject. "Any word from Zag on Ealing's brain?"

"Voicemail. He said, 'If Nestor calls me one more time before I say I'm ready, he's banned from setting foot in here for a year.'"

"He loves me, but he's conflicted."

Daily let a small smile escape. "You bring out the beast in us all."

They discussed their split for the rest of the day. While Daily was at Temperel, Nestor would hardline the remaining opens: one pop diva, two record execs, an ex-Dodger-turned-sportscaster, a director, a senator.

Nestor was deadpan. "Beautiful people. I live for their tang."

"Their *tang*?"

"Their essence. A balm of power and success bestowed only on the anointed."

"Guess it's not nearly as compelling if their success is just dumb luck." Daily looked at her watch. "Let's touch base around five, if something doesn't come up before."

She stuffed the last of her items in her knapsack. The soft image of Alma Morada's photo on one of the task force flyers caught her in the chest. She blinked back sharp pain behind her eyes, found her breath. The young woman's gaze carried a fragility that was more knowing than the girlish smile below.

"Beautiful—but breakable." Nestor said. "Certain people, there's just something in the eyes. It's like they know before they go—they're not in for the duration."

I know.

The words wouldn't pass the catch in her throat.

TWENTY-EIGHT

"WHAT WAS IN THE message from Mike's Gifts, Davis?"

The assistant news director turned to Paulette. "So now you need information, huh?" The newsroom was buzzing since the arrival of the email. "The detective that's here told us to keep it confidential, so they can check its veracity."

"Who's the detective?"

"Pierce. Karen or Taryn Pierce, why?" Davis rubbed his eyes. "Look, it wasn't ominous, it's just kind of sick."

"What am I, a Dick Tracy decoder ring?" Her irritation burned.

"That's all I can say." He started back toward the newsroom. "I appreciate your going on air to do the profile, Paulette. I really do."

"That wasn't a profile."

"Whatever. Helps our cred. And right now I need all the cred I can get." His normally brisk steps dragged. He stopped, looked at her. "If you're still up for doing more background on Eddie Ealing, try Cray Wrightman." Davis named the network news anchor from New York.

"Had a big falling out with Eddie Ealing a few years back. They were childhood friends."

"He have something to do with today's gift?"

"Not that I know of. Forget the email, Paulette, it's probably just a hoax. When Maddie Edwards gets in, I'm going to tell her to find out what Wrightman can tell us about Ealing's early years. If I can't get my news in real time, I'll go back in it."

"I'll call him."

"You're not my investigative reporter, remember?"

"Touché."

He looked at his watch, and Paulette got the impression he didn't care who got there first, Davis just wanted news that Channel Six didn't have—and soon. "Maddie gets the assignment in twenty minutes," he said. "Cray's private number is on my desk and I'm, uh, stepping out for a smoke . . . okay?"

TWENTY-NINE

THANKS TO THE WIND's hot and intermittent gusts, the LAPD's Special Flights Cessna made one loose excuse of a landing at the small Santa Barbara airport in Goleta. Queasy, Daily confirmed her pick-up time with the pilot and said goodbye to the two detectives escorting a prisoner to a murder trial in Fresno. On the tarmac, Daily swept the hair out of her eyes and searched for a place to get out of the wind, call a cab. Maybe she'd call SBPD and see if Litton was free.

A pole of a young man approached her, his frame all angles, his toothy smile pure Christmas morning. "Can I help you?"

Daily said she needed a taxi. He lifted a faded NYPD baseball cap, the kind from memorabilia stores. "Shucks, I'd be happy to give you a ride, ma'am. Uncle Alex doesn't have me giving a lesson for two more hours, so I'm just polishing the polish at this point."

Daily hesitated. He looked a little too happy. Speed-happy? Mad-happy? On closer inspection, she decided he was just goofy-happy.

"Seriously," he said. "I'd be honored. You were on the police flight from LA. You a lawyer? Forsenic expert?"

"Forensic," Daily corrected his pronunciation. "I'm a detective."

"A detective? No shit! Sorry, it's just—you don't look—no disrespect—" Bigger smile. One tooth almost sideways in its berth. "It's a deal then. My ride's right over here."

In the five minutes they'd bumped along in his Jeep, Yuri Tsu told Daily he had always wanted to work law enforcement, especially since a couple of his army buddies had gone that route after getting out. But his uncle Alexi needed help with his helicopter charter business and, since the man had been a surrogate father to Yuri, he owed him. "I'm still going to apply, though. Maybe the sheriff's department. Maybe SBPD."

"Good for you." Daily tried to picture Yuri arresting someone, couldn't see it. Then again, they'd said the same thing about her at the academy.

"Russian and Chinese," Yuri said. "You're staring at me, trying to figure out what I am. Russian on my mom's side, Chinese on my father's. He died in a crash. Uncle Alexi says the only way to get over something is to get back on the horse that threw you."

"What horse?"

"My fear of flying. That's why I didn't go into the air force, went army. When Dad died, I told Uncle Alexi my fear had been some kind of premonition about his death. He said that was bull—uh, nonsense. Just an excuse for staying stuck in one place. Made me fly. First few times I about shit my pants— sorry—but now I love it. Give lessons. You ever fly a chopper?"

"I'm not much for flying."

"Thought you looked a little green when you got off that plane. Your first lesson's on me, then. I'd be honored to instruct a detective with the LAPD. And maybe you can put in a good word for me up here, with the sheriff or SBPD."

"I have a lot to do before I learn to fly." Daily told Yuri Tsu where to turn. The naiveté in the young man's face was replaced by something much older as he pulled into Temperel's driveway. Daily thanked him for the lift, waited for a response.

"You should get right on top of that horse, detective."

"What horse?"

Again, the wicked grin with the reckless tooth. "The horse that threw you."

Daily told Dr. Ross about the monkey hair. The scientist paced in front of her three computers for more than a minute.

"Clearly you feel that narrows things down," she said.

Despite what Lt. Powell had suggested about downplaying it, Daily's gut told her not to diminish the hair's importance with this woman, nor discuss the many ways a defense attorney could dance off the incriminating follicle. Daily didn't buy any of them, and she didn't think Dr. Ross would, either. She wanted her on edge, making choices.

Dr. Ross tapped keys on one of her computers and a printer whirred into action.

"I'm printing a list of everyone who has access to the labs with rhesus monkeys. The database can do that, since those monkeys are only kept in certain labs."

"Subjects or staff?"

"Both. We have to keep an incident like this low-key. We already have enough trouble with the animal activists. Then Eddie's situation. We can't afford to have any more problems, like a possible suspect here. Not with the venture capital I'm rallying." Dr. Ross worried her French manicure with thin fingers. "It's not good that you went to the local sheriff and police yesterday. Alma Morada may have nothing to do with all this; plenty of our maintenance people just leave. You also stirred up the mess over the GHB arrests."

"I have to cover everything."

"Those boys were expeditiously ferreted out of Temperel. We made sure they were prosecuted. There's no tolerance for that here and digging it up now doesn't help."

Daily was tired of checking her tongue, tired of Dr. Ross' vacillations between helpfulness and defensiveness. "Digging's in my repertoire, Dr. Ross, and I'm sorry if it doesn't 'help matters' but if I have to excavate every inch of this place and interview every person here to find out who killed Eddie Ealing, I will. Frankly, I thought you cared about getting at the truth, too."

The doctor's face softened. "Please understand. My protectiveness is for the research. Everything's at such a delicate stage right now. I guard this place like my own child." Her eyes burned. "Some aspects are private matters unless we make them public. You really want other agencies getting involved in a case that's already so dense with people? We can help each other, detective. I'm on your side."

Daily weighed her need for Dr. Ross's cooperation. "Show me."

———————

"The emergency board meeting convenes in two hours," Dr. Ross told Daily as they walked the corridor. "You're welcome to speak with the members afterward."

"I'll do that. In the meantime, don't go into detail about why I've returned. Don't mention the hair or the GHB." Daily looked at the list Dr. Ross had given her. Eleven names. "As you show me these people, let me lead the conversation, even if I'm making small talk. Truthfully, I just want to watch and listen."

What Daily didn't mention is how closely she would be watching Dr. Ross herself. They entered LAB D first. On the opposite side of the room, five rhesus monkeys moved in cages. A sixth cage was empty. In the back of the lab, a row of computers processed data on preset sequences. Dr. Ross pointed to the four names on the list that corresponded to the people in this lab. Two men, two women. She recognized one, the senior subject and lab tech Daily had cornered yesterday. Karen wouldn't meet her eyes; she focused on the clipboard in her hands. Daily recalled the background notes pulled on her: *Karen Rae Lester. Born Fresno, California. Santa Barbara City College, then UCSB. Hadn't graduated. Aptitudes: art, literature. Counselors said Karen was a loner, bright when she chose to apply herself.*

Daily watched the body language between Karen and the doctor. Nothing. She small-talked Dr. Ross. "You said you verify the accuracy of memories by measuring a person's recollections against some baseline proof, like home movies, pictures, dates, so on. You called it calibration, I think."

"Right. We check variance from what someone thinks they recalled to what really happened during the course of those events. We dub those 'template memories.'"

"When your new subjects record a calibration recall, who else is present?"

"Each person records those in isolation. There's someone manning the board, but the tech's only privy to the subject's vitals. Another presence would affect the raw input."

Daily tried to get her mind around it. "How does someone record their recollections?"

"Oh, it's *very* high-tech. Tape recorders and videos." Dr. Ross smiled at Daily's fluster. "It's not a bad question, given all the propaganda about digital chips in brains and whatnot. But remember, Temperel's specialty is trying to reconcile what a person thinks happened against

205

what really happened. In the case of the template memories, we already have the data on what actually occurred: an actual phone message, a wedding video, a parent's tape of a game, security cameras from crime scenes, intersections, an office, a hotel. But our best measure of a person's perception, and the way they warp or filter memories, is still their retelling of it. Right now, anyway."

"Who has access to those records?"

"Each subject can play back their own. In calibration, a tech can view selected pieces. I can view all of it." Dr. Ross anticipated Daily's question. "I occasionally scan for calibration segments, but I couldn't possibly assimilate the entire catalog. Nor would I want to. We have hundreds of study subjects, thousands of discs."

"That's a lot of personal information."

Dr. Ross bristled. "I'm not interested in exploiting anyone's secrets, if that's what you're getting at. Just how memories and their recall synchronize. Or don't."

"Did Alma Morada ever record anything here?"

At the mention of Alma, tech Karen stole a full look at Daily then glanced away.

"No," Dr. Ross replied. "Some of the board members and venture capitalists have tried it, but never any of our maintenance people."

"Did Eddie?"

She snorted. "Eddie was opposed to anyone recording him."

"Then why be on the board of Temperel?"

"His mother's wishes. The only person he never said a bad word about." The doctor tore at a computer printout, then motioned for Daily to follow her into another lab, toward a worktable displaying two mazes with mice inside. Quietly, Dr. Ross said, "The four people who work in the previous lab also work in this one. There are our forgetful mice. A Northern California group developed the vaccine for the ones with Alzheimer's."

Daily had to chuckle. "How do you know if a mouse has Alzheimer's?"

"Transgenic mice. Bred especially to have the condition, which presents physically with a protein that accumulates in the nerve cells."

A white mouse looked up at Daily, sniffed the air, then scurried down a course that was blocked. The mouse reversed its path, looked both ways at a juncture, then proceeded back to the dead end it had just met. Dr. Ross led Daily through doors to a third lab. A peal pierced the room and Daily turned to see a chimp rattling its cage. Dr. Ross touched the chimp's fingers.

"This is Frieda. She sustained damage in part of her brain, yet she's fine now. We used to think that once a nerve cell died, that was it. Science now shows nerves can reorganize to operate and retain memory. We may someday retrieve memories at the molecular level."

"I speak jive," Steven Woydyno said as he entered the lab. Burg. Daily recalled his background notes: *From Pittsburgh. Navy after high school. First based in Norfolk, then San Diego. Moved to Los Angeles. Film studies at UCLA. Dropped out. Spotty work history up and down the coast.* In search of something . . . but what?

Burg's dancing blue eyes locked on Daily's to see if she'd caught his film reference. She had, but Dr. Ross hadn't or wouldn't acknowledge Burg's playfulness. Deadly serious about everything. Even so, Daily wondered why Rena Ross didn't seem to engender the same respect Peter Ealing did among these techs.

"Imagine the impact on crime," Dr. Ross continued, ignoring Burg. "A record of a victim's final impressions. A snapshot into the mind of an eyewitness."

Burg began to feed the chimp fruit. "Or Dr. Ross's private life."

"The animals in C should be attended to first, Burg."

That took the grin off his face. He dallied, shrugged, and sauntered out.

"Wood also works in this lab," Dr. Ross added. She seemed to have forgotten Daily's direction to let the detective lead the conversation; excitement accelerated her speech. "As I was about to say, we don't have explanations for all brain phenomena—yet. What we don't understand now will be explained by science soon enough. Did you realize, as recently as President Garfield's assassination, doctors would just reach into a body with unsterilized hands and feel around for a bullet, oblivious that they were spreading infection? It seems so basic now. That's how it will be with the brain sciences. Once the answers are clear, we'll wonder how we all could have been so blind to them."

Not unlike many homicides, Daily thought. The scientist prattled on with the passion of a zealot. Passionate enough to kill anyone who endangered the institute's future? Had only the family been told about the change in Eddie's will? If Dr. Ross had Eddie murdered, if she was found guilty, Doc and Peter might take control of Dr. Ross' forfeited stake in Temperel. That would give them more than enough to offset Eddie's percentage and it would keep their hands clean. It would be truly Machiavellian on the part of the Ealing family, but Daily wasn't putting anything past these people. She reminded herself that she was here to collect information on the rhesus monkeys. These disparate elements were related, yet how they came together, she couldn't yet see: Eddie . . . GHB . . . Alma Morada. The doctor motioned for her to follow.

Dr. Ross told Daily to keep quiet as they passed through a room marked RECALL LAB #7. Behind glass, several subjects sat in isolation booths, small electrodes on their pulse points and temples, wrap-goggles on their eyes. Above each booth, projected inside Plexiglas, an assortment of small images seemed to float in midair. Daily recognized them as fragments of holograms. Some grew more complete as her point of view shifted. Images appeared, then changed. People's mindscapes, pieces of daydreams.

Two kids squealed with glee on a merry-go-round. Puppies were born as a child swooned with wonder. Smiling people cheered as a bride and groom kissed. A father slapped a child. Lovers embraced, touched each other's faces. An attractive woman in a yellow sundress passed an open window. A parachutist leapt from a plane. The last image fluttered, then split and dissolved. Dr. Ross waved for Daily to follow her next door, to the recall lab's control booth.

"You lost calibration on seven," Dr. Ross said to the technician sitting at the console. Then to Daily, "It's all right, we can talk in here."

"Those holograms—those aren't actual memories—"

"No. Just computer-generated models based on their initial recollections versus later memories. That's where the templates come in. Someone remembers a woman wearing a yellow dress in a window; later, their recall shifts to orange because they saw a similar-looking woman on a TV commercial wearing orange. The original recording, such as a home video they haven't viewed in years, tells us how each subject is most likely to mutate their recollections under different conditions—relaxation, excitement, stress, anxiety, time constraints. But it's still all mathematics and projection. Probability. For now, the imaging models are the best we can do."

"Seems pretty good."

"At Stanford, Karl Pribram suggested that memory works very much like holograms. Laser beams overlap and form 3-D images. The whole is in each of the parts. There's a chance that entire memories are reconstructible from their fragments. By replaying the ones we're sure of, and by honing the subjects' recall through hypnosis and some mild chemical enhancement, we may be able to latch onto the rest of their memories and rebuild them accurately. Each subject in the recall lab is honing a particular segment right now, in 3-D, in their goggles."

Daily filed the chemical enhancement remark for later discussion. On the master screen in the control booth, the technician enlarged the image of the woman in the yellow dress. She undressed inside a window, turned, realized she was being watched, smiled.

Dr. Ross punched several buttons on the console and the word SEARCH flashed on the screen. Four small inset screens popped up below the image of the woman in the yellow dress. Images flashed faster than Daily's eyes could register them.

SEARCH RESULTS appeared.

Dr. Ross clicked on the first inset box. It enlarged to show another woman in a yellow dress. Ross split the screen and set both images in motion. Woman number one's mannerisms were eerily similar to the woman on the master screen. The two women both smiled and waved. In a booth, a male subject laughed and waved back, smiling in bliss behind the goggles. He shot the control booth a thumbs up.

Dr. Ross said to Daily, "You've heard the term 'on someone's radar?' That's more accurate than we know. Brains actually record information in a 'trajectory of sensation.' We've put all kinds of names on it—sixth sense, intuition, premonition. In fact, it's a combination of very real information. Subconscious signals send an internal alarm when data adds up, from sensing earthquakes to guessing someone's terminally ill. It's empirical in ways we're just beginning to see. It will change science forever." Dr. Ross smiled. "It will change laws and law enforcement. It will change you."

Daily's eyes widened at the visual echoes before her. "Impressive stuff." She imagined proof-solid memories of murder. "Trace evidence suddenly seems primitive."

The doctor nodded and led her through a door marked CONTROL BOOTH—RECALL LAB #8. The booths behind the glass were dark and empty.

"The man you saw working the console in there, Bryce Weller, works with rhesus monkeys on rotation. Also the subject who gave the thumbs-up on the synced images. That's Bench Torres. Eduardo's his given name. He can bench press more than the other guys in the gym. Nicknames. Male-bonding thing."

A muffled cry came from inside one of the dark booths in this studio. In the dim glow of a monitor screen, a woman in white wept.

Daily turned to Dr. Ross. "Private memories?"

Dr. Ross switched on the control booth monitors. "Good grief. *Days of Our Lives*." Incensed, Dr. Ross flicked on the lab lights and pressed the intercom. "Izzie?"

Inside one booth, a cleaning woman looked up, startled.

"Turn that TV monitor back to Channel 3. And get back to work."

THIRTY

PERCEIVED AS LITTLE MORE than ghosts by their employers, service people like Alma Morada and Izzie inevitably took in more information than their bosses realized. Invisible people carried some of the most damning testimony, if they could ever be persuaded to talk. Daily tried to pry Izzie open for ten minutes, but she had "seen nothing, knew nothing, heard nothing," no matter what Daily asked her.

Afterward, Dr. Ross took Daily into a wing marked NO ENTRY—TR-4 PASS ONLY. The smell of ammonia enveloped them as they walked into a hospital-style room with two beds and televisions. IVs on both patients, one an elderly man, the other a sixtyish woman. Dr. Ross spoke *sotto voce*. "The last three people on your list are working this ward today. They are on the LAB A rotation on other days. I'll get you a full schedule."

Daily felt uneasy. "I didn't realize you actually had any human patients here."

"We used to have our TR-4 trial patients stay at one of the local hospitals, but the system became too bureaucratic. It's easier this way.

In our lexicon, a TR-4 trial patient is someone traditional doctors have diagnosed with irreversible Alzheimer's or dementia. People who've been turned away from further medical care or their families because they became too much trouble."

The elderly man was asleep. The small woman turned her head, smiled sweetly. Waved with doll-sized fingers.

"*She's* trouble?"

"When her son brought her in, she'd just taken a bite out of his shoulder in the car," Dr. Ross whispered. "Said she was going to eat all the bad people following her."

They were interrupted by a pretty Latina with a waist-length ponytail. "Hello, Connie." Dr. Ross pointed at Connie's name on the list. Connie checked an IV bag marked TR-4-0107.

Daily mumbled, "I thought you weren't a fan of experiments on humans."

Dr. Ross bit her lip. "These people have no other options. Given the alternatives, they sign on. It's one thing to give test drugs to these people, who are terminal, who agree of their own accord, or their family's, as a last measure. It's another thing to put new substances to market prematurely just because there's demand." She led Daily next door to another hospital room. Two beds, just one patient, a man who would have topped six-four if he could stand. Stringy dishwater hair. His closed lids were sunken, as if no eyes lay beneath them.

"James is in a coma, overdosed on heroin. It didn't kill him, but he never woke up; he's been that way for years. There's no family and his medical aid is long gone. We took him." Dr. Ross went to his bedside, touched his hand. "They pronounced him brain-dead, but I believe we'll give James consciousness and his memories back. He was an angry-at-the-world Vietnam vet. Came back shortchanged and underappreciated. He started using over there, to ease the horror. Kept using when he came back, to forget."

"You sure he wants to wake up?"

"We hope to allow him to remember without the pain."

The sound of voices preceded the appearance of two more women in white.

Dr. Ross tapped on the list in Daily's hands. *Christy Goelt. Laurie Tawana.* Goelt was small and cheery, Tawana tall and serene. When they were alone in the hall, Dr. Ross looked at the clock. "That's ten of the people on the list. Wood is probably in the cafeteria grabbing a snack. You've now met every person who works near the rhesus monkeys."

Including you. Daily cast her net. "Except board members."

Dr. Ross sighed. "I'm more worried that board members may be targets, after what happened to Eddie. Certainly, none of us had reason to kill him, as I'm sure you now realize. In any case, I need to finish my paperwork for the meeting. I'll take you to the cafeteria to find Wood. From there, you're welcome to have your run of the place."

Cooperative again. Daily wondered if Ross was on medication herself.

The Temperel café was a bright room with food stations and hungry people on break. Across the café, Peter Ealing poured himself some hot water, added a tea bag. Daily found it odd that he would want hot tea on such a hot day. Daily asked Dr. Ross if rhesus monkeys were kept anywhere else on the grounds.

"Peter's lab, which is cooler than most," Dr. Ross said. "That's the last place with any rhesus monkeys—I'll let him take you there personally. It's a new development. He'll explain." Daily didn't push it. Dr. Ross led her toward a beverage station and said, "Any data you'd like to process here, you're welcome to our equipment, my people."

"Until the commissioner assigns your methods to the LAPD officially, I'm afraid that bucks procedure."

"I'm willing to help as much as I can. Unofficially. All of this upheaval. It's quite disturbing. It's threatening decades of hard work."

Threatening you? She called her bluff. "Unofficially, then, why don't you check all the digital recordings here at Temperel. Tell me if you find any mention of Mike's Gifts. Also any reference to Alma Morada, violent movies and music, military training, hunting, surveillance, or programming computers."

The scientist meted out words that seemed to have passed some filter in her high-powered brain. "That could take weeks to database—"

"And kuru." Daily dropped the word in late on purpose.

Dr. Ross was stunned. "*Kuru?* What does that have to do with Eddie?"

"Brain disease, right? You study it here?"

Dr. Ross pressed her eyes. Opened them with the patronizing sigh of someone too smart for the rest of the world. "We cull memory-recall findings from the peer review journals and institutions that map to our research; we log the findings. The correlations we don't catch, the computers do. Do we spend any time on kuru here? No. A few dozen cannibals used to have it in the sixties in New Guinea. We work on Alzheimer's."

"Just add it to the criteria if you would."

Her agitation flared. "Why?"

Daily had hit another nerve; impatience or fear, she couldn't yet tell. "You said you wanted to help."

Daily started toward Peter Ealing, but stopped to tap herself a soda refill. Burg and Wood passed her. Daily caught the way the female subjects looked at Burg. He didn't notice the lingering eyes on his sea-sanded complexion, tossed locks, and easy smile. By contrast, Wood's dark hedge of hair stood tall on top, shaved on the sides. The muscles in his jaw and temples snaked as he pursed his lips, wolf-whistled back at Dr. Ross, who frowned at him as she left.

"Don't worry." Wood sidled next to Daily at the soda taps. "Dr. Ross knows we can tell when she's dressing up for Peter-Peter-Memory-Meter. Visionary, but he can't see the stars in her eyes. All he cares about is the gray cells. They're perfect for each other. Asexual. You, however, are very highly sexed, but haven't been laid in months."

Daily's embarrassment flooded her cheeks.

"Now you're deciding whether to slap me or tell Dr. Ross."

Daily set her soda cup down. "Where are you coming from?"

"From you, detective. Just broadcasting what you're thinking. How do you like the tunes?" Grinning, Wood waltzed off toward the chips and fruit.

1-900-MIND-GAMES, Daily thought. Wood was a piece of work. Defense mechanisms, or something more? His mouth chewed on itself; she recalled his background notes: *Jerome Talmadge Martin, AKA "Wood." Born in Hollywood. Stuntman father. Mother was a nurse, LVN. Dad beat both of them silly. The abuse stopped when Dad drove his Camaro into a concrete retaining wall during a stunt. His friends mourned him. Mom and "Wood" were relieved. Wood had some minor scrapes with the law, but teachers said he was bright, just easily bored. Mom worked two jobs.*

"It's just his way of showing affection," Burg tried a light apology for Wood.

"Remind me not to fall in love."

"You find Eddie Ealing's killer yet?"

Daily said no.

"But you're here again."

"Everyone has a different assignment."

"But you're the one in charge, right? And you're here."

"Don't read into it. What does Dr. Ross do in her off hours?"

"Don't know. Don't want to."

Daily searched for malice in Burg's eyes, found none. "Intense woman," she said. "Seems like some of you don't respect her, though."

Burg thought about it. "She's okay. She just gets a little evangelical about the mission. She hovers over every aspect, and micromanages everyone. Sometimes we just want her to quit the doting and let us work."

"Sounds personal for her."

"Personal and business are the same for Dr. Ross." Burg's tone warmed. "In her defense, Temperel's competing with Harvard, Stanford, and the U of Chicago. The venture capital is out there if you're happening. Right now, she and Peter are the leaders in memory recollection, but the other researchers are gaining fast. She has to stay in the lead, for Temperel, and for the VCs."

"*She* has to stay in the lead, you said. What about Peter?" Across the café, Peter Ealing seemed to be talking to his steaming tea cup or to himself.

"Peter's in some other universe," Burg said. "Light years ahead of Ross in IQ. Brilliant, but in waves. She's the tenacious one. If it wasn't for Dr. Ross, Peter Ealing would still be on some beach drawing correlations in the sand. So, yeah, Dr. Ross is a nudge. She has a hard time not telling everyone how to do everything. But everyone knows, on the business side, she makes all the difference."

"Whatever happened to scientists just sharing information?"

Burg took a bite of the apple in his hand. "Money happened. And information became the most valuable commodity. Just like in some of Eddie Ealing's films." He smiled at a private thought she would have given anything to hear.

She said, "You never answered my question, yesterday. About Mike's Gifts. What do you know about it?"

"Good memory." Burg swallowed. "Wood said the guy's a Hollywood legend."

Wood rejoined them, five bags of corn chips and two Gatorade bottles in his arms. Daily ignored the chips taunting her salt cravings. Burg still hadn't answered. She watched the two men trade a look.

Daily shot her chin at Wood's sports drinks, similar to the ones Eddie Ealing liked. "You like that stuff?"

"Good for stamina. Playing ball after work," Wood said.

"You guys were here a few months back, when the GHB thing went down?

Wood scoffed. "Idiots. Deserved to get their Tiffany Johnsons yanked outta here."

"Rave boys with too much money," Burg explained. "Don't ask me about GHB. My worst vices are movies and cholesterol-laden meat products."

"C'mon. You must have hung out with them, played some hoop, had a beer."

Wood moved close; Daily could smell the late afternoon in his breath. "They were the beachfront mansion fucks, man. And it's not like we didn't extend the invitation. The Georgia Home Boys were just too precious. Didn't come to work, came to scam. Definitely didn't come here to hang out with my trash ass."

One bag of chips lost its place in Wood's arms and fell to the floor. Daily picked it up. Wood mellowed at her gesture. She retrieved two of her cards. "You guys want to tell me anything outside of Temperel, let me know. My cell number's written on there. Especially if you know of some way I can contact Mike."

Burg finished his apple, tossed it in the trash without looking and took Daily's card. "Got any hunches on who he is?"

"Could be Dr. Ross. Could be Karen. Could be one of you."

Wood chortled. "I was that smart, I wouldn't be working here, man."

THIRTY-ONE

Peter Ealing seemed pleased to see Daily in the bustling café. "There's news?"

"Not yet. But we've narrowed the leads." She explained the monkey-hair development. He listened intently, balancing his teacup and saucer as he led Daily down a corridor. "Did Wood and Burg answer your questions about Dr. Ross?" he asked.

Weird—Peter had been across the café. And by all appearances, unaware of anything around him. "What makes you think I was asking them about Dr. Ross?"

"I just assumed. You have to ask about all of us."

If Peter was probing to get information she wasn't biting. He led her outside. They walked down a path that snaked next to a creek. The vista behind Temperel was a salve to the senses: a wall of eucalyptus trees edged a meadow filled with picnic tables, barbecues. The brisk smell of the trees furrowed up her nose and into her lungs.

Peter asked if she thought perhaps Eddie had carried the rhesus hair home on a previous trip.

"I don't want to make any conclusions until I've seen everything. It's helpful that Dr. Ross showed me the other labs that hold the animals. She's also provided a list of anyone who has access to working around them. You have the last lab I need to see."

"Correct, but—well, I'll explain inside." The wind fluttered his hair, thick as Eddie's, but short and even. His voice grew hoarse. "Mother of God. I wish I could stop thinking about it." Peter's masculine manner was leavened by a gentleness. Everything about him seemed unplanned, understated, the antithesis of his brother. A low rumble grew pronounced as they walked. Past a rise, the creek forked into a strong current, which ran toward a ledge above a cliff. It was a waterfall. Peter said, "No one expects it. It's man-made; the builders have done a good job of making it look natural in its setting. The canyon was dry and bare before that." The sheet of water pounded on the rocks forty feet below. Lined by dark slate rocks, the canyon widened and disappeared behind a grove of trees.

Daily was amazed. "With water rationing, how'd the county let you build this?"

"It's a prototype for the water-quality improvement plan. It's a tourist town with ecological residents. So, improving the water is just as important as having water."

"How does a waterfall improve water quality?"

"Our cascade falls over filters built into the rocks. Large detritus is captured first and finer filters work down. The water that heads down into the ocean meets the new standards for purity. We recycle the reclaimed water for irrigation, the animal and plant matter as compost. A couple of other towns are actually building systems using this model, it's been so successful. No waste."

"Whose idea?"

He studied his shoes. "Mine, I suppose."

Daily smiled. The man seemed to warm to approval, to need it. They continued toward a narrow, curved structure that rimmed the canyon ledge.

"Where I do my best work." He slipped a pass card into a slot and two glass doors parted. Inside, acoustic walls muffled the low drone of water outside. "Too hard to think in the main complex, all those people and footsteps and noise."

"The sound of the water doesn't bother you?"

"On the contrary. That sound is wonderfully hypnotic." Peter checked several monitors and digital readouts, pressed a button. One of the windows opened.

A blast of warm air washed past Daily. Outside the lab, bouncing on a pine branch, a scrub jay sounded its call; Peter blinked at the bird, shook off a thought, focused back on Daily, his head movements as jerky as the jay's. She wondered if Peter was always this sensitive to sound, or if the stress of Eddie's murder had turned his senses on high. She saw something playing in his eyes. Nothing he was looking at. His hair spilled onto his forehead and he looked like he had forgotten why they were there.

"The monkeys?" she said.

"Right." He led Daily into a back room that was white with two Plexiglas boxes, each holding the prone form of a rhesus monkey, each of their bodies smattered with electrodes. Behind the sleeping animals, EKG machines ran. Respirators stood adjacent to oxygen tanks. Various drip IVs and other paraphernalia spidered toward the animals.

"These monkeys were moved over here a couple of hours ago. With everything going on, I don't want to chance something happening to them."

"Nothing here before that?"

"Just Frieda the chimp. Since February. These two rhesus are co-matose. Parts of their memories are gone, need to be reconstructed. We're hopeful with the smaller one."

"How did they get hurt?"

"They weren't hurt . . . the comas are induced, using a combination of chemicals." He noticed her distaste. "I know—you're thinking the animals might think differently. It's a common reaction when you see them like this, without any frame of reference."

Daily had never given medical testing much thought, but it was something else to see the creatures lying here now, intentionally robbed of consciousness. "What frame of reference makes it okay?"

"Your mother, lying in a hospital bed for five years, just staring at the ceiling. You're positive that she's there, underneath the silence. You're sure she still has thoughts and memories. She may even believe she's conversing with you. But you can't be sure, because she's in a coma. Or she's had a stroke. Things don't link like they used to. It doesn't mean her brain has stopped functioning. It means she's living in her own private hell. Wouldn't you give anything to bring her out of it? Would there even be a choice?"

Conflict tumbled through her. Daily forced herself to imagine how a normal person might feel about normal relatives who loved and watched out for each other. When Daily was in her private hell as a child, her mother and father had looked the other way. Betrayed her.

Focus.

Peter was right, of course, but it felt like a damning choice. How many experiments were necessary to save one human? How many deaths? She was confused and angry at the same time.

His tone pushed. "It's about choices. There are animal activists out there who've painted Temperel and other research facilities as these heartless, malevolent enterprises. You know how many of those same people would be first in line for a new drug for a loved one with cancer or Alzheimer's?"

In Daily's Box of Truth, a person's motivations were everything. "I didn't bring up the activists, Peter. You did."

He rubbed a temple. "Forgive me. We've been under siege the last couple years. The bleeding hearts have broken into our labs, trashed things. They've released animals that were in no shape to be let out in the world. They'll die in pain out there, that's what the activists don't understand. It's so easy for people to make the wrong judgments on pieces of information. On perception. They aren't interested in compromise, they just want to shut us down." Peter opened one of the Plexiglas boxes, lifted the lid and propped it up, checked the electrodes. "We're making small sacrifices to protect the most precious resource we all have—our minds. What good is a healthy, ageless body if your mind is missing? Detritus?" The same term he'd used for the remnants filtered from the water. Shy Peter, now impassioned. "Ironically, the activists will do anything to save the animals, but they're willing to kill and maim humans in the process. Even send in tainted food supplies for the doctors and staff to eat."

Daily's solar plexus tightened. Why hadn't anyone at Temperel mentioned this until now? She asked Peter when.

"Several times. The last incident was this spring. We've eliminated a number of fresh food suppliers, much to the chagrin of our techs and study subjects. They really liked the salads and sandwiches that came in pre-made. But those were the easiest to taint. Now we only make fresh items here, and we go with big suppliers, and double-, triple-check it all."

"Anyone die?"

"No, thankfully, but we had a couple of close calls. Food poisoning that would make anyone's system implode. I wondered if Eddie's murder had something to do with the activists, although that would imply that every board member is in danger."

Daily wanted to chastise him for the late information, but she told herself to go easy. He was still dazed from the murder and his mind worked in some odd way; she could blow it. She kept her voice even. "Why didn't you mention the problems with the animal people yesterday?"

"I suppose the monkey hair makes the matter more germane. Yesterday, we were still in a state of shock. I don't want to believe that anyone at Temperel could have had anything to do with Eddie's death. The ramifications—"

"Tell me about the GHB incident."

He rolled taut lips. "It involved two of the subjects here, students from the U. They were using one of the maintenance rooms to mix batches of GBL—gamma butyrolactone—and sodium hydroxide. Lye. The maintenance crew kept losing their rubber gloves, which is what tipped us off. GHB is basically degreasing solvent, or floor stripper, mixed with drain cleaner. God knows why anyone would want to put that in their body, but—"

"I'm familiar with it. Eddie ever use GHB recreationally?"

Peter's tone grew distant. "He moved with a fast crowd. In the seventies, he was a pothead. The me-me-me eighties, he was coked-out half the time. Swore off alcohol and drugs in the nineties, when rehab became the new compulsion. But he still worked around a lot of young people, and the kids are into GHB and ecstasy now. I thought Eddie was sober the last twelve, but who knows. Maybe he fooled us all."

"Think there's a common thread between the activists, the GHB, Mike's Gifts, and Eddie? Something that would also explain the disappearance of the maid, Alma?"

Peter watched one of the monkey's EKGs run. "Anger. It's the only commonality I can think of. The GHB kids are angry that they were kicked out of here and prosecuted. Mike, whoever he is, is clearly angry, like his messages. The activists are angry. Eddie . . . Eddie was always angry."

"Why?"

"I don't know."

"Anger doesn't cover the missing maid."

"I can't see the connection, either. Unless she was being used by one of the others. Maybe she got in the way of someone or something."

"Maybe she got in Eddie's way."

Peter closed the Plexiglas lid on the rhesus, checked the other one. "The situation with Eddie has—well, everything's off track now."

"And that makes *you* angry."

"Yes, I guess it does. Perhaps that's inappropriate. I'm sorry. Really sorry."

Too sorry, Daily thought. Sorry for being too smart? Sorry for being different? Sorry for being the brother who lived?

"If it makes you feel any better, it's not an uncommon reaction, especially after the initial shock wears off. You imagine what could have been different. You beat yourself up for not being there to stop it. You might even feel anger at Eddie for—letting it happen—for leaving this mess behind."

Peter studied Daily. Had she been too candid? Could he read her thoughts, the ones that still bled like torn scabs every time her mind touched them?

"Thanks for understanding," he said softly. They were silent as they watched the chests of the monkeys rise and fall with the respirators. Daily asked where the two rhesus had been before.

"LAB B. Essentially a quiet room with our comatose monkeys. A and B labs are connected and handled by the same crews."

Wood, Karen, Burg. "Who else has access to your lab here?"

"Dr. Ross, of course. A couple of the senior techs who help us run tests, but they can only come in when one of the doctors is present. The board members, although they would also come through escorted by Dr. Ross or myself."

"The maintenance people?"

"Ah—well, yes. When one of us is here, anyway. Hadn't thought of them."

People who didn't exist. "What's to the south of this wall?"

Leaving the room with the monkeys, Peter led Daily through the main lab into a homey office. "My thinking room. I brought in my oak desk, my piano, the couch. You may say I'm a dreamer, as Mr. Lennon sang, but I really do get some of my best ideas and solutions while I write in here, or tinker on the ivories."

His expression relaxed as he sat at the old piano, unleashed a couple of quick arpeggios. His left hand struck a minor seventh chord, his right hand played several high notes, a bittersweet melody. Peter stopped, played the notes again. The notes touched a sad place in Daily. He moved on to a bit of Chopin, then the Olympic theme song, then hit a couple bars of "Chopsticks." Daily had to chuckle at the hodgepodge medley. Peter dropped his hands from the keyboard; his eyes were bright.

"The brain is like a piano. Impressions are not in the notes themselves . . . they're in the combinations and sequences, the way things are played." Outside the window, the birds chattered on. "This jay's peal? G sharp, I believe." He hit the corresponding key on the piano. Peter Ealing had perfect pitch. "Those sparrows there—a high C and an E." Soon Peter was mimicking the bird calls outside with the piano keys. "The notes come together and each sequence's timing, rhythm, and frequency are unique. Memories are like that. Good memories, a nice, warm chord." His hands spread into a rich C major. "Bad memories. . . ." Peter played a jangle of pained notes. "Songs, smells, pictures—they don't evoke memories by accident. They're part of a sequence that's recorded in your senses, a symphony of impressions."

Were sense triggers what she needed to make *sense* of this case, to order the impressions? "*Sense of Life* focused on those five senses," she said.

"Yes. Eddie heard us discuss the links between memories and senses many times, since Temperel's inception. He even worked up our first business-to-business marketing campaign. He called that campaign *Temperel: Creating Sense of Life*. He was, first and foremost, a shameless promoter. It's no surprise that he would co-opt an idea he liked for one of his movies." Peter said the last word the way Daily imagined he'd say *residue*. "And of course, Eddie could relate to the music metaphor, breaking down memories to their 'notes.' Name a song."

Daily thought about it. "*Deacon Blues*. Steely Dan."

Peter's hands danced into action across the keys; he played a note-perfect verse. "Heard it on the radio a couple times. Was that about it?"

"Exactly." She laughed. "Far as I can remember, anyway."

"That's the point. Say I missed a note. A small omission, not obvious. Your memory fills in the missing note, because of your recollection of the original. You see?"

This enigmatic man was many things: brilliant, sensitive, inconsistent, childlike. It seemed illogical that he could have murdered his brother. And why, if it meant losing control of Temperel? Still, something hammered at the back of her brain. She looked at her watch. "I've made you late for your board meeting."

Peter jumped up. "I do lose track of time. You'll be here afterward?"

She said she was planning to speak with the board members. Peter grabbed a jacket from behind the door, armed his way into it.

She watched him shoot his cuffs and asked, "What do you know about kuru?"

He stiffened. "Pardon?"

"Kuru—you do any work on that here?"

He started three answers, stopped each one. Then, "We studied the effect it had on memory. Years ago, when we started Temperel."

"How'd you do that? Ship some cannibals in?"

He feigned a smile but it played nervous. "Anecdotal accounts, journals. Same things anyone can read. We worry about memory, and kuru's *certainly* not much help on that front. I'm really terribly late. May we continue after the board meeting?"

"Sure." For Daily, his reaction was worth more than the answer. As he strode away, he didn't trip on the path. His feet had stopped shuffling.

THIRTY-TWO

PAULETTE WAS GETTING NOWHERE with the phone number, even if it was Cray Wrightman's private line. Again, she told the newsman's personal assistant her name. With Zen-like calm, the PA told Paulette that Cray was not expecting her call.

"Of course he's not expecting it. I'm calling him."

"I don't have you in Mr. Wrightman's schedule."

"People can't call unless they schedule the call?"

A miffed pause. "Well, yes. Exactly. What's your inquiry?"

"I'm the psychology consultant for Channel Ten News in Los Angeles and I'm—"

"All of Mr. Wrightman's PR calls are handled by Geuze, Houck and Engel."

"This isn't a press call, it's about Eddie Ealing's murder."

Longer pause. Papers shuffling. "Mr. Wrightman has not been in communication with Mr. Ealing since 1989." A statement prepared by Geuze, Houck, or Engel, no doubt.

"Tell Mr. Wrightman I have some information that may have to do with the safety of others and his own well-being. It's in his best interest to call me back."

Appeal to the man's base needs. Survival. Once more, Paulette said she was a psychologist. She had to bang on her title to make it stick. The assistant asked Paulette which school. *Exasperated U*. She gave the woman the name of her grad school and dictated her phone numbers.

"Well, then, thanks for calling."

Paulette dialed her voice to sweet. "No. Thank you for helping me reach Mr. Wrightman."

"Oh, have we scheduled a call?"

"You said he would call me back."

"No, I said thanks for calling."

The line went dead.

THIRTY-THREE

PAULETTE PICKED UP THE phone to call Lane again, dropped the receiver on her foot, then banged her hand on the station's metal desk. *Shit.* If she could just calm down, get her bearings. Sure, she and Lane were friends, but there was still an implicit understanding that she was the sage, the shrink, the one with all the answers. How would Lane deal with a rattled Paulette? Lane answered her cell phone out of breath. Paulette asked about the low rumbling in the background.

"Waterfall in back of Temperel." Lane's words were short, tense. "You okay?"

"We got a Mike's Gift via email here at the station but the boss is keeping the content of the message quiet."

"I'll send one of my people over."

"Already here. Little blonde militant in a preppie blue blazer."

"Taryn Pierce." Daily spat the name.

"That's her. Said talking about the message would compromise the investigation." Paulette paused. "I had to know what it was, Lane. I *had* to. I had a bad feeling."

"Tell me you didn't do anything illegal."

"Not unless standing in the news director's office is against the law. His air vents are linked to the GM's vents. In there, you can hear half of everything the GM says. Probably why the damn news director's so freaked about his job, he knows what the boss really thinks of him. The message from Mike's was addressed to the breaking news mailbox, which goes to the assignment desk, which filters the viable pieces to a producer, then the news director. But the contents were meant to rattle me."

Lane sounded surprised. "How do you know?"

Closing her eyes to the newsroom bustle, Paulette remembered the voices in the vents: *Good God, what are those a picture of?*

Guinea pigs.

Dead guinea pigs.

But they're—

Deformed—geezus, they're each missing the back half of their body— they're just heads and—flesh tails—half animals—

Half stumps. Freaks of nature, man . . . get that picture off of there, it's making me sick . . . and get me the Scotch . . .

Paulette's equilibrium swayed. She tried to speak softly and slowly but her words pushed into each other: "When my parents first came to this country after the war, they had less than ten bucks. Then they had nothing. They were starving, living in a rat-infested apartment in New York City." Paulette felt like everyone in the newsroom was listening to her. She lowered her voice. "I would have done the same thing." Lane told her to go on, but Paulette couldn't possibly go into the whole thing here, not with so many people around. She covered the receiver. "The message came with a photograph of deformed guinea pigs."

"What does that have to do with you?"

There was a pop of static, a muted sound, then a click.

"Did you hear that?" Paulette asked.

"Hear what?"

"Those noises on the line. You didn't hear them?"

"Don't go all *Conversation* on me," Lane said. "I'm the suspicious one, you're sensible. Tell me what deformed guinea pigs have to do with you."

"They're screwed up from the same thing I am—"

"Paulette—explain the connection—"

More clicks. "You don't hear that?"

"Hear *what?*"

Paulette froze. She was sure someone was listening. Or she was losing her mind.

"Are you in danger? Is the message a physical threat?" Lane asked.

Paulette *knew* strange ears were listening. "No. Just memories. Mind games. Now I understand why they call it the Mind Box. Never mind, I'm fine."

"A moment ago you were wrecked, now you're fine. What the hell's going on?"

Paulette couldn't tell Lane about the trial experiments in which her immigrant parents had been involved, not with the possibility of someone eavesdropping. Neither would she say that she was heading to New York to corner Cray Wrightman personally, to get her own answers about this nefarious Mike, before he devastated her family.

Lane prodded, "Are you okay or not?"

"Absolutely fine. Really." Paulette tossed a lilt in her voice and realized how loopy she must be sounding by now. Paulette lied about heading to a psych conference in San Diego. She added that she was driving down with a couple of colleagues, sharing a suite. *Give whoever's listening the wrong city and a crowd.* Then she remembered the dog . . . her husband was out of town on a concert tour. "Hey, can you feed Pavlov for me? Take him out a couple times?"

Lane sounded completely mystified. "No problem, but call me when you get somewhere private. I need to hear the rest."

Paulette was now thinking the same paranoid thoughts as some of her more troubled patients. "Sure. As soon as I can."

"And be safe."

"Of course." She feigned a laugh. "I'm the sensible one."

THIRTY-FOUR

WHY WOULD A MESSAGE from Mike selectively target Paulette? Daily asked herself. Why not any of the shrinks or reporters at the other TV stations? And why wasn't it emailed to her directly? Maybe Paulette was mistaken. Maybe the content of the message had nothing to do with Paulette, she had just interpreted it that way. Then again, aberrant guinea pigs weren't exactly commonplace. Daily called the Hollywood police station. Taryn Pierce picked up Nestor's line.

"Tell me about the message with the dead guinea pigs at Channel Ten."

"How'd you know?"

"Never mind that. Tell me."

Pierce sighed. "Baby guinea pigs. Dead. None of them had hind legs or tails. Just heads, front legs with no bones, little abdomens that tapered off to stumps after that. Like they'd been born half-finished. Station management was half-freaked they got the message, half champing at the bit to go on the air and talk about it. Head guy was yammering about share and ratings and points and exclusives. I said it was a police exclusive until we told them otherwise."

"What's your take? Copycat? Station sent it themselves for publicity?"

"I think it's legit. I think Mike wants them to stop showing Eddie's murder scene over and over on TV. *Res ipsa loquitur.*"

"I don't speak Latin, Pierce."

"You should learn, considering you're half Italian. It means 'the thing speaks for itself.' Ergo, it's to Mike's benefit to have the news stop talking about it."

Ergo. Only Pierce would use such a word.

"All the newsrooms in town got a gift?"

"Well, no."

"Then it's to the sender's benefit to have *Channel Ten* stop talking about it. Not the 'news.' If it even came from the real Mike. The distinctions are important, Pierce."

"Uh-huh." Latin for fuck you.

"Is Nestor there? Put him on." As she waited, Daily watched the waterfall roll past the orchestrated rocks and filters, thought about turning a dry canyon into this wonder. All that work—making one nature look like a different one. Below, a dark pool of water ebbed at the rocks. Seagulls pecked at something between stones. Couldn't get at what they wanted, made noise about it.

"Helmy Ulgrod's been taken to Cedars," Nestor said as he picked up the phone. "Heart attack. He was halfway through telling me about the night of May twenty-second."

"He was on the phone with you when it happened?"

Nestor grumbled in the affirmative. "It wasn't drama to get out of answering. Paramedics say it's for real. Just like Berta's lawsuit will be. Helmy had gone back and checked Eddie's calendar for that day. There had been a board meeting at Temperel; Helmy says Eddie went. He remembered because Eddie was planning to go to a concert afterward and he told Helmy to pack a leather jacket to change into after the board meeting, blah, blah, blah. The show was at the Santa Donia Amphitheater. Liara—new Latin pop singer that's crossing over to mainstream."

Daily reeled at the news. "Latin *singer*. Dear God."

"They're not related. We showed Liara's people Alma's photo."

"No, but maybe Eddie was grooming Alma to be like Liara. Did Eddie go to the concert alone? He spend the night up here?"

"Helmy didn't know if he went with anyone. Said Eddie came back the same night, looking peaked. Two syllables, the way Helmy said it. Pea-ked." Nestor was trying to loosen his nerves with banter, Daily knew, but he was coiled tight. "He couldn't remember what time Eddie got back. That's when he started hyperventilating. Berta started wailing in the background, told me to get off the phone so she could call for help. I told her to calm down, stay on the line while I called paramedics."

"Ask the doctor at Cedars to run a tox screen." She told him about the new information she'd received on the food tainting at Temperel.

"You really think animal activists are behind this?"

"I can't tell. The people here say they want to help, then they don't follow through. When I interviewed Dr. Ross and Peter yesterday, there was no mention of any animal activists. And no mention of the GHB scandal here until we dug it up with SBPD. Not yesterday, but today. *After* we find the monkey hair."

"With venture capital pending, maybe they're worried about bad press. A few million could make any of us omit details. Especially if they don't think it relates."

"Sounds good, but I don't buy it."

Nestor cleared his throat. "The lieutenant's glaring at me. Gotta head to the hospital."

"Don't beat yourself up. You were just doing your job."

"Right. Brutalizing another innocent as a maniacal rogue cop."

"Stop it, Nestor. You're a class detective. Act like one."

"I ain't changed a thing that I've done in twenty years, woman. It's the way people see me that's changed."

Excited that they may have finally found a solid link between Eddie Ealing and Alma Morada, Daily called information to get the number for the Santa Donia Amphitheater. She spoke with a man who confirmed that Liara had indeed played there the night of May twenty-second. When she asked for the guest list, the man told her it was locked in the show file in the general manager's office. The GM was out for the day celebrating his birthday. Daily left her number, asked that he call her at his earliest convenience. She dialed Paulette, caught her on the cell in her car.

"I thought you were going to call me back when you left the station—"

"Not now." Paulette cut her off.

Daily had never heard her friend sound so sketchy, so unbalanced. "Not alone?"

"Not alone."

Paulette was fibbing. Why, she didn't know. Daily would have to get the guinea pig story later but she could try other questions. "Does Gerry or your brother ever do shows at the Santa Donia Bowl?"

"Sure. Lots of bands like it. Great vibe." Paulette's brother was the personal manager to a stable of rock and pop artists.

"Eddie Ealing was supposed to have attended a show there the night of May twenty-second, but the guy who runs the place is out and the files are locked in his office. I need to know if Eddie actually showed up or not. We're trying to track his whereabouts after the Temperel board meeting that day."

"Gerry's on Sydney time, so I'll try my brother first. He knows every major venue manager in the industry, and they return his calls in no time, so let me jump on it."

"Paulette, are you okay?"

"I'm *fine*."

Clearly, she wasn't. Daily had one more thing: she did her best to sing the sequence of notes Peter Ealing had first played on the piano. "You know the melody?"

"It's nice."

"What is it?"

Paulette mimicked the notes. "I can't place it. I'll ask my brother when I call him." She hummed it one more time. "Hmm. Haunting little melody, isn't it?

THIRTY-FIVE

THE ENTRY FOR LANE Daily's ninth birthday was one of Tee's favorites. He read it again:

Mom and Dad got me the new yellow radio I wanted. I played it loud all day until Mom made me stop. SHE got me a book, but I know Mom really got it not HER. Dad says: we are froogal now. I think he means we don't have money cuz he stays home a lot more. Anyway, that was enough presents.

So SHE comes in my room really late. I am reading my new book with the flashlight cuz it is way past bedtime. She says: I know I'm not supposed to get you any more presents but I bought you a bottle of your favorite ginger ale, from that store that has all the sodas from New York. It was in my favorite green glass and she even put in ice and a straw, like the store does.

She says: don't tell Mom and Dad and she sits on my bed.

I said it was a great present and I thought it was really cool, especially cuz she has been so weird for awhile. Like not talking to me when I ask her questions and stuff. Sometimes she acts mad at me and I don't know what I have done. I wish she would like me more. Sometimes she loves me so much I think she's going to smother me, and then other times, she acts like she wants to kill me. She was in a good mood when she brought me the soda.

She gives me the glass and I take this really big drink. It tasted funny. Hot and all salty. She stood up and laughed. She lifted up her nightie and grabbed herself down there. She wasn't wearing any panties.

She says: straight from downtown to you.

She was still laughing when I throw up all over my bed.

THIRTY-SIX

DAILY LEANED AGAINST THE rail of the outlook, clicked off her cell phone. She had never known Paulette Sohl to come unglued. Typically, she was the ballast for everybody else. And Nestor—watching his confidence as a cop crumble was like watching a great batter strike out for weeks on end. Daily herself was second-guessing her instincts, which had grown increasingly unsteady. It was perplexing and painful, and there was nothing to do but solve this case, this mess with too many people, too many crossed signals, too many suspects. The only constant seemed to be the dull ache in Daily's gut, one telling her she was being manipulated, contained from all sides.

A hot breeze swept into the ravine and the scent hit her again. Stale salt air. She looked down to where the birds were prying their beaks into the rocks below. Fresh water from the falls misted them. She sniffed again, closed her eyes. It was gone. As the sun beat down on her, she began to sweat, but she couldn't shake the feeling that her bones were chilled with indecision. Hot and cold. Pushing and pulling. Rushing and waiting. Waiting for word from the Bowl's man-in-charge. Unsure who at Temperel played straight. Most of them helpful in one pass, resistant in another.

She felt inept, like a child again. As if she had lost everything she'd ever learned about her instincts. Why? Why this case? She had nothing in common with Eddie Ealing. And why was she so obsessed with Alma Morada, a complete stranger? Daily knew better than to let it get personal. Yet she felt desperate to find out if someone had harmed this young woman, and what they had done with her. Why she had that look in her eyes. Nestor had said it right: *Beautiful—but breakable. It's like they know before they go—they're not in for the duration.* Daily was in for the damn duration, whatever it took, but she needed to cut free of the tethers. She felt like a marionette being tugged every which way, for an audience she couldn't see. Someone twisting her for fun. Paranoia hit—what if someone inside the LAPD was playing her?

If I go there, I'll unravel. She put the phone away, left her bag on the redwood table, climbed under the railing and stepped out onto the cliff's edge. Breathe deep for stress, Paulette always said. *Follow the strings. If I can just follow the strings, I can find the puppeteer.*

The wind picked up and she grabbed a rail. The notes of the piano tugged at her memory. Just a simple sequence, yet it had made her sad and uneasy. Below, a ledge cut into the cliff, a path big enough for one. Footprints were evident in the softer parts of the dirt. It couldn't be a trail per se, it was too dangerous—which begged the question of why it was there. *Detritus*, Peter had said when describing his waterfall system, capturing it in filters. Making good use of recycling everything. Something odd about the way he said it, as if he had improved on nature itself. Daily took a step down the path, bracing herself against the rock face. Small rocks rolled as her feet knocked past them; they tumbled down into the pool at the base of the waterfall. She watched them splash and sink.

A waterfall in a land short of water. Reclaimed water recycled. What happened to things that ended up in the water that weren't supposed to be there? *Detritus*. Where did that go? Out to sea? It didn't make sense, if the whole point was distillation, purification. Who picked up the crap, the waste, the stuff no one could recycle or would? Where did you dispose of the worst trash, microscopic or otherwise?

Alma Morada must have gazed at this waterfall a dozen times. Why did she disappear within a day of the May twenty-second board meeting? Daily considered asking for a tour of the waterfall's workings after today's board meeting, but that would mean asking for more help from people she couldn't trust. Her left foot slid in the dirt and she caught herself. Gravel and rocks plummeted to the water below, hit, then sank. Her temples throbbed.

The dark water.

The face. The eyes staring up at her again.

Open.

Dead.

Sweat broke out on Daily's forehead and neck. She slid against the rock wall and caught short breaths. When they slowed, she climbed back up to the outlook, dusted herself off. Paulette was losing her head because of a secret. Daily was losing her footing because of hers. In that moment, Daily realized just how powerful Mike's Gifts was. Mike's weapons were an endless supply of secrets, of leverage.

Whatever happened to scientists just sharing information?

Money happened.

Burg had been trying to tell Daily something, in the café, then Wood had joined them and Burg had closed up. If he knew something, why didn't he just tell her? Why the dance? Why the games? Just like the messages from Mike on her computer. Cryptic information that left no trace.

While Daily waited in the lobby outside the Temperel conference room for the board meeting to end, Nestor called.

"Our phone checks on the land lines were a wash," he told her. "But we just got the cell records. Doc Ealing called Eddie's Tuesday morning. Before any of us got to Eddie's. The question is whether Doc was calling to talk to Eddie—or to Helmy. An incoming call right before that came from a pay phone to Doc. Call me imaginative, but I'm thinking Kelly Spreck at Channel Six called Doc, delivered the exclusive. I'll keep you posted." He signed off.

Spreck or someone else. *Mike. Kelly Spreck. Mike. Making your own stories. Making news. Murder.* Daily picked up her cell to dial Channel Six, but down the hall, she caught two lab coats hovering. Watching her. Burg and Wood. Wood disappeared as Daily caught his stare. Burg's eyes locked on hers, his gaze saying something. His hand went to his throat, cut across it, slicing the air. Then he put the hand against his head.

What the hell? This was no time for charades. She started toward him, but the double doors to the conference room opened and the cross-talk of five animated people spilled into the hallway. Again, Burg made the motion, across the throat, then to his head, with his hand.

Dr. Ross was speaking with a tall, well-dressed man Daily didn't recognize, and another stranger, a woman with short silver hair in a severe suit. Trailing were Peter and Doc Ealing. Their chatter subsided when they saw her. Stiffening, Dr. Ross introduced Daily as the detective leading the investigation into Eddie's death. She explained that these were the only people who could attend today's emergency meeting on short notice.

Daily glanced down the hall. Burg was gone.

The silver-haired woman introduced herself as Laramie Fallier, the daughter of the well-known impressionist from France who'd died of Parkinson's seven years ago. Ms. Fallier said she was sorry she'd been so hard to reach, but she'd just arrived back in LA this morning.

Everything about her was warm and strong, from her handshake to her owlish gaze. She handed Daily her card, said she was available to help in any way. She seemed genuinely concerned about finding the killer and preserving Temperel's reputation as a top research institute. Daily bought the line from her, in a way she didn't from Dr. Ross.

The tall man was Gil Amanpour, the man who'd driven Dr. Ross to Eddie's Fourth of July party. Polite and well-mannered, he verified what he'd already told Nestor on the phone. Seemed a straight-shooter. He answered what he knew, didn't pretend to answer what he couldn't. As Daily spoke with Amanpour, she noticed Doc Ealing's eyes were riveted on her, even as he talked to Peter away from her.

Daily said, "I know it was short notice, Mr. Amanpour, but I would have expected more of the board to attend, given the circumstances."

He spoke evenly. "There's the 'board,' and then there's the *board*. A host of the names on the masthead are there for credibility and recognition. Then there's the pick-and-shovel crew. That's us. We do the trench work: budgets, contracts, fundraising, all the stuff that has to get done these days in the world of business and marketing."

Doc Ealing suddenly broke into their conversation: "What's our progress on this Mike fellow?" The interruption was rude, but no one said so.

"Mike may not be a fellow," Daily said.

"Male or female, no one is in custody yet, am I correct? And you're here."

"The hair of a rhesus monkey was found in Eddie's pool house."

"As Dr. Ross has just told us. So you assume Mike is someone at Temperel."

"No one said Mike is the murderer. We're exploring possibilities. How come no one mentioned the GHB situation to me yesterday? Or the problems you've had with the animal activists and the food poisoning?"

Doc's smile toward Amanpour was practiced. "Excuse us, Gil." He led Daily down the hall. His voice grew soft, paternal. "I understand you're quite an investigator, detective. Safford said you've got flying colors in the department in addition to our NOBLE commendations. You have quite a record for someone your age. Thirty, yes?"

"Thirty-three."

Doc faced her. "One thing you learn with time is that we all have our 'one.' The one we'll never grasp, no matter how hard we try. No matter how deep you dig."

Daily was silent. She didn't trust this sudden warmth.

"It may be fatigue, Daily, it may be this case. But perhaps you're concentrating on all these tangents, this maze of details, because you're not seeing things clearly."

"Homicide is hard, painstaking work, Dr. Ealing. Brick by brick, piece by piece. It's not the one-hour slam-and-wrap you see on TV."

Doc's paternal tone caught a sharp edge. "Please, dear, I've got friends in Washington with stripes older than you. I've offered my help, and theirs, several times. I'm asking you, in all earnestness, to work with some of the best people—"

"It's inappropriate, sir."

"It's inappropriate that my son was butchered and turned into a media spectacle. I can't see one good reason why you wouldn't want the additional manpower. And I can't see why I should wait any longer to find out what happened to Edward. I'm quite weary of all this dancing around protocol and turf."

"It's not about turf. And you still haven't answered my questions about the GHB and the animal activists."

"Because they have nothing to do with the cretin that killed my son, that's why. It seems wholly evident that this psychopath wanted Edward dead because of his work."

"Why did you call Helmy Ulgrod the morning of Eddie's murder from your cell?"

Doc blinked, didn't answer.

"Eddie was already dead. You spoke with Helmy. Or Berta. Where were you calling from?"

A pause. "My car."

"Safford driving?"

"Yes. We were going out to have some morning coffee."

Doc Ealing heading out for latté in a cardboard cup? No chance. The maid bringing coffee in china cups on a silver tray—*that* was Doc Ealing.

"You found out Eddie had been murdered, but not from the news. Who told you? Was it Kelly Spreck from Channel Six?"

He sighed. "She said they caught the police call-out. Knew the address."

"What did you say to Helmy? Or Berta?"

The color seeped from Doc's slack cheeks. "It was Berta. And what does anyone say about news like that? What happened? How? When?"

"You didn't ask who?"

"I was in shock, for God's sake."

"Why didn't you speak to Helmy?"

"He was incoherent. Berta's the rock of those two, if you can believe it."

Daily could. "You told Berta not to mention the delivery from Mike's Gifts, didn't you? That's the real reason Helmy was hysterical. Thought it was his fault he didn't take it seriously enough. He blamed himself for Eddie's death."

"I didn't even *know* about Mike's Gifts until they started broadcasting it on the news."

"Why didn't you tell me any of this yesterday?"

Doc's head tilted back. "These things don't matter. You're already short on progress, and now I'm wondering if you're short on vision. You're running on fumes, detective, and I had such high hopes with you. These insinuations. They'd be insulting if they didn't sound so much like hallucinations."

"I thought your daughter was flying in from New York for this meeting."

"She was. But Aubrey's in charge of a large fundraiser for the foundation in New York and the Secretary was unable to change his schedule."

"The secretary of the foundation?"

"The Secretary of State."

Daily bit her lip.

Doc said, "Eddie coerced all his New York celebrity friends to go to that, so I suppose he would want . . . the damn show to go on."

The show indeed, Daily thought. "Haven't seen John Safford today. Isn't he usually with you?"

"He's getting our car."

"I didn't see him come out of the conference room."

"He's not on the board, Daily, I am. He works in the administrative office during our meetings, and pray tell, what the hell does that have to do with anything?"

Doc's eyes scorched through Daily but she refused to flinch. "Did you try to have Eddie's will voided in any way, before the last change?"

His glare darkened. "You're over the line on all counts."

"I guess we'll see."

"Despite our differences, the last thing I wanted to see was Eddie murdered." Doc Ealing fought a tremor in his chest.

Ashamed of his emotion, Daily thought. Doc turned and walked down the hall. For the first time in two days, she believed him.

THIRTY-SEVEN

A Temperel landscaper dropped Daily back at the airport on his way home. She'd hoped to get some information about the waterfall's construction from him but he'd answered all her questions with non-committal grunts. The plane was late and Yuri Tsu's hangar was shut. Daily tucked herself behind a wall to break the wind and called Tim Litton at Santa Barbara PD.

He said, "Like old times, getting all these calls from you."

"I was much older then, Litton." She riffed on the save-the-world verve they'd had when they started in law enforcement. "Any word on those GHB boys?"

"Both claim absolute innocence. Say they were framed. Mind you, these aren't nice kids. Spoiled, but even their names and parents' bank accounts couldn't get them out of serving, as if they expected that. That was the funny thing. Their sense of entitlement, their gall. They weren't as concerned with their innocence as they were with their family connections, who was going to get payback for not taking care of them when they get out. You ask me, they need to serve the time just for their attitudes."

"Your gut?"

"I don't think they're smart enough, cool enough, or quiet enough to run an operation like the one you described for very long. Too lazy, too loose-lipped."

"What were they doing at Temperel, if they're so well-off?"

"They heard, and I quote, 'there was lots of great-looking snatch at Temperel.' Just a couple of horny twenty-somethings wanting action with sensitive young women. Easy prey for these scumbags."

"I have another question, Tim. Unofficially."

"You've come to your senses and you're finally asking me out."

"Clever, but no." Daily explained the man-made waterfall behind Temperel. "I want to know who worked on it, who built it, and I want to know what might happen to the stuff that no one wants anymore. The filtered waste."

"That's County Sheriff turf."

"I said unofficially. Every step I take, Dr. Ross seems to know about it. She knew I spoke with the sheriff and your office on the last go-rounds." Daily spotted the LAPD Cessna in the sky on approach.

Litton said, "What does this have to do with your case? And why don't you just ask them what happens to the waste yourself?"

"Deflection. Trust me. I want to have them think I'm working one angle while I'm really checking out something else. I need this favor—please. I'll owe you one."

"I intend to hold you to it."

Daily laughed. Litton's interest in her had never abated through the years; now she appreciated it. "I was hoping you would."

"You better mean it this time. Checking out the construction permits and plans will be easy enough. The physical part, on site, that's

251

the tough one. If it's private property, you got trespassing and all kinds of warrant issues . . ."

"You still hike, Litton?"

"As if you don't remember that time we got off the beaten path and—"

"So get lost again. Call up one of your Santa Barbara lovelies and take her hiking along the area that leads into the gorge there. Get lost. Go skinny dipping. You're a lieutenant. No one's going to file charges against you for an innocent mistake."

"Innocent my ass."

"See, I knew you could do it."

The sound of the Cessna's engines drowned out Litton's reply.

The muscular Santa Barbara coastline sunned half a mile beneath Daily. She wondered how differently things would have been if she'd married someone like Tim Litton instead of Rob. Litton was good-looking, funny, warm, and he'd never made a secret of his attraction to her. So why had she ended up with Rob Rennick? Location, sure. Rob was LA, Litton was Santa Barbara. Ninety miles away was pretty much the perimeter of geographically undesirable. Sex? Daily's physicality with Rob was as strong as it gets, but that wasn't what had kept her locked in the years with him. Personality-wise, Litton was together, on top of it. By comparison, Rob could be charming one day, stone cold the next. His mood shifts could earn ratings on the Weather Channel. Why marry volatility instead of calm? What was *her* motivation? In therapy, Paulette said she felt responsible for making Rob's moods right, for fixing things. It was an intoxicating and dangerous cycle, their marriage, their stop-and-start divorce. Even now, Daily missed the charming Rob, the nuzzling Rob, the incredible-in-bed Rob. During her marriage she convinced herself his volatility was just the trade-off, that everyone had their shortcomings. That was before she discovered another woman was getting all the good Robs.

That wasn't Daily's fault either, Paulette had told her. Affairs rarely are. Still, Daily felt guilty; a strong career was bittersweet if you lost the man you loved because you moved up the ladder more quickly than he did. The cell phone rang; she hoped it was the GM of the Santa Donia Amphitheater calling back.

"How's the insomnia?" Rob's voice. Resonant. Again, she was shocked that he had called at the moment she'd been thinking of him. She heard the blare of the West LA station on his end of the call. "Bitch of a case, Helena. But if anyone can get through it, you can. You always figure things out before the rest of us."

"That's why my life is such a blazing success. How's yours?"

"Big rise in coke with the dot-commers last few months—what's left of them, I should say. They're snorting to survive the extra hours, then snorting H to come down. Twenty-two-year-old just came down for good last night. Got that and ecstasy taking up three-quarters of our time right now."

Daily explained how they'd nailed a homocidal ecstasy mover right before the Ealing case broke; Rob said he'd been tracking it and offered his congratulations. The Cessna banked inland. Again, she realized how much she missed talking with Rob about casework. He still hadn't said why he'd called. "You rang to give me guidance, counselor?"

"Heard your boyfriend on the SBPD's working your GHB angle."

"He's not my boyfriend; who said he was?"

"You're not the only one with connections in the 805. Look, I've been dealing with a lot of GHB lately. Just thought I could help, if you're interested."

Daily said nothing; the Cessna's engine hummed.

Rob exhaled. "I miss you, Lena."

"You've got your woman. Heather, Muffy, Sissy, Skippy, Buffy—"

"Tessa. We're not seeing each other anymore."

Daily wasn't sorry, in fact, she was thrilled against all reason.

"We didn't have that much in common, actually, besides—"

"I don't need to hear the blow-by-blow."

"Sorry. I just miss talking. That was good between us. A lot of things were good."

Yes they were. Daily smoothed her pant legs, trying to push thoughts of his touch out of her mind. The call-waiting tone signaled. "Got to go. I'm expecting a call from—"

"No need to explain. Just wanted to hear your voice. I'm here if you want to talk."

"I appreciate it." She meant it. With all her soul, she wished it hadn't ended the way it had. Daily clicked to the new call; it was the GM of the amphitheater.

"We had a pretty extensive guest list for the first Liara show," he told Daily. "She did two concerts with us. Eddie Ealing was on the list for opening night, plus one guest. But he never came. I remember because I took his request myself; he said it was critical that his house seats be good acoustically. Said he was bringing someone who was breaking into the business and he wanted this girl to hear how Liara worked her voice live, dynamically."

Adrenaline flooded Daily. "Did he mention who she was?"

"Just some new Latina singer he was working with. No name."

Her pulse roared from her gut to her head. The link. Alma Morada. "You're positive he didn't show."

"Without a doubt. The show was sold out and I got an earful from Liara's manager. When someone like Eddie doesn't show and doesn't call, I'm strapped. Hesitant to release Eddie's tickets in case he shows up late. But when he doesn't bother to call and release the seats, it means we turned away someone important who could have used them. You don't forget that."

"You were angry at Ealing."

"Sure. But what was I going to do? Eddie was one guy I didn't want on my bad side. His anger got much better mileage than mine."

She thanked him and hung up. Eddie had been with Alma the night she disappeared. They hadn't made it to the Santa Barbara Bowl. Helmy said Eddie had returned home that night, looking "peaked." Terrified, wiped out by something . . . or exhausted and spent from murder.

THIRTY-EIGHT

PAULETTE LOOKED OUT THE window of the DC-10. The sun was weak behind the plane and darkening sky lay ahead. Below, spatters of pinpoint luminescence shimmered in the twilight. The flight was somewhere over the Heartland, where things always seemed less distorted than back on the left coast. She remembered the conversation she'd had with her Polish father after his heart attack in January. As a psychologist, she knew thoughts could provoke immense pleasure or damning misery, and so she asked what he had been thinking about when the pain had gripped him.

The Wild, Wild West, he said. Paulette asked if he meant the original TV show or the movie. He'd chuckled, then saddened as he explained what he really meant. He'd been watching the local news. It seemed to him that there was utter madness in every story, insanity glowing from every pixel of his screen, night after night. Sure, there had always been crime and strife, but he felt as if Southern California was on a lunatic bender it would never survive. Not for the first time, he wondered if it wouldn't have been better for the kids, Paulette and John, if they had remained in New York, where he and Paulette's mother had first set foot on American soil. Or Boston, where there was culture, like their homeland. History. Heritage. He had always been vocal about such things, after weathering the bombing of Warsaw in '39. America held out its promise to Paulette's parents and, after they could fight no more, after the camps and then the United Nations hospital, they vowed to start a family under the wings of the strongest nation on earth, hoping that they would never witness the rape of their own soil, flesh, and souls as Poland had. But after a couple of years in New York City, the West beckoned as the ripest of new American promises, and so they left New York, dropped a couple of consonant-thick syllables from their surname and headed to California. First to LA, then to Anaheim. In the shadow of the Matterhorn, Paulette loved to tell her girlfriends.

She had spent every birthday at the Magic Kingdom, and her childhood seemed like a fantasy until reality crashed the party. Paulette's fraternal twin brother, John, nearly died at thirteen, after a couple of local thugs beat him senseless for being a "stupid *Polack*." She would never forget the memory of her pale father in the hospital late that night. John was hemorrhaging internally, and the looks of the doctors and nurses blared louder than their empty assurances. John, his only son, might die, for no good reason. Her father didn't want to be touched in the waiting room, he just wanted to pace. Back and forth. Berating himself for not sending the kids to a better school, some place without cretins and animals, a school with culture and humanity. Then he began tearing himself apart for not going to a different doctor, a different hospital, shouldering all the blame. Paulette didn't know what she could do but hold her mother's hand.

Between fits of tears and grief, her mother muttered about losing one of her "miracle" babies. Endless prayers. The all-night vigil. John's pulling out of it. Paulette had never really understood what her mother's nicknames for the kids meant—*miracle babies*—until then, when her mother had explained.

She said God had given her John and Paulette as a miracle, after she'd been told she was barren. After taking new drugs as part of an off-the-books, cash-only drug trial in New York City had somehow damaged her ovaries. Penniless, Paulette's parents had made the choice—it was better than selling their bodies for sex, better than stealing. They were promised no danger, just a headache, a bit of nausea if they got the real pills and not the placebo. Nobody told them it would wither your insides years down the line. Maybe no one knew until her mother's doctor explained that a strange egg deterioration was the reason they weren't having children.

Until my miracle babies—God saved one good egg in me, and made it into two perfect children, my Paulette. You see what faith can do? We wanted to come to America and start over, have two wonderful children who will have more wonderful children. This will be our legacy—our new family. The reason for all the pain we endured. The reason for everything . . . family. Our new generations. Our bloodline.

Between the war, the loss of their own families to the Nazis, between the cruelty of idiots and senseless disease, Paulette's parents had endured enough tragedy for ten lifetimes. They'd devoted themselves to a good life for their children and their future family.

Now some ghost named Mike was impaling people on their pasts with a quiver full of damaging information. Why had he picked her? She had nothing to do with Eddie Ealing. She'd had one brief conversation with Jordan about Eddie's proposed documentary, one Jordan didn't even want to do. She'd discussed the case with Lane, but hell, you couldn't get more confidential than a shrink and a cop.

Unless Mike was listening.

Paulette's blood iced. If Mike had somehow followed her or listened in on those conversations, it meant that she'd hit on something and Mike had heard it, too. If it was an exchange with Lane, then Lane was being monitored as well.

Call me, as soon as you get somewhere private. I need to hear the rest.

Paulette would have to find a creative way of communicating with Lane that couldn't be tapped or traced. She stared at the plane's air phone, chilled with indecision.

Nope. Not unless you're sure.

Even if Paulette went to a pay phone when she landed, Mike could have every one of Lane's lines tapped. She turned off the air vent above her, pulled up her blanket as the pilot announced they were about to experience some turbulence ahead. Someone was trying to control her through her past, frighten her, make her run away. Not only did they know her memories, they thought they knew what her response would be. Well, she'd be damned if she was that predictable. No one was going to mess with her family now, give her cause to back off, or give her father the second heart attack that would kill him.

Not Eddie Ealing, not his murderer, and certainly not some phantom named Mike.

THIRTY-NINE

DAILY'S NOSTRILS FLARED AT the tang of citrus as she drove up to La Sera Groves in her unmarked. Never mind that she was wearing the only designer sheath she owned, a cerulean Trina Turk she'd purchased at a secondhand store. She was still at the wheel of a Crown Victoria and she still felt like a cop. Six people from Eddie's Fourth of July guest list had heard the rumor of another Mike's Gifts delivery tonight, but the hearsay couldn't be traced to anything meaningful. Nonetheless, Daily's team couldn't afford to miss possibilities, not with the brass, the city, and the media watching.

La Sera Groves Estate was the newest old place to throw a party on the Coast. The Loquitur Man of the Year fête honored the person who had the most positive impact on the media business in the last year. Tonight's honoree was Harmon Whittsedge, the man who owned the second-largest string of radio and TV stations in America.

The valet looked down his nose at Daily's car until she badged him. He directed her to a spot distinctly apart from the Bentleys, Jaguars, and Ferraris in the main queue. She approached the estate's entryway with as much casual confidence as she could muster but tripped on the last step.

Fatigue was already taunting her, and she wasn't even inside. Daily found Nestor near a table of young lovelies charged with guest list duty. High above them, the ceiling was painted with twilight renditions of the old citrus groves that gave the Santa Monica mountain estate its name. Around them, orange blossoms and sprigs heavy with kumquats and lemongrass filled lead crystal vases on the marble staircase. An inordinate number of the women wore white to set off their tans. The dense scents of perfume, body oils, and flowers flooded Daily's head.

"This place looks amazing," she said to Nestor.

"That's not all." He lost himself eyeing Daily head to toe until she asked him to show her the grounds. Nestor didn't look so bad himself, she thought as she followed him toward open doors. The ache for a man's touch teased her, but she chased it off. Pretty bad if she was thinking of her own damn partner that way.

He said, "The techs were here earlier; they briefed us on the most likely points of entry for a perp. Point one—these glass doors that lead out to the garden. It's an intersection of traffic between kitchen, one buffet area, a catering hall, and the garden service entrance."

Nestor led Daily out into the warm orange night, where the full force of orchards engorged her senses. Buzzing with efficiency, caterers cast finishing touches on the food and the flower sprays of yellow, orange, and white. Daily spotted crates of imported white truffles and foie gras. They walked past a winding lagoon that spilled into a dark blue swimming pool, one Daily had seen in the pages of *Los Angeles Magazine*. The photographs didn't impart the sweet moisture in the air, smells that took her back to Orange County, where the kids played hide-and-seek among citrus trees that were far more imperfect than those in this grove.

A sensory pain gored her shoulder; memories of her sister jamming her into the gnarled thorns of an old lemon tree, holding her against the barbs until blood came. Mad laughter morphing to practiced concern as their mother approached, asking what happened. *Nonsense, your sister loves you. Don't make up mean lies, it's ugly.*

Here, high in the breezes of Malibu Canyon, the trees were trimmed of low-hanging thorns and the skins of the fruit were remarkably unblemished, their color glazed and fired by a western sun that never knew when to leave the party. Midway through the groves, three chefs prepared meats on sizzling drum grills. Daily inhaled the marinade, a heady infusion of cumin and ginger.

Nestor's chest filled. "That tantalizing smell whetting your buds is—"

"Jerk fish," Daily finished. "I do cook, Nestor. When I'm not busy."

He looked at her as if she was some other woman, not his partner. His eyes roamed to the tangerine sky. "Think this case is going to become an Elmer?"

Nestor dubbed homicides that weren't solved for decades "Elmers," after Elmer McCurdy, the legendary mummy found in a Long Beach amusement park in 1976, when Universal was shooting an episode of *The Six Million Dollar Man*. After extensive investigation, the mummy, discovered as a glo-painted funhouse dummy, was traced to a crime museum in downtown Los Angeles that had purchased the cadaver of the Midwest outlaw in the twenties for display.

"Not on my watch," she said with a bitter laugh. "God, Nestor . . . is it worth it?"

"If you're talking like that, we're ruining the good ones way too early."

"I've seen things no one should see in a lifetime."

Nestor listened as twilight crickets warmed their wings. "Too many criminals, not enough time. When we do catch 'em, they get off for Twinkies, technicalities, oversights of overworked people. The perps rub it in our faces, 'cause they know they can work the system the way we can't. Not if we play by the rules."

A silo of a security man in a suit passed them, the bulge of his sidearm too obvious. Security by insecurity.

"Peregrine," Nestor dropped his voice. "They should have used ProStance."

"You were going to show me the weak spots. Seems like this entire orchard is a perp's wet dream."

"Not exactly. Security central for the entire estate is right up there— northeast corner, third floor. They have a view of the entire perimeter, the orchards and beyond from end to end."

Daily turned to see the parapet of the main estate, several suited men bustling in its open windows. One had binoculars. Another manned a high-powered telescope. Automated video cameras moved at strategic corners of the building. Daily counted ten of them, and those were just the ones she could see.

"Peregrine has Jeeps cruising the surrounding roads every ten, and they've doubled up manpower on every post with the estate's security team. Anjar even had them put in wireless intercepts to capture any messages that might try to be beamed in from outside the property."

"Fully set. So what are we doing here?"

Nestor smiled. "The chef promised me a piece of jerk fish, before the rich and famous get their taste buds on any."

———

Gingerly, Nestor ate his sea bass. Daily nabbed a bite and told him the latest on Alma Morada, how Eddie Ealing had planned to take a "young Latina singer" to the Santa Donia Amphitheater on May twenty-second and never showed.

"Affirms your Pygmalion theory," Nestor said.

Daily said she had called several recording studios in Los Angeles, Ventura, and Santa Barbara to see if Ealing had brought Alma in for any sessions in the last several months. Then she told Nestor about the strange comments made by Wood and Burg in the Temperel cafeteria and Burg's motions in the hallway outside the executive conference room.

"Throat to ear, what the hell is that supposed to mean?"

"Call me. Stop talking. Stop using my cell phone. Slice my throat. Listen. I don't know. I've left four messages at his apartment. Told him to call me ASAP. Nothing." Daily held her hair back from a warm gust. "Not sure if he knows anything, but it seemed like he was trying to help me."

Darkness flickered in Nestor's eyes. "Let's see how hard we're getting hit up front."

In the foyer, guests arrived in a steady stream—everything from broadcasting executives in Armani to celebrities in khakis and T-shirts. This many acres, this many people, Daily still thought they were weak on a lot of fronts and said so. "Some of these Peregrine boys might be minimum-wagers in a best man's rental."

Nestor chortled. "These guys make more than you and me combined." He launched into a speech about how they guarded Steven and Kate and Goldie and Barbra and James and it paid a hell of lot better to guard the powerful and the beautiful than it did to protect the common and the ugly. In the crowd, Daily caught snippets of conversation that echoed what she'd heard on talk radio during her drive to the party. Lots of chatter about the controversial guest of honor, Harmon Whittsedge.

"... his biggest service is his debt service ..."

"... Loquitur's not a popularity contest, it's about affecting change."

"... affected change all right, the idiot laid off my whole staff with no warning ..."

264

". . . why do they always give the biggest awards to the biggest assholes?"

". . . he's okay in business. Just a sloth personally . . ."

A handsome man approached. "Detective Nestor!" He beamed at Daily. "Your wife?"

"No, my partner. Detective II Lane Daily. Meet Barrett James. Owner of La Sera Groves and host of tonight's awards presentation."

Daily felt herself respond to Barrett James' hazel gaze, though it was hard to feel entirely sexy with a 9-millimeter service Beretta in your handbag and a .22 strapped to your ankle. James grabbed two golden martini glasses from a passing tray, handed one to Daily.

"Cicadas. Made with our own fresh citrus juice." James urged them to try one.

"Can't drink on the job," Daily said.

"A sip, then. Just a taste."

Daily humored him. "Delicious. I assumed the people throwing tonight's awards rented the place from you, Mr. James. You're hosting as well?"

"Oh, yes. I'm on the board of directors, and The Loquitur Award seems to have become *the* industry event of the year. More important than anything. No work of art or editorial can thrive without endorsement from at least one media powerhouse anymore. That's why so many companies are snapping up broadcasters. They've all realized content won't matter unless people are exposed to it. The airwaves and wires have become the tastemakers, not just the pipelines."

"Eddie Ealing realized it," Daily said. "He was buying stations."

Barrett James colored at the mention of Eddie's name. He nodded in the direction of a wide man with a narrow head and silver hair. "Tonight's recipient, Harmon Whittsedge, with the FCC approval of the WindWave merger, he's now owner of—"

"Three hundred thirty-six radio stations," Daily interrupted. "Twenty-eight television stations in major markets, though he'd like more of them to be network affiliates, a string of juice bar outlets, plus a chain of convenience stores that he was going to dump until he realized how many teens hang around them. Now he's decided to keep them and load them with video games to attract even more of that hard-to-reach demographic."

Barrett James stared at Daily. His jaw hadn't dropped, but his mouth was ajar.

Nestor smiled. "She was a business major, before she got a conscience."

"I listen to news radio," Daily said. "Not one of Harmon Whittsedge's stations."

"You don't approve of his programming or the way he does business?"

"I don't mind anyone's business until it starts to infringe on mine."

James' tan paled. "Homicide?"

"My personal business. Whittsedge is gobbling properties in order to broadcast what he thinks is the right message. That rhetoric reads well, but it plays wrong. Like the rest of us 'poor uneducated folk' are too stupid to have any common sense of our own. With deregulation, he doesn't have to buy advertising, he can just buy stations whole, for his 'correct' message."

Barrett James' chin cut the air, searching for the right position. "I must say I'm shocked. Many of my colleagues in intelligence and in law enforcement support Whittsedge's efforts. There's a proven correlation between certain entertainment and crime."

Nestor gave Daily the eye. *Cork it.*

Instead Daily said, "I know all about it. And you're wrong. There's a much greater correlation between crime and bad parenting, or no parenting. But no one monitors parents until it's too late. Until Nestor and I get to deal with the aftermath."

"Well for God's sake, don't take it personally. Harmon Whittsedge and some of us are just trying to clean up the airwaves a bit—"

"I don't have anything against clean, Mr. James. I just don't like people who've never handled a single criminal case telling me what motivates crime."

"I thought she was a NOBLE recipient," James said to Nestor.

Daily answered for herself. "I am. But I don't like being told what to think."

"You clearly have intelligence, good breeding. But the simpler people in society see murder and violence in movies, they think it's glamorous. They think it's cool."

"You ever work South Bureau Homicide?"

James stammered, "Well, of course not. But studies show—"

"I can tell you, firsthand, the kids down there don't think murder is cool."

Nestor groaned.

"What have you got *against* Whittsedge, Detective?" James looked at Nestor. "Is she going to be able to police this event, with this attitude toward our guest of honor?"

Nestor pondered his best Florsheims, then looked up at Barrett James. "She's in charge of the task force on the Ealing homicide, as a matter of fact, so she's not really here to police this event, she's here to look for a killer. And you know the funny thing? She's got one of the best clearance rates in the entire department. She may be opinionated, but she never—I repeat *never*—lets her personal feelings get in the way of solving a murder, even if it's a scumbag that everyone loves to hate like Eddie Ealing. And you know why that's good? Because it means if some other rich jerk died, you know—some posing, pontificating type who goes around trying to wow people with really impressive-sounding but essentially shallow rhetoric—well, Daily would be the woman you'd want on the case, because *she'd* catch the shit who did it."

Barrett James' mouth was now tightly pruned.

"The last thing I should tell you about Detective Daily—she really hates it when people talk about her as if she's not . . . right . . . *there.*"

The crickets seemed to roar in the silence between them.

FORTY

DAILY WALKED BACK TOWARD the estate now gilded with golden lights as night deepened. Nestor trailed her and said, "Why are you tangling with everyone lately?"

"I'm not tangling."

"Yes, you are. What are you so pissed off about?"

"You were going to show me where perps might gain entry."

"Can't be anywhere from the outside, take my word for it. If something happens, it has to arrive as an inside job. Catering, maid, security—"

"Cop."

"Damn, woman, whose side are you on?"

"You said inside. That's pretty inside. How many do we have here tonight?"

"You, me, Clem Burns, Taryn Pierce, Hill, Thomas, six others and Rigor—"

"They brought the dog?"

"Slam had Rig track Eddie's pool house back door for scents, see if it hits anyone here."

"Maybe it's all deflection. Someone doesn't want us somewhere else." Daily saw a chopper above, slicing the dusk. Channel Six. Kelly Spreck's station, owned by Harmon Whittsedge. Not the biggest station, not the most prestigious, but always first on the scene. So true, they'd started using it as a promotional slogan: *Always first with the news.* She said, "Think they'd wag the dog? Make their own news?"

Nestor shook his head. "Too big a risk on this one. And you're getting too paranoid."

In the great room, they found what Daily was looking for: a Loquitur Awards program that carried a bio on Harmon Whittsedge, followed by a roster of his controversial talk-show hosts. A man indicted during a political scandal, now a high-paid voice against immigration, social programs, and government assistance of any kind. Another, a psychologist whose idea of therapy was telling near-suicidal callers to get a life. A list of Harmon Whittsedge's properties followed. Daily's fingers dropped to Los Angeles. KSYX-Talk Radio. KSYX-TV. Channel Six. Not an affiliate of one of the big networks, either. But when Whittsedge acquired enough stations, reached critical mass, what then? Something off Wall Street's radar? Harmon Whittsedge was more potent than a greedy man. He was a greedy man on a mission. *The right message. Always first on the scene. Always first with the news.*

Kelly Spreck was first on the scene of Eddie Ealing's murder all right, but how was her report the right message? Hedonism kills? Here's what happens to immoral people? Eddie Ealing and Harmon Whittsedge were competitors. Both buying up pipelines for their content in the exploding world of media distribution. But Ealing didn't own near the number of broadcasting outlets that Harmon Whittsedge did. Not yet anyway. Like everyone else in the content business, in music and TV and film, Eddie had realized that it didn't matter what you produced or put out if no one heard the music, if no one saw the programs or films. Content was only king if you had a kingdom.

Wearing a headset, a waitress in white passed them with a tray of seared ahi-wrapped asparagus. Daily's attention focused on the receiver at the waitress' waist. She heard tones amid the din. Her cell phone. She opened her evening bag and put it to her ear. Static.

"Hello?"

She realized a man across the room had his cell phone set to the same ringing tone, and he was receiving a call, too. He'd put his hand to his ear as well. Daily's caller said something but she couldn't make it out. A man's voice.

"... *two Mikes ... real one ... make it look ... different ...*"

More static.

"Hello? I can't hear you—" Daily's pulse raced. Another voice broke in. A woman's. Someone else's call, drowning out her caller.

"... *kill the deal ... he doesn't have to know ... after the ceremony.*"

A burst of noise. Then nothing. Adrenaline rushed through Daily. She scrolled back to find the number of the last call: UNKNOWN CALLER.

"Your boyfriend in Santa Barbara?" Nestor smirked.

"Tim Litton is not my boyfriend." Daily put her cell away and told Nestor what she'd heard, the mention of Mike.

"There's a zillion Mikes on cells."

"But the voice said '*two* Mikes.'"

Nestor thought about it. "Could be someone needs two microphones for the public address system here, for the awards ceremony."

"What about 'the real one' and 'make it look different.'"

"The real one, probably the main microphone. Wrap a different color tape on it. Sound guys do that all the time so they know what channel is what on their board. Let's not get distracted with something that's probably nothing."

"I guess," Daily said. "Really disturbing, lately, how much I hear of other calls when I'm on my own."

"Pretty soon they'll just put cell chips right in our heads. We'll be talking, transmitting, and receiving direct. Find your kid, dog, or husband using GPS."

Looking around, Daily let her imagination take her back to Eddie Ealing's party, before his death. Similar people, doing similar things. Eating, drinking, laughing. *Using cell phones.* No cameras were allowed at Eddie's Fourth of July party, but phones were. What if one guest heard a critical part of some other conversation, the way Daily just had? All this wireless information, bouncing around in the air. What was it Anjar had said about Ealing's security system? *It's also wireless . . . people like Ealing have to have the hottest thing . . . But they're not the most secure, in spite of the advanced technology. Eddie's TouchStar screen could do anything he wanted it to. It was his system.* Daily told Nestor her thoughts, and asked, "Do wireless intercepts include cell phone signals?"

Nestor said he wasn't sure and radioed up to security central in the parapet. He nodded as the answer came. "Estate management decided not to track cell phones or paging frequencies. Too many people here would get pissed off; they think Eddie's perp used another band, anyway."

"Great. So the perp could have overridden the security system with something that looked and operated like a cell phone or a pager. Something basic. A gate remote, or a TV remote."

Her cell rang again.

"Same conclusion I came to myself," the caller said. Same man's voice as before.

Daily wasn't sure if it was an authentic male voice, or one affected by those studio gizmos that could make a parakeet sound like Louis Armstrong. She quickly took in the room from all sides, looked up at the mezzanine. Bodies, heads, no one looking at her. Flashes of white uniforms. The catering staff. Two of the guests on their cells, none of their mouth movements matching the voice of her caller.

"We need to talk," the male voice told Daily.

"Who is this?"

"I have the answer."

A waiter passed. Daily studied the small remote pack attached to the back of his belt. The wire that went to his ear. Security, catering, staging and production, all using remote gear, all on different frequencies. Daily tried to catch Nestor's eye, but his attention was on guest of honor Harmon Whittsedge who'd entered the other end of the great room to cheers. He looked angry.

"Don't tell anyone where you're going. Not even Nestor," the caller said to Daily. Strange voice, but something familiar about the cadence. "Meet me at the pool. I'll explain."

"Here?"

"No—the first pool." Then something unintelligible.

"I couldn't hear the last part . . . what did you say?"

No answer came; she heard only the noise of the party. In her frustration, every laugh sounded like a taunt to Daily. Every murmur was about her ineptitude. *Contradictions. Two Mikes?* Hell, she couldn't even nail one right now.

Taryn Pierce approached them in a rush. "Harmon Whittsedge just received a message from Mike. Follow me." Nestor and Daily trailed Pierce into a library, where a wall of monitors played clips from the guest of honor's life. The three detectives broke through a circle of people. Barrett James, Harmon Whittsedge, and Clem Burns stared at the center monitor. On it was a video image of a silver box topped by a blue card reading Mike's Gifts.

"I received a cell call," Whittsedge bellowed. "The man said there was something I needed to see in the library. Probably a ruse, but it's extraordinarily irritating."

"When did the call come?"

"Moments ago."

"Did you recognize the voice?"

"No, but it was a man. It's pretty noisy here."

"Have you played the clip?"

Whittsedge shook his head. "I don't need to be bothered with practical jokes tonight."

Daily could hear her own pulse in her head. "Who's been in and out of this room?"

Barrett James held his hands up. "It's open to the guests. The clips play off the disc and tape decks down there in the corner."

Daily reached into her bag for a Latex glove and started checking the nine decks that fed each monitor. Three sheriff's deputies from the Malibu Sheriff's Office broke through the crowd. One of the deputies said, "We should probably handle this—"

"Sorry." Daily found the deck that correlated to the center monitor. "Ties to my homicide. If someone's going to screw up the chain of evidence, you want it to be me, not you." The deputies hovered until she told them to call Lieutenant Powell; one of them did and they backed off. Daily ejected the silver disc and read the writing:

MIKE'S GIFTS

"It's an inside job, all right," Daily said. "Whoever delivers these gifts is more than authorized to be around, except this time he left the disc here. That's a switch."

"Run it already," Pierce said with too much edge.

Daily made everyone leave the room, except for her people and Whittsedge. She wanted to view the content before the news blared it everywhere. She slipped the disc back in the deck and hit the play button.

Harmon Whittsedge's face paled to a sick gray as he watched. "My God . . ."

Pierce grabbed his arm to steady him. "What's wrong?"

His eyelids fluttered. Then Harmon Whittsedge dropped to the floor.

Daily didn't care; she felt violently ill.

Pierce groaned and kneeled. "Daily, can you give us a hand here?" Still staring at the video image, Daily couldn't feel the floor; her vision clouded.

"Hey, Daily, do you mind?" Pierce's yell faded beneath the icing silence in her head.

She could hear none of them.

FORTY-ONE

HARMON WHITTSEDGE HAD BEEN so affected by the images of a woman's bathing suit that when he woke on the floor of La Sera Groves' library he promptly vomited. But there were two images on the screen. Behind the shot of the woman's striped pink one-piece that had sickened Whittsedge, Daily saw a weathered sign from the Newport Pier, its municipal code announcing its location:

NO DIVING

To Harmon Whittsedge and the others, the sign was only a prop, a backdrop for the bathing suit. But Daily recognized everything about the sign, from the forked crack in its upper right corner to the uneven paint job on the 'N', and it devastated her.

It was her sign, from her pier, from her nightmare past. Someone knew everything about her. *Everything.* More than she'd ever told Paulette, her own doctor, in two years of therapy, for God's sake. Secrets that would ruin her as a cop, as a human, and as a daughter all over again. If Paulette discovered the lie, she'd disown Daily as a friend and a former patient, and that would be nothing compared to the rest. The chill in Daily's spine deepened; her gut liquefied and she felt as if her blood had stopped flowing altogether.

A gift with more than one message. Dazed, Daily had the passing notion that she would just explain it all.

Really . . . I didn't mean for it to happen.

She'd lost her mind. That would be professional suicide. Daily was numb. Nestor, Burns, and Pierce were talking about the bathing suit that made Whittsedge cringe, trying to figure out if a smear near one strap in the clip was rust, dirt, or blood. The suit looked old, Nestor was saying. The kind his ex wore in high school, and that was in '67.

Pierce tugged at Daily's arm. "Earth to Daily." She snapped her fingers quickly: *snap, snap, snap . . .*

Daily seized Pierce's wrist, held it mid-air. Rage filled her and seared to a hot point in the fist that held Pierce's offending hand. She wanted to crush it.

Nestor tried to break it up, but Daily couldn't look at him. Barrett James asked everyone left to move out of the library. Daily maintained her hold on Pierce, then, as reason shoved anger aside, she let go.

Pierce rubbed her hand. "Geezus, I was just trying to save you from looking like a fool. You were a million miles away, talking to yourself. You're supposed to be in charge; act like it."

"And you're supposed to be a team player, so be one."

Pierce's pout turned malevolent. "Come off it, Daily, you manipulate everything so that only you know what's really going on. You're a control freak, not a leader. You can't take anyone challenging your decisions because you're not even sure they're the right ones. You keep it all tucked away, figure maybe no one will see you're not really the hotshot you're cracked up to be. It's all a damn act."

Daily couldn't respond. The rage had left her body. In its place was an empty void, a maw of fear. Pierce's moneyed education was good for something after all. She had just looked straight into Daily's soul and seen what was there.

———————

Dizzy, Daily finally found Nestor upstairs, in the master bedroom. The fragrance of the groves through the open windows had mingled with the smell of the vomit from Harmon Whittsedge, who was now prone on the bed. Barrett James and one of the Whittsedge execs were negotiating a day on which to reschedule the award ceremony. Only Nestor seemed concerned about Whittsedge himself.

Daily hoped Nestor wouldn't notice she was dying inside. Hoped he wouldn't mention it, anyway. Not now. Her latex glove still on, she took the disc from Mike's Gifts and studied it, trying to find her voice. "I'm going to take a look around. You good here?"

"Yeah. I'll stay with Whittsedge until he comes to. Find out what's so freaky about a pink bathing suit from the sixties. Our perp's long gone by now."

Daily stood at the window, looked down at the crowd of hundreds surrounded by rows of citrus trees. "I'm not so sure. Maybe he's still here, sipping on a martini."

"Mike's going to stick around after that?"

"There's easier ways to hurt people than these gifts," she said. "These are theatrical. I think the giver hangs around to see the effect of the pain, the impact of throwing someone's worst secrets in their face. Power. That's what gets him off."

She thought she saw a flash of blond hair in the orchard. Eyes looking at her, then nothing.

"Daily?" Nestor said it like it wasn't the first time. "You never told me what the caller said the second time."

"The pool . . ."

Daily's eyes shifted toward the winding pool of the estate, now surrounded by confused and chattering guests.

Meet me at the pool. I'll explain.

"The pool here? What about it?" Nestor asked.

No—the first pool. Eddie Ealing's pool?

Don't tell anyone where you're going. Not even Nestor.

At least Daily knew one thing: the caller wasn't Nestor, he'd been right next to her. But if the caller was able to hear what she'd said to Nestor earlier, maybe he could hear it now, too. She didn't want anyone following her. "It wasn't anything. I'll take the disc and the deck, get SID working on it. On my way out, I'll drive the perimeter a few times, see what I can see."

"You okay to drive? You seem a little out of it."

"I'm fine." Daily's head warmed again and she staggered.

Nestor watched her steady herself and said, "Yeah, I can tell."

FORTY-TWO

AT THE HOLLYWOOD STATION, Daily tried to suppress her anguish as she completed the paperwork on the message disc for Harmon Whittsedge. His Mind Box. His worst fear. Everyone at the party assumed the NO DIVING sign went along with his message, only she knew otherwise. She tried to keep her pen steady and failed as the silent inquisition in her mind raged. In her mind, the truth was out. She was already downtown, at a Board of Inquiry hearing:

You really expect us to believe you didn't want your sister dead, after all you've said?

I just wanted her to act normal.

You'd had enough of her madness; now you wanted her *to die. Isn't that right, Detective?*

I don't know.

You better know, you're an officer of the law. Can't have murderers on our police force.

I'm not a murderer.

Your own mother and father didn't mind if your sister hurt you or killed you, you said. Perhaps you're exaggerating things, Daily. Maybe your sister never tried to kill you. Maybe it was just the usual sibling stuff, nothing more, nothing less. And your imagination.

That's not true. She tried to kill me.

So you had to take matters into your own hands?

No! It was an accident . . . an accident . . . the sign said NO DIVING.

The memory of dank saltwater stench surged through Daily's head and she was there again, on the pier that day. She willed the thoughts away using techniques Paulette had taught her, and a separate wave of guilt filled her. Paulette, her dearest confidante, and even she didn't know Daily had left out the filial aspects of her worst wipe-out, leaving Paulette thinking she was simply afraid of the chaos of crashing waves, not that of blood and mind.

The phone jarred her; it was Lt. Powell calling from home. She told him about the gift to Whittsedge, said she was sending the disc to the SID lab with a patrol officer heading downtown. Powell asked if there was anything else he should know.

NO DIVING. *It was an accident.* But Mike's Gifts knew all about her. Everything.

Daily said no.

As she hung up, her stomach heaved. The skin on her neck and throat burned with a flush so intense she felt sunburned. Now she understood Paulette's reaction to Mike's Gifts. More than one message, only horrific to a recipient, depending on one's point of view. Only one thing would stop her meltdown, and that was the case. Working the problem. Organizing someone else's madness. Finding order. Reasons. Motivations. Tonight, the main message had been sent to Harmon Whittsedge. A rumor of the gift had preceded it. Did Ealing's gift have similar forewarning? With that many people, someone would have said something, and so far no one said Eddie's gift had a harbinger.

It had been helpful for Daily to be among the guests at La Sera Groves, to imagine herself at Eddie Ealing's party. The web of remote signals dancing through walls and air to small devices. Eddie Ealing liked to record things. Daily wondered if Eddie himself was listening in on all that was said about him, all the time. What if that was what gave Eddie his edge in business? His power of information?

The first pool. Don't tell anyone where you're going.

Eddie Ealing's pool. How could the caller gain access with the LAPD still watching the place? It gnawed at her. Daily would be safe with the officers on watch, and she had two firearms on her. She called Berta Ul-grod as a courtesy, apologizing for the hour, but explained it was imperative that she visit pool house tonight. She didn't have to divulge her reasons; detectives often returned to their crime scenes.

With manic energy, Daily drove into the hills. The angrier she became, the more the pieces of waste fell away. The core of the case was rage; she felt it now, understood it, became it. Eddie's power was his anger. Someone who wanted to alter the balance of power had killed him, someone who feared the momentum of Eddie's temper. Mike. An imitator of Mike. She couldn't see the perp, but she could sense him. He was filled with the same darkness she was. Worried enough about her progress to threaten her, to frighten her. The person who'd put the NO DIVING sign in the virtual delivery had miscalculated. In a way, she had less to lose than Paulette. Daily's parents had all but disowned her the day their favorite daughter died. Her ex-husband's love had been as fragile and conditional as his ego. If Mike was going to ruin the one remaining thing Daily had faith in, her career, then she had nothing to lose by taking Mike down with her. Funny how pure it was—the fuel that fired her as soon as she didn't have to work inside the rules.

At the gate to Ealing's estate, Daily surprised the two rookies standing guard. She figured it was the evening gown. The house was dark, save for the entryway lanterns and the light in Helmy and Berta's bedroom window. Daily parked and walked toward the pool house. She heard Officer O'Rourke's radio before she saw him emerge from the darkness.

"Did I forget to pick you up for the prom?"

Daily's laugh was fake, too loud to her ears. "We were up at La Sera Groves—"

"Heard all about it. The guy keeled and barfed. What's shakin' here?"

"Need to see something in the pool house."

O'Rourke turned the flashlight on Daily's face. "You feel all right? Your eyes are glazed. And you're weaving into the hedge."

"I'm all right. The first problem's called no sleep. The second problem's called you-try-walking-on-a-lawn-in-spike-heels-sometime."

"Pass." O'Rourke tossed his light onto the path as they walked. "Been quiet up here. Except for Berta Ulgrod's *stöllen* and caffeine, I'd be narcoleptic."

"What's the latest on Helmy's heart condition?"

"He's stable, but Berta said it with a pretty unstable look on her face. Like she's afraid she's gonna get the news any second." O'Rourke opened the door to the conservatory and Daily stepped inside. The wet heat of the day had condensed on the windows. Behind the bushes, droplets edged down the panes. She realized that Ealing couldn't have seen outside the pool house the night he died. O'Rourke asked if he could help. She told O'Rourke to go ahead, finish his *stöllen* and coffee, she just wanted to do some thinking at the scene. The patrolman gave her a tired smile, said he'd either be on the terrace above the deck or circling the grounds.

Daily went to the chaise where they'd found Ealing dead. The cushions were now at the SID lab. She touched the spot where the victim's head had bashed against the frame. It seemed heavier and cooler at night. Fingerprint dust was everywhere and she moved to avoid getting it on her dress. Noxious smells hit her. Pinch traces of the muriatic. Oxidized blood. Daily looked toward the skylight. Waited for the voice that had called her to come. Her senses were on high. Eddie had looked up at the steeple of glass, and past it, into LA's starless night. What was he thinking before it happened?

He'd had a Scotch, neat, after years of teetotaling. Why? Coroner Zaginsky had mentioned that Eddie might have the same condition his mother did—early-onset Alzheimer's. But if he knew, wouldn't Temperel be the first place he would go for treatment? Unless he didn't know. Or he knew and had a reason for *not* going there.

Before and during his swim he'd downed a PowerAde, according to Helmy Ulgrod. If dosed with GHB and mixed with alcohol, it was a potent and possibly deadly combination. Seizures. Coma. Death. Daily had seen it too many times with the immortal kids who could stay up dancing for nights on end, immune from all reality. GHB was not a drug Eddie Ealing would take himself, Daily felt sure. The Scotch was another matter—that was the wildcard no one had anticipated.

What had the vic heard and felt as the alcohol had hit him? The party was over. It had been a windy night. Everyone said he liked to play his recordable CDs, they gave him more pleasure than any album—the Eddie Ealing Berlitz course in power plays. Daily went to the stereo, found a CD that SID had deemed noncritical, and slipped it in. Pressed play. Jeff Beck. She turned up the volume to the same level as the night of Eddie's death, then walked outside, looked up at the Ulgrod's bedroom. Moments later, Berta Ulgrod opened the window and peered out. O'Rourke waved his flashlight at Berta, told her it was just Detective Daily. Berta cursed in German and slammed the window shut. It verified Helmy's story that he could hear the stereo at that volume. Daily walked back inside the pool house and pressed the intercom button.

"What is now?" Berta Ulgrod's anger roughened her accent.

"Just testing the intercom, Mrs. Ulgrod. Sorry," Daily said.

"Works good. Now you leave me quiet."

"My apologies." So far, so good. Daily put herself inside Eddie's head:

I'm losing my memory . . . I'm sick . . . I refuse to have my own family's center treat me for it . . . Alma Morada . . . Mike's Gifts . . . rage . . . it's what you leave behind . . . Good God; had Eddie Ealing staged his own murder in order to trigger the clause in the will that would screw them? The penultimate fuck-you? She thought she heard footsteps. Anticipation roped her veins.

"O'Rourke?" she called. She went to the pool house door, leaned out. The wind picked up, maybe that was all. Then, the clank of metal. Again she said his name. The grounds were dark but for the dapples the moon dropped through the cypresses. Her pupils adjusted. She saw motion by the hedge. Her own breaths sounded distorted and amplified. Something light or white was out there. Something shiny. Hair. Blond hair. Short.

"Pierce?" Daily removed her Beretta from her bag. "Taryn Pierce, is that you?"

No answer. From the side opposite the hedge, O'Rourke hurried toward Daily. His flashlight bounced with each stride; his breaths were dense rasps.

"I thought I saw something," Daily told him. "Over there, by the hedge."

"I heard you calling Pierce's name?"

"I thought I saw her." Daily grew hot at the recollection of Pierce's threat at La Sera Groves; she was grateful for the darkness that hid the flush warming her cheeks.

"Lots of jackrabbits around here. Raccoons, too," he said. "Better if no one else comes tonight, actually. Berta's pissed as a wasp in a wet

285

nest. You do talk to Pierce or anyone else, tell them to come in the morning."

"Sure thing." If Pierce had been watching Daily, she certainly wasn't going to step out in the open now and admit it. And O'Rourke's noisy return would have scared off anyone who might have been approaching, like her anonymous caller. Maybe Mike. Frustrated, Daily started back toward the front of the Ealing estate and her car. She tried not to let irritation creep into her voice. The officer was just doing his job. "You take care, O'Rourke."

He exhaled and said, "No worries. Safe and sound, all around."

Daily had the deep and sickening feeling that nothing was that way anymore.

FORTY-THREE

BONE-DEEP FATIGUE HIT Daily as she walked into her loft. All the driving, maybe, or the lack of substantial food. As her eyes adjusted to the darkness, she saw blue irises in a glass vase, drops of wetness rimming the edge, on the counter. She reached for her gun.

"I remembered you like them."

Daily froze at the voice. In the corner of her living room was a dark silhouette. Something reflective caught at her heart. A badge.

"Good lord, Rob, you scared the hell out of me."

He walked toward her, his face illuminated as he hit the entryway. "I remembered you liked them," he repeated, wiping sleep out of his eyes.

Daily had forgotten what it was like to be close to Rob, but her senses remembered. His smell. His split-amber eyes. His even and resonant words.

"I was just going to drop them off, but your cleaning person was here. She said you'd be home any moment. Asked who I was, told her

I was the ex. She said I looked like a nice 'boy,' thinks we need to stop being exes and get back together."

"I think I need a new cleaning person."

He laughed. "Don't blame her. I was going to leave right away, but I was beat, so she made me sit down, went to make me some coffee. I nodded off, didn't hear her leave."

"She could have let in a uniformed psychopath."

"She checked me out pretty hard, did the heavy-duty badge scan. Said she'd seen fake ones on *The Justice Files*." Rob adjusted his rumpled uniform shirt. "You look really beautiful in that dress, Helena. Sorry I scared you. I'll get going."

Daily dropped her bag on a barstool and sighed. "The flowers are lovely. My nerves are just raw from this thing."

Rob scanned the walls of the living room, where Daily had taped her spreadsheets and notes. Everything from her latest Box of Truth grid to histories on the people involved.

"Still believe in organizing every detail, I see."

"It works for me."

His soulful eyes searched hers. "I brought you a pound of your favorite tiger prawns from Bartelone's, too. In the fridge. Plus some lemons, some extra-large capers."

Her taste buds sparked at the recollection of their dinners. Safety. Warmth. Suddenly she was very hungry for real food. "Rob's scampi?"

"Only kind I know how to make," he said.

———————

The smell of garlic infused the kitchen as Rob chopped and sautéed. He had taken off the uniform shirt and Daily tried not to stare at his shoulders in the white T. Still taut, but a few pounds leaner. She'd heard his last girlfriend was a lousy cook. She went to the refrigerator and took out some romaine, an egg, a lemon, some parmesan cheese, then found the bowl big enough to make a Caesar for two and couldn't recall the last time she'd used it. The kitchen had always been a good place for them, the busy work of preparing a dinner together a pleasant respite from a day's unfinished business. He added basil to his pan, another splash of olive oil. She said it smelled wonderful. His familiar scent reached into her even amid the aromas of food. Rob asked her to keep the garlic moving on the heat as he strained the capers. Daily suddenly felt as if they'd never divorced. Pangs tickled her belly and a different hunger shot through her body. As her fingers moved past the heat-resistant handle and onto the pan's rim, heat singed her.

"Damn." She dropped the spatula to the floor.

Rob took her hand carefully and grabbed some ice from the freezer. He wrapped the cubes in a dish towel and held them against her burn. "Food, talk, and first-aid. We were always good on those counts."

Neither of them stated the obvious omission. They were best at sex. It had been their joke, their truth, and finally, the reason for their split. Rob's libido had cooled in direct response to her rapid career track, their sex growing cold, infrequent, and perfunctory as the gap in their ranks widened. She wondered if he was past it by now. The recent spate of calls, his concern, his support—it was as if he was saying he wanted to try again. His face seemed softer than she remembered. More lines. More maturity. Being this close to him made her nervous; she began prattling about the case. The web, the tangents, which mattered, which didn't. She left out the NO DIVING sign, unwilling to confide her worst darkness to anyone. She would deal with that one alone.

He had her sit with the ice and asked her if she wanted a mojito, her favorite drink. His memory was good, indeed. She said she kept mint in a clay pot outside on the balcony. He returned with two of the best sprigs, dropped one in each glass. He crushed the leaves into sugar and lime juice, then tossed the spent halves of a lime into each highball. He filled the glasses with ice, poured in white rum, stirred. He added club soda and set the drinks on the counter.

"One full lime mojito for Helena Saggeza Daily. Nothing halfway about you."

He dished up steaming plates of scampi with linguine and set them on the bar. She gave him more background on the case while they ate. As the conversation flowed from her, she realized just how much she missed marriage. She'd been denying it, putting it in a place where she didn't have to face the ache. As the mojito rode her blood, the ache mellowed. Maybe they had to lose what they had to appreciate it. As they talked, she wondered how different it would have been if they had just met now. He seemed so much more grounded.

The phone rang; Zaginsky from the coroner's office, returning her call. "I've tried you a few times today," he said. "Didn't want to leave this on your voicemail. You were right on the GHB. Ealing showed levels high enough to cause a coma. Then again, he was no flyweight. Good thing you ordered the test as early as you did, or we would have lost the window on it."

"Anything on the brain sections?"

"As I told that excuse of a partner you have—"

"Okay, okay, Zag, let me know when you do. Thanks for calling back." She told Rob about the GHB kids who had been making batches of the drug on the sly at the research facility. "They say they were framed."

Rob chortled. "Don't they all?"

"Either someone inside the deal didn't get caught, or someone on the bust side isn't coming clean . . . " Daily stopped. She'd never come clean herself. The cocktail couldn't quell her new swell of fear. Her secret. As Rob waited for her to finish, she deliberated telling him, then veered off it. No one would understand if her own parents hadn't. If Mike was going to try and obliterate her career, she wanted this one last night, this resolution of warmth and respect between them. Ironic, she thought, that you could live a life as right and as true as the sun, and still, one dark moment, one sin . . . She wiped her warming face. "Doc Ealing said something weird to me today, before I left Temperel. He said 'We all have our one.'"

"One what?" Rob asked.

"'The one we'll never grasp, no matter how hard we try.' That was his answer."

"He speaking from experience or taunting you?"

"It felt like a little of both, actually. He said I was denying help from his friends in higher circles because of my ego."

"Are you?"

Taking a long sip of her drink, she asked herself why she cared now, if Mike held the trump card. Rage. She had rage, too. Plenty of it. The rage of trying to understand madness and its damage and its utter lack of sense and reason. The rage of trying to organize it into something she could grasp, and analyze, always failing. If Mike was going to ruin her with her past, she'd take him down with her. Screw reputation. Screw the rules. None of it would matter, anyway. Rob was looking at her funny, and she realized she hadn't answered his question.

"It's a no-win." She swallowed. "If we bring Doc's cronies on, they'll take over and it won't be my case anymore. He'll circumvent the LAPD anytime it suits him. On the other hand, if we don't bring *his* people in, if we don't find the killer, it will always be our fault. My attention to detail always serves me well, but I can't see this one. The answers are right there on my walls, on those pieces of paper. Maybe there's more than one answer and they're at odds. More than one agenda."

"Unsolicited?"

"Sure."

Rob touched her. "You're exhausted. Nothing operates right when it's overheated, underfueled, and out of tune. I know you think you're

Superwoman, but you'd see more clearly if you slowed down and had a night's rest." He studied her eyes. "Insomnia really bad?"

Daily nodded.

"Let me see that burn." Rob took her finger, turned it into the kitchen light. "Need to put some antiseptic and ointment on it." His voice was soft, his breath warm with spices and lime.

Daily felt a burn in her eyes and heard her laughter fill the room. Her words seemed to come from someone else. "Detective II Lane Daily found crying over blistered pinkie. Garlic breath found to be powerful new disinfectant."

Rob laughed with her and cupped his own mouth, smelled. "Whoa. We're a pair." He pulled her hand to his lips and gave the back of it a tender kiss. Caring, not sexual, Daily noticed. Playing it safe. She didn't want to play it safe. Not now. As he stood to hug her, his barstool tipped back and hit the floor. Neither one of them did anything about it. She rested her face in his shoulder, looked up at him; her mouth searched for his. His hand combed through her hair and more memories fired. As they kissed, something at the back of her brain tugged.

Not now.

She shoved it aside. She pulled his T-shirt from his pants, let her fingers roam on his chest, his stomach. He pulled her injured hand away and held it, protected it. Rob undressed her, then himself. She led him upstairs to her bed. It was yesterday, it was now, it was no time at all. He kissed her breasts, and need rolled through her. She reached to touch every part of him—his arms, the small of his back, his thighs. His breathing was close and clear; it was inside her head. As he arched over her, his tongue played against her nipples, then her stomach. She pushed all logic aside. His smell was hers, her taste was his. They were practiced lovers who still remembered, and the ache she felt now was wonderful. Rob rolled her to one side, held her hand to his cheek, out of the way. She didn't bother to tell him how little she was thinking of the burn. She trusted every nerve in her body now. This was good, it was right, it was essential. It was okay, Daily told herself, as she sank deeper into the pillows and Rob.

It was okay.

———————

Daily squinted at her Braun clock in the dark. Hit the illumination tab.

Twelve forty.

She felt fuzzy. Hot. Garlic mouth. Rob's cologne. Rum on her tongue. Rob.

Rob.

She turned on the bedside lamp. Noises below. She threw on her robe, walked down the stairs to see Rob sitting in the corner of her open living room, staring at her file of case notes. He'd turned her desk lamp toward the wall to read her latest scribblings. The bottle of rum was next to him, open. A glass was in his hand.

He sipped. "Can see why this one's keeping you up. The thing is, Lane, you always overanalyze it. You keep trying to work it out this way, hell will freeze over five times."

She sat on the bottom stair, feeling more naked robed than during sex. Her head hurt. "Okay, Obi-Wan, who did it?"

"Don't get defensive, I'm just saying—maybe your Box of Truth method is the wrong way to come at this one. And don't make that face. You know you get too precise sometimes. Chop it up so fine, you don't see the big picture."

"I'm not making a face, I'm asleep. Can we finish the critique tomorrow?"

"It could be Bingus Korr. He's out and active, according to the bureau—"

"The feebs lost him at LAX. It's not Bingus Korr."

"I don't get that about you, Lane." Rob tapped his index finger on her notes. "You do all this busywork on Ealing, but then you can make one premature judgment that sweeps a real option right off the radar."

"And you spend less than an hour looking at my notes and make equally sweeping judgments about it."

"Pierce says you're not being very open-minded about things."

It felt like someone had filled her gut with gasoline and tossed a match down her throat. "You've been talking to Taryn Pierce about this?"

"I called the station for you, she answered your phone. Don't get wiggy."

"I'm not wiggy. Just don't talk to Pierce about this."

"Right, I forgot—you can ask me questions when you want to bounce your theories around. When you're calling the shots. But I'm not allowed to tell you that you're being myopic and I'm not *allowed* to talk to Pierce."

"Talk to me first. About Pierce. On the rest, you can do what-ever—"

Rob saluted, stood. "Yes, ma'am. Think maybe my sorry sergeant's ass has worn out its welcome. I forgot how much you like to be on top."

Damn him. Why was he doing this? She started to apologize and stopped herself.

He stood and weaved—hard. He reached for balance and flailed, ripping Daily's taped notes from the wall. Cursing as the sheets fell to the floor, Rob hit the desk and they both watched the rum bottle fly, roll, and drench Daily's mangled work.

"Shit."

Daily sped to her pages. Some were salvageable, some were sopping wet.

"It was an accident," Rob said, his voice flat and unemotional.

"You would have been more careful if it was your work—"

Rob held up his hand; the definitive sign that he wasn't going to argue. Stone mode, the coldest part of his psyche. Daily was amazed that apathy could be such a brutal tool. When he waved her feelings aside with that hand, his indifference tore at her, reminding her of their silent and horrible last months together. When they'd loved each other, arguments meant he still gave a damn. But as she'd passed his rank in the department, he'd stonewalled her. It made her want to scream then, and now.

He collected himself, buttoned and smoothed his shirt, gathered his belongings. On his way out, he touched one of the irises in the vase, rearranged it.

"This is the part where we aren't so good."

He shot her a cold smirk and left.

Daily felt sick as she showered. She cursed herself, then Rob, then herself some more. So much for trusting her judgment. Trusting the rum was more like it. The ache she felt now was all pain, the aftermath of alcohol and sex. She felt vulnerable, stupid. The worst pains of her life with Rob played her mind like a hideous slide show. She wondered how she could have ever forgotten the power struggles, the silences, the words that left her black and blue in places no one could ever see.

She was an idiot.

She dialed the water from hot to cold. Steamed and nauseated, she entertained the notion of never drinking again. Then came the maybes. Maybe he wasn't expecting her to want him after everything. Maybe he'd just wanted to lend support, be friends. Instead, she'd projected what she needed into the situation: sex, passion, a mate, even if it was the ex.

Stop it. She shut off the shower. It wasn't her job to figure him out. That was the old pattern. Worrying more about making life right for Rob than for herself. For everyone else. Dangerous prescription. The medicine she needed now was sleep. No more thoughts of Rob. Paulette was going to take her to town for this. Paulette . . . Paulette was in New York . . .

Take the dog out . . . Pavlov. Damn.

Dripping, Daily threw on clothes, ran downstairs, out the door and down the street to Paulette's condo. The dog cowered in the entryway. Daily smelled it before she saw it. Pavlov moaned his apology.

"It's my fault, boy. I'm sorry." How could she have forgotten? She cleaned Pavlov's mess while he watched her. "You'd make a hell of a therapist. Got that nonjudgmental look down." Pavlov's tail whacked the tile. A beach run would have to wait; she still felt sick, and the mess didn't help. "I'm sorry, boy. Maybe in the morning."

His tail played two more beats, then fell to silence. With a groan, he dropped his head to the floor. Outside, Daily dropped the trash bag in the bin. Back in the condo, she gave Pavlov a pat, filled his water dish using the good bottled water, one of Paulette's requests, then turned out the lights and locked the front door.

Five strides down Second Street, she heard him. A wailing that would shiver the Headless Horseman's hide. A surfer leaned out of his window and bellowed for the dog to shut up. Moments later, a young woman appeared on her balcony, said something stronger and slammed her sliding door. The dog sounded like he was dying. She went back. She heard Pavlov's tail beating in anticipation as she opened the door again. The whining stopped. Hot dog-breath warmed her shins. She could swear the dog was smiling. "Okay, come on."

Walking Pavlov back to her building, Daily thought she saw someone standing between her building and the next. Her imagination? The moist air clouded visibility. She stopped and focused. Nothing.

Back in her loft, Daily marveled at the insanity of going to bed with her ex-husband. The brief security she'd felt was an illusion. In reality, she was heading straight for the rocks; Mike's latest 'gift' was a clear threat for her to back off or lose her job, the only thing that mattered to her anymore. Agitation kept her pacing the living room. Pavlov watched awhile, then lay supine, angling for a scratch. She paced right over him. She needed to find Mike, she had to face the ghost.

She gave Pavlov a slice of turkey, cleaned up her desk, then sat down and turned on her laptop. The hard drive whirred to life. Pavlov didn't ask for more turkey, he just slid between her legs, and nuzzled her feet with a wistful sigh. Probably missed Paulette, who spoiled him rotten and gave him the too-well-fed belly that Daily now scratched with her toes. He groaned.

"You camp here, chubs, it's going to be Lean Cuisine. None of that gourmet stuff."

The dog didn't respond. His hot, even breathing slowed to the rhythms of sleep.

FORTY-FOUR

THE NIGHT BEFORE, THE stranger online had copied Daily's computer files, according to tech Anjar. Since then, she'd updated her notes on paper only and kept them close to her. A male voice had called her at La Sera Groves and suggested they meet at the pool. *The first pool.* He hadn't shown. The fact that Mike had gone online to take Daily's notes ruled out someone on her task force—they were all privy to the Box of Truth. Her team could call Daily anytime for her theories; they shared trust, except for Pierce.

Come off it, Daily. You manipulate everything so that only you know what's really going on. You want to keep the rest of us in the dark.

She didn't think of herself as a control freak, there just wasn't time in the day to explain every move, every nuance. Nestor and Burns had never had a problem with her leadership.

You can't take anyone challenging your decisions because you're not even sure they're the right ones. But you keep it all tucked away, figure maybe no one will see you're not really the hotshot you're cracked up to be.

To Daily, Pierce acted more like some young bureau colt than a cop. *The bureau.* But provoking her to what end? The auditors looking into police corruption since Rampart were from the Department of Justice. And Lt. Powell had said not to worry about the Florian Corporation angle on the will, it was "being covered." Was Pierce a DOJ mole? Daily accessed the government sites she'd bookmarked on her computer and entered TARYN PIERCE in the SEARCH fields. No hits. She queried other search engines for photos, articles, awards, scholarships. Nothing. Okay, if Pierce was policing the police, she wouldn't use her real name, but it would mean she had been put on the case by higher-ups. The lieutenant had no choice, so who issued the directive. And why were they policing Daily?

The cursor on her laptop jumped across the screen.

Her hands had been resting on her knees. If she found herself on-line with Mike again, the LAPD techs had told her to send an innocuous message to a specific email address. That message would be the trigger for one of Anjar's computers to start an automated trace, which in turn would launch FBI computers on a separate search. Granted, she'd only seen the cursor move. No message from Mike, but she had the feeling he was there, watching. What did she have to lose? She opened her email program, hit "new message" and typed in the code line:

```
Anjar—reminder—bring "Crime and
Punishment" to the potluck—Daily.
```

Daily sent the message, waited, listened to her laptop whirr. Assuming Mike was still watching her keystrokes, she tapped out new notes and pretended to work.

```
Eddie Ealing: commonalities with Harmon
Whittsedge?
```

```
Wealth.
Success in business.
Own broadcasting properties.

Differences:
Morality.
Politics.
Eddie Ealing murdered.
```

Daily sat back, closed her eyes. Her laptop signaled a new message and she clicked it open. No sender. No title. Just text:

MIKE'S GIFTS DOESN'T DO DEATH.

She had him again. Her pulse quickened. She typed:

```
Prove it.
```

The cursor blinked on screen. She hoped Anjar's computer was putting the trace in motion. Hermosa Police were to be silently alerted, too, and they would scan areas within a two-mile perimeter where Mike might override Daily's laptop by remote. A new message arrived:

FRIEND, NOT FOE. MIKE'S GIFTS DID NOT KILL EDDIE EALING.

Daily thought about this. Played out the options. Again, she typed:

```
Prove it.
```

The cursor moved away from the email message to her laptop's program bar, opening her notepad program while she watched. He could control her entire PC. The reply pecked itself out before her eyes:

WHY WOULD I CONTACT YOU IF I KILLED EALING?

Daily had to keep him engaged as long as she could without losing him. She typed:

```
1. Because you think we can't catch you.
2. Because you're insane.
3. Because you're too clever for me.
```

She sat back and waited. Mike added his own line:

4. BECAUSE MIKE'S GIFTS DID NOT KILL EDDIE EALING.

She had to make him say more. She wrote:

```
You told me to meet you at the pool. You
didn't come.
```

This pause was long. Daily worried she'd lost him. Then:

NOT ME . . . SET-UP . . . THEY HAVE YOUR PAST.

No kidding. But he had typed the word *they*. They have your past. Who were they? How many, and how could she possibly contain them? She imagined the news on air. *Should we have law enforcers who may be killers themselves? When we come back, we'll delve into the childhood of LAPD Detective Lane Daily, a woman with a past she doesn't want you to know about—the death of her sister at her own hands.* They'd get it all wrong; they'd mangle it and twist it into something vile and incendiary. She told herself to calm down, keep Mike online. Her heartbeat was louder than her typing.

```
Why should I trust you?
```

After a long silence, the response pecked itself out on the screen:

THE DOG HAS BEEN POISONED. TAKE HIM TO THE VET. NOW.

Daily sat up. She pushed on Pavlov's belly with her bare foot. It was cold. He didn't move. She slid to the floor, leaned under the desk and wrenched the dog's mouth open. Bits of turkey and a trickle of thick bile coated his limp tongue.

Pain burned her arms as she dragged Pavlov by all fours, as if he were hogtied. Shaking him did no good. His heartbeat was weak; faint breaths came from his dry nose. She threw her bag over her shoulder, heaved Pavlov from the floor, and headed for the door. It took her three tries, not because of his fifty pounds, but because his lobbing head threw off her balance. Daily looked back at her laptop. A new email had arrived. The subject line read:

```
ERROR! Mail message to anjar77@vector.gov
undeliverable.
```

Frozen, Daily watched as her cursor moved of its own accord, closing out the email program and the notepad with their discourse. It slid to the window that held her new notes and saved them. Daily couldn't do a damn thing with the dying dog in her arms.

FORTY-FIVE

DAILY SAT ALONE IN the waiting room of the Beachside Veterinary Hospital. Sickening sounds came from inside the surgical suite, where the doctor and an assistant worked on Pavlov. Pumping sounds. Steel banging steel. Liquid. Gas sounds. Agitated murmurs, their urgency clear even though the words weren't.

Dr. Nichols, a small bald man with kind eyes, had arrived first. Daily had Pavlov prone on the passenger seat of her car, and together they'd carried him into the surgery room. Nichols's nurse arrived next, a young Ava Gardner, even at four AM with no make-up.

For a half hour, Daily's mind toggled between Pavlov and the person hacking into her computer. He had warned her, told her to save the dog. An animal activist, after all? Was he inside Temperel, posing as someone else? Or had he simply poisoned the dog and then alerted her in order to get her out of her apartment? After all, the trace alert to Anjar's program was aborted. This guy was more than a hacker; he was better than the top pros.

In her bag, she found a packet of herb tea that Nestor had given her weeks ago. *Serenity Infusion.* She unwrapped it, dropped it in one of the styrofoam cups by the water dispenser and pressed the red lever for hot. She could use some steaming peace. A violent retching sound came from inside the surgical suite and she hoped it was a machine. Her heart raced. She didn't know what she would tell Paulette.

I forgot about Pavlov because I slept with my ex-husband.

I forgot about Pavlov and he was poisoned.

Pavlov is dead.

Daily set aside the tea and dropped her throbbing mess of a head in her hands.

Her darkest moment was in someone else's possession. *They have your past.* The word *they*: two or more. Maybe Mike was lying. Why the hell should she trust some cyberphantom anyway? The blood flow in Daily's temples shrieked, or was it the sound from the surgical suite? The grind reminded her of a Stryker saw, the kind used to slice skulls in autopsies. She heard panic through the door.

Hold it! Now! Down, down. Harder! Clamp!

What kind of lousy friend was she? Paulette had always been there for her, but she couldn't keep the simplest promise. All because of her inability to manage any other part of her life around her work. All for a puzzle with no solution, a cackling riddle with no bottom line. *The first pool.*

Daily had assumed the voice meant Ealing's pool, where this case began, but now she feared it referred to another place. One where her thoughts were hidden, thoughts now tripping her fast and mad, hurdles laughing as she hit them. She hated this case. She hated Eddie Ealing, Taryn Pierce, the Temperel people, the press, her ex, and everyone else who couldn't stop second-guessing and *monitoring* her. She hated herself for not seeing the answers. And this *Mike.* Omnipotent, all-knowing, motherfucking Mike. Mike's power was information. His advantage was time. Mike knew all about Daily, and she knew nothing about him.

All sound in the surgical suite stopped. Then, soft murmurs. Whispers? Whispers were bad. She closed her eyes. When she opened them, the vet stood in front of her.

"Someone slipped him poison. Maybe with chicken or turkey."

She couldn't ask.

"He's pretty weak right now, but he'll pull through, I think. A half hour more, you would have lost him. Good thing you got him here when you did."

She exhaled. "I'm the one who fed him the turkey. Right before he went to sleep."

The vet frowned. "I see. He didn't have anything else but clear liquid in his stomach, and he definitely presented as drugged. Does he drink tap water?"

Daily shook her head. "No, Paulette—his owner—she only lets him drink purified water. From the big jugs. She's worried about the chromium thing in LA water. Ever since she saw *Erin Brockovich*, and the reports in the news."

The vet and Ava Gardner stared at her.

"But I ate the same turkey and I'm fine. So what did they use as poison?" she asked them.

"Won't be sure until we run it through a lab in town," the vet said. "No odor to speak of."

Clear. No odor. GHB? Just a salty taste, which a dog wouldn't be able to describe. Too much sent you dreaming forever.

Dr. Nichols asked, "Did the dog have his own drinking water, or did he use the same supply as your friend?"

"Same supply."

"And your friend is out of town."

The realization hit her. The water wasn't meant for the dog—it was meant for Paulette.

FORTY-SIX

Instead of using her garage, Daily parked the Crown Vic a block away. If someone was watching her place, she didn't want to announce her return. She slipped through the passage between her building and the one next to it, went to the back stairwell. The metal door screeched as she opened it. A dim bulb illuminated a layer of dust on the unused stairs. Three steps up, she saw a single footprint close to the rail. Male size eleven, Daily guessed from experience. Sport-shoe tread. A couple more stairs up, another.

Her senses spiked for any sound or movement. She climbed the stairs on the side against the wall, away from the footprints. When she opened the door to her floor, she was met by more silence. Her ears rang from tight blood flow and the pitch of intense listening. The shoe print was consistent with her impression that it was a male who had been watching her. No one she knew. Rob was a ten, Nestor a twelve. The one guy who lived in her quad complex, probably a seven. She checked out the hallway, then entered her loft. Sickened by the night's events, she swallowed the bile rising in her esophagus. Her heart wouldn't calm down. Hypervigilant, she tried to remember how she'd left everything. The laptop was still on. She jiggled the mouse. Nothing new on the monitor. Garlic hung in the air. Spilled rum. The scent of Rob's sex. Senses as hot buttons to memories. Dr. Ross had a point. Memories triggered and perverted by sensations. Corrupted. Right now, Daily wished she could discern what was real without emotion. She couldn't tell if anything was out of place, not with this kind of trepidation turning her mind into a funhouse mirror. Her hand on her firearm, she walked the entire loft, downstairs and upstairs. Satisfied no one was inside, Daily tried to remember the last time she'd been to her other place. The forgotten place. The place she kept her confidences.

The first pool.

Was *that* what the caller had meant?

From the pegboard inside her cupboard, she grabbed the key on the old dolphin logo keychain. She didn't think of it as a pool anymore, because it was dry. Waterless.

Daily left her building and walked the side street that ended at the sea, in back of the power plant across the city border that divided Hermosa Beach from Redondo Beach. A cold wall of black faced her. Unseen waves rumbled; there was no seam between the sea and sky at this hour. She waited for her eyes to adjust. Above a fence was the sign with half a dolphin that matched her worn keychain's logo, and two-thirds of its letters:

a py orpo se wim Sc ool.

What used to be the *Happy Porpoise Swim School* was a seaside motel before that. But neither a cut-rate hotel nor a pool to teach tykes the freestyle could flourish so close to the clamor of the sloppy saloon to its north or the stench of the water reclamation channels to its south. The bar's trash bin reeked of hops and food fried in rank oil. Daily jumped the chainlink and edged her way around the long-empty plunge. As her pupils dilated, she made out the sweep of waste in the pool's deep end. To make sure no one had followed her, she climbed the rusty three-meter diving board frame craning above her. One rail creaked at her grip. She stood alert, waiting for more sound, shifts of noise or motion. Nothing but the sea's rhythms, the hum of the wind.

A can scraped the pool bottom, startling her. She shook the anxiety from her hands when she realized how hard she was gripping the rails. She climbed back down, paced to the pool's shallow end and jumped inside. Running her hand along the chipped edge for balance, she walked to the deep end, her head sinking below the surface level of the rim around her. A fence sign above the three-foot marker read:

NO DIVING

The damn phrase mocked her again. When she got to the pool's lowest point, Daily dropped to her knees, moved the pile of detritus off the drain cover and set it aside. She reached into the dark space for her metal box, wrapped inside thick plastic and rags, realizing how odd it was that she kept these few items. She returned to them rarely, always in moments of stress, as if studying them again would reveal some previously undiscovered cipher to her life. The small lock clanked against the metal box as she set it on the pool bottom. She set her penlight between her knees and inserted the key. The lock dropped open, she removed it, opened the lid.

Her breath caught in her throat.

Her journals were gone.

They have your past.

The box was empty.

FORTY-SEVEN

Thursday, July 7

THE NEW YORK HUMIDITY was stifling, even this early in the morning. It wasn't air, it was soup. Paulette waited outside the studio
door,until *TimeLine*'s Cray Wrightman and two dark-haired females
exited and walked down the street to a Cuban bakery and restaurant.
Paulette stayed a few paces back and watched as they greeted the host,
who led them to a window booth at the back. The newsman and the
host broke out in laughter at something one of them said. They weren't
strangers. The smell of fresh bread and coffee mingled with the scent of
cumin, onions, and garlic. Outside, Paulette pretended to read her *Wall
Street Journal*. Wrightman patted his forehead with his napkin. The
woman with long hair wiped something from the corner of his mouth.
He smiled and wrapped his fingers through hers. The three of them
broke into more laughter as he gesticulated with large hands. The
short-haired woman held an electronic organizer and poked at the air
with her finger.

Paulette had considered several options; she decided on the one that seemed to fit the moment.

She entered the restaurant and made a beeline for the eatery's host. Slouching and rubbing her abdomen as she spoke, Paulette recited her script. Annoyed, the host shepherded Paulette down the hall to an alcove near the kitchen. He commanded her to wait. From behind the service counter, she saw the host approach Wrightman and whisper in his ear. Wrightman looked startled, then frowned. The host again said something private to him. Wrightman glanced at the two women. Flustered, he stood and motioned for his female companions to stay at the table.

He strode toward Paulette. There were still traces of pancake make-up and powder caught in the folds of his neck, and the crags in his weathered face were more pronounced in the alcove's stark light. The salt-and-pepper hair that seemed so distinguished on national television looked harshly dyed. Like lasers beading on her, his hooded eyes targeted Paulette. He moved too close and she took a step back.

"I've never seen you before in my life," he spat. "I am not having a child with you, and I certainly don't owe you any money."

She crossed her arms in planned response. Play indignant. "I'm Dr. Paulette Sohl, Mr. Wrightman. And I'm sorry if that's how you interpreted what the host just told you. I said that I've been trying to reach you regarding our mutual problem and that you hadn't been returning my calls. I explained that I had no choice but to come inside to get what you owed me."

Confusion clouded his gaze. "He said you were a pregnant woman pointing to her . . ."

"Sorry if he misunderstood. My upset stomach has nothing to do with why I'm here."

"What kind of bullshit ruse—I don't have any mutual problem with you—I don't owe you anything—"

"Eddie Ealing has been murdered. It's already affected me, and it's about to affect you. Personally."

His cheeks fired. "I haven't spoken to Ealing since '89."

"As your assistant told me every time I called. But—as she clearly didn't convey to you—this is a matter of your own safety and security. If you don't believe me, call Detective Lane Daily with the LAPD. She's the lead investigator on the case. She'll vouch for me." Paulette handed her own card and Lane's to Wrightman. He held them each to the light, squinted as he read them.

The voice from his office came from behind Wrightman. The Zen voice. "What's going on, Cray? Is this person bothering you?" The short-haired woman. Zen eyes that didn't blink. Too small nose. Lips that looked terse and hard despite collagen.

Wrightman ignored his assistant and said to Paulette, "I already spoke with the LAPD. Someone called about my name being on his party list. I had nothing to say then; I've got nothing to say now. I have no idea why I was even invited. We didn't like each other anymore, and I don't know anything."

"But we share a mutual problem, so I thought you might appreciate speaking to me off the record. Before I air what I *do* know."

"Air?"

"I'm the psych consultant for Channel Ten News in LA and I've been asked to do a profile of Eddie Ealing's killer."

The long-haired woman now joined them, wary. She said softly, "Cray?"

"Mother of God, woman, I told you to stay."

Stay. Like a pet.

He turned and glowered at Zen. "Why didn't you tell me she called?" He stuck Paulette's card in front of her nose.

Zen tripped on her words. "Well—I assumed—"

"A doctor of psychology profiling the Ealing killer called to warn me about my personal safety, and you didn't tell me?"

Zen blinked. "Cray, if you knew all the things people make up to try and get to you—"

"Did you call LA, check her out?"

"We were *insane* this week—I referred her to the PR company—I can't personally check out every kook—"

"Go sit down. Both of you." Wrightman cursed under his breath as his assistant and girlfriend slipped away.

He turned to Paulette. "Impossible to find good help these days. Little tyrants, all of them. Stock options, that one wants. I've got a new option for her." The newsman caught himself and leaned against the opposite wall. "All right, Dr. Sohl, save my life in five minutes and tell me why you'd bother."

"Eddie Ealing sent you an invitation to his Fourth of July benefit for the Temperel Alzheimer's Foundation. You didn't attend."

Wrightman said nothing.

"Did Eddie ever try to contact you about a story on the brain disease kuru?"

"Yes . . . wacky messages. He said it was in the context of an exposé; something at the highest level, whatever that meant. Everything with Eddie was hyperbole: 'the biggest, the best, the most.' I didn't take it seriously. His family was mentioned, some garbage about ripping the facade off the Ealing legacy."

"How far did your discussions go?"

"There were no discussions. As I said, Eddie and I didn't speak."

"But he tried to reach you."

"He went nuts with the calls. My assistant handled them. Another assistant. She took copious notes, unlike . . . " He shot his chin in Zen's direction.

"What were you so angry about that you wouldn't take his call?"

Wrightman wiped fresh sweat from his forehead. "We had a falling-out years ago. Woman thing."

"How serious?"

"He married her. Then he treated her like shit. Then he divorced her." Wrightman glanced at the two young ladies in the booth. Shook his head with something just north of mild disgust. "She was the only woman I ever really gave a damn about."

"She's single now."

"Yeah, that's what I thought after Eddie dumped her. But she's damaged nineteen hundred different ways from that marriage. Not the free spirit I fell in love with. Goddamn Eddie. Wrecked everything and everyone he touched."

Progress. Still, she was careful. "You and Eddie were close as kids."

"Tight as hell. Lived in the same building in the city, summered at each other's beach houses, went to the same camps. Fell in love with the same woman." His face brightened at a thought, then darkened. "God, I wish I could forget this shit, but I can't. Stays with me like a damn tick." Flecks of Southern in his voice.

"You're not from New York, are you?"

"Houston. Dad moved to the city when I was nine to work at Tyan headquarters." The third biggest oil conglomerate in the world.

"So Eddie took you in, the new kid in town, showed you around?"

Wrightman chortled. "Hell, no. I showed him around. Eddie was a wallflower when I met him. Stayed in his room, read books all day. I had to drag him outside to do anything. Being from Texas, I wasn't used to being cooped up, even with our own floor and a view of the park. I wanted to get out all the time, see things."

"*Eddie Ealing?* A wallflower?"

"Third fattest, second-string everything, and the number one shyest kid at the academy and camp."

314

"What happened?"

Wrightman pulled at his chin, the same way he did on TV, right before he asked the killer questions. "Around the time he was fourteen he lost his baby fat, got more edge to him. The germ of his infamous attitude, I suppose. Started making home movies with Doc's eight-mil. Eddie was the director; he let me produce and act—badly, but I looked okay on film. Plots just poured out of him. We used different kids we knew to play the other parts."

"What kind of plots?" Paulette asked as casually as she could.

"Typical adolescent bullshit. Scary stuff, gore, psychos. We used Heinz ketchup for blood, sausage for guts, marbles for eyes. Our cooks let us use poultry gizzards and anything else we weren't going to eat."

She used that reference to ask Wrightman about the heart in the virtual message delivered to Ealing.

"Eddie could outgross any of us kids. Something like that, even a human heart, probably wouldn't register on his Richter scale out of context. You know what they say about these Mind Boxes. Meaningful only to the recipient. I don't know the context on that delivery and don't want to."

He was closing up again. She needed to find out who was threatening her and her family, but aggression wouldn't work on a man with a PhD in surly. She shifted to neutral. "You guys ever make the typical boy movies—cops and robbers? Military stuff?"

"Nope. Underneath that gentle facade of Eddie's was the Eddie the world grew to know and hate. Used to blow my mind, the weird things he'd think up. Guess that dark side was there inside him all along."

Maybe not. Kids replay what they see and hear and feel. Try to express it, change the outcome. "You remember any of the stories he made up specifically?"

Wrightman sighed, then made funny clicks with his tongue. "One was an Abbot and Costello riff, spook flick in a lab. Another mimicked *The Hand*. The original, not the Caine picture. One had spiders. Eddie used dead spiders from his brother's insect collection for that. Got in a hell of a lot of trouble from Doc. There was another one where a kid poisons his brother and gets away with it."

Paulette exhaled hard but said nothing.

"That one gave me the creeps, and I told him so. He said someday people would listen to his stories. Someday people would pay for them. He was right, except he paid the ultimate price."

Something in Wrightman seemed smug, if not pleased, that Eddie had died the way he did. That kind of relative morality sickened her. *Bracket your emotions, doctor.* "Where are those home movies now?"

"I have no idea. My old things are in storage in Connecticut. I'll have Priscilla check into it. You might also check with Eddie's sister, Aubrey. She was always a bit of a pack rat."

Paulette asked if he had Aubrey's private number, and Wrightman lost his patience.

"You were going to tell me about the terrible danger I'm in and all you've done is ask me questions. You're a shrink, all right. Stop manipulating this conversation and get to it."

"Mike's Gifts," she said.

"Yeah, yeah. We're doing a piece on it this Sunday. Violence in the media. And don't try and scoop me on any of what I've told you, because it doesn't matter, it doesn't play on a national level, and I'll have your job if you do."

"Don't run it."

"It's already in post."

"Take it out of the show. Run something else. Anything."

Wrightman studied Paulette's fear, which seemed to tell him more than her words had. He rubbed his temple, then shook his head. "This is lunacy. Do you know how many times I've been in danger as a reporter? Serious danger? I don't run scared just because—"

"This is different. Why do you think Eddie Ealing was trying to contact *you* about doing the kuru piece? When he had all the media contacts in the world, even his own company? He was calling you because *you* saw, heard or know something related to this. Has to be something that happened when you two were young. I don't know what it is, but somewhere in your memory, you do. And that's why you're in danger now."

Wrightman was silent.

"And right now, your memory is the one thing we still have. Someone else has more of the pieces of something they don't want exposed. They don't want us putting them together. They want to control who gets the information and exactly what they get. They've already let me know—in no uncertain terms—that I better stop trying."

Wrightman's chest filled. "Look, I've been threatened by terrorists and nuts the world over. I'll call in a favor from my DC boys, beef up my security. But I'm not killing my piece."

Paulette fought the rapids in her chest. She had to let *him* make the decision or she'd lose all traction. He was that kind of man. She said the word softly. "Okay."

"What are you doing with your face?" he growled.

"I'm not doing anything."

"Yes, you are. You've got that, 'Okay, go ahead, walk right into the maelstrom' look."

Paulette gathered her breath. "The way they got to me didn't have anything to do with guns or armor or protection, Mr. Wrightman. They got to my family's secrets. Things no one knows. Things that will kill my father if they come to light. And if they got our secrets, they can get yours."

FORTY-EIGHT

A BUTLER SHOWED PAULETTE into Aubrey Ealing's penthouse on the Upper East Side. In a bright living room Aubrey stood over two prim women seated on an Anglo-Indian gilded sofa upholstered in green damask. Eddie's sister was taller than Paulette expected, with the same bone structure as her brother: large chest, high hips, wide abdomen, slim legs. Highlighted hair that brightened the darker Ealing ash. The two younger women surveyed samples of elegant gifts and favors topping a Japanese Edo coffee table. Tall iced teas sat on a silver tray.

"Ms. Ealing-Hollingsworth . . . Ms. Paulette Sohl."

Paulette didn't correct the butler's introduction. The three women looked up nonchalantly, as if callers were a regular occurrence. One of the young women asked Aubrey what she should put in the contents of the gift bag for a well-known mogul who had everything. Twenty-something was worried that well-known mogul would sneer at the offerings, which were only worth four or five hundred dollars in total.

"Let them sneer," Aubrey said. "Everyone else will recognize that kind of behavior as gauche. This is a charity fundraiser for a very good cause. Don't worry about the jerks."

"Truer words were never spoken," Paulette said as she approached them.

Aubrey offered a hesitant hand. Her sentences came out as questions. "Cray Wrightman's office called on your behalf? Said it was urgent that I see you? Lord, I haven't heard from Cray in years. Guess I still haven't, since it was his assistant who called." Her wide-set eyes took in Paulette with a note of recognition. "You'll forgive me if we've already met but—"

"You may have seen my piece on Eddie from Channel Ten in Los Angeles. The network picked it up, ran it a couple of times. But I'm not here on behalf of the media, believe me."

Doubt rode Aubrey's gaze.

"Whoever killed your brother has my family on their radar now," Paulette said.

"Oh? And why should they?"

The two young women eavesdropped until Aubrey snapped a look at them. They gathered their papers and retreated to another room.

"I'd like to find out," Paulette said. "I've had no other association with Eddie than the fact that I've been asked to comment on his killer by my newsroom. As a professional."

"Journalist?"

"Psychologist. I generally consult for News Ten on mainstream issues like marriage, teenage angst, job stress. Before that, I worked criminal cases, principally high-profile crimes and their perpetrators. It took a little too much out of me."

Aubrey frowned. "A lot of experts are spouting their opinions on my brother's killer. Why would someone target you?"

"I was hoping you'd help me find out." Paulette pulled one of Lane's cards from her purse. "You can call Detective Daily, she'll vouch for me. I give you my word, anything we discuss is off the record, only for my own family and my peace of mind."

"The detective on my brother's case is Pierce. Taryn Pierce."

"Daily's in charge of the case. Pierce works for her."

Aubrey's eyes rested on her phone. Paulette suggested she try Daily's private cell first, said it was the easiest way to reach her when they were working a case. Aubrey dialed the Hollywood station first, verified Daily's cell number, then dialed it. Paulette waited while Aubrey asked Daily the expected questions, starting with an update on the case. Walls and tables full of photos surrounded them, dozens of Aubreys. Aubrey and Doc Ealing at a formal dinner. Aubrey and her banking-scion husband at Christmas. Aubrey with two Scottish terriers. Aubrey, her brother Peter, and her father at a beach. Aubrey receiving a plaque from the First Lady. Aubrey with the President of the United States. Paulette saw the same affliction among many of her patients. *See me. Love me. Notice me.*

Aubrey hung up. "Detective Daily said they have a new lead in the case, but she didn't want to say more about it yet." Her face quivered. Hundreds of dollars worth of make-up couldn't paint confidence. "About your problem . . . I understand your concern, and I don't mean to be rude, Ms. . . ."

"Sohl. Dr. Paulette Sohl."

"I don't mean to be rude, Dr. Sohl, but I really don't see how I can help you right now."

I can barely help myself, her tone said. Stalwart over tremulous. Aubrey Ealing wasn't doing so well, after all. Her nervous eyes glanced at another table, where a guest list and photos of a white estate in the Hamptons lay next to the drawings of a party planner.

"Looks like it's going to be quite an evening," Paulette nodded at the sketches of the fête: champagne grapevines across tables, swatches of ivory damask beneath an outdoor stage, trellises of willow, wheat grass in tall, bark boxes rimmed with beech. "At first, I was surprised to hear that you were still going ahead with it, but now I can see how much effort you've put in."

Aubrey blinked. A glimmer of pride, followed by suspicion. "My effort has nothing to do with it. The Secretary couldn't change his schedule. He's heading to the Middle East tomorrow."

That Secretary.

"Eddie was responsible for a lot of the guests who are coming. In a way, this is the best tribute we could have had. He would have liked how much money we've raised for the Foundation. Not some morbid, somber thing." Aubrey's voice dropped. "The coroner in LA won't release his body yet. That's morbid, how much they're drawing this out. Used to be you could die in dignity, with some privacy. Now everything's public property." A single sharp laugh. "And here I am blubbering about it to some media—"

"My reason for being here couldn't be more personal or confidential."

"Credentials don't guarantee truth. Why should I believe you?"

Weighing her options, Paulette told her about the message delivered to Channel Ten, its content, its implications in her life. When she was through, Aubrey Ealing sat stunned and pale.

"Mother of God. How do I know you're not making that up—just to get to me?"

"Could you make up what I just told you?"

"I couldn't have thought of it." Aubrey hesitated. "What is it you want?"

"Can you tell me about the relationship between your father and your mother?"

Aubrey grimaced. "I need some fresh air before I get in the car for the Hamptons. Follow me." She led Paulette out to an expansive terrace that overlooked Central Park. As if he'd read Aubrey's mind, the butler delivered a tray with cookies, lime wedges, a decanter, ice, Belvedere, tonic, and highball glasses. Without asking, he added two cubes to each glass and poured two vodkas with a splash of tonic. Aubrey consumed half her drink immediately. Paulette sipped hers to be polite.

"My parents met in Vietnam, in the fifties, when the French were still there," Aubrey said at last. "Father was there with my grandfather, who advised our government on foreign affairs. Mother worked in one of the hospitals. She'd had some bad experiences during World War II in France, when she was young. It depressed her for years, but eventually, she went to work as a nurse outside Hanoi—the hospitals were in need, the whole Vietminh ordeal—the work was supposed to distract her from her bad memories in France. Father met her while touring the facilities. He had to ask her out ten times; she was so hesitant. He didn't know why—yet."

Aubrey didn't elaborate but her eyes spoke to Paulette, woman to woman. Her mother's "bad experiences" were of that nature.

"Your father played white knight."

"Salvation personified. He rescued her in all ways, brought her home to New York." Aubrey smiled sadly. "She didn't even know Father was from a well-to-do family. Part of the reason he fell for her, I guess. Over here, he always had a million hens chasing him, or so I hear."

"Did your mother feel safe in America?"

"At first. But eventually—well—my mother's demons always sang just a little bit louder than her angels." Aubrey poured two more fingers of vodka for herself. "I didn't notice it as a child, but by the time Eddie was born, Mother was drinking regularly, taking Valium every day. Father often wasn't around, so he didn't notice as much as we did.

When he was home, he didn't want to see it or acknowledge it. He was too busy changing the world."

"You noticed." *Even when no one noticed you.*

Aubrey shrugged. "I'm not into all that holistic stuff, but I've heard that sometimes people with a lot of pain can actually make themselves sick. I know it's not possible with Alzheimer's, that's as scientific as it comes. But there's a part of me that wonders sometimes—if it isn't what Mother wanted deep inside . . ."

"What do you mean?"

"To forget." Moisture trembled in Aubrey's eyes. "To forget all her pain."

Aubrey finished her third vodka as the butler announced that the car would be ready to depart for the Hamptons in an hour. He asked if "Mrs. Sohl" would be joining them.

Aubrey shook her head. She asked if Paulette needed a refresher.

"No, thanks. You know, this morning, Cray said Eddie was actually shy until he was a teen."

"That's true."

"Speaking as a professional, a drastic shift in personality doesn't usually happen on its own."

"Meaning?"

"What changed in Eddie's life around that time?"

Aubrey rubbed a temple. "What does this have to do with his murder?"

"It has to do with his *identity*. It's an essential factor in why he was killed, and how."

Aubrey had grown more agitated with each drink. "Hey, it was 1968. Martin Luther King, Jr. . . . Robert Kennedy . . . Vietnam. Who wouldn't grow angry and cynical?"

"With all due respect, Eddie was what, fourteen?"

"Thirteen."

"In my experience, thirteen-year-old boys are more affected by what happens to them personally. They're conscious of current events, but they're more narcissistic at that stage."

Aubrey chortled. "No kidding."

"Developmentally speaking."

"Oh, no. You hit it right on the head."

Paulette could almost feel the jealousy steaming off her. She asked if Aubrey was close to her parents.

"Peter was Father's pride and joy. Eddie was Mama's boy."

Leaving Aubrey out. The boys mattered. She didn't, and she still resented it.

"How awful of me to say these things, right? Just two days after Eddie's passing."

The right words, little remorse. Years of jealousy, or something more?

Aubrey stood. "I'm sorry, doctor, I have to change or I'll be late. Is there anything more I can help you with?"

"Actually there is. Cray Wrightman said you might have some of Eddie's old movies. The ones they made when they were friends."

Aubrey sighed. "That's all they did for several summers." She walked inside and Paulette trailed her through the living room and into a library. Aubrey pressed a button and a panel of shelves opened to reveal an entertainment center. Beneath the TV screen were rows of discs, videos, and other items, all labeled neatly. "I had the family films transferred to disc five years ago. They're as tedious as all home movies, and Eddie's attempts at directing were abominable, even for his age." Aubrey looked at a clock. "I'm leaving soon. Whatever you want to view in that time, be my guest."

324

Alone, Paulette fought her frustration and focused instead on the faint hope inside her. She had less than sixty minutes. She chose a disc marked *SUMMER '68.*

FORTY-NINE

THE EALING BOYS ON horses. Eddie more chubby than Peter, the dazed dreamer even then. His steed is a droopy Appaloosa that doesn't respond to his goads. Eddie, on the other hand, kicks and whips his palomino. The horse stops and Eddie yells silent curses at the animal, whips it harder. Hardly the shy mama's boy Aubrey and Cray had described.

Cut to . . .

The Ealing family stands in front of the riding arena. Americana personified. Doc Ealing, tall and proud. His demure wife, Monique. Aubrey, the prim young lady, sits on the rails. Peter Ealing's arm wrangles around Eddie, who tries to shake it off. Odd, Paulette thought. The film ended. Paulette ejected the disc and pulled out another: *CAMP '67.*

A silly face in the lens. A younger, rounder Eddie Ealing with an Australian sheepdog. He pets it, hugs it. He cajoles the dog to a picnic table, feeds it snacks, claps with glee, and runs circles around it. New scene, new place . . . *Peter and Eddie. A campfire burns. Fish in a pan. Peter's arm around his younger brother. Eddie reaches to touch the frying pan and Peter slaps his hand away.* "Hot," *Peter's lips read. Peter wraps his hand in a towel, then grabs the pan's handle to move it. He puts his arm back around Eddie. His affection toward his younger brother is apparent. Almost theatrical.* Paulette watches as Peter's hand dangles over Eddie's shoulder. Where's the other hand? *Across his own knees, the hand against Eddie's thigh.* Misplaced touches? Not really. Not that she'd seen yet, anyway.

A new film followed on the same disc. *A cabin. Boys on the porch steps. Peter feeds himself a bite of a sandwich, then Eddie. Eddie doesn't want any, his attention goes to a squirrel. Peter pulls Eddie back.* Not affection. Something else, but not sexual.

Paulette went for yet another tape—way back this time: 1959. Peter would have been five years old, Eddie four. *Christmas morning. The same building Paulette sat in now. Huge Christmas tree. Fifties icicles and lights. Peter opens a chemistry set, places the equipment on the living room floor. Doc admonishes him to move it. Peter doesn't. Doc pats Peter on the head and laughs it off. Everyone laughs with Doc, even a maid. Eddie, a ball of a boy at four, chases a wind-up toy across the living room floor. Peter grabs young Eddie's arm. Gleeful, Eddie tumbles into Peter's lap. Laughter, tickles, but Peter keeps Eddie pinned down. Doc smiles and waves at the boys. In the background Aubrey tugs at her father's pant leg. He seems annoyed. With Eddie's head still in his grasp, Peter takes one of his medicine droppers from the new chemistry set. Fills it with something clear from the kit—what?* Water? Oil? Vinegar? Had to be something harmless, it was a toy, after all. *Peter squeezes the dropper and liquid falls onto young Eddie's belly. Then his face. He's howling and kicking.* Paulette couldn't tell if it was real or mock pain. *The maid looks nervous, but Doc laughs again. Everyone laughs with him. Lots of silent laughter. Eddie kicks, his arms flail.* The pain is real. *Peter keeps him close.*

What is it Paulette is seeing? Not affection. She watched more; there it was.

327

Possession.

Paulette's empathy for the young Eddie swelled. Peter Ealing was oblivious to his younger brother's identity and separateness in every scene she'd watched so far. Throughout, he behaved as if Eddie belonged to him, like a toy or a dog. Paulette checked her watch. If Aubrey was on schedule, she only had five minutes left. She went back to 1968, pulled the disc subsequent to the one she'd first watched.

A baseball game. Well-coifed parents in the bleachers. Eddie on the mound. Leaner in the legs, still thick in the chest and stomach. Decent pitcher. He strikes the batter out. Next to bat is Peter Ealing. A tan Doc Ealing stands behind the fence, claps at Peter and imitates a swing. Eddie's pitch is a strike, catches Peter watching. Two balls, then Peter swings and fouls. More instruction from Doc behind the backstop. Was Eddie's scowl at his father real? Either way, Paulette found it odd that Doc was so clearly championing his one son at the expense of the other. *In the stands, Mrs. Ealing sits in a white dress. She raises her hand at Eddie, as if sensing his need. Eddie smiles at his mom. The smile fades as he looks at his catcher. Eddie nods. The wind up, the pitch . . .*

Peter was down in the dirt before Paulette realized what she had seen.

She rewound the tape then advanced the picture using freeze frame.

Eddie's pitch hit Peter squarely in the left temple.

Peter goes down. The people in both sets of bleachers rush toward him.

She watched it three more times then let it play on. The film went sideways there. *Jagged shots of grass, running feet, then the end of the film.*

Paulette thought of head trauma, the grenade pin that could pull shaky minds into full-blown pathology. After years of resentment and abuse, had Eddie aimed the pitch at his brother on purpose, or was it an accident? She didn't realize she was holding her breath until Aubrey's voice came from behind.

"Renquist shot all our family films when we were young. He taught Eddie how to use the camera. Eddie never had Renquist's eye, though. Isn't that right?"

The butler's tone was as flat as his gaze. "You flatter me far too much, Ms. Aubrey." He straightened and resumed his role. "The car is waiting."

Aubrey said to Paulette, "I hope we've been of some help to your . . . situation. As you said, this is all off the record. Anything to the contrary will incur the full wrath of my attorneys."

Renquist took the discs, replaced each into its slot with a smack and closed the cabinet.

Paulette had to get away from these people, this toxic house. She had much to tell Lane and many new questions. If Eddie's murder was part of the secrets in this house, then it meant Mike was tied to these souls. Eddie's rage, Peter's possession, Aubrey's indignation. Paulette needed air; she felt boxed in from all sides. The walls in this home bore more tales than she could possibly absorb in one sitting.

FIFTY

AT KINKO'S, TEE MADE a copy of the final entry in Daily's green journal, the most incendiary one he'd taken from her lockbox. This was the passage that would shake her for months, if not forever. He might first send Kelly Spreck at Six the best segment, the end, to fuel things. She'd been the perfect chump for his anonymous call to leak Eddie's murder, spinning the "violence in art" retaliation angle. Ironic that Eddie's own film poster gave him the idea when things went wrong that night. All things considered, he'd wiped out most everything, and he had to admit, there was something poetic about using the fucker's own film story, his own recordings, at his death scene. Except that wasn't the plan. Nonetheless, Spreck was all mouth, no fact-checking, and that bought him precious time.

Now he needed more time to get rid of the damn shrink who was tight with Daily, a complication he hadn't expected until he'd intercepted her cell call in the unmarked that first day, then shotgun-miked her loft at night while Daily and the shrink had dinner. The poison injected into Dr. Sohl's water bottles had, of all things, reached the damn *dog* first. Next time, he'd make no mistakes.

And this journal would cinch it for Daily. Soon, the story of her uncontrolled anger would spread: above the fold in the local papers, maybe even the nationals. The damage would be done. She should have listened, should have picked up her cues. It was her own damn fault she was throwing away her career. He read her adolescent words once more:

> *Really hot. Like weird hot for this time of year. We got to go to the beach, all of us. Mom wants Dad to get out. He stopped going to work. Mom says he's tired. We swam forever. There were no life-guards because it's not summer. Mom and Dad watched me do the backstroke.*
>
> *After lunch the waves were really good so we went to go body-surf. Mom and Dad acted like out of it or something.*
>
> *She started it when we were in the water. She wraps her legs around me and pulls me down. I try to get away, but she's HOLD-ING me HARD. When I come up she laughs at me. Mom and Dad give us this stupid wave. They think she's like tickling me or something. Then she gets both her legs AND arms to push me down. I'm TRYING to come up and I can't. I feel really sick and when she lets me up I say: that's not funny and water comes out of my nose and mouth when I talk.*
>
> *She goes: I think it's funny!!!*
>
> *I start to run out but she pulls me down <u>AGAIN</u>. I choke on more water and I can't see and I guess I scraped her trying to get up and she pulls me up and SCREAMS at me for SCRATCH-ING HER!!!*
>
> *I say: stop trying to drown me!*

She says: DROWN? You aren't DROWNING. This is drowning!

She pushes me down and I can't breathe. She's mean no matter how I am to her—nice or mean. It got black. It got even darker.

Then this huge wave hit us. Sand and rocks scrape me and go in my mouth. Sand gets in my bathing suit and everyone laughs at me when I get out. I barfed. They thought that was REALLY funny. I told them what she was doing and Mom says: don't make up bad things. God doesn't like liars. It made me so MAD. But then I wonder if maybe they don't believe me because they like her more or she's stronger and stuff and I'm not. Like she wouldn't RE-ALLY let me DROWN right? Maybe she's just trying to make me more like her. She's NEVER scared. Of anything. I'm scared a lot. Mostly of her.

Tee laughed. The next segment was what he'd slip to the media, in Daily's own childhood scrawl:

Maybe I AM crazy like mom says sometimes. She IS my sister.

So we're on our towels and she rubs sun lotion all over me and Mom says: isn't that nice? See how NICE?

Later she says: let's go up on the pier. We see a bunch of fishermen and fish and some had no heads and were in buckets. Some flop around but the fishermen don't do anything even if the fish are STILL alive. It smelled like REALLY bad. She said some boys dive off this spot that's in the middle of the pier. Between the booey and the ladder on the side of the pier. She says: let's jump. I say I don't want to. She calls me a wimp. CRY-BABY CRY-BABY! She pushes me to the rail and her fingers are jamming my stomach HARD and she doesn't stop until I climb up on this stump with her. Where the guys dive. There was this awful smell, like, <u>SICK</u>. There were these dead fish just ON the pier.

She says: we'll dive together I'll hold your hand and laughs.
I say: I don't want to.
She gets super mad and calls me all these bad names.
There's this sign right in front of us that said NO DIVING.
I say: I don't want to break the rules and she says: chicken shit, grow up and be a real sister. Then she RUBS my arm and acts like she likes me all of a sudden.
She goes: we can do really cool things together cuz we're the same, Helena the same flesh and blood. We're SISTERS.
Her eyes got that look again. I go to climb down but she's got my arm and she goes: we are in this together. On the count of three, OK . . . one . . .
I say: I DON'T WANT TO, and she goes:
TWO
So I try to pull my arm away but she pulls me back hard and says:
THREE
I hated her then. I HATED HER for everything. I scream and push and I hit her hard in the head <u>HARDER than I EVER HAVE</u> so she will <u>LET ME GO</u> but then she grabs her head where I hit her and she falls and there's this really awful SLAM and a splash.
These two fishermen looked over the rail. They looked BAD.
So I get up from where I fell and go look down. She was all loose in the ocean. Her hair was all bloody. There was blood on the ladder on the pier too.
People all around me yelled for an ambulance and stuff.
I couldn't move. I just stared down. Her body was floating and it swished over from this wave. Her head rolled back and she looked at me.
She <u>LOOKED</u> at me.

This fisherman dove in. They laid her on the sand . . . said she was dead. Mom and Dad were crying.

I killed her.

I killed my sister.

FIFTY-ONE

Lt. Tim Litton called Daily at home. "We found the body of a young Latina woman this morning. Washed up near Coal Point, near Isla Vista. Might be your Alma Morada."

Hope filled Daily; her breaths grew short.

"The body's been in water for some time. The CI says she had enlarged lymph nodes and she'd been operated on. The ME will decide pre or post, but it looks like post. Her brain is gone."

"What?"

"It's not in her skull, it's missing. There's a saw line, the kind from a Stryker. The stitches came apart in the ocean. First time I've ever seen anything like this before autopsy."

Her uncertainty condensed into fury. Some monster was using Temperel as a front for truly bizarre deeds. Whether it was Dr. Ross or someone posing as the mysterious "Mike," they were doing things that would never be sanctioned in the light of scrutiny. This was beyond comprehension, and it drilled an enmity into her that she didn't realize she was capable of feeling.

"One other piece of news. We received an anonymous call this morning. Female voice. Said we should check out an apartment in town. We sent a unit over, the door was open, place was a mess. Someone was there looking for something, but they left in a hurry. Place is rented by one Steven Woydyno."

Her breath stopped. "Burg. It's his nickname—Burg."

"Looks like Burg's your Mike fellow, then. Found clippings of Eddie Ealing everywhere. Photo of the girl we found on the beach, when she was alive. Bunch of cards that say 'Mike's Gifts' in a drawer. Maybe he had a thing for the maid, didn't like Ealing moving in on her."

The chill in Daily's veins hardened. *Burg as Mike. Burg killing Alma. Burg killing Eddie.* Lightheaded, outside of herself, she forced herself to inhale, then processed what Litton had just said again. It wasn't right. Every synapse in her brain was firing in protest.

"You there, Daily? I thought maybe I'd hear something—like, 'Thanks, Tim. This is worth a year of lasagna, Tim.' or 'Wow, I'll be right up, Tim.'"

Logic had left her. Thoughts were forming faster than she could articulate. "I appreciate it, Tim. More than you know." She couldn't explain it now; she had to move. If it wasn't Burg, then someone was setting him up to take the fall. "You call here first?"

"Tried you at the station. Spoke to a Detective Clemson B—"

"Burns. Thanks. I'm on my way."

Daily called the Hollywood station and asked for Burns. She was greeted by Lieutenant Powell instead.

"Come into the station, Daily," he growled before she could utter a word. She tried to address the Santa Barbara developments, but he cut her off and said, "I'm aware of everything. Come into the station immediately." Something was wrong. Powell's tone was punitive.

"I'll be right there, sir."

Alone in his office, Powell told Daily to sit down, the first time in years that he'd barked at her like that. He stared, questioning her eyes. "Where were you last night?"

"La Sera Groves. The assignment."

He gave her a *no shit* glare. "After that."

"Here, filing the paperwork on the gift sent to Harmon Whittsedge. I called Nestor to close out the night—"

"But you didn't *close out the night*, did you? Didn't I tell you no maverick stuff this time? Isn't that what I said?"

No one could tap dance for Powell, but she heard herself try. "When I was at the party at La Sera Groves, it gave me some ideas, about what guests might have seen and heard at Eddie's party. I wanted to go back, put myself there. Think things through."

"Who was with you?"

"No one. I mean, besides the officers at the gate, plus Berta Ulgrod and O'Rourke."

Her heart heaved beneath her ribs. Did Powell know she'd gone to meet the anonymous caller? She couldn't explain the wordless motivation that had pulled her there.

Powell slumped, shook his head. "O'Rourke is dead," he said. "One shot, nine, back of the head. Taryn Pierce is in a coma at Cedars."

The explosion in her head blinded her; it stopped her from speaking. She wasn't sent to Eddie's place to meet anyone—she'd been set up. When she found her voice, it was distant and small. "I swear to you, O'Rourke was alive—"

"I'm going to need your weapon, Daily. Once ballistics runs everything—"

Her expression pleaded with him, but Powell turned away. Daily removed the ammunition from her service Beretta and set it down on the desk. Powell pulled some forms from a file and recited the advisements regarding paid leave. She signed her name as disgust tickled her throat.

Powell coughed as if to get his own voice back. "Stick around, case they want to have the BOI hearing sooner than later."

Board of Inquiry. Internal Affairs. Her head was a ball of pain; she couldn't even respond. As Daily walked back toward the homicide desks, she saw Burns talking to Nestor. Their eyes clouded at the sight of her.

"I didn't hurt anyone," she said. The entire floor of the station seemed to be watching and listening.

Burns nodded once. Nestor didn't move. His glare devastated her.

"I need to leave the car here," she mumbled to Nestor. "Give me a ride home?"

With a tone that could only be called professional, Nestor said, "Sure."

———

Nestor drove too fast down the Hollywood Freeway, barreling through downtown to the Harbor Freeway interchange. Daily tried to explain. "The caller said not to tell anyone. My going alone has nothing to do with you—"

"It has *everything* to do with me," Nestor bellowed. "It means you don't trust me enough to tell me what's going on. It means you hold things back. Pierce was right, you aren't—"

"I was trying to make sure *you* didn't step knee-deep in *my* shit, okay? Pierce went there to track me." She searched his face, but he wouldn't look back. "Look, I feel like hell about what happened, but she hasn't been policing the case, she's been policing *me*. If she wanted to find Ealing's killer, she would have made herself known when she arrived last night. No harm in saying, 'Hey, Daily, it's Pierce, I'm here, too.'"

"Guess you can ask her when she comes to."

Neither one of them said it: *if she comes to.*

The muck of tension filled the car. "I'm sorry."

Nestor changed lanes too close to an eighteen-wheeler.

"I said I'm sorry, Nestor."

"It's just what I was talking about the other day. Can't trust anything anymore."

"I trust you."

"Right."

"It may not seem logical to you, but there was a linear process to my decision—"

"God, listen to yourself! You're real good at *lines*, aren't you?" Nestor spat. "Boxes, lines. *My decision.* Deciding what I should know or not know."

"That's not true—"

"Trust ain't about logic and details and your damn spreadsheets. You're like the Tin Man in *The Wizard of Oz*, Daily. Great mechanics, but missing your heart."

Deep blow from Nestor, that one.

"You know better." She yearned to explain her reasons, but that would just enrage him more, for hiding yet more from him. He continually overcompensated for Daily saving him from a fatal shot. Who knew what he would do now, if she trusted him with everything? She refused to complicate the life of the man she cared for like a brother. If she was going down in a BOI hearing, or in political machinations, she refused to drag him into it. Her eyes burned with tears that she refused to let go. Again she said, "You *know* better."

"Do I?"

"Now you're saying you don't trust me anymore?"

Nestor blared his horn at the truck and snorted. "I don't know what I'm saying."

Daily closed her eyes and pain swelled inside her.

Twenty minutes later Daily was still in Nestor's car when her cell chirped. From New York, Paulette prattled a nonstop recap of her encounter with *TimeLine's* Wrightman, the piece he was doing on Mike's Gifts, media violence, the details of his childhood with Eddie Ealing.

"It wasn't about patching things up with old friends, Lane. Eddie wanted Cray Wrightman to do the exposé on the Ealings, on kuru, because Cray could *vet* it in some way."

Daily kept trying to talk, but Paulette was lost in a nonstop stream. All about the Ealings, Cray, the home movies.

"Dammit, Paulette listen to me, I'm trying to tell you something. I've been leaving messages on your voicemail for hours. Didn't you get them?"

Trepidation slowed Paulette's speech. "No. Not one."

"It's Pavlov. He was poisoned." Paulette's cry pierced the cell phone. Daily explained, "He's okay. I got him to the vet in time, they got it all out. I can even pick him up tonight if he's ready."

Paulette's voice was shrill. "How? What—"

"His drinking water. The vet's sending his stomach contents to the lab."

Paulette's words choked. "My God. His drinking water is *my* drinking water."

Daily was silent as Paulette cried. She knew they weren't tears of fright as much as violation. Daily tried to offer the best consolation she could by phone—she told her friend the Hermosa Beach Police were checking the condo, and they'd promised to test her water and watch the house and the alley on a heavy rotation. She finished by saying she'd uttered a hundred prayers of thanks that Paulette had never sipped one drop. "But there's one thing I can't figure out—the water was there all day. So was Pavlov. Why he hadn't—"

A stilted sigh. "Pavlov drinks out of the toilet downstairs when I'm not around to spank his ass."

"Saved his life and yours. Before HBPD arrived, I checked things out, saw a small hole near one of the seams in the plastic water jug. Size of a needle on a large syringe. You store your water outside, in back, right?"

"Yeah, they deliver twelve at a time."

"Who knows you're really in New York and not San Diego?"

"Just you and Gerry."

"And the airlines and Cray Wrightman and his assistants. I'd feel a lot better if you were on the next plane home."

"Home." Paulette's voice was raw. "Maybe I'm safer here."

Daily didn't want to cause Paulette more grief, but she had to know. "One of my detectives told me what was in the message from Mike's Gifts delivered to Channel Ten."

A long pause. Sniffles. "Right."

"Why are deformed guinea pigs so mortifying to you?"

Again, Paulette said she didn't want to talk about it on cell. Paulette blew her nose. "I'll explain later. And why do I get the sense there's something else you aren't you telling me? Is it something more about Pavlov?"

Daily took a deep breath, looked at Nestor. Two hands on the wheel, eyes straight ahead.

"No. I've been suspended."

"God, Lane, I'm sorry. Why?"

"It's a mistake. I didn't do anything wrong. Everyone will realize that soon enough."

Nestor's knuckles grew white on the steering wheel.

"You're not alone, are you?" Paulette realized.

"No."

"I'll call you later. I'm making good headway on Mike."

Daily sighed. "That's why I'm worried about you. So was I."

FIFTY-TWO

ONCE SHE GOT HOME, Daily trashed the rum-tainted spreadsheets on her desk. Box of truth, box of lies. The Mind Box. Bullshit. She'd been trying to solve the murder remotely, watching the case like a viewer outside one of those miniature Plexiglas worlds with plants and creatures and its own ecosystem. But she would never catch this perp from the outside, watching like a lab tech, or minding the rules like a law-abiding peace officer. Hell, no. She was going to have to go dark and deep into the most primal parts of herself to reach him. To be like him. No more *lines.*

She grabbed a satchel, threw in some clothes and eyeglasses to fit the plan congealing in her mind, plus her personal .22. Funny what a catalyst rage was. In its burn, all indecision fell away, leaving only a core of pure, incorrigible will. It was all riptides until last night. Leads swirling, just taking her farther away from the real problem. She'd been fighting it until she started seeing things from Eddie's point of view. Someone didn't like it. Someone who knew she was at Ealing's. Someone who had watched her, followed her, nearly killed Pierce and murdered O'Rourke. A copkiller. Some cold-blooded, stone asshole *motherfucker*, a word cops reserved for the lowliest of creatures, some creep with no soul, no conscience. Daily intended to find him. If she was going to burn for that asshole, he was damn well going to burn with her.

————————

Daily eased off the gas of her '66 Mustang as she coasted down the steep Conejo grade on the Ventura Highway and into the flatlands of Camarillo. Wearing wide-brim hats, farm workers worked in the even rows of green, their hands busy in neat quadrants of artichokes, peppers, and squash. Hand-painted signs beckoned drivers to stop and buy fresh corn and flowers. Industrial complexes squatted in the middle of farmland, like the first spores of urban sprawl.

Cyrus Services housed an entire complex at the end of a long road, past fields of tomatoes and green beans. The sun-leathered faces of farm workers looked up as Daily drove by. She tucked the Mustang behind one of the farm stands selling produce down the road. For good measure, she purchased a peach, two enormous tomatoes, two cobs of sweet corn, and a bouquet of gerbera daisies. Eating the peach in her car, she checked out the road leading to Temperel, then called Tim Litton at the Santa Barbara Police Department. He was out. She reached him on his cell. She explained that she wouldn't be coming up to see the body of the young Latina victim after all. He said he'd heard about her situation and offered condolences.

She craved disclosure. Instead, her jaw tight, she said, "It'll work out."

"I'm sure it will." Litton's tone didn't match his words. "I'm at this Woydyno guy's place now. Looks pretty cut-and-dried from here."

She tried to sound neutral. "Uh-huh."

"You don't buy it?"

"Nope. Too pat. Too theatrical. Just like Eddie's murder."

"Well, the body that washed up at Coal Point was anything but theatrical."

She felt the argument rise in her throat then swallowed it. Debating instincts would be futile now; she wanted only her singular focus. "I'll talk to you later, Litton. When you're alone."

Daily had tried Eddie's point of view, now she was going to try Alma Morada's. Alma had come to Temperel through Cyrus Services. Daily took off her white shirt and pulled on an old Virgin Gorda T-shirt that had seen better days. She wrapped a worn bandana around her head, kerchief-style. She left her bag, her ID, and her purchases in the car, locked it, then walked the quarter mile to the Cyrus complex.

She practiced remembering the missing-P file Litton showed her two days ago:

"This one looks like you when I met you…"

Cedella Rayborne. 28 . . . Olive skin, mixed heritage, the angles, the full hair. Born: Jamaica. In US on student visa. Hotel management. Missing since last December. Parents in Kingston say she never came home for Christmas. Last known place of employment: Minton Hotel. Maid.

A pale woman sat in the guard booth at the Cyrus gate. Her security uniform was too tight and her cap was too big. The voice was nasal California country. "Got an appointment?"

"No ma'am. Come to find out about work." As a kid, Daily and her two brothers had listened closely to their father's Caribbean relatives when they came to visit in Costa Mesa. Privately, they would spend hours mimicking the dialect.

The guard was churlish. "Go in, head down to that far building on the left there, where it says personnel. P-E-R—"

"Yes, ma'am, I can see it."

"She can spell and she can see. Two points. Ask for Jimmy Lugo. What's your name?"

"Cedella Rayborne." She iterated each letter.

The guard spelled it incorrectly on the clipboard and made her sign. Inside the personnel office, Daily was blasted by frigid air conditioning. Around her, on plastic chairs and wood benches, were a dozen people sitting with their fears.

"You Rayburn?"

She turned to see a tall man in a blue work shirt and jeans. Hair so blond it seemed translucent in the fluorescent lights above. Gray eyes that scanned Daily. The ID badge clipped to his belt said: *J. Lugo.*

"Yes, sir. Rayborne with an 'o' and an 'e.'"

"All right, Rayborne with an 'o' and an 'e.' Come with me." Jimmy Lugo laughed at his own rhyme. He walked in long strides and didn't look back. Daily hurried after him, down noisy corridors that had walls but no ceilings, to an open warehouse. She could hear the sound of forklifts and machinery. Metal doors opening. Commands and responses yelled in English and Spanish, a couple of other languages she didn't recognize. A radio played Ranchero music.

"You read and write English?"

"Yes, sir."

"You a citizen?"

"Student visa."

"What are you studyin'?"

Daily double checked her memory. "Hotel management."

"Ambitious. You ever work at a hotel?"

"Yes, I did." Daily didn't mention the Minton, because she didn't want him checking there. "Some hotels in Jamaica. As a maid."

Lugo smirked. "Have a seat here with Victor and he'll see if there's something that might meet your skill set."

She sat on a formed plastic chair with wobbly legs. Victor, a sprout of a man behind the metal desk, looked up and asked her name. Daily repeated her false identity, explained that she had not expected to be interviewed today, that she had simply come to inquire what positions might be open.

"Here now," Victor said. "May as well go through with it. Got ID?"

Think, Daily. "Have my papers up in town, where I'm staying. I was just coming by to check the job board, you know."

Victor seemed to buy it. "Okay, Cedella, tell you what—why don't you go ahead and fill out these forms, then come back tomorrow and show me your ID so we can make copies. Formality. Fact is, we need some new people right away, so I'd prefer that we burn rubber, try to match you up to our job database ASAP."

Daily gauged the danger in filling out papers here, now.

Victor misread her blank look. "Burn rubber? Get a fast start?"

"Right." Daily ventured an uneasy smile. "Glad to hear there are openings."

She was mortified when she saw how little attention Victor paid to her finished application. He told Daily to follow him down the hall, into a hot quad between the buildings, then back into the door of another freezing cube of concrete. This building had better amenities. Some employees wore lab coats over their jeans and T-shirts. They entered a room filled with the smell of ammonia and a host of test tubes filled with blood.

"Jiggy!" Victor yelled in a most unprofessional manner. "Jiggy, I need you! Now!"

Daily put herself in Cedella Rayborne's head. "What's this part?"

"Need to run the standard tests on you. Our employees work with some medical firms and stuff, need to see what you have and what you don't have before we send you anywhere."

"I'm healthy."

"I'd say so." Victor eyed her a little too long, then frowned in irritation at the still-missing Jiggy. He told Daily to have a seat with the other people, handed her a piece of paper. "These are the tests I need

347

Jiggy to run on you. Tell him I need the results by tomorrow at three, latest." He walked away.

Daily sat between two women waiting in the connected school-style chairs lining the hallway wall. To Daily's right, a porcelain-skinned woman with sad eyes and straight hair had her nose in a book. Russian. The girl to Daily's left smiled at her.

"I been waitin' for this Jiggy to come back for half an hour." Southern dialect. Too much conversation could get Daily in trouble, so she just nodded. The woman said, "Heard you say you're healthy. That's good. Get more choices that way."

She couldn't have been more than thirty, yet her ebony skin was like paper, missing its shine. Patches of her hair were missing.

"Ovarian cancer," she said, answering Daily's unspoken question. "Now don't gimme that look, I don't want no pity. We gets the cards we're dealt, gotta play 'em. Thank God for Cyrus Services. One of the only places that will hire someone like me. Got insurance to cover some stuff, but I'm also trying a bunch of experimental therapies and they ain't covered by nothin' and my insurance is all tapped out in a month anyway. This lady in my support group told me about Cyrus, says they got programs for people like us who can still work, and they don't hold the cancer against us or nothin'. They even work with you on the flow, 'cause you know you go through spells, good times and bad times, depending on chemo and whatnot." The woman looked up at a small-boned young man who jumped with nervous energy. "Well, finally. Jiggy's a good name for him, don't you think? You take care now."

The woman went in to have her blood drawn. Jiggy took enough for three test tubes and the woman sat through it patiently. A pro at being sapped, pricked, and prodded.

Three more people, then it was Daily's turn to sit in Jiggy's small lab. He jabbed the needle into her vein with too much impact. She watched the tubes fill with her blood and felt the spread of uncertain fear.

———————

Daily was given brief but unclear directions to the exit and she purposely headed the wrong way. In the bowels of Cyrus Services, she found an internal hallway that seemed to connect all the major buildings to one another. Without an employee badge, she could get kicked out at any moment, but she had her excuse ready and she carried herself with confidence. Attitude was everything. She passed what looked like a food-services center. Through waiters' doors, she saw dozens of workers prepping food: they chopped, steamed, sauced, and shrink-wrapped. A cordon of people placed containers into trays and stowed them on large metal dollies with rolling wheels. At the end of the kitchen was an open loading bay. She saw the back of a truck, several of the dollies already on board.

A man in a blue Cyrus Services windbreaker addressed her. "Can I help you?" Beside him stood another man in an identical jacket.

"I just finished my job interview. I left something off my application and I need to—"

"Who interviewed you?"

"Victor—he didn't tell me his last name."

"Victor Reed. Maintenance. You want to head back that way. Keep going this way you'll end up in waste management, dear, and that's not where you want to go."

Both men laughed. Daily started in the recommended direction. When they were out of sight, she circled back. Waste management. What was so funny about trash? Ahead and to the right was a door marked NO ADMITTANCE—W PASS ONLY in three languages. She hovered near a bulletin board, pretending to read the posted notices, waiting to see if anyone went in or out of the W door. No one did and after a few minutes, Daily decided to take her chances.

The noise that met her as she went through the door nearly deafened her. Conveyor belts that transported metal containers clanged and churned in dissonance. The men in this warehouse wore ear protection, the kind airport workers used to muffle the roar of jet engines. The odors were a fusion of rotten and sweet; some like she'd smelled at murder scenes, others unlike anything she knew. Lights hung over staging areas for the pallets. Large bulbs, canopied in metal, lit the path of each conveyor belt's winding path to the workers loading metal containers. Beyond the key work areas, however, no one could be accused of abusing electricity. Around the perimeter were plenty of areas with no illumination.

No one noticed Daily standing along the dark edge; she tucked herself into a corner and slid behind a pallet holding a large metal bin. She watched the workers sort items in open containers for recycling: plastics, glass, metal, white paper, colored paper, other trash. Closer to her, men handled closed containers marked *Basura*. Some of the large metal boxes had the toxic warning symbol painted on them, the same icon found on disposal containers of used needles and medical waste. One line of men wore masks and heavy-duty gloves. In spite of the room's chilled temperature, several of them were sweating. The noise was too loud for them to talk. The loading dock closest to Daily rolled open, and light flooded in. A buzzer sounded, and voices erupted into animated discourse as the machinery stopped. Lunchtime or break. The entire warehouse cleared out in three minutes. Speaking English, three men huddled on the loading dock. The first was the man in the blue work shirt, Jimmy Lugo. Next to him was a ruddy Caucasian with a basset hound neck and a bulldog attitude.

And the third man standing with them was none other than John Safford.

FIFTY-THREE

DAILY WASN'T JUST SURPRISED to see Safford at Cyrus Services, she was amazed at the way he spoke to the men—he was clearly directing them. Lugo used a phone on the wall to make a call, then hung up and told Safford that a driver was on the way. Safford went outside on the loading dock. Lugo left the warehouse and came back with two workers who seemed perturbed about being called back during their break, but Lugo silenced them in Spanish. One of the workers manned a forklift to move two of the metal containers out to the loading dock where Safford waited. One bore the "toxic" icon, the other did not. The other man helped load containers into the open truck, slammed its doors shut, then both workers headed out for the rest of their break, muttering several of the choicest curses Daily knew in Spanish. Safford bid farewell to Lugo and called the other by name—Pearson, his voice familiar from two days ago, when she'd called about Alma Morada. Safford jumped down from the loading dock and climbed into the passenger side. Pearson mounted the driver's seat and the truck pulled away. Daily had to get to her car.

Lugo wasn't leaving the loading dock.

Think.

If she made a move, she'd be noticed in the now empty and quiet warehouse. But she had to follow the truck with Safford, had to know what he was doing and where he was going.

A set of ear protectors sat on a crate just out of reach. She edged herself in their direction and, using her index finger, inched them toward her until she had them. Summoning her focus, she tossed the protectors toward the middle of the warehouse. Good arc. They landed on one of the metal bins with a clang.

Lugo jumped and moved toward the sound. Daily crept back around her pallet, keeping it between herself and the man's sight line. She slipped quietly between the bins, but she missed one step and tumbled toward a container. She sucked in her breath and twisted her body so that she missed the collision with metal. Her rear caught the impact of the concrete floor instead, and the pain was excruciating, but thankfully, silent. She bit her lip as blood pressure bored through her head. She waited, watched. With Lugo looking at the floor in the middle of the warehouse, she stepped out.

Daily found her way to an exit door and walked as briskly as she could toward the guard gate, which opened for the truck. The guard ignored her as she passed. Running, she made it to her Mustang in less than a minute. There were four shoppers at the fruit stand, and she squealed the car out of the parking lot, kicking up dust and frightening two dapper men holding cartons of brussels sprouts. As the green orbs spilled and rolled, Daily pulled a twenty from her purse and let it fly out the window, hoping it would cover the vegetables in her wake. Ahead, the Cyrus Services truck turned for the on-ramp: 101 NORTH.

She kept the Mustang a few cars back; her pulse vacillated each time she'd lose the truck and race to locate it through uneven traffic. Her cell phone chirped midway through Ventura and she steeled herself for Lt. Powell's voice, delivering news of the BOI hearing, or maybe Pierce's condition. She said a silent prayer for both Pierce and herself to make it through this.

Instead of the loo, the caller was a stranger. "Lane Daily? Fred Hibbs here, from Mysterious Discoveries Bookstore in Charlotte, North Carolina. You were on the Internet the other night, looking for an out-of-print book? Well, I emailed you a couple times but I guess we're not hooking up or something. My messages came back to me undeliverable."

Daily's mind fractured—the Cyrus truck was picking up speed, but she was concerned that emails hadn't made it to her. Mike again.

"You've got me now, Mr. Hibbs."

"Well the books you're looking for, *Vertical Sins* and *Mimic's Poison,* they're impossible to find. I assumed you knew . . . they were both written by the same man, writing under a pseudonym, Lathanore, a special forces agent who saw action in two wars and a number of other, uh . . . situations. I know because I served with him, before he went off to work intelligence. Is this a bad time to talk? I don't want to bore you with my old vets—"

The word *intelligence* hit Daily in the solar plexus. *Information.* The only thing the varied guests at Eddie's party had shared, according to her grouping analysis, her Box of Truth. *Stay calm.* "This is a great time, Mr. Hibbs. Just great. Please."

A cement truck blared its horn at Daily's sloppy lane change.

"You're driving?" Hibbs said.

"Yes, but please continue." Her thoughts roared. The films Eddie *hadn't* made. Daily wished she could download what this man knew instantly, but his speech was slow.

"See . . . a few of us, his pals, we were all pretty intrigued when we heard that the first book was coming. *Mimic's Poison.* Scuttlebutt was that it was our guy telling the real stuff. Given what we heard he'd been up to, well, we were just surprised he'd be spilling, is all."

The Cyrus truck pulled away from her again and she jammed on the gas. "Go on."

"Next, there was all this fanfare in the newspapers here, where we're from, up by Banner Elk. That his story had been bought up by the movies. This one and a second book, too. And this was before the first book was even out, you see."

"I've heard it works that way sometimes."

"Well now, you can imagine how excited we all were to read it. 'Cept the books never came out. The first one or the second. I'd ordered twenty of *Mimic's Poison* alone, for the shop here, just given the rumors. That's a fair order 'round here. Simply never came out."

Daily hit the steering wheel in frustration. More something that ended in nothing, like so many other leads in this case. Her voice sank. "I appreciate your call and the background, Mr. Hibbs. Can I send you some money for your trouble?"

"Well, it's not all bad news and trouble."

Daily's heart torqued. "What do you mean?"

"There were some proofs, you see. Advance copies that get sent out for reviews and all that? Some of them had apparently already been printed at the time everything went belly-up. I'd been looking for these things for years, but I'd been told they were all destroyed. Then I found one copy at an estate sale. Critic died, and so I guess he never sent it back when the publisher requested it. Only copy I know of."

Daily checked her excitement. "Did Lathanore say why the book never came out?"

"That's the strange part. He died way too young. Heart attack in his sleep, or that's what they said, anyway. Damn cursed history, you ask me. Seems this book wasn't supposed to see the light of day. Guess the movies weren't either, from what I know now."

"You've read the proof?"

"I have."

"Is there . . . something about it?"

"It's not pretty, the things it says. But we've seen worse by now, in our books and movies. Guess it's right on par with your *Silence of the Lambs*, all that kind of thing. I think what makes it more disturbing is that it's true."

Stay calm. "Mr. Hibbs, I didn't expound on the email, but I'm a detective with the LAPD and this book may have something to do with a case. A homicide. If you'd be so kind as to send that proof to me, FedEx, I promise I'll ship it back to you as soon as I can. I'll also reimburse you for your time and consultation." Daily left out the part about her suspension.

His consideration seemed interminable. Finally, he said, "No need. You can send me a check for the overnight-service part, but consider the rest . . . just a debt I'm paying down the line."

"I'm not sure I understand."

He struggled with the words. "Sometimes, we don't all do the right things while we're here, you know. As we get older, we see what we could have done better, but there's no way to go back. So we leave some pieces of ourselves, some history instead. We hope that it might help someone down the line, going forward. Maybe that's the best we can do. Help people remember."

An odd sensation filled Daily—one that she didn't completely understand and wasn't sure she trusted fully. She gave Mr. Hibbs the address of a neighbor who could sign for her with Paulette out of town. Then she thought about how much Mike knew about her life, her phone calls, her secrets. "You're not worried about the conversation we just had on the phone?" she asked.

"We've been talking for less than four minutes and I'm on a se-cure line here. Ninety-eight percent secure. Encrypted anyway," Hibbs replied. "Your end, I can't speak for, so I hope you don't mind that I took some liberties with my own name and identity."

Solar-plexus hit number two. "You're not Fred Hibbs of North Carolina. And you don't just run a bookstore, do you?"

There was a smile in his voice. "I've been asked for this press proof more times than you can imagine, detective. I've never admitted that I have it until now."

"Why this time?"

"Received a call from a man I know. Name of Mike. A right good man. Heart's in the right place and he said yours is, too. I owed Mike a favor."

What the hell was going on? The Mike she'd been chasing was some-one who eluded the law, who worked his own system of justice, his own rules, his own punishments? Mike who terrified tyrants like Eddie Ealing, Harmon Whittsedge? Mike who threatened her best friend Paulette? Mike who cavalierly invaded her privacy, her com-puter and her own past with the virtual delivery at La Sera Groves? Then there was the Mike who'd warned her that Pavlov had been poi-soned in Paulette's absence, saving the dog. Now, here was Mike help-ing her find the story behind a book tied to Eddie Ealing, and possi-bly his killer. It didn't make sense. If he killed Eddie, why help her?

There were crosscurrents, two agendas. One trying to help Daily solve the case, one trying to prevent it, neither one wishing to be identified. She wanted to rip the skin off this damn thing, to get to the sinew and bones of it all. She hated the feeling that she was so ex-posed in the eyes of all-knowing forces while her own vision was blocked, her progress manipulated.

She slowed the Mustang for the *Winchester Canyon Road* exit and trailed the Cyrus truck as it turned in the direction of Temperel. Sparse traffic gave her less cover. The truck drove past the Temperel entrance, opting for a service road toward the back. She parked her car behind a hedge of oleander, then walked the far side of the service road, where the eucalyptus trees provided camouflage. Steadying herself against one, she watched the Temperel loading dock. Safford got out, stretched his legs, and lit a smoke. Pearson emerged from the driver's side, greeting some Temperel workers. They used a rolling ramp to remove one container from inside the truck, then replaced it with another from the loading dock. Safford climbed back into the truck as Pearson started it up again. Soon they were heading back down the service road.

Daily darted back to the Mustang. She thought she'd lost them until she saw the CS logo turning at an intersection ahead. The truck ambled for miles, past orchards and homes and eventually down toward the harbor. Traffic grew congested closer to the sea. They weren't going back to Cyrus. She followed them to Cabrillo Avenue, the road hugging the ocean. The truck had a hard time negotiating lane changes when they reached the tourist-heavy marina and Stearns Wharf, and Daily followed it into the lot. The Cyrus truck finally parked near a working ramp to the boats. She parked in the visitors' lot, between two SUVs.

When she was out of the car, she removed the bandana she'd donned as Cedella Rayborne, and pulled off the T-shirt. Underneath, she wore a black one-piece maillot along with running shorts. After adding a straw hat, she changed to bright, oversized sunglasses, making her look like a tourist strolling the marina, nothing more. She tossed her purse in the trunk and left the Mustang's windows open to keep the car cool; this would be a short stop. Her Swiss Army keychain went inside her shorts' velcro pocket so she wouldn't jangle as she walked. She watched Safford and Pearson greet two men at a boat down the ramp.

Some kind of sportfishing vessel, from the looks of it not as long or as nice as the Hornet humming past, but substantial. The boatmen had well-lined, sun-mottled skin. One had a large, crooked nose; the other had a big brown mole on his cheek. They rolled up the back of the now-unlocked Cyrus Services truck and whistled for a couple of their helpers to unload the container inside.

As she meandered between parked cars, Daily overheard Pearson say they were heading to Longboard's Grill to have a beer, adding that they would be back in twenty minutes to pick up the empty truck. Safford handed Mole an envelope, shook his hand, and they were off toward the wharf. Dozens of people walked the waterfront and the pier. No one cared about the metal container being loaded onto the fishing boat from the Cyrus Services truck. Scoping out her options, Daily approached from the far side of the dock. By the time she got there, the container was on the vessel, flush with the stern rail. Mole lifted the container hatch and looked inside. It said TOXIC WASTE, yet, with no glove on his hand, he reached in and moved things around. Couldn't be very toxic.

The men conversed in a language Daily didn't recognize. Mole gave two of his loaders some cash from his envelope, then made a comment that pried a laugh from all of them. The loaders walked to an '85 Toyota truck and drove away, leaving only Mole and Nose aboard. Safford and Pearson were off having lunch.

The vessel grew quiet. For a few minutes, Daily heard just the voices of tourists and demanding seagulls until the boat's motor choked and coughed to life. Mole and Nose spoke at the front of the boat, away from her. Mole, the man who seemed to be the boss, had looked into the metal container without hesitation. It would only take a second. Ten strides got her to the container. She peered in; cold hit her face. Ice? Dry ice? Smells she recognized but couldn't identify. Meat or fish, maybe both, and something else.

The boat's engine rose in pitch.

Hurry up, Daily.

She moved to the left, against the toxic markings on the outside. They had to be bluff symbols, cover for contraband, given Mole's actions. She lifted the metal hatch again. Glistening were light and dark shapes she couldn't identify. Cold blasted her once more. The boat bobbed as it lost its tether to the dock. *What the hell's in there?* Their backs turned, the two men were still at the front. Daily leaned farther inside. Her last chance to see. Something wet and shiny. Dark circles against something light, viscous.

Eyes.

Validation gripped her: if the person inside wasn't dead already, they'd been doped into a stupor. She pictured Alma Morada within, before she'd been hauled out to sea and dumped, her brain carved out for some unspeakable reason. Shoes still on the dock, Daily reached for the penlight on her key chain and shined it into the icy container. She was *sure* the person was a female. Something about the eyes.

The boat canted left and surged forward, pulling away. Daily grappled for balance on the sides of the five-foot square container, but it was too late, there was no longer anything beneath her feet. Pain shot through her arms as she struggled not to slip off the back of the boat. She had to know who was in the bin. Hoisting herself up, she dropped headfirst into the dense wetness of the box. A cold substance muffled her landing; at least she hadn't landed on the body inside. Finding a tentative footing on ice blocks that rimmed the container, she lifted the hatch and looked out. Water spanned between her and the dock. No way back that wasn't wet. Quickly, Daily turned and crouched so that only her tennis shoes were touching the ice blocks beneath her. It was fine, she told herself. The man on deck had reached in here with bare hands. It couldn't be harmful if he touched it without any protection. Every one of her senses was heightened.

The boat's speed increased. Daily set the hatch ajar to let in a crack of sunlight, enough for her to see. John Safford was definitely involved; now she just had to find out how far the web extended within Temperel. Dr. Ross managed the institute; she had to know. Maybe Doc, maybe the whole board. If the woman in this bin was still alive, Daily would try and revive her. If not, she would wait until the men weren't looking and drop off the boat, then swim to shore, call for assistance. They were still in the marina after all, not too far.

Stay calm.

Deep breaths. The crack of sunlight illuminated a thin slash of the bin's floor. She needed to see more. She pressed her penlight, shot the beam in the direction of the woman.

Jesus almighty.

Daily clamped her mouth to stop the retch. The eyes did not belong to a woman. They did not belong to a body. All around her, wrapped in soft containers, were brains.

Human brains. Animal brains.

The dark circles of hematomas had fooled her, mimicking the irises of eyes. They weren't eyes at all, they were dark, circular bruises of brain tissue surrounded by undamaged, pale tissue.

Daily fought to stay still. Rational. At the back, in something like a large Rubbermaid refrigerator container, were a dozen organs she couldn't identify because so many of them pushed against each other. Each brain had its own plastic "cell," wrapped separately. There were dozens of brains, packed in a liquid that tossed as the boat rode the water. Daily shuddered. Her own sight had tricked her. In her mind, she had seen eyes—they became a woman. Of course. Never would she have envisioned *this*. She grew lightheaded. The boat lurched over a swell and the metal lid of the container flew up and then down against the top of Daily's head before she realized what had hit her. As she dropped down in pain, she was no longer thinking about the abhorrent cargo that coddled her fall. She watched as the slash of sunlight above stippled to blackness.

FIFTY-FOUR

WHEN SHE CAME TO, Daily's hands pushed against the edge of the dark bin; her breath was the only thing she recognized. Aches seeped from her skull into her spine. She remembered the two men on the boat. The engine was quiet—the vessel was floating now. No footsteps, only wind and the groaning sea swells. She had no idea how long she'd been unconscious, no idea how far the boat had traveled. If Mole and Nose were aboard, they were quiet. She stood to take a look out the hatch but her tennis shoes slipped on the melting ice and softening organs and she fell. She stifled a moan. The air in the bin was growing tepid and foul; it took everything she had not to lose her stomach. She reminded herself that she had seen these same body parts and organs a hundred times at autopsies.

When you're in control, eh?

She heard Pierce's taunts in her head. This case was doing her in, suspending her senses and her career. All her bullshit about being so smart, so organized, so on top of her game—it was all a crock, a ruse to cover the utter lack of sense she had about anything in this Godforsaken world. She had no clue. Laughter echoed in her memory, uncertainty throttled her. She was a girl again, and she could feel her sister's hands pushing her head under the waves, where she couldn't breathe. Gagging, she put her head between her knees until the nausea subsided. She shook and wondered if she was indeed going crazy, or having a nervous breakdown. She almost wished it would happen, then maybe she could see it all from the inside—she would finally understand what it meant to burn with the conviction of insanity. To hell with divining right and wrong; screw the Byzantine maze called justice. Where had it gotten her? Suspended. After the BOI hearings and the secrets and the press rakings, everyone would know the truth. She wasn't the steely detective with the stellar record the department liked to tout. No, inside, she was a quivering mass of lies. She was a scared little girl with no answers, who to this day couldn't decide if her own hand helped steer God's the day her sister died.

Tears dripped into her open mouth now and only the most primal survival instinct prevented her from crying out in anguish. Stuck in this abominable tin of freight, her mind was crumbling. *Box of Truth, indeed.* All her analyses, her attempts at insight and logic and control led her to this moment where there was no truth, just the never-ending collisions of chance and the inexplicable horrors of humanity. How arrogant of her to think she could control any of it. Time and memory and sickness hit her, and she simply wanted to fall unconscious and die.

Alma Morada's image loomed in her mind and wouldn't leave. Daily had never even met her, but by all accounts she'd been a vital, happy spirit. A damn maintenance worker, yet cheerfully, beautifully, she sang, they said. Again, Daily looked at the clear containers of liquid and organs surrounding her. When she'd first peered into the bin, her mind saw eyes. Female eyes, for some reason. They weren't the eyes of her dead sister, laughing at her; not this time. Instead, she'd seen the eyes of a helpless victim, pleading with her from beyond life, asking her to make things right. She thought of John Safford and his cronies slaying Alma, cutting her head open and removing her brain. For what possible reason? Who were these human beings, now surrounding her in pieces; who had they been? How had they become innocent victims of such a warped agenda?

She wiped her face and her eyes, cleared her head and heart of self-pity and despair. In their place she directed all her anger, pushing it and concentrating it into a white-hot point of clarity. She couldn't let Alma Morada die for nothing; there had to be something left behind that stood for her soul, something good. The devil's logic twisted her mind: *there is no justice, there is no good.* But what Daily couldn't see for herself, she could see for Alma Morada. She wasn't going to let an innocent go down for something wicked. Not without a fight. Even if it was only in memory of Alma, she owed it to her.

She found footing, slipped once more, then tried again. Slowly, she lifted the hatch with her throbbing head. The fresh air braced her. Against the late sun, she saw the man with the crooked nose looking out to sea. From the first few lights of the shore and the size of the buildings in the distance, Daily guessed they were about three miles from land. The boat was positioned in a vector between two of the offshore oil derricks.

She couldn't see the other man, the guy with the mole. In the distance, she heard a motor, a powerful and rapid crescendo. Nose appeared right next to her bin, the bulge of a gun in his pants. Daily dropped down inside. The two men spoke to each other as the sound approached. She had to get out of there. Daily peeked again, fixed on the men. They both stood at the front of the boat, awaiting the arrival of a vessel with jet engine lungs. As it neared and drowned out all noise, Daily found her ballast, pulled herself from the bin, stepped onto the stern rail and dropped into the Pacific.

As she swam, Daily didn't look back. Under the surface, she pulled strong and straight to get out of their sight. Later, when she was tired, she could slap at the waves. She tried to forget she was out at sea, where terror of the void swelled under her. She forced herself to imagine that she was in the clear waters of her pool, just doing her laps.

She would be fine.

Just three miles.

She ran that distance four times a week, at least. She tried not to think about how deep the ocean was, or what creatures lurked beyond her vision. A cramp of anxiety tugged at her, but she had to keep going. Now away from the boat, she reached underwater and removed her tennis shoes, letting them go. A swell blindsided her and she swallowed water. Treading as she cleared her throat, she struggled to take off her sodden socks. A pair of her favorites—red bird dogs chasing flying fish—but this was no time for sentimentality. Something hit her foot. Hard. She turned in the water, looked around. Just the sea. Again she reached down and felt a force knock against her legs. She stopped moving and let her limbs hang in the ocean against every contrary instinct pulling at her. Motion would attract attention. She turned so that her feet were in the shadow of her torso, their colors unlit by the departing sun. After an eternity of waiting to her hammering heartbeat, she slowly slid her socks off and tossed them as far as she could. They slapped onto the sea surface. Not ten seconds later, there was a snap in the water and one was gone. The other bright sock twisted and undulated in the ocean. A flash of something moved it away from her.

Daily turned and looked to shore.

Just three miles.

She could do it. She was sure of it.

———————

"Mom, look! There's a lady coming out of the water in her shorts and she looks like shit!"

The mother on the twilight beach wasn't as concerned with Daily's appearance as she was with her boy's foul mouth. Her spanking and his howls of protest seemed like distant echoes in Daily's dazed brain as she trudged from the break.

Across Cabrillo Avenue, the lights of a hotel glowed a warm gold, but they were spinning. Daily dropped to the sand and rolled onto her back, staring up at the sky and thanking the first star she saw. It was most certainly an angel. Her lungs were raw. The swim had nearly killed her, and she couldn't even remember it—the entire crawl was a blur. The water had been colder and more turbulent than she'd expected. The swells became onslaughts as her resistance had waned. Not that she'd had much choice. The numbness in her legs and arms ebbed to a cold burn. When her head finally stopped spinning, she realized there was a great deal she needed to tell someone.

———————

Back at her Mustang, she blessed her Swiss Army key chain—it was still in her pocket. She opened the car trunk, removed her purse, threw her beach towel around herself and dried off.

The inside of her car never felt so reassuring. Daily found her cell phone and composed her thoughts. What would she say to Lieutenant Powell, to Nestor? She had to get it right. Letting the engine warm, she turned the heater to high, to thaw the chill that had seeped into her bones during the swim. Crazy, needing the heater in the middle of July.

It hit her. The cafeteria. The hot tea.

Peter.

She looked out toward the darkening horizon and the silhouettes of the offshore oil derricks, the lights on them starting their burn for the night.

"Peter was cold," she said aloud. "He was drinking hot tea because he was cold. Peter was out there yesterday."

"Yes, he was," said the voice behind her.

Daily felt the barrel of a gun against her head. She looked into the rearview mirror and saw Burg.

———————

He forced her to down a quart of orange juice, a large 7-11 coffee and an Italian sausage sandwich. Finally, Burg insisted that Daily eat a pack of small powdered donuts. Keeping the gun in his free hand, he finished off a pack himself. Her trepidation mixed with confusion as the coffee warmed her and the food replaced the pang in her belly. After the last twenty-four hours, Daily was convinced there was more than one Mike, more than one agenda. If Burg was Mike, or one of two Mikes, if he was planning to harm her, then why *feed* her? His sparse directions told her only to drive the 101 south. Thirty minutes later, with the hulking backs of the Santa Ynez Mountains and La Conchita nudging the water's edge, he spoke.

"Sorry, Daily. Couldn't talk until we got here. Take the next exit. There's a dead spot in the grid."

"What grid?"

"*The* grid. Just take the exit. Pull in there, next to that banana tree farm. Park at the far end of the lot."

Daily turned the Mustang onto the dark road, remembering the grove of banana trees tucked in the elbow of the mountain range, a small jungle that didn't belong in this stern patch of the California coast. Burg told her to shut off the ignition and get out. She heard the occasional car blaze the highway, the sounds of the sea and the breeze rustling hundreds of banana leaves. In the wind-whipped moonlight, dense bunches of green fruit swayed. Burg led her up an incline, toward a spot beneath two power poles. The gravel protested their steps and trunks of current hummed above them. Daily's eyes fixed on the Glock automatic in Burg's hand. A nine.

"Why here?" she asked.

He looked up at the power lines. "Screws surveillance. Static privacy."

"The power grid?"

"The information grid." He noticed Daily's look. "I'm not some kook. I've worked for them."

"Who—"

"The people who firewall—hell, the people who *monitor* information."

She swallowed the bolus of fear in her throat. Before she asked what his last comment had to do with Eddie Ealing, Mike's Gifts or Temperel, she contemplated his sanity. If he wasn't insane, a host of things made sudden sense—from people hacking her laptop, to the LAPD's atypical handling of the case, to the news leaks. If he was psychotic, he was one of life's brilliant lunatics who could play at sane and pull it off, the sort of manipulative deviant who would feed her before he eviscerated her. Either way, she had to take him seriously.

"Don't gauge how to play me; you know I didn't kill Eddie," Burg said. "They'll do anything to nail me for it—it solves their last problem. They don't want us teaming up, comparing notes."

"'They' meaning Temperel and Cyrus and Safford and whoever else is involved in those abominable shipments?"

"Yes."

"So they're removing brains, doing some kind of monstrous experiments or conducting black-market transactions. It doesn't jibe with any one of them arranging Eddie's murder. Temperel doesn't benefit from his death; he dies, they lose control of the operation. An outside partner comes in—a hostile one. A clean one."

Burg shook his head. "They're setting it up to look as if *Eddie* killed Alma, and they're setting me up for Eddie's death. If Eddie committed felony murder, his will is null and void, his assets are seized and the family—Doc and Peter—regain Eddie's votes. Temperel keeps control."

If Burg wasn't in with Safford, Cyrus, or Temperel, then he was working at cross-purposes with them—the crosscurrents Daily had felt, the two agendas.

Some aspects obsessive. Careful. Others screaming impulse. Mess.
Burg could be a magnificent liar.
Certain things matching. Certain things missing. Contradictions.
Two killers? One killer with two minds?

Questions screamed in her head. "Which one of them killed Eddie?"

"I'm not sure—yet. Eddie gave Temperel an ultimatum. Let a clean partner come in and take over, or he was going to the media about what they're doing. Extended research on unsuspecting subjects. Chemical tests on new substances and enhancements. Not exactly approved, not exactly using the proper protocols or channels."

"Not exactly memory research."

"Every bit memory research. It's what information's all about," Burg said too sharply. "The human CPU, the master hard drive, our precious gray matter. Hack into that with the right juice and the right conditioning, it's an all-access pass to someone's entire life."

"You think they're all involved?"

"Maybe, maybe not. It only takes one."

Almost the same words Doc had used in the hallway the day before. "If you don't know for sure, then why are they worried about us comparing notes? Sounds like you don't have anything to compare."

"I have plenty, and so did Eddie. It's why he's dead."

"You're Mike."

Burg's eyes flickered. "No."

"Who is, then?"

He didn't answer. What was it he'd said? Who he worked for? *The people who monitor information.*

"Your people don't want them to have that kind of access to memories. What is it, some government thing? Is Mike a code word for some operation? You don't walk, talk, or look like a feeb, Burg. You freelance?"

"You could say that. Now."

"Stop with the cryptic comments and give me some clarity. If you're not insane, you're doing a lousy job of convincing me otherwise."

The Glock punctuated his anger. "*I* warned you about the dog. *I'm* the one making sure you get the only remaining copy of a certain incendiary manuscript written by an ex-intelligence operative. *I'm* the one giving you pieces you didn't know about Eddie. I'm the one trying to help you here."

Daily searched for the rapid blinking, the sporadic darting of the eyes that rode the paranoids. Maybe he was going to bring out his foil hat and his bent-hanger antenna. Instead, she saw nothing but will and intelligence. "You didn't answer my question."

"I can't get into details. It's what has to be done. Eddie tried to stop it and it killed him. Someone has to finish the job. It can't be me, not directly. I can only help."

He was buying time, hedging on straight answers and she wasn't sure why. He seemed torn—wanting to tell her something, while honoring some other obligation. Choices seemed to be ripping at him.

She said, "If they wanted to solve the Eddie problem, there were easier ways to do it. They want a felony situation, why not nail him with a gunshot, frame him in a drug deal gone bad. Create a mess with

370

a dead prostitute and a stiletto. What happened on Mulholland was hard. It was messy. It was *no* perfect murder."

"No kidding. That's why we have to share everything. Every fact. Every hunch."

She chortled. Why should she trust him?

"You have to trust me." His eyes ached with a private grief.

A weird sensation filled her, but it wasn't a bad one. "For some inexplicable reason that goes against every ounce of logic—"

"Bullshit," he said. "At a level below consciousness, you've compiled a billion different bits of data about me and the situation. Maybe you can't articulate it, but it's the most powerful thing you have going for you. If you listen to it."

"I'm listening."

His breaths were heavy. He didn't seem unstable, but if he were psychotic, the shift in his mood would be sudden and unexpected— she knew all too well from the years with her sister. She felt for the cell phone she'd placed in her shorts, found it, and moved her finger to Nestor's one-touch number; she wanted someone to hear what was happening. She coughed to cover any sound her phone might make.

"I wouldn't call Nestor just yet," Burg said.

Daily's hand jerked and she dropped the phone to the gravel.

He raised his gun arm. "It's what I'd do, too, but only if it got ugly here, which it won't. Besides, I just told you, this is one of the few dead zones on the Pacific coast."

"If we're being so friendly and trusting, get that Glock out of my face."

"Insurance. Until I'm sure I have your word. You'd like nothing more then to regain your reputation, and I don't feel like being the bait. There's a bigger picture here."

"My *word*?"

"Yes. I'll trust your word."

She would have laughed if it weren't so absurd. "Doesn't mean a thing anymore."

"It means something to me."

"Big of you. I don't even know who in the hell *you* are." He was still behind the gun. "Fine," she said. "I give you my word. Not that it matters; there's an APB out."

"C'mon, Daily, I'm not going to leave Mike's Gifts evidence sitting around my place with a bunch of Eddie Ealing clippings, for God's sake. How staged." He dropped the Glock to his side.

"Then tell me what went down between Eddie and Temperel. Exactly. And tell me why you're involved."

The wind seemed to sigh with him. "Eddie knew, saw, and learned too much. He didn't have Peter's IQ, but he was an amazing study. The guy could read something, hear something, and it was there— like a copy burned on his brain. He was a master at recycling it, using it, playing it to his advantage."

"Dr. Ross said Eddie was thick."

"Wrong point of view. He was repeating questions to nail the fine points. Check out any Ealing film, the details are pristine. Not like *RoboCop*, where the setting is Detroit but they're using California codes on the police radios."

Daily chuffed; he was right. Burg had said he was connected to Eddie—who knew Burg as . . . what? Her memory rifled Eddie's films . . . the key characters . . . *a loner . . . a down-and-out musician . . . an NSA agent . . .* It slammed into Daily. *The details are pristine.*

"You work for the NSA—"

Burg hesitated. "I work for different people."

"You said you *worked* for the people that monitor information. Past tense."

"Everything's changed." Burg shifted his weight. Two long breaths, then a rapid-fire credo shot from his mouth, as if recited a hundred times before: "'*Information superiority is the capability to collect, process, and disseminate an uninterrupted flow of information while exploiting or denying an adversary's ability to do the same.*' That string of rhetoric is the NSA's 'Joint Vision for 2010.'" He chortled. "But you know what else it is? It's the operating philosophy for every one of the world's biggest information technology corporations, the new media conglomerates, even your damn cell phone provider, now that they're delivering everything from real-time stock quotes, pizza, and music downloads to you, Helena Saggeza Daily, thirty-three, of Hermosa Beach, California."

"So it's a little 'Big Brother' out there . . ."

Burg howled. "Big Brother came and left the building before we were *born*. No such thing as privacy anymore." He waved his free hand at the sky, his laugh bitter. "We got a damn satellite parking lot over the equator, it's so congested now. Thirty-eight more satellites still waiting to be launched, and that's just from one private company. From Hong Kong to the Cayman Islands, they're sending more of the pups up, so they can rent space or resell data packages and information. Those are business terms, man, not spook talk. Terms of commerce and trade. Never mind all the unrented space funded by those ventures that aren't quite making projections right now. That means Deals. Unused Inventory. Bargains."

A dread crept into Daily. Whatever remnants of privacy she thought she still had, Burg had just ripped away. He sounded more outraged than crazy.

"The NSA? The government? World leaders? Please. You got Malaysia and Indonesia launching their own satellites in the interest of 'informing their people.' A TV in every home from Bali to Bandung.

And here, Uncle Sam's right in there with them. Any transmission or sound that comes out of a mouth, a body, a phone, a wire, a cell, or a groundhog's asshole can be tracked . . . no brainer. I've worked for the whole gamut of them. People can now see and hear all, just like God. Problem is, they make all-too-human judgments about others. That's why real memories and the truth are more important than ever."

The hatred she had toward those above the law shot through her and erupted.

"Ah, truth. It's okay to watch anything—listen to anybody—in search of *your* truth?"

"On the contrary." Burg's words burned. "When the whole world's a stage, all you have are more actors, not more truth."

FIFTY-FIVE

PAULETTE HAD BEEN TRYING Lane for the last few hours with no luck. She tossed and turned. A sick fear kept her awake, not the sounds of Manhattan. Someone hadn't thought twice about trying to poison her. About trying to kill her. No one was trying to kill Kelly Spreck or Gozman, so it wasn't just about the media coverage.

Why couldn't she find Lane?

Paulette worried she might do something headstrong after being suspended. *Lane Daily suspended*, of all things. For Lane, her reputation and her job were her life. When Paulette was counseling her through divorce, she'd known Lane was holding back something. Powerful and potent, it demonized Lane as much as it drove her, but she wouldn't acknowledge it. She had never divulged it, not then, and not since they'd moved on to friendship. Paulette worried about its silent metastasis, something so virulent, suppressed for years. She occasionally caught glimpses of Lane's rage, and the triggers always surprised Paulette. Violence didn't affect Lane nearly as much as passivity over its damage; criminals didn't rile Lane nearly as much as those in power who looked the other way over illegalities. And though she still didn't know what it was, Paulette was worried that one day Lane's demon was going to explode inside her. She only hoped it didn't kill her in the process.

FIFTY-SIX

Furious at Burg's words, Daily crossed her arms and covered herself. *I only watch what needs watching.* Her cheeks burned as she wondered how much he'd seen. "You were the man on the beach. Two nights ago."

"That was Safford. I was watching him. He'd been watching and listening to you."

"The surfer in the window across the street, last night."

Burg's eyes flickered. "I was the bitchy girlfriend. I do a great bitchy."

"Why is the NSA monitoring Temperel?"

"I didn't say it was the NSA."

"You didn't say it wasn't. God almighty, you people think you can do anything in the name of intelligence—"

Burg howled. "You really are a Girl Scout under all that attitude, aren't you? The government doesn't give a shit that you shower twice a day and brush your teeth five. Or that Burns refers to your lieutenant as 'that Negro' when he's alone with his family. What bureaucratic clusterfuck could possibly keep up with the free market? Your grocery store, your credit card and cable companies know more about you than the NSA, the CIA, the FBI combined, with a fraction of the legal restrictions placed on intelligence or law enforcement."

Daily felt small and bare.

"No contest. The government doesn't have the latest or the greatest anymore. They've got one tool left. Exposure. As long as there are taxes and crimes, licenses and fines, they can decide when, where and how to give somebody a hard time. On that front, people still have to play ball. Make deals. Trade-offs."

"Sales spikes on Baggie scans as DEA tip-offs? Someone's too-blue Tivo selection?"

"Laugh all you want."

Daily heard a series of waves break on the rocks across the highway. "You're avoiding my question. Why is the NSA monitoring Temperel?"

"I didn't say it was the—"

"Fine," she snapped. "Let's say, theoretically, *some* government intelligence operation was watching Temperel. Why?"

"It's not simple. About the time you and I were born, some people saw what was going to happen. As technology raced ahead, more firewalls would be needed to protect information. But the smart ones knew that technology would soon outpace the control systems. Then, look out—one giant info swap meet. Access to information on anybody, anywhere, for the right deal. These people I mentioned—major players in world politics, big business—returned to the least corruptible of all transactions. Agreements made only on handshakes and memory, with, say, one impeccably-vetted witness on each side. The deals are made silently or out of context. A harmless discussion about a fine meal, a certain piece of art. No records. Just *memory.* The terms of those deals can never be exposed in any written, wired, or electronic manner."

"It means people can forget they ever made those deals."

Burg looked at her with startling intensity. "Not these people. Not these stakes. If any of these deals come apart, it's only with the understanding and blessing of both sides. That's how important they are."

"How do you know?"

"I worked for one of those men."

"You still work for him?"

After a long moment, Burg shook his head. "I failed him." He agitated gravel, kicked a rock into the night. "It was my job to be vigilant. To pay attention, never let my guard down. I was tired. I failed him in the worst way possible, and I'll never forgive myself." It was clear he wasn't going to tell her the man's name.

"Did he die?"

"Depends what you mean by death." Burg's breath quickened, his eyes were moist. "My failure impacted other things down the line. There, plenty of people died."

"Was he 'Mike'?"

"Mike is bigger than any one person. When you get the galley proof of the book, you'll understand."

"Why must everything be so damned cryptic? Just tell me—"

"—In 1989, I was still assigned to the man I mentioned. Years ago, there'd been an operation called Mike's Gifts in intelligence, the original MIKE, an acronym, not a person. It was tucked away, no longer in use. My boss called, said he'd received word that someone was out there sending new deliveries called 'Mike's Gifts.' A copycat. The fact that someone was using that name was trouble. It meant they knew about the original. Nothing serious in the gifts themselves. It was the Christmas trees on the lawn thing. The house of that jerk who wouldn't give people a Christmas holiday."

"Could have been coincidence. The Mike's Gifts cards came from stationery catalogs."

"It wasn't the name; it was someone else using *the method*. It's not about the contents, Daily. Mike's Gifts is a Rorschach test for the soul. It's a way of finding out if someone has a *memory* of an incident or not. A guilty conscience or not. Harmon Whittsedge sees his message, most people see a pink bathing suit from 1972. But Harmon Whittsedge sees the cabaña girl who wore it. The one he impregnated and strangled when she threatened to tell his conservative and extremely pious wife of forty years about their baby. One she never would have aborted had she not been killed. Mrs. Whittsedge put the seed money in that marriage, you see, not Harmon. He gets all the fanfare, but it's the little lady's empire."

Daily's ribs tightened. "That bathing suit was for Harmon Whittsedge. But the NO DIVING sign was for me."

"The story of Mike's Gifts is out there now—in Goddamn wide release. Whoever sent the sign knows about you, they're trying to manipulate you and blame it on 'Mike.' I think it came from Temperel."

"How did you know what the bathing suit in the message looked like?"

"I watched you open the video message."

The flash of blond hair in the groves. The feeling that someone was watching her. "You said in '89—"

"We were trying to track who was using the Mike's Gifts angle, sending the pranks, but more importantly, trying to find out how he even knew about the original operation in the first place. We might have never known—until he got tired of his own private game and decided to option the story and make a film out of it. With his ego, his stones, he made the announcement to *Variety* and *The Hollywood Reporter* before he'd even found out that the thirty-year-old book was not only out of print, it had been erased from existence."

The blood left her head. "*Mimic's Poison*. Eddie Ealing was sending the gifts. Eddie was Mike Number Two."

"Eddie had heard of the original operation somehow. Given that the book never made it to market, there were only a few people who knew of it. We ran traces for years, no luck. Got to hand it to him—if he hadn't tired of playing Mike, if he'd never made the announcement to the trades about his new film, we might have never found him. He was a very good Mike."

"Why couldn't the book come out?"

"It would have eroded our ability to do our own work."

"It was fiction—"

"It was all too real." Burg paused. "You know how many novels have been locked away because they're too close for comfort? Because someone buys them *off* the market? There are writers and geniuses out there, some of them literally out of their minds, who've either created crimes too sick or too perfect. Some people don't want them to see the light of day. Then, there are the true stories—the one that are called fiction because they're too heinous; no one would believe them. *Mimic's Poison* was one of those. If Eddie made that film, it would expose a program that was too important to national security. To our firewall. Years ago, the original book was killed by the people in charge. When the copycat Mike's Gifts began in '89, word slipped up to my boss. The project was intact from the old angles; we couldn't find any leaks. Most of the original people were dead, and don't give me that 'we-knocked-them-off' look, Daily. They died because they were old."

"I didn't say a thing. Go on."

"I'd been working for ten years trying to find out who the new Mike was, and how he knew about Mike's Gifts in the first place. A couple years ago, Eddie's press announcement led us to him. He never copped to it and we couldn't prove it, but it fit. Everything he'd ever done under the guise of Mike's Gifts was legal, mind you; he was just messing with assholes, and no one at the agen—on the inside—felt too bad about that. My new boss made an agreement with Eddie:

he would never make the film, never discuss the contents of the story or its topics again. He was well-compensated for his cooperation, and he kept his end of the bargain until he died."

Daily's thoughts tossed. "Then why did he die?"

"Keeping tabs on Eddie was my assignment, something we do after deals are struck. Everything was copacetic until Eddie started working on kuru. Eddie was the ultimate quick study, but he couldn't think up an original idea if his life depended on it. That meant the kuru notion had come to him from somewhere else. The disease has been all but eradicated, so if Eddie was getting all worked up about it, it meant he had seen it or heard about something new with it. And given what kuru is, I assumed—"

"That Eddie heard about it at Temperel. Why didn't you just ask him about it?"

"He didn't know about me. My job was to keep an eye on Eddie, not to blow my cover. He only communicated with my boss in preordained ways. Eddie's brainchild for the kuru project came from something he saw or heard about at Temperel; that sent up a flare. I signed up, got in as a subject, worked my way through the system there. At first I couldn't trace it. There was no active work on kuru anywhere at the institute. Everything seemed legit, from the labs to the certifications to the protocols. There was the GHB problem, but they got rid of the jerks. Someone was messing with the food later this year, animal activists; they changed suppliers, reworked the menus and food system."

She said, "Now the food comes from Cyrus Services. I was there today. Pretended I was someone like Alma, from another country—Jamaica. Told them I was just checking into openings, didn't even have ID, but they whisked me into an interview and lab work before I could finish saying 'student visa.' That's when I got curious."

Burg's eyes widened.

"I looked around and ended up in the warehouse. Saw Safford there. He was tense over a shipment on a Cyrus truck, rode with it back to Temperel, stayed with it when they made an exchange of containers. They took it out to sea, and they were hooking up with another boat. They're shipping organs in the containers, at least in the one I was in—"

Burg cursed. "Safford's getting bold. I've never seen him interface directly with the Cyrus people like that. He and Peter have been meeting down at the harbor; they've been taking low-life charters out. But if Safford was actually riding in one of the Cyrus trucks, he's worried about the cargo. They're moving things quickly, getting them away from where they can be found or traced."

"Are they dumping the brains and organs?"

"No. Incineration would be easier. It's what we do with the parts and collateral at the labs. Incinerator's right there."

The same sick feeling she'd had on the boat came over her again. "Was Alma Morada shipped out in one of those containers?"

"Do I have proof? No. Do I think so?" He nodded sadly. His eyes fixed on a star above the banana trees. "Alma was fragile, you know? She was the type that would apologize if you bumped into her. But God, what a voice." Burg hummed the arpeggio of notes that Peter had played on the piano.

Shivers shot up Daily's spine. "That song—"

"The melody Alma used to sing while she cleaned. Eddie heard it one day, and suddenly he was very interested in talking to her. He couldn't move fast enough. He spent an hour with her that night, after work, taking her out for a glass of wine, just listening to her talk. Sing-talk, that way she did."

"You joined them?"

The wind shot through Burg's hair and he took a long breath. "I watched from a distance. Things moved quickly. Ealing was laying it on thick, like he did with the women he chased for sex, but this was business. A wonderful new talent dropped in his path. He set her up with some cash, a place, got her new clothes, told her to keep working at Temperel like nothing had changed. Privately, he arranged some gigs in out-of-the-way places, to help her hone her voice. I went a couple times. She was dazzled by all his promises: record deal this, tour that. When he felt she was ready, he had her lay down some tracks at remote studios. Didn't want anyone poaching his new discovery."

"I called dozens of recording studios—"

"Eddie booked under false names, and used enough money that folks weren't going to talk. Not even to the LAPD." Burg cleared his throat. "At one studio up in Ojai, Alma's memory failed. First it was just a few times a session, then it screamed downhill."

A bitter taste filled her mouth. "Alma was barely out of her teens."

"According to one engineer that hung around the local bar and told his Scotch about it, Eddie couldn't figure it out either. One time, the 'new singer' forgot her name. Another time, the 'new singer' forgot where she was."

"You think Alma was drugged?"

"No. And I don't think she had Alzheimer's. Not at that age."

The sick implication hit Daily. "Kuru causes dementia—but you have to eat the brains of the infected person, or it has to be injected directly into one's brain. You can't catch it like a virus or a bacterial infection. Alma wasn't eating brains—"

"Not knowingly. But the maintenance workers got a free lunch, provided by Temperel each day they worked there. We know Cyrus Services was up to a lot more than maintenance and food supply. The food scare—the bleeding hearts—it's all theater. Something to fall back on. They can blame it on an animal activist who 'infiltrated' Cyrus."

It made perfect sense. It gave Temperel the ideal alibi, distancing them for any abhorrent act they might be accused of. A fictional bunch of kooks as a cover for something dreadful. Some kind of research or science that wasn't legal, wasn't sanctioned, wasn't ethical. Daily's heart ached for the young woman who had been drawn into the institute's sick experiments. And she was just one . . . how many others were there?

"Did Alma know she was losing her memory?" Daily asked.

"No. She was giddy, happier than ever, when she wasn't forgetting what day it was. Eddie seemed to care more than she did."

"And then she was gone."

Burg nodded. "Yes. And then she was gone."

FIFTY-SEVEN

DAILY SAID TO BURG, "Tell me what you know about the night of May twenty-second, after the board meeting, Alma was supposed to go to the Santa Donia Amphitheatre with Eddie. The Liara concert."

"She worked the day shift, got fuzzy toward quitting time. It was as if she had forgotten that she'd just worked one shift and started another. She washed the same counters again, mopped the same places on the floor. I didn't see her after she left LAB A that day. Her name was paged on the intercom. She smiled and walked down the hall, in the direction of the cafeteria and the maintenance locker room.

"A while later, Eddie came through in a storm. He never found Alma, but ran into Peter instead, started going off at him, saying, 'Where is she? You mess with her like you messed with mom?' Stuff like that. Couldn't hear everything, but words like *suicidal* were thrown around. I thought they were talking about Temperel's future, not Alma's. Then Peter and Doc took Eddie into the conference room. I couldn't stick around; I bumped into Karen who was eavesdropping more blatantly. I waited outside where I could watch Eddie's Jag. He came out of the institute steamed, but his eyes were wet. The great and ferocious Eddie Ealing had been crying. I never saw Alma Morada again, and neither did he."

The knowledge made her short of breath. Testing unwitting subjects with kuru, then disposing of them. But another option screamed at her. "What if it's the other way around?"

"What do you mean?"

"At Cyrus today, I met a woman who had ovarian cancer. She's terminal, but they'd signed her up for a job. She said it was one of the few places that people like her could find work."

Burg's face grew somber. "Use people who are dying already?"

"The competition's breathing down Temperel's neck, Peter said. Maybe it's time to find out if TR-4 works in human trials or not. Use human guinea pigs who will never complain, because they're immigrants or illegals that have something to hide. Some eat placebos, some eat trial drugs. Neither group ever knows. Big upside, no downside." She watched Burg pale. Thoughts of crawling among the brains sent an involuntary spasm through Daily. "Nothing happens at Temperel without Dr. Ross controlling it, right? She even tells Peter what to do. That means he's involved, even if she's manipulating it."

Burg said, "I can't tell if he's just protecting the family and Temperel, or if he's integral to it, but he's been out on the ocean with Safford the past couple days. Maybe he's just upset about Eddie's murder, and Safford's under orders from Doc to keep him quiet. Then again, maybe Peter's behind the whole thing."

Clarity buzzed through her. "If Safford's that deep in, Doc has to be. You said your people can hear every transmission or sound that comes out of 'a mouth, a body, a phone, a wire, a cell, or a groundhog's asshole . . .' so why don't you just arrest them?"

"What I know was acquired using means that don't exactly meet your DA's standards for admissibility. We need more."

"Did you send Eddie the gift message with the heart and Alma's photo?"

Burg smiled. "Eddie sent it to himself. He knew Helmy Ulgrod read through his calendar and all the messages in his in-box. It was his own test to see if Helmy was loyal, if he knew anything about Alma Morada. No calls to Doc or Temperel, no suspicious behavior."

"But when the news hit that Eddie had received a delivery from Mike's Gifts, it meant that Eddie's killer had to look at the possibility of a Mike who also knew about Alma Morada."

"And the people who want to find Mike have been using the process of elimination. There's rewards. It's a witch hunt. Someone gathering as much info on Mike as possible to find out what 'he' knows about the Temperel problem. About Eddie's death. About Alma Morada." The gun was still in Burg's hand, now dropped at his side. "The Temperel people *need* Eddie to be Alma's killer, which solves the problem of the will. They *need* me to be the loose screw that infiltrated Temperel, fell in love with Alma, and killed Eddie. It all keeps the integrity of their precious research institute above question."

"Why aren't you a thousand miles from here?"

"You." Burg's voice was intense and low. "You don't go with the flow. You're willing to fight, to dig out the truth, even if it's uncomfortable. What really happened deserves to come out. I'm taking a chance."

With a warm grip, Burg handed her an odd-looking cell phone, not like any commercial model she had ever seen.

He said, "Stop using your regular phone to call anyone. I was trying to tell you that in the hallway the other day, to stop using your cell. Use this one instead, and only where you can't be overheard. It encrypts better than anything." He hit function keys so quickly she couldn't follow them. "This direct dial key—seven—is good for the next twenty-four hours. Seven reaches me and me only. You may not hear me say anything, but I'm there. I've got your back, and I'll be with you all the way. I'm taking a leap of faith, and I never trust any-one. Just like you."

That remark hit her harder than anything else Burg had said. Her eyes stung as she thought of her sister. "You must have a hunch," she said. "About how this actually went down. About which one of them killed Eddie."

Burg didn't answer. Instead, he said, "You need to call that nice vet and tell him you're coming to pick up Pavlov."

"We were talking about the murderer." As she watched him listen to the ocean, she wondered if she was wrong again. If she was a fool, once more trusting someone she shouldn't, betting on insanity.

"That's a good dog, Daily. One good dog." Preoccupied, Burg walked toward the highway.

"You must have a hunch," she started after him. "An idea . . . "

Daily watched Burg pace toward the road through the grove of fruit trees. A VW van pulled past. She heard it brake and idle behind a thick row of plants. A large truck sped past on the highway, its tires kicking up gravel and dust. Daily covered her face.

"Burg?" she called as she arrived at the front of the empty lot.

She waited for his reply and got none.

FIFTY-EIGHT

In spite of Tee's prayers, Jay had died a long and painful death in that hellhole of a jungle in a part of a stepchild war that no branch of the military and no government would ever embrace. Jay would never get any acknowledgment. Tee was left with only memories.

The horrors.

Back in the US, he had thought maybe the nightmares would finally stop. But the smell of cooking meat still made him sick. The sight of children and babies sent him into tears or mania. People treated him as if he was crazy, and no one would hire him, not the military nor the police, not even the departments in second-rate suburbs. Some security companies were intrigued by his extensive knowledge of surveillance and new technologies, but they always balked after the second interview. He got impatient, lost his cool on the inane personality profile questions. He'd be damned if he was going to be some minimum wage rent-a-cop, anyway. He had to do something. He had Jay's ID. He was planning to take it to Jay's one living "relative"—an elderly foster mother, to tell her he had died an honorable death, serving . . . whom?

For what? There were no records. They were the government's ghosts, its nasty secrets.

She would ask, *How did he die?*

Tee knew he could never tell her. It would be better to leave her alone, let her wonder. Let her mind paint heroic masterpieces of her lost soldier until her own passing. Christ, the sad reality was all his fault. Maybe that first Navy psychiatrist had been right. Tee wasn't wired for service. He'd gone the private-contractor route, sure he would prove them all wrong, and look what had happened. He'd choked and now Jay was dead because of it. There'd been only one choice.

That brain of a guy he'd met as a kid at summer camp, now working on the new stuff with memory at the U. He was easy enough to find, getting tons of press and coverage. Breakthroughs—well, he could use a fucking breakthrough. When Tee showed up at the place and signed up for a clinical trial, they had asked him for ID. In his bag he had two.

And at that moment, Trent Edward Eisen killed himself, a weakling in the sick memory of a jungle halfway around the globe, as he gave new life and a hero's future to John Jay Safford.

FIFTY-NINE

HAPPY TO BE BACK at Daily's Hermosa Beach loft, Pavlov crawled onto the couch and Daily let him stay there. The vet said the dog would need plenty of pure water and rest over the weekend; she would supply all she could.

Paulette called from New York, rattled with anxiety but relieved that she'd finally reached her. Daily said she wanted to call her back on a different line; Paulette gave her the number of the Plaza Hotel. Daily walked down the street and stood underneath a web of power lines next to the Redondo Power Plant, a whale of a building which the city had attempted to beautify with paintings of gray whales, dolphins and other cetaceans. She called back using the odd cell phone from Burg.

"Why all the subterfuge?" Paulette asked.

"Don't want people listening in. I'll explain later."

"Hey—don't go all *Conversation* on me." Paulette's sarcasm sparked when she was stressed.

"I'm truly sorry I ever said that." Daily explained everything and Paulette listened without interrupting. Daily finished with Burg, the special phone she was talking on now, and why.

"For God's sake, Lane—how do you know this Burg is who he says he is? That he isn't a sociopath?"

"He isn't."

"Some of them are remarkably charming. Convincing."

"Sociopaths or intelligence types?"

"They're not mutually exclusive," Paulette warned. "Create the crisis so he can save you from it. Classic."

"I didn't imagine what happened at Cyrus, and he didn't create what I saw in that boat's containers. I trust him, all right? And he might be listening, so be polite."

Paulette's tone cut. "Great. Super."

Daily asked what had happened in New York. Paulette detailed the headway with Cray Wrightman, Aubrey Ealing, then added, "She refused to let me see any more tapes until she returns from the Hamptons—after Labor Day."

"I'm not waiting on Aubrey or anyone else."

"I'm not either, believe me."

"You going to tell me about it now?" Daily asked.

She could picture Paulette in consternation, her free hand worrying her blond hair.

"Burg can find out whatever he wants anyway. But he's *with* us. He saved Pavlov."

She sighed. "That does mean something." Paulette's voice sounded younger, smaller. "When my parents first got here from Poland, they tried to get work in the medical field. They'd been studying to be doctors when the Nazis bombed Warsaw. But after fighting in the underground, they had no credentials, no proof they had medical training. By the time they got to New York, finding work was nearly impossible.

There were ads that asked for volunteers to work at clinics. Medical trials. They were told there were no real dangers, but they had to sign all kinds of forms, signing away their rights if anything ever went wrong down the line."

Daily could feel it coming. *It went wrong.*

"My mother couldn't give birth for years. Each pregnancy terminated with an unformed—"

"Like the animals in the gift message that was sent to Channel Ten."

"Right." Paulette swallowed. "When she finally gave birth to me and John, she said it was a miracle. Because we were okay. We were whole. Nothing wrong with us—or so they thought. Each time she tried to give birth after that, back to the same damn thing. She cursed herself for ever signing up for those trials—but I don't know what choice they had. They were desperate."

"But your mother told you about this—how can they threaten your parents with what they already know?"

"It's the part they *don't* know." Paulette's voice broke.

Daily wished she could hold Paulette, console her. "Tell me."

"They came to America to start a family, okay? That was everything to them. The whole point. When things went wrong, they thought they were cursed or something. Then, they had us, the twins. They always talk about when we'll have their grandkids. Keep the legacy and the bloodline going. When my brother's wife died, it wiped him out emotionally; I don't know if he'll ever fall in love again, let alone have kids. And me—" More stilted breaths, then her friend let the grief come, unable to stop it.

"Paulette—what could possibly be so terrible about you?"

"I can't, Lane. I'm not whole. Inside. The drugs my parents took in the trials—my ovaries, my reproductive tract—they never developed right. They're these strange malformations of what a woman is supposed to be, and I don't have the heart to tell them. The deformities are a rare result of the clinical trial drugs they took—to make money when they came here—to start a *family*, to keep the heritage, you see?"

"But you could have ended up infertile on your own . . . it happens . . . you could adopt . . ."

"No. This is fate's cruel joke. The very thing they did to keep their dream alive damaged its reality. My Dad's heart is already frail. I can't let that sick news, which I thought was private, get to him. Never. He'll feel responsible and it'll kill him."

Daily didn't know how to stop her friend's pain, nor how to protect Paulette's parents from the information. "Whoever sent the message to the station had two agendas. They knew your newsroom would use the 'gift' to spike ratings. And they thought the deformed lab animals would get you to back off your research—but that means you were on to something. And they were wrong about you."

"Dead wrong. And now *you*, my dear Helena. You have something to share with me, too? Something you never told me?"

Daily's body tensed. "What makes you say that?"

Paulette seemed to be thinking about her answer. "When you were recapping before, you danced a little too quickly past the gift delivered to the guest of honor at La Sera Groves. You didn't say what was in the message."

She chewed her lip. "I was just moving fast, trying to cover as much as I could."

Paulette didn't say anything.

"It was a bathing suit, all right? From a woman he'd impregnated and killed in the seventies. Whoever sent it is blackmailing Harmon Whittsedge. The implied threat is telling his wife; she's a religious conservative who gave him the money for his company."

"What else was in the gift?"

"What makes you think there was something else?"

"My gift had two agendas, but mostly it's your tone of voice. I *know* you, Helena."

Daily considered lying but knew she couldn't pull it off. "A NO DIVING sign."

"Something heavier than your friend's suicide in high school, yes?"

Shards of pain in her mind's eye—unbearable. Images of her sister heckling her. Taunting her. "It's a long story. I had a sister—older than me—"

"You never told me."

Daily took several short breaths, couldn't seem to get air. Her eyes hurt. Sense memories playing tricks.

"What happened, Lane?"

"No one ever believed me." Her voice didn't sound like her own; it was feeble and distant, the echo of a faraway child. "My sister wasn't—who she seemed to be. To everyone else, she was this amazing girl. Full of energy. Brilliance. Ideas. Charisma . . ."

"And to you?"

Daily's lips wouldn't move.

"Did she hurt you, Lane?"

The words propelled from inside; she couldn't stem the force that spewed the pent-up rage coming now. "She tried to kill me."

Paulette was silent.

Daily was shaking. The noise in her head was loud, shrill, and high; every one of her nerves burned. She'd never talked about her sister to anyone since the day of the wake, when she'd tried for the last time to explain it to her father and mother.

Her father had mumbled that she was nuts; her mother had slapped her, then chided her for blaspheming her sister's memory. Daily begged them to understand, reminding them of the "accidental" burnings, and the "games," she had always tried to tell them about. The "play" in the waves was just the last in a string of horrors Daily had endured her entire childhood. She'd said they hadn't listened. They'd looked at Daily as if she was the devil, then they'd left her room and never allowed the subject to be brought up again. The chasm between Daily and her parents had grown wider and colder with each passing year.

Daily wiped the heat from her brow, and tried to catch a decent breath. She told Paulette about that last day at the beach with her sister—being held underwater, being told to dive off the pier against her will. How she'd finally found the courage to fight her sister off, how it resulted in her death. Daily's guilt rocked her down to her soul.

"My God," Paulette's voice quivered. "I can't believe you held that in all these years."

"My own parents didn't believe me; why would anyone else?"

"I want you to have some sessions about this, as soon as possible; I'll recommend one of my best associates. You *cannot* carry this shit around. That's dark, noxious stuff they laid on you. Not just your sister—all of them."

"They didn't mean to hurt me. They just couldn't believe their precious princess was—"

"She was ill, Daily. Very, very ill. I want you to stop beating yourself up and get into therapy on this. ASAP."

"I've got bigger problems than my head. If word gets out that one of the LAPD's detectives might have killed her sister when she was a kid—"

"You didn't kill her. You were protecting yourself."

"Point of view. Imagine what the news would do with the story."

"The story I care about is your sanity. You have to deal with it or you're going to implode. God, I wish you'd trusted me with this before. It explains so much."

Daily said nothing. If you learned as a child that your own flesh and blood could "love" you one moment and want to kill you the next, you were rarely surprised or shocked by anything ever again. You had seen the worst a human could be. You just didn't understand why.

"You must forgive yourself, Lane."

Her voice was weary. "No one believed me."

"And you've been trying to justify your existence ever since," Paulette said. "The NO DIVING sign—whoever sent the gift to the party knows—how?"

"Someone took my journals. From a place I was sure was mine alone. It's just like Burg said. There's no privacy anymore. Everyone can find everything now. Even my memories."

SIXTY

Friday, July 8

FRIDAY MORNING, DAILY TOOK Pavlov out for a convalescent walk, just two blocks to the ocean and back. On the way up the steps she saw her next-door neighbor, who said she would be happy to sign for a Federal Express package if it came while Daily was out.

Back in the loft, she heeded the vet's advice and only allowed Pavlov a small amount of dry food and some broth until his stomach healed. Daily opened a bag of potato chips for herself: breakfast of champions. She scanned the morning news, Channel Ten first. Burg's name and photo floated above the anchor's shoulder.

"New evidence in the bizarre death of media mogul Eddie Ealing now verifies that this man, Steven Woydyno, was in fact at Ealing's house the night of the killing. A small strip of shoe rubber was found in the area adjacent to Ealing's pool house door, the entrance the killer used, according to police. It's a perfect match to a rare type of custommade hiking boot, the same kind of boots that were discovered in Woy-

dyno's closet when Santa Barbara authorities searched his apartment Thursday morning . . ."

Daily switched to Channel Four.

"*An all-points-bulletin has authorities throughout California working together, and Lieutenant Theodore Powell of the LAPD's Hollywood Division homicide team says he's confident that they will apprehend Woydyno soon.*"

Channel Six. . . . Kelly Spreck.

"*Woydyno, who others at the institute describe as 'off-center' and 'often strange' . . .*"

Daily switched back to Ten. There was a piece on Officer O'Rourke's grieving family. Taryn Pierce was unconscious but holding at Cedars. The only reference to Daily said she was still suspended pending an investigation into Wednesday night's shooting at Ealing's estate.

Nestor reached Daily after her shower, elated about the shoe rubber match. Cognizant that she was perhaps being monitored, she measured her words.

"You don't find it weird that SID missed a strip of shoe outside Ealing's pool house door? Kerns worked that scene, and Kerns is a fiend for detail." She didn't want to say she thought it was a blatant frame of Burg, that someone had dropped it there long after Eddie's murder, probably the same night that they had shot O'Rourke and cracked Pierce on the head with the gun's butt.

"Pretty unusual for him, but hey, even the best of us make a mistake once in awhile—" Nestor caught himself. "Sorry. I didn't mean . . ." His tone was conciliatory.

"Don't worry about it."

"I'll keep you posted on everything."

"I said don't worry about it."

"What'd you do yesterday? I called you five times."

She wanted to tell him but couldn't—not yet. Not on this call, not on this phone.

"Took a drive. A long run."

"You should do that kind of thing more often." Nestor told Daily what the assignments were for the day. Attention on the whole crew had shifted to the manhunt for Steven Woydyno. "It seems pretty clear this guy's our man. It looks like he was pissed at Ealing for killing Alma Morada, but somehow, I don't think he was in this alone."

Daily deliberated. Acting cagey would tweak Nestor's antennae. "I'm not sure. Something's nagging at me, but I haven't put my finger on it yet. Think I'll sleep on it a little."

Nestor laughed at that. "Sleep. There's a concept. You eating chips this early?"

Daily crunched. "Nope. Celery. Like you told me."

She took Burg's special cell phone outside, again walked toward the power plant's hum. Something had to be done about Temperel, and no one in the department was going to help her do it; the homicide team was being diverted, full force, to the wrong perp: Burg. Someone was using the maintenance staff at Temperel for human experiments. Something to do with kuru . . . and profit. It was Ross who had offered as much help as possible, then backpedaled and waffled. Why? Acting? Or something else? Burg had said that neither Temperel nor Peter would have made it without her—Ross was the one who kept the institute's gears meshed, organized the board, launched the new trials, sparked investors' interests. Faced with Eddie's change in the will, she could have conceived of his murder, had him executed, then used neatly seeded contingencies that explained how Alma's murder was tied to Eddie. Criminal activity voided Eddie's shares in the institute, giving her and Doc control again.

Safford—if he was involved, either Doc had to know and approve . . . or Safford and Dr. Ross were working things in tandem, behind Doc's back.

Peter—according to Burg, he was brilliant, but he couldn't run or manage anything to save his life. He needed someone strong to tell him what to do. He needed a director. Dr. Ross had always been there for him. Daily dialed Temperel.

"Detective Daily?" Dr. Ross sounded surprised at the call. "Thought you were . . . out."

Daily fought the urge to set the truth straight. She needed to appeal to Dr. Ross from a weak position, to garner her sympathy. "There's been an unexpected problem, but maybe you can help. Tuesday, you said that some private investigators had used Temperel's methods to— help clarify things. In cases where there was conflicting testimony, or eyewitness accounts."

"Yes."

"I'd like to try that."

Dr. Ross's breath caught in her throat. "You said the LAPD can't —"

"This is just for me. I'll pay. I've thought long and hard about it. I'm even willing to try some of your trial drugs. The TR-4. Whatever. I've got an LAPD Board of Inquiry coming up and I need to figure out what I saw Wednesday night, when I went back to Eddie's house. I need to remember 'the truth' as you said. An uncorrupted memory. I didn't kill Officer O'Rourke, and I didn't hurt Taryn Pierce, but maybe I saw something that will tell me who did." Daily paused for effect. "I'll do anything."

Dr. Ross ruminated. Her answer would tell Daily where she stood.

Hesitation. "We have the CapVen people, an investment firm, here for the Alzheimer's Groundbreakers tea and reception at four o'clock. They've tendered an offer that's most attractive. I need to prepare—" A long pause. "Excuse me a moment." Daily's call was placed on hold.

Dr. Ross was either checking with someone or thinking about it. Making a choice. She came back on the line. "I'm sorry, I just won't be able to help you with that."

Daily had to be sure it wasn't just the schedule but Dr. Ross' conscience making this decision. "How about tomorrow then? Or whenever's convenient?"

Dr. Ross' voice cracked with tension. "I'm sorry. I *can't* help you. I really think it's better if you—"

Don't come to Temperel?

"—let your situation work itself out on its own."

"I understand. Congratulations on your deal. Thanks anyway."

Something was wrong. If Dr. Ross was masterminding this operation, she would have jumped at the chance to mess with Daily's mind in a lab. That meant she was covering for someone else. Which one of them? Safford alone? No, he didn't have the scientific know-how to run the experiments on humans or their brains. There had to be a partnership. Daily hung up, dialed Temperel again and asked for Wood in LAB A.

Wood was defensive the second Daily said her name. "I don't know where Burg is and I'm not involved—"

"Chill out, Wood. I'm calling for another reason. Frieda the chimp. Is she in your lab?"

"Yeah. They put all the monkeys back in here, now that—Burg didn't kill nobody, man."

"I know he didn't . . . Frieda's there right now?"

"Yes."

"Do me a favor. Sing this." Daily hummed the melody she'd heard Peter Ealing play on the piano. The same one Burg said Alma sang while she cleaned.

"What are you, cracked?"

"It's not a joke, Wood. Sing it and tell me what the chimp does."

"Shit. All right." Daily heard his steps. Then his voice, singing Alma's song.

The chimp's shrieks shot through the phone.

"Christ, man, what the fuck! She's going nuts. What kind of—"

Adrenaline flared through Daily. "What's she *doing*, Wood—tell me—"

"She's smashing her head on the bars of her cage, man! Hitting them! She's out of control . . . like some fuckin' demon is in her head, killing her, makin' her hurt like she's *dyin'*—"

Daily's last doubts were gone.

SIXTY-ONE

AFTER LUNCH, PAULETTE TOOK an unpredictable walk through midtown Manhattan. At a pay phone, she called her parents in Anaheim for the second time. Since the message to News Ten and the poisoning of her water, she'd been averaging three or four calls a day to them. While they were overjoyed with the sudden flurry of communication, they had no idea Paulette was terrified that they'd be the next recipients of a malicious delivery, or worse. As long as her parents greeted Paulette's calls with cheer, she knew they hadn't received anything, but she hated feeling like she was on constant watch. She wanted to throttle the sender, the one who had tried to get to her family, to her. How did they *know*? She wanted to see the creep face-to-face. None of this shadow crap.

Mike's Gifts is a Rorschach test for the soul. It's a way of finding out if someone has a memory of an incident or not. A guilty conscience or not. A secret to hide or not.

That's what this Burg guy had told Lane. Either NSA, if Lane was right, or now part of some intelligence alliance that watched other intelligence organizations, companies and countries trading information. Monitoring deals that existed in no records, only in the minds of the powerful. An old program called Mike's Gifts resurrected in the modern day. Eddie Ealing riffing on Mike's Gifts for his own purposes. Now a malicious copycat was using the Mind Box to go way beyond reactions and reads on people. It was blackmail. Intimidation. Murder. The thought of living in this constant state of hypervigilance made Paulette dizzy. She stumbled and leaned into the wall of a building. A man in a suit asked if she was all right.

Since when do people here notice? Had he been watching her?

Briskly, Paulette walked away from him, then turned to see if he was following her. No. She walked to the nearest phone and called Cray Wrightman. It was a long shot, but she had nothing to lose— just her sanity, her reputation, her entire patient list if Wrightman decided to blast her on TV. Zen answered; Wrightman was out.

"This is Dr. Sohl. Please ask Mr. Wrightman to call me as soon as possible."

Zen was pure ice. "Of course, *Doctor* Sohl. What shall I say this is regarding?"

"His story on Mike's Gifts. It's different than he thought. And much bigger."

"Of *course* it is." Heavy on the sarcasm. Zen said she knew the Plaza number.

By the time Paulette returned to the hotel, she was hyperventilating. All the rhetoric she used to help patients decompress seemed painfully trite now applied to herself. She couldn't slow her own breathing. Her chest felt tight and there was pain. Maybe she'd been poisoned—maybe the water she'd had at lunch, or tainted food—like those people Lane had told her about at Temperel, the ones eating God-knows-what in their free employee meals. No—no one knew where she was going to eat lunch. A heart attack, maybe. People had heart attacks in their forties.

More like a panic attack, Sohl. Chill out.

She collapsed onto the bed and shut her eyes. Slowed her breathing. When she felt better, she sat up and noticed her message light was on. She scrambled to hear it.

Wrightman. His own voice, not the insufferable assistant. "Dr. Sohl, I hope you aren't planning on leaving town. I'll explain when I pick you up at five."

SIXTY-TWO

Daily saw expensive summer dresses and serious suits emerge from expensive cars as she pulled into the Temperel driveway. She told the valet not to bury her Mustang in back; she wasn't staying long. Inside, she told the security guard Dr. Ross was expecting her, lying with such command she surprised herself. In the corridor she called Nestor on Burg's special cell and reminded him of the plan they'd discussed during her drive.

"You clear on the sequence?" She hadn't told Nestor about Burg or his code-thwarting phone, not yet. Her own cell sat tucked in her pocket.

Nestor said, "You want me to call you on your cell. But you want me not to hang up when we're done."

"Right. Cell phones don't always click off so good, so let's say I'd finished talking to you and I accidentally forgot to hit the 'end' button."

"Uh-huh." Nestor sounded skeptical.

"So the call's still live. Say what you hear starts to get real interesting . . . as in essential to Eddie Ealing's murder."

Nestor exhaled. "Powell said no renegade shit. You're not even—"

"You really think I've lost it?"

"Hey, I sure don't want to. But honestly—"

"I should have trusted you and I didn't, all right? I'm trying now. Put all the risk on me if you're worried. Dial my voicemail at home first, leave me a message but don't hang up. The station noise always keeps it recording, it's so loud. 'Accidentally' hit the conference function on your phone, so the calls are together, then call my cell on the second line right away. That way you can say *my* voicemail recorded it all, and you're clear."

"It won't be remotely admissible, and that's if it even works right."

"Never mind admissible; I need to be heard. If it's only in the court of public opinion."

"You say so. What's the spin again?"

"You're making sure I'm okay while I'm on leave. I'm depressed."

"You try St. John's wort?"

"Whatever you want to say. One more time: call my machine first, hit conference, then get me on my cell. And don't forget to mute your end once you reach me by cell. I don't want Ross to hear the station squawking out of my jacket."

She cut him off in the middle of asking what the call had to do with Dr. Ross and hovered in the restroom alcove. Hopefully Nestor was dialing her machine in Hermosa Beach right now. The seconds on her watch moved far slower than her pulse. She felt for the other small item she'd picked up before the drive. Secure in her pocket.

A vibration stirred in Daily's hand and she answered her regular cell. Nestor, going with the script. He said he'd tried her at home and missed her there, then asked how she was. She did her best to sound melancholy. He told Daily to stay strong and recommended herbal supplements for low moods. She thanked him for his concern and, without ending the call, tucked the Nokia in her pocket and clipped the headset's mic under her lapel, out of sight. She heard her partner hit mute to silence the Hollywood station's hum. Her nerves wired, she walked down the hall and hummed to keep the recording live. She found Dr. Ross in her office, rehearsing her speech. The scientist's voice was stilted, unlike the first time Daily heard her speak.

"While the concerns of business must never navigate—" The doctor damned her notes and resumed. "While the concerns of business must never *dictate* the path of science, the perfect partners know exactly how to navigate business, freeing Temperel's researchers to reach new goals. Dictate, then navigate. Dictate then navigate—"

"Dictate he did," Daily said. From her pocket, Daily pulled out the tiny hearing aid she'd picked up and set it on the desk.

Dr. Ross caught her breath and turned. She stared at the small device.

"Eddie Ealing recorded everything."

Dr. Ross didn't move.

"I couldn't figure it out," Daily said. "Here's a guy who records most of his phone conversations, keeps a library of them, plays them back at people all his life. So they won't *forget* what they said. I couldn't figure out why he would suddenly break his own routine the night of July fourth. The answer is, he didn't."

Dr. Ross picked it up. "This is a hearing aid."

"That's what we all thought the first time we looked at it. Our criminalists included. But it's a microphone and a transmitter. It picked up what Eddie said and what people said to him. The recordings are elsewhere. Eddie said a couple of names out loud before he died. Yours included. A message he knew was being recorded."

She watched Dr. Ross' fears churn. A gut calibration locked inside Daily as she watched the doctor's face and hands begin to tremble.

"Nestor and the others are coming to arrest you. They're on their way now."

Dr. Ross shook, as if trying to convince herself. "*No*—for what *possible*—"

"Conspiracy to commit murder in the death of Edward Boyle Ealing. Nestor's going to say you have the right to remain silent. Anything you say can and will be used by all the media people outside at the reception, not to mention the ones who'll be listening to the police scanners as they drive you back to the Hollywood station—"

Dr. Ross erupted: "If you really heard anything, then you know I had no part in Eddie's death—you *people* don't understand the first thing about me."

Daily waited for evidence.

Ross gripped the desk with both hands, her knuckles blanched, her face contorted. "I would *never* jeopardize my research—what it will mean to millions of people who are losing their minds each year. I couldn't have a megalomaniac like Eddie destroying everything I've—" Wetness filled her eyes and caught in her throat. "God, all I wanted was to work in peace. That's still all I want."

Daily watched Dr. Ross wrestle with choices. Another news van arrived outside. The scientist glared at its transmitting equipment and steeled herself.

"If I tell you certain things, then my choices are what—exactly?"

"You can tell me whatever you want. It's off-the-record until I'm reinstated or until I give the recordings of Eddie's last moments to Nestor."

"And Nestor?"

"He'll have to speak with the DA, see what he can do if the information you give him is salient."

Dr. Ross chortled. "*Salient.* Maybe I should just call my lawyer now."

It was Daily's last chance. "You need to be on the dais in a few minutes. Maybe Nestor can read you your rights out there. In front of the investment bankers."

Dr. Ross looked out the window as a cameraman piled out of the news van. She said, "I wanted to help, detective. From day one, I wanted to help you catch the killer."

"Until you found out who it was."

"You don't understand—you have no idea." Her hands weaved anxiety. "I can see how it would look now, how you would misunderstand. But Peter's brilliant. The work he's doing will heal millions."

Peter. Repugnance tugged at Daily's tongue as she thought of the dead young maid, her brain cut from her skull. "Peter's work won't heal Eddie. It didn't heal Alma Morada."

"This isn't about *Alma!*" Dr. Ross slammed her hand on the desk. "All of this, every bit of this should be about *making things right.* About what science can do to improve a human's quality of life. And instead, it's become a battle of wills. Of control."

"And that's hard to accept, isn't it? You can't fathom that there were things going on at Temperel that you weren't apprised of. Life-and-death decisions. You defended Peter because he's 'not of this world.' He needs someone strong as a partner, and you thought you were that partner. But someone *stronger* was managing Peter. They left you out of it, because you're a purist, Ross. You really are a scientist, I'll give you that."

"No one planned—"

"No one *planned* on one of the Godforsaken maintenance people attracting Eddie's attention," Daily continued. "Alma sings like an angel, Eddie gets to know her, keeps it quiet, records some songs in out-of-the-way studios, where no one can steal his find. Everything goes swimmingly until Alma starts forgetting things. Big things. Like her name. Where she is. She's too young to have Alzheimer's. That's when

Eddie asks Alma about her work history here. Under pressure, she comes clean, tells Eddie she's dying anyway, from something that has nothing to do with memory. Cyrus Services hires people like that—the word's out on the terminal grapevine. That's when he realizes Alma's been a human guinea pig. Infected with TR-4."

Daily could see the rancor coursing through Ross.

The scientist's words were a hiss. *"That's not it at all."*

"That's exactly it. Cyrus Services has been supplying Temperel with humans for testing. People who didn't have any other options. And it was happening right here, under your nose."

"Plenty of firms use Cyrus—"

"But only Temperel works with Lyle Pearson. You mean to tell me you never had suspicions? You never realized what Peter was *doing* to these people?"

"I didn't—" Tears spilled. "Safford came to me Wednesday, told me you weren't backing off, that you were headed down this path. He said you might come making crazy threats, wild accusations."

"And, as always, you asked Peter about it."

Dr. Ross swallowed. Her voice was shrill, her words desperate. "Peter said Alma was going to die anyway. Lymphoma. Her options were to die a slow and painful death in a filthy hospital, or to come here and take part in a revolutionary drug trial and make thousands of dollars doing it. She changed her family's *destiny* by making that choice. She helped science even as she died. And she did it willingly."

Daily fought the explosion of reactions in her gut. It sickened her to hear the warped reasoning of those who tried to justify life's most heinous acts. "You bought it. You had to. Too much at stake, Temperel to lose. But when Eddie found out, he went ballistic. He claimed it proved Peter was more dangerous than ever. Eddie gave Doc and Peter until the Fourth of July to sell Florian a majority stake, or he was going to the media with his story. The Ealing family exposé, told by one of the Ealings. Did Eddie have proof that Alma had been infected?"

Dr. Ross' breaths grew heavy. "The causes of kuru and its analogs are still in play—it may be a prion, or a prion byproduct. The disease can only be diagnosed post mortem, on histology. Regardless of proof, Eddie was ready to imply that Alma had been infected with TR-4 on purpose. Never mind what I've just told you. The media and the accusations would ruin Temperel's reputation, our ability to raise money, forge alliances, Safford said. It would destroy everything we've worked on. For years."

"What was Eddie offering in return for the Florian deal?"

"Silence." Dr. Ross scoffed. "A promise Safford said Eddie would break like breathing. He couldn't be trusted."

Daily locked onto Dr. Ross' eyes. "Safford works for Doc. Did Doc Ealing order Safford to murder his son?"

Dr. Ross dropped her head. When she looked up, her eyes were wet and cold.

"No. That's just it—don't you see? There was never supposed to be a *murder*. Eddie Ealing was never supposed to *die*."

SIXTY-THREE

PAULETTE DIDN'T REALIZE CRAY Wrightman was taking them to a helipad until they emerged on the roof of the skyscraper housing his network. The Sikorsky S-76 copter, a charter, was ready. Cray didn't offer an explanation, just hurried Paulette into the flight cabin. Soon they were two hundred feet over the city, spiriting toward La Guardia.

"The airport?" Paulette asked Wrightman.

"East Hampton. We're paying a visit to an important friend of mine."

"Aubrey's party is tonight. In East Hampton."

"He'll be there."

Paulette noticed the tape in Wrightman's hands. Old-looking videocassette. He wouldn't let go of it.

———

The sounds of the orchestra swirled into the second-story library of Aubrey Ealing's beach home. Wrightman inserted his tape into Aubrey Ealing's deck. Paulette and Aubrey stood on either side of Cray as he used the remote to fast forward it. "It's from camp," he said. "Took hours to dig it out from storage in Connecticut, but you were right. Eddie knew I had it. That's why he was calling so relentlessly. Eddie shot this film the summer of 1969. Our family transferred movies to tape a while later."

Paulette and Aubrey watched as Eddie and Cray acted out Eddie's story. Rough, but the gist of it was that one brother kills the other, Cain and Abel in Kodacolor. Teenage Eddie, dressed as an American soldier, spasms and rolls on the ground in a histrionic death. Young Cray uses a knife to "open" Eddie up and pulls out his "organs," one by one. A boy's gore-and-gut fantasy.

"Those were the animal parts the cook at the camp let us use," Cray explained.

"Who was shooting this?" Paulette asked. "Peter?"

"No, some other kid from camp. Trent Eisen. I brought the camp yearbook magazine, it has everyone's picture. I'll show you when the film's through."

"Was Peter around?"

"Keep watching."

Young Cray gathers the 'organs' and a new figure walks on. Peter Ealing, dressed as a soldier, carries a crate into which young Cray places Eddie's "guts." They pack the box with letters from inside the dead Eddie's coat, then shut the top of the crate. On the side of the crate is an amateurish but readable stencil:

M.I.K.
GIFT

Cray froze the image. "I didn't remember the crate in the background, and now I know why. Eisen and Peter hung around together that summer. It was those two who worked on the props while Eddie and I rehearsed the death scene. I was so worried about my role as traitor that I wasn't paying much attention to the set."

"What does it mean?" Paulette asked.

"I had to look it up, I didn't remember. In German, *Gift* means poison. And I checked with a World-War-II professor we use for research at the network. The initials allegedly stood for *Medien Information Kommission*."

"Propagandists?"

"*American* media propagandists. US citizens hired to work as propagandists and lobbyists for Germany."

"Private contractors?"

"In some cases. In others, they were actually large firms. Not unlike some that do media work for foreign countries and companies in the US today. To help them 'spruce up' their image." His eyes swept the room. "Whether the *Medien Information Kommission* was a real organization or not, the people hired to do such work were very real, and they did a fair amount of it. For money."

"God." Paulette dropped to a chair.

"The Foreign Agents Registration Act was legislated in 1938 because the practice was going on. It has some bite against foreign governments hiring propagandists or PR firms here now to manipulate the media. But it doesn't stop a foreign government from using one of its private companies to hire a US media firm to do the same thing."

Aubrey said, "Whose idea was it to paint the crate? Peter couldn't have known about it. And Father wouldn't allow it if he knew. Not after what happened to Mother . . ."

"It was Eisen's," Wrightman said staring at the screen. "Something about his dad. Took me until now to realize the implications of that."

Paulette needed to find Lane. "You have that photo of Trent Eisen?"

Wrightman pulled a thin black and white leaflet from his satchel. On the front was a logo: SAN DIEGO SAND AND SURF BOYS CAMP 1969.

"San Diego?" Paulette asked. "I assumed you went somewhere in the Northeast."

"Hell, no. California, every summer. Couldn't beat the girls or the weather. None of that damn humidity." He flipped the pages, came to the headshots. "Here he is, front row: Trent Eisen. Know him?"

"Never seen him in my life," Paulette said.

Aubrey paled. "Mother of Jesus."

"What?" Cray said impatiently.

"He's changed his hair, but those eyes. That's Safford. I'm sure of it. John Safford. Father's right-hand man."

SIXTY-FOUR

DAILY LEFT DR. ROSS standing in her office to let fear have its way with her. She wondered what the scientist would say to her audience now. She pulled her cell from her pocket. The call was still live and she ended the connection without saying a word, then dialed Nestor back on Burg's phone.

"Holy shit, Daily—how did you know?"

"She was a warrior for this place. Until she started to crumble."

"But the hearing aid—Zag said it was just that and nothing more—how'd you figure Eddie used it to record what happened?"

"He didn't."

"It's just a hearing aid?"

"Just a hearing aid. I told a saleswoman at the Hearing Center I needed to show my infirm grandmother how small it would be, to get her to buy the thing. Told her I was LAPD, she let me borrow it for the day."

"That's so many kinds of trouble I can't know about."

"So forget it. Ross' fears were inside her all along, I just gave them a name and a shape. You going to get your ass up here, or you going to sit down there dumbfounded at my brilliance?"

"I'll tell the SO to cover. Powell and I will chopper up. Where are Peter Ealing and Safford?"

Daily looked out the hallway window to the terrace up the hill. The audience was now seated and she could hear the opening rhetoric piped in via the PA. "Peter's on the dais giving a lovable-genius speech about Temperel's trial drugs. Doc's on the dais too, glowing with pride."

"Dr. Ross?"

"Still in her office, regrouping. There's only one way out and I'm standing there."

"Safford?"

"Can't see him. I'm heading outside now; I'll check it out."

"Stay put," Nestor barked. "And this time, watch your back."

———————

Daily scanned the guests at the roped entrance to the terrace, where women welcomed late-arriving patrons and matrons of charity whose faces she recognized from the society pages of the *Times*. She roamed between tables. The sun was high in the sky and the ocean was turbid. Sailboats skimmed the horizon. Ringing crystal heralded a toast to a new era in memory recollection. On stage, a taut woman thanked everyone for their generous support of the Foundation and acknowledged Peter Ealing's "inspiring" remarks.

She introduced others. Doc's name received great applause, but behind the crystal glassware, both Doc and Peter had left their seats. Dr. Ross sat in a red-eyed daze.

Daily's regular cell chirped: Paulette telling Daily to call her back on the encrypted phone. She did. Quickly, Paulette said she was at

Aubrey Ealing's place in East Hampton with Cray, then launched into a high-speed download on Peter and Safford, someone named Trent Eisen, something about propaganda, media, information. She was going too fast; Daily said to tell her once again. As Paulette repeated it, Daily eyed John Safford's place card, but his seat was empty. Napkin folded, water glass full, salad untouched. She had to move. Peter, Doc, and Safford were disappearing and Nestor's call hadn't produced a single sheriff's deputy so far. Paulette pleaded for her to wait for back-up.

"Burg's my back-up."

"You don't even know if he's there."

"He's there."

———————

Daily hastened inside Temperel. The door marked OCEAN CONFERENCE ROOM was ajar. People had left half-finished bottles of Pellegrino and wine on the wet bar. No one was in the room except Doc, his hands clasped behind his back, staring at the sea.

Daily approached him. "Missing the biggest day of Peter's life?"

No reaction.

She moved alongside him, followed his gaze to find what he was fixed upon. Something she couldn't see. "I know what happened to Eddie." Daily fought to keep her voice even. "The use of TR-4 is illegal in humans. Any intent to render part of someone's body useless is mayhem. Even if it's his anger, memories, it's *his* brain. That's aggravated mayhem and extreme indifference with malice and forethought. Murder One."

Deep, even breaths rode Doc's chest. No words.

Damned if she was going to let him get away with his stoic bullshit. This *scion* of righteousness. "The felony-homicide law applies to co-conspirators."

Doc's voice was a rumble. "The idea that we would have anything to do with harming Eddie is preposterous. You said yourself we wouldn't want Eddie dead. No matter how bad he got. If he died, we lost Temperel."

"Exactly why Peter used GHB to put Eddie into a *coma*."

Doc's eyes flared. "That's not what happened."

"That's *exactly* what happened. Dr. Ross just confirmed it."

"Dr. Ross has no idea—"

"She asked Peter about it yesterday, when she couldn't deny it anymore. Peter said he was just trying to *help* Eddie. To soothe his anger. To buy time until Eddie could be *treated* up here at Temperel like some new lab rat. But Peter didn't count on Eddie going off the wagon that night. Alcohol and GHB. Perfect cocktail for a seizure. Eddie seizes, cracks his skull. Peter's at a loss for what to do. So you have Safford clean up, make it look like a psycho thing. The only way to invalidate Eddie's will now is to implicate Eddie in a crime. Create a trail that pins the problem on Eddie. Neat solution, given the change of circumstances. Make Eddie the bad guy, nix the will, keep full control of Temperel. And your secrets."

Doc turned toward Daily. His eyes burned.

"Peter is a *scientist*. His only motivation is to help people."

Daily rifled through the information Paulette had given her about the Ealing family. Like the hologram she had seen in the Temperel lab, the image came together in Daily's mind. Young Eddie was shy, afraid of his older brother. Mrs. Ealing was always afraid of Peter, her own son. She knew his potential, and she died . . . early onset Alzheimer's, or so they thought. Peter's recent activity not a new development, just more in a lifetime of entitlement. Of life-and-death decisions. His alleged genius.

"Peter gave your wife—his own mother—poison."

"More of Eddie's old slanderous paranoia. You people—your psychologist friend—manipulating her way into Aubrey's home and mind. Into our life. Abominable."

"After what you've done?"

Doc's jaw trembled in indignation. "You have no idea. My wife used to *beg* me to kill her. Monique was incredibly fragile. As a ten-year-old in France, she was sodomized and raped by ten soldiers in one day. *One day*. The last man finished with her as the sun rose. She said she'd never forget it. It was the most perfect, beautiful morning. The sun hit her bloodied, swollen face through the slats of the barn where they tore her young body apart. The birds sang as the cretins stumbled away, drunk and spent. When she finally found the strength to crawl outside the barn, the first thing she saw was a garden of lilies. For her, the dawn, the birds, and flowers would always mean one thing. Horror. A ten-year-old *girl*, detective. When I met her, she was contemplating one fate only. Suicide."

His voice grew louder.

"She was at a French military hospital outside Hanoi—taking care of patients round-the-clock to cover the fact that she was hoarding pills each day to *kill* herself. Because of her memories." Doc's words were bullets of vitriol. "Every single day she lived in her own walking purgatory, half alive, half dead. Too frozen to commit to either one. Do you understand? She was haunted by those ten animals, their ghosts."

"But she didn't kill herself. She went on to marry you. To have three children, to lead the charity foundation for Temperel—"

Doc scoffed. "You're naive for someone with your intelligence. So is Dr. Ross. Every second was a struggle. Going to sleep was a nightmare. Waking up to the sunshine was sheer terror. I gave her my love, my money, my sons, but none of it could ever erase her memory. It was as if she was living with a terminal disease. Her own trauma."

Daily was there, in Doc's head; she could see it through his eyes, even as it repulsed her. "Your doctorate at Harvard was in behavior modification. You went to Vietnam to work with men who had been subject to war horrors. To modify them. You always promised your wife you would make her better, too, but you couldn't, not even after decades of trying. The nightmares wouldn't stop. Why not commit her?"

"She knew too much about hospitals. No, the only way was to keep her under our watch, at home, round the clock."

"A heavy burden for the family."

"Not as heavy as her suicide would have been. It was the one time in our life when we were actually a team, working toward the same thing. Her survival."

"And when Peter finally injected her with one of the test analogs from his lab in San Diego, he didn't stop to think it might kill her instead of help her?"

The arteries in Doc's neck throbbed. "Don't you dare get righteous with me. Not now. We were all doing everything we could to save her. Peter took a risk. Did I know about it beforehand? No. I'd have stopped him and he knew it. He had the passion of youth, of *possibility*. He believed he could cure her. He believed that someday there would be a way to remove the trauma and to keep the mind. Now, by God, he's right. It just came too late for her."

Even now, Doc couldn't see Peter for what he was, Daily realized. "He erased more than the trauma. He ruined her mind."

"She was dead long before that. Peter was only trying to help."

"After years of constant vigilance for a woman whose despair knew no bottom, Peter relieved you of a tremendous burden. And he won your eternal protection. A deal made without words."

"Now you're delusional, Daily."

A wrath deeper than she had ever known spewed from inside her. "Am I? Why didn't you punish Peter for injecting your wife with a drug you didn't know about? That ended up destroying her brain?"

"What *good* would it have done?" Doc bellowed. "For the first time in years, she became remotely happy. Her last few months, she could actually look out the window at the sunshine and smile. The birds made her laugh for the first time since I knew her. Peter brought a bouquet of lilies home as a test, to see if she had any bad reaction to them—" Warmth flickered in his eyes. "She adored them. Arranged them!"

Daily scoffed. "The first test of memory and emotion. But then she forgot who she was altogether. Then she lost her life. Peter killed her."

"No! He gave her a sense of life she never had! A *real* sense of life!"

Revulsion enveloped Daily. He was a monster worse than Peter—he had a conscience, yet he chose to look the other way.

Doc leaned into her. "Since that failed attempt to save his mother's mind, Peter's sentence has been to live in his own personal hell. That's why he practically sleeps in that damn lab to find the answer. And he's done it. In learning how to track the recollection of memories, he's also learned how to block out the ones that should *never* be replayed. He's learned how to filter out the damage. It'll give an entire generation a world with less rage, less crime, more peace." Doc's voice grew suddenly seductive. "What if you could *forget* the things your sister did to you, detective? What if you could find it in your heart to forgive her, to love her again after she nearly killed you?"

Daily froze.

"What if you could forgive yourself for making the decision that saved you and killed her?"

Her skin went numb. The air in the room disappeared.

Doc's eyes bored into her. "Remembering the sounds and smells of that day all over again? The memory? The guilt? All this nonsense about Eddie thinking Peter tried to kill him. You're *projecting*. Your sister tried to harm you time after time. She nearly succeeded in killing you. Later, your own subconscious rage made your choice for you, on that pier."

Molten fury coursed through her. Daily shut her lids, but images of her sister and Peter Ealing kept firing in her mind's eye.

"You disgust me, Daily. Your guilt, your weakness of choice. You just keep digging in the dirt of your homicides as a distraction for what *you* can't really face. Some petty penance for not having the courage to admit you made a real decision. Your life against hers."

Daily fought a shaking deep inside her. Her head slammed with pain; her ears rang with her sister's laughter. "It was an accident."

"You don't believe in *accidents*."

He knew her every word. She and Eddie Ealing had both known what their siblings were capable of, yet no one had listened or believed them—they didn't matter. In different ways, they had each spent the rest of their lives trying to prove that they did.

"Eddie wanted people to remember what happened," she said.

"Eddie was disturbed. He made things up."

She remembered what Paulette had told her about the family, about what she'd discovered in New York between the tapes, Cray and Aubrey. She stepped closer to Doc. "Eddie was a shy, quiet kid until thirteen. Only then did he begin to act out. The bluster and the attitude were defense mechanisms because he didn't feel safe. He was scared to death of Peter, and no one but your wife believed him. Peter killed the only ally Eddie ever had in his life—his mother. And he never trusted a single soul again."

Doc was practically laughing at her. "Speaking from personal experience again, are you? I keep waiting for you to slip and say 'I' in-

stead of 'Eddie.' You're stuck in the smallness. You're living in the past."
He chortled. "I was wrong about you. You don't have what it takes to
make the tough choices. To fight the bigger battle."

"Some soldiers go to war because they have to; others go for the
excuse to kill. It's the nuances that define who we are."

"The same could be said of cops. In your case, ex-cops."

"And scientists. For every person who's tried to solve the mysteries of the mind, there's always a few ready to exploit it."

"You dare throw Peter in with mercenaries and rogue cops?"

"Peter experiments on human beings. On his own relatives."

"He does no such thing." Doc closed in, his height bearing down
on her.

Daily stood her ground. "Peter was behind the 'animal-activist'
food tainting. Peter was behind the GHB 'scandal'. Both set up, with
great care, beforehand, to indemnify Temperel from anything that
went wrong later."

"That's a crock."

"Alma Morada was one of the illegal immigrants that Peter had
brought into Temperel under the guise of maintenance workers, cafeteria staff. People who had been diagnosed with terminal diseases in
other countries, who were funneled to Cyrus Services with new IDs,
to work at Temperel. In exchange for undergoing *Peter's* experimental
therapy, they were paid handsomely. They sent their money home to
Russia, Mexico, wherever. As people destined to die too early, it was
the greatest gift they could leave their families."

"Absurd. I don't believe a word of it."

"You don't have to. Dr. Ross has already told me what she knows,
and Peter confirmed it with her. TR-4 has been refined, but it's *not*
perfect. And it's certainly not fit for trial on humans. Dr. Ross said
TR-4 still destroys more memory than it saves."

His voice broke, "That can't be—"

"Your son with a conscience found out about it. Believe it or not, Eddie offered you the one solution that would save your reputation and your pride. Sell Temperel and he wouldn't expose or ruin the *decent* work that had been done." She circled behind him, saw that his shoulders had caved. Defensive suddenly. She'd be damned if she'd let him delude himself out of this. "Under Eddie's proposed plan, Peter could still do research, but he'd be accountable. I'm not so forgiving. Officers are on their way here now."

Doc crumbled under the weight of it. "No—"

"You didn't heal things, Dr. Ealing, and you didn't forget. You looked the other way. And denial is the worst crime of all. Because you could have *stopped* it."

"I didn't—he would never do those other things and not tell me—"

"You knew what Peter was capable of—"

"—Peter's whole life is about *saving* people—"

"It's about saving *certain* people. At the expense of others."

He suddenly looked much older; he gripped Daily's arm. "You can't let him be arrested. He won't make it. Peter's far too sensitive to endure anything like—"

"He poisoned people. He used them."

"Healing. Peter only wants to heal."

He stammered, desperate for any illusion. "If they were terminal, they must have known what they were asking for. Certainly they *asked* for it, by God, they asked for it. We allow people to plead for their own deaths, but not this—there are people who simply can't live with their diseased destiny, others who can't bear the weight of their pasts. They can't live with their memories—"

"He took Eddie's, without his consent."

"No, this is all wrong. Peter is a good man. A brilliant man. But Eddie—" His mouth quivered. His eyes glazed, surrendered their strength. "Maybe God threw the ultimate test at me. To have the devil

428

for a son." He walked unevenly toward the window and set his hands on the ledge. The lion in him was weak now. "We know there's no redemption for true psychopaths. They can't change. But those of us with a conscience—you and I—we make choices and sometimes we fail. Sometimes, in those cases, the most humane decision we can make is to look the other way. To move on."

Daily swallowed her hatred. "Don't include me in your 'we.'"

"Peter's no psychopath. And I'm no accessory to murder."

"No. You Ealings think you're God. And that's just as dangerous."

SIXTY-FIVE

Doc slumped into a leather chair next to the window. "The CapVen people shook on our deal before the reception started. Rena's our best speaker and she didn't even have to utter a word. That's how impressed they were with Temperel's new drug."

Daily wondered how impressed they'd be when they found out how far it was from ready. How much they'd like a photo opportunity when the Santa Barbara SO and LAPD showed up to cuff Temperel's *Wunderkind*.

"Your people will give Rena some kind of immunity, I imagine," Doc said, drained.

Daily didn't answer. Outside, deputies from the Santa Barbara County Sheriff's Office appeared at the edge of the berm. Two closed in on the dais. Two more uniforms, on radios, looked down toward the building complex. Daily bolted for the door, identified herself to the lead and briefed him on Doc Ealing inside and Dr. Ross at the head table. Said they were both accessories to murder. Daily then hurdled up the slope to the terrace.

Peter wasn't anywhere in sight. Neither was Safford.

She sprinted to the valet in front, described the Jaguar that Safford drove for Doc, asked if it had left, then demanded the keys to her Mustang. The valet guarded his key board until she flashed her gun grip, got in his face. He said the Jaguar had shot down the south fork of the main road. She found her keys, ran for her car, slammed the key in the ignition, floored the gas and skidded out of the lot cursing options. To the freeway? Too easy to track. The harbor again? Possible. The marina would be a good place to get lost. She tried reaching Burg on his phone. Nothing, just a click and dead air. She recalled his words and spoke to him as he'd instructed; imagine he was there. She tried cells for Nestor and Powell with no success, left word at the Hollywood station. Finally she tried Litton at SBPD. Out. Left him a voice-mail that probably sounded as frantic and disjointed as her driving.

This close to nailing the perps and now they were gone. She was on her own. She needed to see them, see it all from above, as the crow flies.

———————

Yuri Tsu had a mound of banana bread in his mouth when Daily found him at the small airport in Goleta. He offered her some with a greasy hand. The other held a wrench.

Daily ignored the banana bread. "I need a ride."

"Gonna get on that horse, eh, detective? When do you want to go?"

"Now."

"Now?" Yuri spoke with his mouth full. "We usually start with ground training."

"I need to get up there. *Now.*"

He swallowed. "Got the urge, don't want to lose the moment. Know how it is. But you got to start with ground training."

"Dammit, Yuri, I don't want to fly the frigging thing, I just want to get in the air. If you can do that, tell me."

"I got to put something in the log, for the boss. Where to?"

"I've got a suspect on the run. I don't know what direction he's headed and I won't know until we get in the sky."

His eyes brightened. "Suspect? Why aren't you using the PD's chopper?"

"Unavailable." Daily laid out a credit card. "This is for your log." Next, she gave him all the cash she had. A little over a hundred dollars. "This is for you. If you get me in the air in the next ten minutes."

Yuri stared at the money. "OK. But only if you tell me what's going on."

———————

The Bell 206 Bill Jet Ranger wheezed its way toward the coast, over the marina and Stearns Wharf. Daily asked Yuri to circle the harbor. There—the Jaguar's rear peeked from an alley garage off Cabrillo. Could be a lookalike, but her instincts hit the sweet spot. Using Yuri's binoculars, she scanned the faces of tourists and fisherman. She searched for yesterday's boat. Nothing. It was midday, and a number of slips were open, their vessels out working the water. Safford and Peter couldn't be that far gone if they'd left shore in the last fifteen minutes.

Daily looked at the isles in the sea, the exposed backs of sleeping giants hulking beneath the surface. The Channel Islands and the derricks both blocked an open view of the water; if Cyrus had been moving illegal cargo, or bodies, there was no better place to do it than behind the cover of one of them. Her senses on high, she scanned the ocean. Most of the boats were cruising at a languid pace; only one seemed to be in a hurry. The vessel gashed across the waves.

She shouted at Yuri over the copter's rhythms. "See that boat, there, with the wake at ten o'clock? Can we get over it?"

"Say the word." Yuri's flying finesse didn't match his bravado; the old Jet Ranger jerked forward with a lurch. Daily hit the window with her head and Yuri apologized. Two minutes later, they were over the motorboat. Daily saw Burg at the wheel. Her heart swelled with relief. He'd been listening. He'd been there. He glanced up once, then looked at the helicopter again and waved. Daily gestured back. Burg pointed at a larger wake ahead of him.

"Your partner?" Yuri said.

"You could say that. How long until he catches that boat in front of him?"

"He won't catch it. Not in that thing."

Dammit. There was no way she was letting the perps slip away. Not now. "We can make up the distance?"

"Sure."

"Then drop down and get him."

"You want me to drop down and let your guy *climb* in my chopper?"

"That's what I said."

Yuri looked uncomfortable, but his youth wouldn't let him admit it. "No problem. Long as he can handle an old rope ladder with you up top."

The copter jerked Burg up and away from above the now-dawdling motorboat.

"Burg—Yuri," Daily introduced them.

"Nice to meet your machine, Yuri. How long you been flying it?"

"A couple."

The copter dropped, then lurched forward.

"Weeks?" Burg said under his breath.

Daily watched as Burg checked his holstered Glock plus a sheathed knife. "They're going to swing by that derrick there," he told Daily. "That's the one they've been traveling to the last few days. They either need to pick something up or dump evidence attached to it. Then they're heading out to open sea. There are two vessels just outside territorial waters right now. One's headed for Peru. The other for North Korea. Safford's meeting one of them. We need to get to them before they board."

They gained on the boat below. Low, gray, and sleek, it moved with incredible speed. She couldn't see anyone beneath the housing on the boat.

Burg read her thoughts. "The cabin's all facade. Below, it's a knock-off of one of our Mark Vs. Can hit forty-eight knots, low radar signature. Long range, high maneuverability."

Yuri stared at Burg. "You're no cop, man. What are you?" The copter veered to the right.

"Eyes on the road, Yuri," Daily said. Her stomach felt as choppy as the swells below. She turned to Burg. "What the hell does Peru or North Korea want with Safford or Peter?"

"They want what they've got."

"An Alzheimer's drug that doesn't work yet?"

"It works just fine," Burg said with rancor.

"No—Dr. Ross confirmed it an hour ago—the new compound *doesn't* help people remember any better than TR-4—"

"Exactly."

He seemed to be talking to someone else, missing her point.

"It destroys more memory than it saves," she said.

Burg's eyes locked onto hers. "Exactly."

Daily listened to the blades above her. She was the one missing the point. "My God, they don't want it for Alzheimer's."

"No, they don't."

Daily's gut felt like it had dropped through the copter's floor and into the ocean. "They want it to erase memory. In a way that can't be traced."

"No one said biological warfare had to be loud and obvious."

The rotors seemed to crescendo around Daily. In a moment of utter clarity, she saw it all in resolution. All of it, the madness, the murders— it wasn't about remembering, it was about forgetting. About voiding memories.

"Is it contagious?" Yuri interrupted.

Burg said it wasn't and told the pilot to stay low, to fly just past the spray of the boat's wake as long as he could. They were gaining.

"Where's your support team?" Daily asked Burg.

"Don't have one. I don't exist, remember?"

Whatever agency or consortium he worked for, they'd crucify Burg if he failed, she realized. He was beyond deep cover, there would be no fleets or troops coming to rescue him. The boat below was now a good seven miles from shore. Five more miles, less than minutes to go before they were in international waters. Still no word from Nestor, no vibrations on the cell against her chest. Nothing on Yuri's radio. She pulled out Burg's phone and dialed Paulette, recapped the situation: "Get someone out here to help us. Or Safford's going traveling." After the call, Daily turned to Burg. "The man you used to work for—you said you lost him and you'll never forgive yourself. But you didn't lose him to death, did you? You lost him to this. Someone destroyed his memory and you think it's your fault."

Burg's eyes closed, reopened in the affirmative.

"You said the people operating on memory deals were world leaders, pretty high up. How about your boss? Where did he rank in the mix?"

Burg looked out the Jet Ranger's window. "About as pretty high up as it gets."

SIXTY-SIX

THE GUESTS ROAMING AUBREY Ealing's party had finished their dinners and were now enjoying the lull of soft music and fine wine. Three of Temperel Foundation's supporters had thanked the audience at various breaks through the evening, but everyone was eager to hear what the Secretary of State had to say.

The Secretary realized this as he gazed out Aubrey's library window, at the sloping grounds and the sedate night sea. Paulette, Aubrey, and Cray Wrightman stood waiting. The Secretary addressed Cray first. "You realize what you're insinuating?"

"All too well, sir."

The Secretary studied Paulette. "And you? You stand by this story about the illegal immigrants being used for drug trials? Unauthorized drugs?"

"Completely. The call I just received confirms it."

"Do you two understand the geopolitical ramifications? That we allowed something like this to be developed on our own soil? That it was used to lure unfortunate people to America who had nothing else to live for? That they were used like lab animals?"

"Yes, sir." Paulette's anxiety rose as she thought about the Secret Service men outside the library door.

The Secretary wiped his brow. "I can't very well go down there and stump for Temperel considering what you've all just told me, Aubrey."

"Of course not, sir," Aubrey said.

"Who else knows about this?"

"Detective Lane Daily, of the LAPD, sir," Paulette said.

"They'll handle apprehension of the suspects, then. That's a good buffer. We can figure out the rest once they're in custody."

Paulette searched Cray's face. His eyes told her to speak up.

"There's just one problem, sir. They may need a little help."

SIXTY-SEVEN

AT FULL THROTTLE, YURI'S copter sounded like a tubercular dog, thanks to its questionable condition and equally questionable pilot. Burg's face grew dark as Safford's boat edged away from them. "We're losing them—" Burg yelled at the pilot.

"You want to fly, frogman?" Yuri's defenses were piqued.

Daily scanned the sky. Not another chopper or plane in sight. Where the hell was Nestor? Was some bureaucratic bullshit dragging him down, even now? Yuri pushed the old bird to its limits, and finally they gained on the boat. A man emerged from the cabin—Safford. Daily saw him reach inside his jacket.

"Bank it, Yuri," Burg bellowed. "Left, man. Left."

"Left what?" Yuri yelled. "I thought you wanted me to catch up to them!"

"Dammit, drop left! Now!"

Bullets flared from Safford's gun and Yuri veered the copter in a steep air skid. Daily couldn't see who was at the wheel of the boat.

Yuri cowed in his seat. "Shit, man, you didn't say anything about bullets." The pilot started the copter back toward the coast.

"What are you doing?" Burg shouted.

"I'm trained to fly, man, not die."

"You need more practice." Burg pulled out his Glock and held it at Yuri's head.

Yuri whitened and brought the chopper around. Burg told him to fly the Jet Ranger in erratic patterns as they approached the boat. Vary the speed, vary the direction, don't make the same move twice. As they edged ahead, the boat on their right, Burg told Daily to aim her gun into the cabin below to try and hit the hidden man at the wheel.

"Feel free to help," Daily said to Burg. He was on the same side.

"I'm going down." Burg pulled a Ziploc from his pocket, put his Glock inside.

"From here? When?"

"Soon as you stop talking and cover me."

Safford fired at the chopper again and retreated into the cabin.

"Cover something or I'm outta here!" Yuri yelled at both of them.

The copter dropped and banked. Daily fired three shots. The gray boat's stern shimmied, hit a swell, then spun to the right. Daily hit something. Buffeted by the swells, the vessel now moved in a slow, tight circle.

"Get me over it, now!" Burg shouted. "Hurry up—"

Yuri dropped the chopper again. Before Daily could say a word, Burg had jumped out the side. His splash looked like it would crack a back. He was gone. The seconds elapsed and she feared Burg had been whipped unconscious from the drop. Finally, his head emerged. She was surprised by the protectiveness she felt. Strong strokes moved him toward the boat.

Two more shots raced past them, and Yuri throttled the helicopter up and to the left. Daily saw Burg grab the boat's stern. He cut at something. The wake dissipated; the boat's engine died.

Enraged, Safford emerged from the housing; he moved toward the rear. Burg ducked underwater. Daily caught Safford looking up at the copter. He turned toward the boat's cabin, yelled something, then tucked his gun in his pants and started to work his hands inside the engine compartment.

From the side, Burg hurdled on board. From behind, he bull-ran Safford and the two men hit the deck hard, wrestling for control. Burg held Safford down with one arm as his free hand went for Safford's gun. From the chopper, Daily aimed for Safford, but Burg kept getting in her line of sight. No clean shot. Safford jerked on deck— Burg must have pumped a round into him. Safford went limp, his gun loose on the undulating deck. Burg grabbed the gun, patted Safford's body, then dragged him toward the cabin. A swell rocked the boat and Burg reached the rail for balance. As he did, Safford rolled to a fetal position, hands gripped around a leg trailing dark venous blood.

Ambivalence filled Daily. Burg had control for the moment, but she had no idea who else was on the boat. Safford had spoken to someone in the cabin. She looked around. Still no sign of Nestor in the sky. Burg leaned against the boat railing below, spent. Perhaps the worst was over. He didn't seem concerned about any other threats. Yuri stabilized the chopper over the boat and Daily's stomach started to settle. Below, she saw Burg pull a box from inside the cabin. He set it on the engine compartment, smashed the lock with the butt of his gun and opened it. Daily couldn't make out the contents. Burg stood over it, shaking his head, his sandy hair drenched and dripping.

It was as if an invisible blow hit Burg from behind. His back arched, then his head lashed back and forward. He was over the rear of the boat and in the ocean before Daily realized Safford had hit him with something. Another gun? A knife? Burg's arm flailed, then disappeared underwater with the rest of him.

Daily unloaded her Beretta into Safford's prone form on deck. She turned to the pilot. "Get me over Burg! Now!"

"I can't see him," Yuri pealed. "I can't see where he went . . ."

Daily spotted Burg, unconscious, head bobbing, face forward in the ocean. "Christ, he's going to drown."

"What do mean he's *going* to drown, he's already toast. I want outta—"

"Yuri, take me down."

"I'm as close as I can get now."

"Get closer."

"I can't."

"You won't."

"I like my life. I'd like to keep it."

Cursing him, Daily opened her door of the chopper. The wind was wicked and cold, yet she was sweating.

"What the hell are you doing?" Yuri yelled.

Angry swells tossed Burg's limp body like kelp. His form sank and surfaced again. Yuri was right. If Burg wasn't dead already, he soon would be. A rolling muscle of sea washed over Burg's head; his hair splayed into sharp rays. Another swell rose under Burg's body and his head rolled back. His face stared at hers.

Burg's eyes. Open but not seeing.

Her sister's eyes open in the sea. Looking at her. Daily smelled the sense memory. The stale air. Heard her sister's taunts.

Laughing. Always laughing at her. Knowing her fear.

Daily choked back the anxiety. Felt her own arms move her to the copter's rail. She looked down again.

Laughing.

Dammit, Daily, it's Burg. Not her. Help him.

A gust hit Daily and pinned her against the copter's frame.

Help him.

She was unable to move. Her mind wanted to jump, to get to Burg, but each time she looked down she saw her sister. Staring at her. Knowing her fears better than she did herself. She could smell her breath, feel her hands pushing at Daily, testing the boundaries. She felt the burn on her thigh as if the flesh was freshly singed. She tasted the urine, felt the legs wrapped around her throat. Stiff with fear, Daily looked down. Burg was sinking. She pushed away the memories, thought only of Burg. Her sense of him. His laughing eyes. His clean smell. His voice.

He'd gone under.

She saw a glint of gunmetal on the boat, a movement of Safford's hand. He was injured but he wasn't dead. He was aiming up, in her direction.

Do it.

Daily leapt out of the copter, felt the air rushing past her. Her arms windmilled to cant her drop. The hit was hard and cold. Her vision cleared and she fought not to choke on the saltwater that roared into her nasal passages. She swam back to the surface. The sting of the sea marred her focus. She dove and searched for Burg.

Nothing.

He was gone.

She dove again.

Hit something. Rubber or leather.

A shoe. *Burg.*

Diving down, she located his holster and used it to trawl his body up. She checked the boat. Safford wasn't at the rail anymore. She held Burg as best she could in the rise and fall of the swells.

She shook him. "Wake up. Dammit. Burg. *Wake up.*"

Blue hues iced his skin. Burg's head lolled forward.

"Come on, come on . . . " A shockwave hit her gut. "Breathe, for God's sake."

She pulled his head back, shook him again, then slapped him. Nothing. She dropped underwater, clenched her arms under his ribcage and heaved as hard as she could. Then again, until she felt a spasm rock him. As she surfaced, seawater spurted from Burg's mouth, and his eyes opened. He was coughing, but breathing.

"Where are you hit?" she asked.

"Chest," he rasped. "Upper left."

"He missed your heart, thank God."

"Shit, Daily. Us freelance types have no heart. Didn't you know?" Burg's eyes glazed. He fell limp again.

She struggled to keep his head above water, difficult to do with him slipping in and out of consciousness. She looked up but couldn't see Yuri in the chopper with the glare. Safford's silhouette on the boat was another matter—he was now leaning on the stern railing. Bullets hit a peak of sea to her left, then grazed the copter above them. Yuri veered away from them and turned toward the coast.

"Useless wimp," Daily spat at Yuri's retreating copter.

Another round skidded on the sea. The boat rocked Safford off-balance and he dropped inside it.

Burg roused in Daily's aching arms and gasped, "My gun . . . in the bag . . . far side of engine compartment . . . he doesn't know I left it there. Go get it."

"I'm not leaving you here."

"*Go, dammit!*" Burg's words were strong, even with his weakening lungs.

Daily looked at him, then back at the boat.

"Christ, Daily, *commit.*"

"I'm staying here. Help is coming."

"If it's like your pilot up there, it's not much good." Burg choked on water.

Safford's form rose at the stern and he fired two more rounds, the second almost nailing Daily.

In the distance, they could see a ship, its markings foreign but not distinguishable to Daily. A smaller craft spirited toward Safford's lame boat.

"Go," Burg said. "Or he'll make the rendezvous and we'll lose them for good."

This stranger, who'd given his trust to help her, was dying in Daily's arms. Yet if Safford eluded them, the damage would be irreparable. Torn by the choice, Daily loosened Burg's holster from his body. She hesitated; she still couldn't leave him.

A laugh sent more saltwater from Burg's windpipe. "Go on. I won the Red Cross award for treading water when I was ten."

She couldn't turn away; she didn't trust that he would still be there.

"Let him think he's hit you," he told her, "then go under."

Another shot scored the air next to Daily, closer than the last.

"Now," he said.

Emotion flooding her, she released Burg. A swell poured over her and he was out of sight. She held her breath and dropped beneath the surface, swam toward the form of the boat. She could see the sun casting Safford's rippled shadow over the water as he scanned the waves. Her lungs were about to burst. Safford couldn't last much longer, not with that kind of blood loss.

His shadow dropped away.

Daily broke the surface for air. After waiting for sounds of Safford's movement and hearing none, she grabbed the rear of the boat and hoisted herself above the rail. A bleeding Safford stared in the direction of the large ship and its approaching speedboat. In the cabin,

Daily saw Lyle Pearson, dead from her shot through the roof. In the corner, huddled and dazed, sat Peter Ealing. His eyes looked right through Daily. Drugged.

Daily reached into the half-open engine compartment and felt for Burg's weapon. The Ziploc bag. A strong swell pulled Daily down into the sea, tugging on her will. When she came up, Safford was wrapping his belt above a blood-soaked rag high on his thigh, his attention focused on the wound. Again, she searched the engine compartment, found the bag and Burg's gun grip. As she took the weapon, her anger steeled. She hoisted her legs from the water and straddled the back rail. Balancing herself with her left arm, she trained the Glock on Safford.

"Good at taking care of yourself, eh?"

Shock curdled Safford's face.

The boat rode the swells, and as much as Daily tried to hold her target, the sea was now Safford's ally. He put his hands up, but warning signals shot through Daily. Too easy. She followed Safford's eyes as they topped the next roll of the ocean. As the rise hit the boat, Daily used one hand to grip the rail and her gun's aim wavered.

One of Safford's hands reached back and grabbed something under the bench. Daily saw steel—sharp and curved—a tool she didn't recognize. He fell to his belly and hurled it at her. She pulled back, but the metal grazed her shoulder—impact, then hot pain. Without thinking, she emptied the Glock at Safford. Two bullets missed him, the third caught him in the forehead.

He jerked back.

Breathing hard, Daily watched Safford's movements ebb to involuntary spasms. Bright blood spread across the deck.

Peter Ealing hadn't moved through it all. Locked in some faraway place, perhaps on one of his own wipeout cocktails. The ones Safford was going to sell on the black market—memory loss on demand, the latest twist in a world spinning off its axis. She went to Peter and touched his face. Alive, but not present. Oblivious. Gone for hours or for good? By his own choice or Safford's?

Another swell slammed the boat and Daily turned to look for Burg, to tell him everything was all right, but there was no sign of him. She searched every crest, every dip of the ocean within sight. Nothing.

Burg was gone.

SIXTY-EIGHT

ON THE BOAT WITH the two dead men, John Safford and Lyle Pearson, and a brain-dead Peter Ealing, Daily stood alone. Burg was nowhere to be seen, lost at sea, Yuri had disappeared from the sky. The foreign ship with the odd markings loomed ahead and a signal flashed on an approaching speedboat. She was going to have to use her boat's radio for help, but right now, unintelligible squawks were coming from it. A male voice repeating two words she didn't understand, impatience evident in the tone.

Daily heard the thunder of noise behind her before she saw copters emerge from the rim of coastal clouds. Navy, Coast Guard. The transmissions on the radio stopped.

The Coast Guard chopper waited over Daily while the others passed, heading toward the large ship ahead. The approaching speedboat made a hasty U-turn. From above, the copter's ladder dropped in front of Daily. Once she was up and inside, two of the Coast Guard men climbed down to deal with the aftermath on deck.

In the back of the Coast Guard copter sat J. D. Nestor and Lieutenant Powell. Relief flooded her. More importantly, vindication. Their faces blared silent apologies for doubting her, for questioning her motives and her sanity. Her instincts had been right. She was happy as hell to see them.

Daily gestured at the Navy choppers ahead. "What'd you do, Nestor, call the Pentagon?"

Nestor laughed. "You have no damn idea."

Powell broke open a first-aid kit and attended to the gash in Daily's shoulder. Searing pain cut into her as he poured disinfectant onto the wound. She thought she saw slivers of moisture rimming his deep brown eyes. He saw that she'd noticed, shook his head and conjured up a stern look. "Thought I told you no maverick stuff, Daily."

He caught her looking away, down at the sea.

"You okay?"

She looked for Burg and there was no sign of him.

"Daily?"

She tried to say she was fine but the words wouldn't come.

SIXTY-NINE

CRAY WRIGHTMAN HIT THE final stretch of the interview. His eyes beamed in the studio's bright lights. Daily waited as he paused to check his notes. Paulette watched from behind one of the Channel Ten cameras.

Wrightman asked Daily, "What happens to the $4.1 million that Trent Eisen, the man you knew as John Safford, stashed in various foreign bank accounts from reselling TR-4 and the kuru analogs?"

"We've actually discovered even more money with help from the FBI and other agencies," she answered. "It's going to the victims of the crimes, and some will be earmarked for restitution to the one living relative of the real John Safford, who died in what's called a 'combat other than war' situation in South America. The real Safford was an information specialist with a government contractor called Archipelago Technologies, which designed the programs for the type of security that Ealing used at his home. We now know that our 'John Safford'—really Trent Eisen—made inroads with a number of less-than-scrupulous security concerns here, including Peregrine. He greased palms there and used a Peregrine patrol car to leave Doc's house unnoticed the night of July fourth. He was able to roam to Mulholland unpoliced. He overrode Eddie's wireless system and made it look as if Eddie Ealing had been brutally murdered by someone with an agenda related to his movies."

"So the *Sense of Life* angle was all a ruse?"

"A ruse born of complications. The original plan that night was to put Eddie Ealing into a coma, not to kill him. They needed him alive because of the will. When Eddie's unplanned drink of Scotch mingled with the GHB-spiked sports drink to cause *death*, Eisen was in trouble—he had to think quick. The movie posters on the wall gave him the idea to mimic the film's murder, to set the investigation and the media down the wrong path. But some aspects of Ealing's death didn't match the movie's, because Eisen had to use what was on hand to cover his tracks, like pool chemicals."

"The appearance of a media-related murder bought what—time? Distraction?"

"Both. After Eddie's death, Eisen and Peter Ealing were just trying to stay ahead of us at every turn. To set up false leads for the findings we would reach next."

"Hard to believe Doc Ealing wouldn't know his own man was so corrupt."

"I don't think Doc Ealing *wanted* to know. Eisen was working both sides. He would be rewarded handsomely by Doc if Temperel made legitimate breakthroughs on the Alzheimer's and brain science fronts. But he and Peter found alternate uses for the drugs that didn't get approved. And for terminally ill human beings. He didn't let anything go to waste."

Cray Wrightman adjusted his pince-nez, looked at his notes. "I have a confidential report here which says that Eisen's father was a lobbyist for several European concerns. His uncle was a propagandist for hire. This is a family of men who worked for money first, their conscience second. How about Peter Ealing? Is he just a brilliant scientist, who, when put in orbit with someone like Trent Eisen, spins out of control? Or is he the real operator in this equation? Was Peter the one who influenced Trent Eisen to do his dirty work?"

"That's a question for the psychologists. One that may not be answered soon, considering Peter Ealing's condition. He's still in the same state in which we found him on the boat Friday afternoon. The doctors working on him now aren't sure if the damage is permanent or not. It's highly likely Eisen drugged him on the boat, as insurance, although I think it's just as likely Peter drugged himself, seeing the options that faced him as things unraveled."

Cray Wrightman removed his glasses and leaned toward Daily. "You really believe Doc Ealing, a man revered for his morals and principles, had no idea that his son and his right-hand man were doing these despicable things?"

People don't see what they don't want to see. Daily chose her words carefully. "Ted Bundy's wife saw a loving husband. O. J. Simpson's mother can only see her loving son. I think there are signs, but if they challenge our beliefs, we tuck them away, put them in some dark place. Because facing them might be too difficult.

"People were abused and murdered because Doc Ealing turned away from reality. Because Peter's colleague, Dr. Rena Ross, didn't want to explore what must have been internal alarms going off for some time."

The bolt of anger that reared in her was something she recognized now, a familiar beast she'd have to deal with the rest of her life. "I think turning a blind eye to those signs is perhaps just as heinous an act as the crimes. Because we have a conscience. We know better. We can change things, if we choose to, before they get out of control."

"Both Doc Ealing and Dr. Ross face a variety of charges now. What do you think will happen to them?"

"I'll leave that to the legal eagles. I know you have a host of them on this show."

Wrightman smirked. "Indeed. But if you had to project—"

"Dr. Ross is a good scientist. Beyond the charges and whatever penalties she'll face, perhaps she'll be allowed to continue her work somewhere, maybe in something like the government program at Florian."

"Doc Ealing? Think he'll look into another book, perhaps from prison?"

Daily took a long breath. "I think he should look into his soul."

"And Mike's Gifts . . . now that the story of the original organization has hit the airwaves across the globe—"

"Eddie Ealing was the best copycat and he's gone. Trent Eisen was using the method to keep us off-track and he's dead. I imagine we'll have a rash of imitators, but I doubt we'll ever hear from anyone associated with the original program."

Daily thought of Burg with a private sadness.

Wrightman congratulated her and the LAPD, and tossed the program back to the *TimeLine* anchor in New York.

When they were off the air, Paulette helped Daily remove her lavaliere mic, told her she looked and sounded great.

Cray shook Daily's hand, asked if she'd be available for a book he was thinking about doing on the case.

Daily said, "Not wasting any time, eh?"

Wrightman shrugged. "I know more about Eddie Ealing than most people. Better that I do it and get it right."

"Your book will sell better than anyone else's."

"Except maybe yours, detective."

"No, thanks."

Wrightman turned to Paulette. "You ready for Tuesday, my dear?"

Paulette laughed. "I don't know that anyone's ever ready for an interview with you, Cray. But I'll do my best."

Outside the television studio, Paulette walked Daily to her car and said, "Nothing is what it seems, eh? You're the tough-skinned cop who's really an idealist; I'm the open-minded shrink who's actually a cynic. Sometimes I think we should trade jobs for a while."

Daily started to argue that she was as cynical as they come, but realized Paulette was right. Every peace officer she respected still chased the notion that they were making a difference. Absent that ideal, they became something else altogether. "We're having a celebratory meal at Musso Frank's. You're welcome to come."

"Nah, you wouldn't want to hang around a bunch of *my* cronies drinking and comparing war stories." Paulette smiled at Daily in the late sun. "One more thing, Lane. The GM, the PD, and the news director called me in. They want to up my deal and offer me a show of my own."

"You're kidding."

"Hey, I'm not that bad. *The Mind of Murder.* That's what they want to call it. A half hour each week on why criminals do what they do."

"Not as through with forensics as you thought you were, huh?"

"There would be travel. Not just the states—Europe. Asia. Anywhere celebrated and strange cases confound humanity. That's their pitch."

"Sounds intriguing. I'd watch it."

Paulette hesitated. "He wants me to have a cohost. An investigator." She paused. "You."

Daily blinked, then laughed. "Oh, no, no."

"Think about it."

"I just did. See you back at the beach."

Paulette bit her lip. "Uh—I hate to be the one to tell you, but I think you'll be asked to consider it again . . ."

The oldest restaurant in Hollywood was alive with homicide. Nine detectives, five patrol officers, and Lt. Powell crowded the Musso & Frank Grill's rear tables. Daily approached the booth coddling the loo, Nestor, and Burns. Chatter broke into cheers as Daily arrived. Everyone told her she did great on *TimeLine*; she'd made the force proud.

Be polite, she told herself. Her issues were with Powell.

"Daily, sit down." Powell motioned for the waiter. "She'll have a Belvedere, rocks."

"Coffee, black," she corrected.

"And get her a hot lamb sandwich."

"No, the sand dabs."

"And a pile of fried onion rings. Got to have the onion rings."

Telling her what she was going to eat. What she was going to do. Damn Powell.

Daily's voice stopped conversation in the room. "Why did you tell Channel Ten I would do this new show, loo?"

Powell didn't blink. The lieutenant waved the waiter off, told Daily to sit. "The mayor, the governor, some of the folks at DOJ thought it would make strides for the department. Put a good face forward. For years, we've been trying to stay out of the limelight; all we get for our trouble is bad press. The new brass thinks it's time we go on the offensive. Show just how much we get right."

"You offered me up without asking me?"

"It's either you or Fumpidtch at RHD. You're a lot better . . . on camera. And you got a lot better name than Fumpidtch."

Deadpan, Nestor said to his drink: *"And now, the latest insights from Detective Fumpidtch."*

Clem Burns frowned. "What's wrong with that?"

The waiter set a vodka on the rocks in front of Daily. "I said coffee."

Nestor stole her cocktail. "You gotta do the show, Daily. For all of us."

"I'm not doing a 'show,' no matter how much I love you all." Daily changed the subject. "I just got a call from Zag. Neuropath came back on Eddie Ealing's brain sections. The sections are consistent with one of the prion conditions of the brain. Creutzfeldt-Jakob disease, mad cow disease . . ."

"Kuru," said Nestor.

"Maybe. They're going to run some more tests. Could be coincidence."

"Right," Nestor said. "Peter was a busy boy. Killing them softly . . . before Eddie's discoveries and threat of an exposé moved them to coma-mode. They were already erasing his memory; they just needed a fast forward with the GHB."

Daily would never forget it. "It's certainly a new one for the DA."

Lt. Powell said, "Got good news from Cedars. Pierce is groggy but conscious. She ID'ed Eisen's mug in a six-pack. He was the one who hammered her and shot O'Rourke up at Ealing's. Could've been you, too, Daily."

"I'm glad she's okay. I have some things I need to get straight with that woman. Or should I say G-woman, loo? DOJ?"

Powell sighed. "What do you want me to say? They'd been after someone inside NOBLE for a while, but had to watch how they approached things because Doc was tight with too many people in Washington. Pierce was sent to us in March, as one of the DOJ watchdogs, to keep an eye on detectives who didn't always play by the rules."

Daily's emotions flared at the irony. "Don't look at me."

"They figured they'd save budget and put her on the NOBLE thing, too." Powell chewed on some onion rings. "We can talk about it when you come back. After O'Rourke's funeral. After your vacation."

Daily pondered those precious days off. How this whole case had started on one of them. A case that had seen memories gained and lost, stolen and delivered, a case that had seen one of her fellow officers murdered. A case that had thrown Daily into the path of a stranger who had forced her to trust again for the first time in years. Burg—or "Steven" or "Mike"—the man who had changed the course of this whole case—was gone, missing at sea, most likely dead in its depths. No organization would ever acknowledge his existence or his passing. Sadness overwhelmed her; everyone at the table was looking at her and she wondered if they could see her thoughts. She didn't want to have to explain the strange bond she'd felt with Burg, whoever he really was. He had saved her in more ways than one.

She raised a glass in a toast. Her voice was unsteady. "To O'Rourke."

"To O'Rourke," everyone chimed, their glasses held high.

Under her breath, Daily added, "And to Burg."

After Musso's, Daily's body was weary but her mind was too busy to sleep. She drove the Crown Vic fifty miles south, into Orange County, past the Costa Mesa neighborhood where she had grown up, to the Newport Beach pier. She didn't tell her parents she was coming; she needed to have this conversation alone.

She parked, walked onto the pier, to the pylon where her sister had tried to pull her down for the last time. Where Daily had fought back for the first time in her life and watched her sister die because of it.

She let the tears come. Heaves of grief rolled through her; she couldn't stifle the pain that purged from within. She cried for what her sister could have been, for what she really was; then Daily grieved for herself, for an innocence lost before the age of ten and never regained. A couple of surf rats stared at her as they passed with their short boards, but the fishermen on the benches paid no mind. They had seen their share of tears here.

She stared down into the water, remembered that day.

The eyes, open . . . staring at her . . .

This time the memory didn't elicit fear. She studied the images in her mind's eye. Daily thought about her sister, then about Peter Ealing. Both favorite children; both left undisciplined or unquestioned because of it. As kids, they had each been missing something else; some barometer or conscience. Was it learned, or was it embedded—some genetic aberration? To the world around them, both Peter Ealing and Daily's sister appeared to be gifted, charming, exceptional. But their siblings knew their manipulations, their lack of limits. In an extraordinary case with an unexpected twist, Daily had found herself identifying with Eddie Ealing—by all appearances, someone nothing like her—but someone whose life and personality had been changed forever in fear of his own flesh and blood. Something in the Ealing dynamic had tapped warning signals buried inside her. Regardless of wealth, lineage, education, or ethics, she and Eddie Ealing had each built different walls and different worlds to protect themselves. To create safety. To survive.

Doc was right about making choices, but he was dead wrong about Daily. She *had* made her choice, at a level that she couldn't have possibly understood as a child. She did the only thing she could have. Eddie Ealing had amassed wealth and walls to exert pressure on those he feared. Daily became a cop. Only now did she comprehend how her biggest secret had been driving her decisions ever since.

Damage. Daily recalled the first day she heard Dr. Ross talking about the research at Temperel, how someday they would be able to capture pure memories, untainted and unwarped by emotion. She wondered

457

what would happen now if she could actually show her parents what her sister had done—would they understand? Would they ever accept *her* truth, *her* reality? Daily knew the answer. No matter what people were shown, they would always make their own choices about what they believed. And, in the end, that was the only truth that mattered.

The eyes in the water were no longer looking at Daily; they were gone. Below the pier now she saw only the dark, undulating ocean.

The delivery interrupted an epic beach morning.

For the first time since she'd joined the LAPD, Daily truly wanted her days off. She had slept deeply the night before. Now her body was loose and languid in the sun chair; she imagined herself enjoying a blissful series of naps in the coming week. Now, she wasn't secretly hoping for a new case to distract her, and she wasn't wondering about anything back at the station. It was time to let her soul roam, to finally mourn the past and move on. To forgive. It would take time, lots of time, alone.

The shadow suddenly blocking Daily's sun belonged to Tad, the guy with the yellow beach house and the breakfast burgers. "Hey, Lane. Saw you on TV last night. You're the big hero now, huh?"

"Heroine."

Blank look. "Right. Hey, this messenger just rode by on a bike, asked if you were out here." Tad handed her a green box. White ribbon. The gift card attached to it read:

PHIL'S PETS

"Thank-you gift, huh? Bet you're getting tons of them. That dog I see you with—funny mutt. Seems to love you. Barks a lot, though."

Daily smiled. "Thanks a bunch, Tad."

He waited. It took him a couple minutes to realize she wasn't going to open the box with him standing there, and she wasn't asking him to sit down. "Guess, I'll see you around then, Lane. You want to drop by for a drink later—"

"I know just where to find you. Thanks."

With Tad out of sight, she rushed to open the box. Inside was a yellowed manuscript. Notes and marks, stains, torn pages. The title page had just two words:

Mimic's Poison.

Burg's note was tucked a few pages in. *He* had sent it to her, not some bookseller in North Carolina. She looked at the date. Saturday.

He was alive. He wrote in a strong, slanted hand:

This is the only copy that remains. I know you'll understand when you've read the story in its entirety. Some of us try to make amends for the past. We try to learn from them, make right, do better. Others just repeat the damage.

You're a maverick, just like Powell says you are. I don't know if you'll ever find the resolution or satisfaction you're looking for in your current job. Maybe. But if you ever decide you're looking for more, you have a permanent job offer with us. I'll tell you more about "us" at that time—if it ever comes. The phone no longer works, as you know. It's not traceable, so don't waste the energy. Get rid of it.

I wish you well, Daily. You got heart, a conscience, and one hell of a freestyle.

Daily set the box in the sand and looked up and down the well-peopled beach. Sun-streaked blond hair topped every other head. She scanned north and south, looked for a bike, for Burg. His face. His shoulders. There? The one in sunglasses who'd just turned her way? No.

An oddly personal longing kept her looking and as each hopeful match turned into the wrong chin or the wrong arms or the wrong lips, she wondered if she would ever see the man with the smiling eyes again.

She wanted to know so much more about his secrets, his gifts, his pain, his desires . . . and perhaps she never would.

But he was there, somewhere, in the endless sea of people.

*

ACKNOWLEDGMENTS

TECHNICAL ACKNOWLEDGMENTS

Department of Justice: Fred Cotton of the SEARCH Group, and agent Jeff Thurman of the FBI.

At the Los Angeles Police Department: Detective II Mike Pelletier, Hollywood Division Homicide; Theresa Esquivel-Solis, South Bureau Homicide; Lieutenant Edward Alba (retired); Sergeant Eddie Zalaya; Sergeant John Pasquarello. At the Santa Barbara Police Department: Lieutenant John Thayer; Sergeant Jim Lohse; Detective Jill Johnson. At the Los Angeles County Sheriff's Office: Sheriff's Homicide Deputy Louie Danoff.

Forensics and crime scene evidence: Craig Harvey, Chief of Coroner Investigations/Los Angeles County Coroner's Office; Chris Rogers, Chief of Forensic Medicine/Los Angeles County Coroner's Office; Scott Carrier/LA County Corner's Office; Barry A. J. Fisher, Crime Laboratory Director of the Los Angeles County Sheriff Department; medical examiner Tony Manoukian.

Information Technology and Surveillance: Christine Nail/Santa Barbara Police Department of Information Technology; Cliff Chabot;

Nathan Crawford/WESCAM Operations Manager; Rick Miller/ WESCAM Information Technology; Dale Chermak/WESCAM Software Engineer; and the extraordinary aces: Jeff Schroeder; Anthony Improgo; Van Ngyuen.

Telecommunications: W. R. Wayne Perrin, Security Investigations Manager/Pacific Bell.

Military and war history: Don McQuinn (USMC-Ret.); Maria Skierska; Slavek Szymanski; Wanda Diehl-Kielek; Maria Nirenberg; Moss Jacobs; Ambasada Izraela-Warzawa; The Holocaust Martyrs' and Heroes' Remembrance Authority.

In the Los Angeles District Attorney's office: Deputy DA Daniel Bershin; Deputy DA Karla Kerlin.

News: Jamie Ioos, News Director KVBC-TV/Las Vegas (NBC); David Peterson, Managing Editor WPTV/West Palm Beach (NBC); news professionals at KABC/Los Angeles; KPIX, San Francisco (CBS); KGTV/San Diego (ABC); Steve Hochman/LA Times.

Psychology and Forensic Psychology: Claire Greene, PhD; Michael Gross, MD; Jennifer Munell Rapaport, PhD; Mary Moskoff, PhD; Irwin Jacobs, MD.

Medicine/Bio-Sciences: Bruce Jacobs, MD; Rich Hubbard; Douglas P. Lyle, MD.

Aviation: Michael B. Kelley/King Aviation; Steve Phillips/Sun-Val Aviation; Tom Baum/Baum Aviation.

Security: Cory Meredith and StaffPro; also the SaMo team.

Because of the nature of the material in this novel, some who offered technical experience have asked to remain anonymous.

SPECIAL ACKNOWLEDGMENTS

This story owes its publication to Richard Marek, author, editor and publishing legend extraordinaire. I'm thrilled to be one of your 'students,' of writing and of life, and am honored to be in the company of the amazing authors you've nurtured.

My heartiest gratitude to the wonderful publishing staff at Midnight Ink: acquiring editor Barbara Moore for her enthusiasm and faith; designer Joanna Willis; editor Valerie Valentine; Gabe Weschcke; Eric Sneve; Connie Hill; Kelly Hailstone; Jennifer Spees; Alison Aten; Kevin Brown; Karl Anderson; Amy Martin; the entire launch team.

Susan Schulman, a fine literary agent (with projects that daunt mine) who still took the time to nurture this one to publication.

Thanks for the mentoring of Ron Howard, David Koepp, Jay Bonansinga, and everyone at the Maui Writers Conference.

To Don McQuinn, my guru. You're so much more than a great author. Your strength, vision, and wit are priceless. If I can pass along even a fraction of your sagacity, talent, and insight in this lifetime, I'll have done good work.

To Chavarria, Tiger, LC Cookie, Mitch, Joe Torsella, Laura Linton and the rest of my fellow tour colleagues – your souls and smiles are priceless, on rough roads and smooth.

Sara Thomas, you're a genius; and Heather Sorensen, a genie who gave me far more than three wishes; Jason Lavin, formula one navigator of all things cyber. Thank you all for your hard work on the site, themindbox.com.

To the best coaches a writer could ask for: Cindy Bowell;Mark Felsot; Tommy Ginoza; Danielle Gordon; Tara Kai; Rhonda Kraus; Tim Link; Fran MacFerran; Benita Wally; Chuck Wilson. Blake Kuehn: did you get the TPS memo?

To a new team of angels: Terri Budow; Mayra Victoria. Couldn't do it without you.

To new inspirations: Susan Vernon; Mandy Clevenger; Mary Dukes; Arlene Krausz; Rudy Youngblood; Patrick Mirabal.

Much gratitude to my brother Andrew, Daniel Randolph, and Tommy Gill for eagle-eye editing.

Thanks to Diane Golden of Katz, Golden Sullivan for her amazing legal mind.

And most importantly, to all the booksellers and salespeople who work endlessly to present new authors and stories to the reading public; you handle thousands of new releases each year, and I'm honored that so many of you took the time to help this new book make its way to light. Thank you.

If you enjoyed *The Mind Box*, read on for an excerpt from
the first book in Richard Greener's The Locator series

The Knowland Retribution

COMING SOON FROM MIDNIGHT INK

AN UNHAPPY HIGH SCHOOL counselor once told Walter that few people know much in advance what their life's work will be. Some doctors perhaps, because their parents make the decision for them when they are born. Some sons of business owners who must prepare to become *& Sons*, often to their lifelong chagrin. Conceivably, a handful of precociously pious pastors get the call in the cradle. But how many children tell their friends, "I want to sell office equipment"? How many college students look in the mirror and practice asking, "You want fries with that?" And few if any, Walter learned, ever intended to wind up teaching high school physics to the underequipped, let alone advising profoundly limited youngsters on their career options.

Walter Sherman was called neither to God nor medicine. He had no father, not even an uncle who owned a business. He sold his share of french-fries but never considered teaching physics or anything else. He joined the Army at eighteen, on his birthday, in 1970. He had nothing better to do. As he still sometimes said when thinking it was appropriate, it seemed like a good idea at the time. At the time he was a high school graduate working as a car washer and gopher-boy at a local Ford dealership. He was living in his mother's house just outside of Rhinebeck, New York. Before he could say, *"I made a mistake!"* he was in Vietnam. He could not remember why he re-upped, but he did. When he left the Army at 25 he had no better idea of how to make a living than he'd had seven years before. The army had trained him with guns and knives and hand held explosives. If Dutchess County New York had that kind of work available, he didn't know where it was. Nor did he know anyone who needed to be found.

Colonel DeScortovachino called Mrs. Sherman's house on a rainy Sunday in the spring of 1977. The call gave Walter's life direction.

"Walter!" the Colonel began in a false-hearty tone.

"Who is this?"

He introduced himself as "Colonel D" and explained that Walter's Vietnam CO was now attached to the Colonel's unit, hence Colonel D's "fortuitous awareness" of Walter.

"Son," he intoned, "I need your help," The Colonel was assigned to The School of the Americas and lived near Fort Benning just outside Columbus, Georgia. His sixteen-year-old daughter, Jessie, was nowhere to be found.

"She's not really missing," the Colonel said, "She just ran away. Her mother says we . . . Shit, that's not important. My point is that Jessie's gone." His voice changed just then. Its theatrical flourish fell away and a strange, melancholy pleading rose to soften the Colonel's military twang. Walter didn't recognize it then, but over the years he came to know that sound well. It signaled a desperation only someone who's *lost* someone feels. It was all about *lost* and *missing*. *Dead* may or may not kill you, but, Walter learned, *lost* and *missing* rip the insides with hot knives. *Lost* and *missing* produce a perpetual frenzy of mind that makes many people think they are close to insane every minute of every day. Such people always had, when their energy flagged, that sorrowful sound in their voice.

Walter didn't need to ask why a Colonel a thousand miles away, a man who didn't know him from Adam's uncle, would make such a call.

In the absurd jungle that was Saigon in the early 1970s, Walter was often called by the descriptive nickname: *Locator*. It wasn't a funny nickname like Bonehead or Lardass, or chummy, like Chip or Chief. It wasn't the kind of nickname you used to bum smokes. Nobody said, "Locator, got a butt?" This was a nickname of the highest order. It was earned. The earning of it started with a member of Walter's platoon who'd gone AWOL.

There were, as Walter recalled, two reasons most soldiers ran away, which was all that AWOL really was—running away, escaping jail, dashing to imagined safety somewhere. Either they went temporarily nuts—from the combat, from the drugs, from the simple unrelenting madness of what was going on—or they went over; defected. American MP's in Saigon took little joy in finding the nutcases. They followed the drugs; followed the girls. They usually found their AWOL soon enough. But after a week, if the missing soldier wasn't found, he became a "motherfucker," a political deserter. MP's got off on them because the reward for becoming political could be death. The order of the day was no longer "find and return," but "dispatch." More AWOLs turned up as combat deaths than anyone talked about.

When Freddy Russo, a hard drinking, drug using, pussy chasing Chicago hitter took off, the MP's searched for a week but couldn't find him. Walter knew they'd kill him when they did. Walter and Russo had hardly spoken, but an odd, insistent impulse moved him to see his CO and request permission to find the man before headquarters issued its next order. On the spur of the moment Walter lied. He told the CO that Russo had saved his life one night in a very notorious bar. In truth, no such thing had ever happened. Freddy was no friend of his, but Walter knew they would kill him and he knew he could prevent it. He asked for two days, certain he wouldn't need that much time. Walter did not think of himself as especially well organized. His mother, however, always marveled that her son, so unlike most children, never lost anything. And if something—a pair of socks, a jacket, a book or a toy—was missing, Walter always found it. Should his mother misplace her purse she called for Walter. As a teenager he never "forgot" where he parked the car, lost his keys or his wallet; and his knack of finding other people's lost belongings became a mysterious aspect of his personality. Walter thought too much was made of it.

He found Russo the next morning—never said how—happily lounging in a ditch behind the whorehouse where Russo had never saved anyone, where in fact, he once watched coolly, smirking, while Walter talked his way past two drunk Navy Seals bent on mayhem. Russo was covered in God knows what, still drunk and narrowing his eyes to work the last quarter inch of a joint that smelled like buffalo dung. Walter returned the ungrateful Freddy to his platoon. The CO covered his ass by sending the MP's a report saying there had been a mistake, that Specialist 4th Class F. Russo had been injured while off duty and had thus been unable to contact his unit until that morning. The written report credited Pfc. Walter Sherman with the "rescue."

Walter's Vietnam was an evil funhouse with no sense of proportion and few secrets. Everyone soon had a version of the event—and the Locator tag was born. Two weeks after, Walter's CO received an order assigning Walter to Headquarters Company. Now he was to find someone else—not an AWOL, not a political. This one was a bona fide POW. They air dropped Walter in the middle of fucking nowhere and he cursed himself all the way down. Still cursing, he trudged alone into the buggy jungle to find a captured American helicopter pilot. The officers who sent him on this mission and the helicopter crew that delivered him never expected to see Walter Sherman again. He turned up three weeks later with a gangrenous toe and identifiable fragments of the pilot's body. Walter was soon a Sergeant and his only job after that was finding people. Sometimes he looked for Americans, other times Vietnamese. He found them more often than not, mildly bemused that others could not. Then Walter went home to civilian life, too old and too wise for college.

When the Colonel called, Walter was working whatever hours he could for a food distribution warehouse. He pushed boxes of fruit juice from here to there and loaded cases of canned vegetables onto trucks. Some weeks he worked seven days and overtime. Other weeks he had no work at all.

"What do you want me to do?" he asked the Colonel.

"Find her. Bring her home."

"Well, I got a job now, and I have to work . . ."

"I'm not asking favors, son. I have money and I'll pay you whatever it is." That sound again.

"Okay, sir," said Walter. And so saying he stumbled onto the path that brought him a better life.

He found the Colonel's daughter four days later in Panama City, Florida. She was over her head in sex, drugs and rock 'n roll and not always rock 'n roll. He didn't clean her up. He just took her home. The Colonel paid Walter $1000. During much of the flight to New York he kept his hand in his pocket, on the money.

Locator.

Reputations grow most quickly in sensitive lines of work. Walter had a talent made for an apparently insatiable market. The sons and daughters of notable people—rich ones, celebrities, public figures—mostly, in fact, the daughters—were opting for the AWOL life in very impressive numbers. Almost all of the younger ones, the kids in their early teens, were into sex and drugs. Once they had some of either they couldn't get enough. For the older ones, the college kids, it was parents driving them over the edge—and they just had to get away. Rarely did any of them have any idea of how to avoid being captured. Their survival skills amounted to a credit card and a Holiday Inn. They were easy for Walter, if not others, to catch.

He found wives who'd slammed the door and peeled off in the Mercedes and forgotten the way back. There were endless embarrassing family members, the boozy, brawling brother-in-law, the loving husband gone deep underground, the off-kilter auntie who thought the better of coming home from the club one day. It might be the CEO taking a breather from heterosexual pretense, so much in love that he failed to notice the passing of the time. It might be his horse-hide-happy spouse. The kinkier the sex, the more anxious the contracting party, the more the client was more than willing to pay.

Famous, wealthy, and public people, Walter quickly discovered, can be embarrassed by almost anyone close to them. When those close disappeared, when they went *missing* or *lost*, and especially when they seriously intended to stay that way, Walter was the man their protectors found to find them. He much preferred the droll situations, the high-priced peccadilloes. It was the melancholy Walter could do without, the hard-core human interest.

He made it his business to offer his clients the commodity they held most precious: Privacy. He didn't start a firm. He didn't promote himself. He did not become *Walter Sherman, P.I.* He didn't print cards, open an office, have a secretary, not even a phone. He worked only by referral. You couldn't get to him unless you knew someone who knew someone who knew someone else. Consequently, he did not do this work often—and for another year continued his shifts at the warehouse. But that, his mother pointed out, was how to really advertise discretion.

Back then, if you did your due diligence and actually managed to talk to Walter Sherman, you did so on his mother's line. And before he stepped foot out of her house, you'd had someone hand-deliver a box full of fifties and hundreds.

Award-winning writer **A. J. Diehl** has been featured as a spokesperson on radio and television, and in newspapers such as *USA Today* and *The Los Angeles Times*. Previously a senior news editor who worked with ABC, CBS, and NBC-affiliated newsrooms, Diehl also freelances for regional and national publications. A member of the RTNDA (Radio and Television News Directors Association), the LA Press Club, and the SPJ (Society of Professional Journalists), Diehl graduated from USC with honors in journalism. *The Mind Box*, her fast-paced debut novel, took "Editor's Choice" stripes at the San Diego Writers Conference. The manuscript was originally discovered by Richard Marek, editor of *Silence of the Lambs* and many Robert Ludlum novels. For more information, see www.themindbox.com and www.ajdiehl.com